Into the Wonder
Book 2

The Devil's Due

Into the Wonder, Book 2:
The Devil's Due

Published by Puggle Press

ISBN: 978-0692375822

In memoriam
Hazel Pruitt Piercy
and
Otto Piercy:

hard workers,
storytellers,
good country people

Acknowledgements

The Devil's Due has been a fun ride for me, and I hope it will be for you as well. It's only fair that I take a minute to thank the folks that made it possible:

Those who read and left such glowing Amazon reviews of my first novel, *Children of Pride*. You made it worth the effort!

My amazing beta team for their affirmation and suggestions for improvement.

Jennifer Whiteley Becton for fact-checking my limited equestrian knowledge.

Dave Jones for his technical expertise.

And most of all, Connie and Rebecca for once again putting up with me spending way too many evenings at the computer.

Table of Contents

The Summer Court   The Winter Court

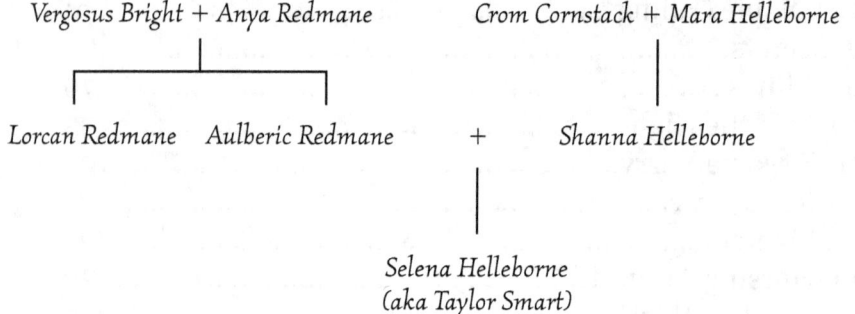

Vergosus Bright + Anya Redmane   Crom Cornstack + Mara Helleborne

Lorcan Redmane   Aulberic Redmane   +   Shanna Helleborne

Selena Helleborne
(aka Taylor Smart)

Chapter 1

The Dream

The air was muggy and damp, as if it had just rained. The ground was squishy under Jill Matthews's bare feet. The mist began to clear, but her mind still buzzed as she fought off sleep.

"Take your time," the woman said. "I don't mind."

She had heard the voice before. But what was she talking about?

In another second, she realized where she was. New Orleans. Gethsemane Cemetery. Above-ground crypts and mausoleums stretched out in every direction, punctuated by trees and religious statues. The pressure in her head got stronger. She shivered and let where she was standing sink in. She looked around, not frantic but curious. Before she saw it, she knew it had to be there.

Of course. It was right in front of her. Her Pawpaw's crypt.

"Wh-why have you brought me here?" she said. "Who are you?"

"All in good time" was the woman's only answer.

A small bouquet of flowers appeared in Jill's hand as if by magic. She gasped and stared at them.

"Go ahead," the woman said. Tentatively, the girl bent down and set the flowers in the stone vase provided.

As she rose, she spotted where the voice was coming from. The woman was seated on a stone bench only a few paces away underneath a statue of an angel. Her black hair blew free in the gentle breeze, as did her flowing green gown. Her fair, slender arms gleamed in the gray, predawn light. She smiled. There was no question she was very pretty, but something about her seemed a little too perfect. Her fierce dark eyes were brighter than should have been possible. Her voice had been just a bit too silky. With every word, she seemed to exude a subtle power that communicated she was not someone to be trifled with.

Jill slowly approached.

"What do you want?" She was tired of games. Scared and disoriented as she was, she wanted answers.

"Only to help you, my dear. Only to help you."

"By bringing me here? To my grandfather's grave? My parents—"

The woman laughed. "Darling, you have much to learn. Look around." She gestured regally. "Pay close attention."

The girl took in her surroundings. This was definitely the cemetery where her grandfather was buried, but something wasn't right. The birds in the trees sang harmonies she had never heard before. The air exuded the slightest hint of spice. The color of the slowly brightening sky was ever so slightly off.

"This is some kind of dream."

"Yes...and no," the woman said. "This place does exist, I assure you. You've simply never seen it from this...ah...angle before. Graveyards usually exist in the Wonder as well as Top-side where you people build them. That is especially true in a place as full of magic as New Orleans."

"I-I don't understand. What are you talking about?" She set her hands on her hips. "And what do you mean, 'you people'?" No, this white woman didn't really go there, did she?

"No offense intended, my dear," she said with a smile, and Jill couldn't help but believe her. Her voice was so compelling... "Everything will become clear soon enough. But as I was saying, this is New Orleans—after a fashion. And you are quite right: it is also a dream."

"And you?"

"'Such stuff as dreams are made on,' perhaps. Although I am quite real, I assure you. I thought it would be helpful for us to

2

meet in a place like this, a place you hold close to your heart." The woman leaned forward. Her eyes flashed once more.

"I've brought you here to warn you, child."

The girl shuddered. "Warn me?"

The woman nodded.

"You are only now beginning to awaken to your potential. It can be a disorienting experience with no one to guide you."

Jill's neck-hairs got fidgety. Something in the pit of her stomach told her this dream, or whatever it was, was about to get worse.

"Oh, you may not know in your head what's coming, but I'll bet you can feel it in your heart just the same. You've always been quite perceptive, haven't you?"

Something shifted in Jill's vision, like the shimmer of air over the pavement on a hot summer day. All at once, the trees seemed to grow wilder, twisting in tortured angles. It was as if the cemetery were in a haunted forest and not in the middle of a major American city. She suddenly felt exposed, vulnerable in her nightclothes.

She became aware of movement all around her—dark figures darting about, hiding behind the crypts and grave markers. As soon as she locked eyes on one, it was gone. There must have been a dozen of them, some large, some small. They slithered and skittered among the tombs, whispering to one another in the shadows.

"There's no telling what you may see when your mind is fully opened to the Wonder," the woman said.

"I-I want to go home."

"Of course, child," she said. "Go home to your family, your friends. But in time, you'll realize that you need what I can offer you. When you do, I'll be there." She smiled broadly. "I promise."

Jill sat up in bed, breathing heavily, sweating like she had just run a mile. Her alarm clock said 5:03. It took her a minute to convince herself of where she was—her grandmother's house, in the guest bedroom at the end of the upstairs hall.

Every time she had the dream, it had gotten worse. More vivid. More like something real.

There was a quiet knock at her door.

"Jill? Are you okay?"

It was William, her twin brother.

"Go back to bed," she said in a shaky voice.

Instead, he cracked the door open. "I heard you from the bathroom," he whispered. "Are you okay? Have you been crying?"

"No," she said. She wiped a tear from her cheek.

"You can't lie to me, sis," William said. "You never could. Something's wrong." He stepped into the room.

She decided to take a chance. She switched on the lamp on her bedside table, drew her legs up under her, and patted the side of her bed. William sat down next to her.

"Did you ever have a dream that seemed so real you'd swear it really happened?"

"Y-yeah?"

"Only, it couldn't have happened, because...there were things in the dream that...that just couldn't happen in real life?"

"You mean, like a nightmare?"

"Worse than a nightmare."

"What's up, Jill? You sound serious."

"It's probably nothing," she said. "It's just...It was so real. It was like I was there."

"It's just your imagination," William said. "Like all those times you thought somebody was spying on you and Taylor."

Jill was suddenly wide-awake. What if somebody was spying on her and her best friend?

"You know, Danny Underhill never came back to school," she said.

"What's Danny Underhill got to do with anything?"

"Maybe nothing, but you've got to admit, it was weird for a kid to transfer into school in February and then transfer back out in April. They said his dad's company moved him around

4

a lot, but to only spend three months in Macon? That's just ridiculous."

"Jill, I know you never liked Danny, but do you really think he's part of some kind of conspiracy to spy on you? And how in the world is he supposed to track you all the way to New Orleans?"

"You're right," she said, defeated. "That would be crazy... But you've got to admit, right before he left town was when Taylor started acting strange."

"I remember," William said, shaking his head. "Being all polite to her teachers. Flirting with all those guys..."

"You know she still thinks you're a dork, right?" Jill scolded. William blushed.

Jill resumed her train of thought. "And then, just when Danny left, she went back to being herself. Only, not really. She was...I don't know...not right. One minute she was looking over her shoulder like somebody was coming to get her. Then she was walking around in a daze. I don't know how she ever finished the school year like that."

"Since when has Taylor Smart ever cared about school?"

"Yeah, well, she was acting weird, even for her. And now, every time I go over to her house, she keeps looking at me funny. Like there's something she wants to tell me. You ask me, something happened to her last month. I've got a bad feeling Danny did something to her...."

In her mind, Jill pictured her former classmate, his bushy eyebrows, his curly black hair, the weird way his eyes glowed yellow when he was startled or embarrassed. Those eyes reminded her a little too much of something from her dream.

William yawned.

"Listen, let's just get back to sleep. Okay? You had a bad dream, and you're worried about your friend, and both things got all jumbled up in your head."

"Yeah."

"Besides, Germaine and Tonya are coming tomorrow."

That, at least was a pleasant thought. As soon as their cousins arrived, they'd have kids their age to hang out with for the rest of the weekend.

"Thanks for listening."

"What are brothers for?" he said. "This time tomorrow, the only thing you'll be dreaming about is having another bowl of Maymay's jambalaya."

Jill smiled.

"You're not too bad—as brothers go. You know that?" She tossed a pillow at him. "Now get out of my room!"

Chapter 2

Between Two Worlds

Taylor Smart kept hoping things would get better, but they didn't. The world was dull and gray. She had little to no appetite. Her favorite songs sounded tinny and distant when they played on the radio. Even something as relaxing as sitting at the piano and practicing her lessons left her unenthused. It was as if someone had turned a giant, invisible dial and watered down everything.

If Taylor were an ordinary thirteen-year-old, she might have just been in some weird hormone-induced funk. Nothing a hot fudge sundae or a trip to the mall with Jill couldn't fix.

But nobody had ever mistaken Taylor for an ordinary thirteen-year-old. It wasn't just that she was very bright. And it wasn't just the vibe she gave off that told the world she knew full well she was probably the smartest person in the room. There were plenty of quick-witted, snarky teenagers in the world. That didn't even set her apart at Bulloch Middle School. (Although she was reasonably sure she was in the top five.)

"Morning, sweetie," her mom called from the door.

"Good morning," Taylor said. "Time for work?"

Her mom nodded. "I just wanted to say goodbye before I left. Are you still sure about this?"

"I'll be fine. You and Dad go on to work. I can fix myself breakfast."

"Are you sure you'll be here okay by yourself?"

"I've got my cell phone," Taylor protested. "I can call if I need anything."

"Whatever you want. I can have Mrs. Dibney check in on you if you like."

"That's not really necessary!" Taylor said. She tried to keep frustration out of her voice. The last thing she needed was their nosy neighbor snooping around—least of all today! "Besides," she continued in a more even tone, "it's just for one day. I can handle it."

"Of course, you can. I love you, honey." Mrs. Smart moved on.

Taylor sighed as she stumbled to her closet.

Get a grip, Taylor, she told herself. *Just a few more minutes.*

She rifled through the shirts hanging her closet in search of something to wear. She couldn't help but grin when she thought about what she had planned for the day. While her parents were at work, Taylor was going on an adventure that might—just might—break her out of her funk.

Taylor's problems all started in April, when she met her birth mother for the first time. That was when she discovered the truth: she was not entirely human. She was, in fact, a faery.

"Fae," she corrected herself. Her Kind didn't like that other word—though she still wasn't entirely sure why. Whatever they were called, her birth parents were from a race of magical beings that had lived alongside humans in secrecy for thousands of years.

A month ago, she found this out when her classmate Danny Underhill kidnapped her on orders from her grandmother. Since then, she tried not to think too much about her biological family. It was enough to know that her true father, Aulberic Redmane, was dead—the victim of a deadly feud that pitted his family against that of Taylor's mother, Shanna Hellebore. A lot of people thought *Romeo and Juliet* was a beautiful love story. They must have not read to the end, where everybody dies. But whatever the case, that was pretty much the story of Taylor's biological parents. Fortunately, her birth mother survived and, after fourteen years in the Hellebore dungeons, was finally safe, living with Fair Folk in North Carolina.

But Taylor was stuck between two worlds. She wanted to fit in with her Topside friends and her Topside parents. But she wasn't very good at it—even before magic started getting in the way.

And she still hadn't figured out how to tell her parents about all this.

Maybe this little field trip she had planned would clear her head.

She got a quick shower and then put on the clothes she had picked out: khaki shorts, tennis shoes, and a royal blue top. It was cute and casual but not grungy. Perfect. She threw a few things into her new beaded purse—a souvenir from her first visit to the Wonder—wallet, some sunscreen, her cell phone, her asthma inhaler, and a few other odds and ends.

She also packed her seeing stone, a smooth, black stone with a hole in the middle. Her Kind used stones like this to communicate with each other over long distances. Actually, it was through a seeing-stone conversation that Taylor learned about Ichisi, a nearby fae town. When her new friend Ayoka scryed her right at the end of the school year and said she would be coming to Macon soon, Taylor's heart did a somersault.

Now, at last, the day had come.

By the time she came out of her room, the house was empty. It was the first Friday after the end of school. If her best friend hadn't gone to visit her grandma in Louisiana, she would likely be hanging out with her all day. But something better came up, so it was just as well she didn't have to worry about Jill.

She hadn't figured out how to let Jill in on her secret, either. She had meant to tell her everything. But how do you explain something like that to somebody who's been your best friend since fourth grade? *By the way, Jill, it turns out I'm a mythological being. Cool, huh?* No, she had to find a better way. Ease into it somehow. Maybe she could think of what to say over the Memorial Day weekend.

She grabbed a granola bar and a glass of orange juice. She watched a little TV. Then she pulled back her long, straight hair in a ponytail, donned the floppy sunhat she bought at the beach last summer, and headed out the door. She checked the time on her phone. It was a little past eight.

Taylor locked up the house and got on her bike. Twenty minutes later, she had reached her destination. The gate at the Ocmulgee National Monument was already open. She wheeled down the park road past the Welcome Center and kept on going. The shadow of the trees kept the heat from feeling unbearable. Birds sang. She had the park pretty much to herself.

The Ocmulgee Indian Mounds had been inhabited since prehistoric times. Now, it was a national park in the middle of Macon, Georgia. The park hosted an annual Indian powwow every fall, and a lot of school groups took field trips to the place. Taylor hadn't been there in a couple of years, but it wasn't hard for her to get her bearings.

In another ten minutes of cycling, she arrived at a small parking lot at the foot of an immense artificial mound, taller than a five-story building. The sign by the side of the road identified it as the Great Temple Mound. A footpath led to stairs creeping up one side. A family with two young children stood at the very top, enjoying the view.

She chained her bike to the sign and continued on foot.

"Any mound should do," Ayoka had told her. "Just pick one near the river." She gazed up at the top of the mound and sighed. It was a long way to the top. She decided to veer off the footpath and head to the Lesser Temple Mound, which was both closer and smaller. She tried to take her time; it didn't take much for her to get out of breath. Even though she hadn't had an asthma attack in over a month, she wasn't ready to take any chances.

The family on the Greater Mound above her was no longer in sight. It wouldn't be long until they reappeared on the path, however. It was time.

She took a deep breath and imagined a magical mist surrounding her like a blanket. Danny Underhill had taught her that. Confident she was effectively invisible, she hiked up the wooden stairs to the top of the Lesser Mound.

She paused to take in the view. Not only could she see several of the other mounds in the park, if she looked off to the west, across the Ocmulgee River, she saw the buildings of downtown Macon.

She checked the time again on her phone. If she left by 4:15 or so, she should have plenty of time to get home before her parents, and they would never have to know she had left the house.

But first, she had to get to where she was going. She pulled down the brim of her hat against the glare of the sun. She bit her lip and gazed at the top of the mound, looking for the telltale shimmer in the air.

There it was, right at the edge, where the mound ended abruptly as it looked over the parking area. She took a deep breath and took a couple of tentative steps toward the spot. What had Ayoka told her on the seeing stone? "It's something like putting on a veil of magical mist, except you imagine the magic seeping up out of the ground. Use your hands if you have to. Oh, and singing sometimes helps."

Here goes, she thought. She took another breath as she closed her eyes and imagined a billowing cloud of mist rising from the ground. Without even thinking about it, she gestured with her hand, like a conductor leading a choir to sing louder.

She felt ridiculous.

And then it happened. A swirling wall of gold and silver lights erupted from the mound, a shimmering circle ten feet across. Taylor suppressed a giggle and plunged straight in.

Immediately, she was in a different world. She was still atop the Lesser Temple Mound, but the mound itself was huge—maybe three times larger than it was before. To the west, the downtown buildings were missing completely. To the north, the two deep railroad cuts—one still in use by the railroad and the other turned into the very park road she had taken to get there—were also missing. Instead, a vast, broad plaza stretched out from where she stood all the way to the Earth Lodge a quarter of a mile away.

The plaza was dotted with dozens of houses, some ancient and traditional, others more modern. And hundreds of people filled the entire complex! These were the Fair Folk: the people to which Taylor's birth parents belonged. Most were nunnehi, Native American fae like Ayoka. Some were in traditional dress and others in regular street clothes. Some were white or African American. Some had pointed ears. Others had tails or snake-like eye slits. Some were little folk: dusky-skinned and only three feet tall.

Taylor had slipped into the Wonder.

None of this existed Topside, of course, and nobody Topside had any inkling that a whole other world existed right under their noses (although Native Americans told stories of "spirit warriors" who sang and danced at the mounds). In this version of the Ocmulgee Mounds, in the town of Ichisi, there was no city just beyond the trees. Everything was wild, untamed. Free.

She looked up into the sky. As expected, the hue was more turquoise than the blue it had been Topside. The air was filled with the smells of exotic foods and the hubbub of conversation. In the distance, fans cheered some kind of sporting event. That, she knew, was her destination.

Taylor came down off the mound and made her way through the crowd toward the sound of cheering.

From inside the open doors, she saw women cooking untold delicacies in huge copper cauldrons. Young children ran willy-nilly through the streets, laughing and playing. A couple of men were haggling over some sort of magical implement. Others, both men and women, had stopped at the corner for an impromptu a cappella jam session.

Further down the street, a teenage fae dazzled a crowd of younger kids by creating rings of colored smoke out of thin air and sending them skyward.

A man and a woman—Native Americans both at least ten feet tall—stooped to converse with another fae with an open suitcase filled with a multitude of jars, cases, and vials of multicolored liquid.

It was almost more than Taylor could take in.

It wasn't home. It was anything but. Even so, something about it put Taylor at ease for the first time in weeks.

Chapter 3

War's Little Brother

She picked up her pace as she wandered west toward the river and soon arrived at an open-air sports arena. A thousand or more fans sat on blankets all around a large, flat depression between two mounds. The place was bigger than a football field, with sixteen-foot tall poles at either end.

Two teams were going at it: running up and down the field, each player with a stick in each hand. The sticks had little mesh cups on one end, and they used them to carry a little ball back and forth. There were about twenty on a side, and Taylor had seen nothing like them.

It was a fast, brutal game. Apparently, you were allowed to tackle the player who had the ball, because players were constantly slamming into each other. They didn't wear any padding. In fact, they played barefooted, wearing just a loincloth and war paint, with a horsehair tail trailing behind them.

But something else was also going on. Occasionally, someone would lunge at an opposing player, only to have his target vanish into thin air with a flash of light. Then, he would reappear somewhere else on the field and continue his run toward the goal post. At other times, a runner would stop short, magically blasted off his feet by a member of the other team. Or else he changed course unexpectedly as if he saw an opponent rushing him even though no one was there.

It was like a non-lethal form of combat, with generous doses of magic added in.

"Taylor!"

She looked up from the game. Ayoka was weaving toward her through the crowd of spectators.

"You made it!" Ayoka smiled. She looked like an ordinary teenage Native American girl, dressed similar to Taylor. No sooner had the two girls hugged each other than the crowd erupted in wild applause.

The girls whipped around to see one team, dressed in red loincloths, lifting one of its members into the air in exultation.

Ayoka groaned.

From somewhere near the field, an amplified voice called out something in a language Taylor didn't understand, followed by, "Ichisi goal by Shupco for one point. Ichisi 13, Tsuwatelda 10."

"They've been on fire for the last half hour," Ayoka said. "Four unanswered points!"

"Uh...right," Taylor said. Ayoka and her family were visiting from Tsuwatelda, or what Topsiders called Pilot Knob, North Carolina.

"My parents are saving us seats," Ayoka said. "This way."

Taylor followed her friend through the maze of spectators. Ayoka kept one eye on the game, which wasn't easy when fans jumped up to cheer for their team or complain when they did something wrong.

"You've never seen stickball, have you? At least, not the way we nunnehi play it?"

"Not the way anybody plays it." Taylor winced as two players went down in a flash of crimson light.

"It's pretty simple," Ayoka went on, weaving among the spectators and their blankets and coolers. "The goal post has two marks: one halfway up and another one between the middle and the ground. Hit the goal with the ball between the two marks for one point, above the midline for two points, or the very top for three."

Taylor noted the oblong wooden finials at the top of each goalpost. "And you're allowed to use magic?" Taylor said.

"You can't charm the ball or the sticks—yours or another player's—and there's no shapeshifting or size-shifting allowed. Other than that, yeah, pretty much anything that won't cause a permanent injury is fair game. Blinking, blasting, invisibility, glamour diversions...whatever you can think of, as long as you're at least ten yards from the goal post. See those circles on the field?"

Just then a player in a black loincloth leaped into the air and used one of his sticks to fling the ball toward the nearest goalpost. It slammed into the finial, which spun around like a weather vane in a tornado. Ayoka shrieked and pumped her fist in the air while most of the fans around her shook their heads.

The announcer said something again, then translated: "Tsuwatelda goal by Tsisgwa for three points, and the score is tied at 13."

"That's my cousin!" Ayoka beamed.

"I remember," Taylor said. She had seen Tsisgwa from a distance back in April. Her heart fluttered as the young fae spun and dodged on the field, his bare chest heaving with exertion, a look of fierce concentration on his face. She looked away before she started to blush.

They soon found Ayoka's parents seated near what Taylor would have called the fifty-yard line.

"You remember my parents, don't you?"

A nunnehi man and woman smiled at Taylor. She nodded and took her seat on the blankets they had spread out.

"I don't see a clock," Taylor said. "How do you know when the game is over?"

"They play to fifteen points, so there's probably just a few more minutes left. They've been at it since sunrise."

"No way!"

Ayoka nodded, then jumped up to cheer something that happened on the field.

"You're really into this, huh?"

Ayoka nodded again. "I wish girls could play—I mean, on this level. Everybody plays when they're kids, of course. But I qualified for the exhibition game—only kids age twenty-five to fifty. That starts this afternoon."

Taylor had nearly forgotten that Ayoka had just turned twenty-six years old, even though she only looked about thirteen or fourteen.

There was another bone-crunching tackle. A couple of players from both teams sprawled on the field. They were quickly escorted off, however, and play continued almost immediately.

"And I thought football was violent," Taylor muttered.

"Is football how Topsiders train their warriors?" Ayoka asked.

"It's mostly how they keep the big dumb jocks all in one place so they can keep an eye on them. Wait a minute: this is warrior training?"

"Sure. We call it 'little brother of war.' In the past, the nunnehi have even used it as a substitute for bloodshed. Whoever wins the game, wins the war."

"Wow," Taylor said. "That's...intense."

Everyone around her was suddenly on their feet. The Ichisi team was driving toward the goal, the ball in the possession of a giant of a man who muscled through the Tsuwatelda defenders like they were children. Tsisgwa flew toward him in a flying tackle, but the Ichisi player blinked away in a flash of super-heated dust, appearing just outside the no-magic line. Just as suddenly, another Tsuwatelda player blasted him with an explosion of purple flame, and the ball came loose from his stick.

Players from both teams scrambled to retrieve the ball. It looked to Taylor like an honest-to-goodness riot was about to break out, when at last an Ichisi player swatted the ball into the cup of an awaiting teammate. This player wasted no time: he flung the ball toward the goal just as four Tsuwatelda players piled into him.

The ball sailed through the air for thirty feet and struck the goalpost above the midline.

"Ichisi goal by Enomako for two points and the win. The final score: Ichisi 15, Tsuwatelda 13."

"Arrgh! We almost did it!"

"Maybe next time," Ayoka's dad said. "Come and eat something before you have to get ready."

Ayoka's mom opened a picnic basket and offered both girls sandwiches and fresh fruit: a delicious selection of apples and plums. Ayoka scarfed down her sandwich like she hadn't eaten in a week.

"Slow down, honey," her mom said. "You'll give yourself a stomachache."

"I'm just itching to get started," she said. "Can I have some cookies?"

"Sure," her mom said, digging into the picnic basket.

Taylor's eyes wandered across the playing field, now empty except for attendants smoothing out the densely packed earth and spreading out a fine coat of sand.

The spectators were a sight to see. If anything, they were even more diverse than the residents of the town of Ichisi she had seen on the way in. Fae of every conceivable size and appearance were there: young women in dresses made of leaves, pointy-eared men no taller than children in bright tee shirts and tennis shoes, bronzed men in buckskins who stood nearly seven feet tall, green-haired, barefooted maidens in diaphanous beach cover-ups. Across the field was a man whose tee shirt said, "The Wild Hunt – 1997."

With the playing field in order, a nunnehi musical group began to sing an upbeat song in their own language. Many in the crowd began to join in.

When she turned back around, Taylor saw that Ayoka had finished off her second cookie and was opening a bag of fruity candy.

"Hungry?" she scoffed.

"Stuffed," Ayoka said, "but I'll need my magic for the tournament."

"Oh, right." Sweet snacks helped to power fae magic. Taylor wondered how many cookies those stickball players had to put away to do the things they were doing.

"I'd better get going," Ayoka announced. "Taylor, you can go with me if you like. Get a front row seat?"

"Are you sure? I don't mind sitting with your parents."

"No, I think I'd like you to go with me." Ayoka glanced at her parents, the three nunnehi exchanged subtle grins.

"If you say so," Taylor said said. She finished her sandwich and put her apple in her purse. Ayoka took up her leather pouch.

The two girls weaved up the side of the embankment and off to a wooden structure, a dressing room where athletes prepared for competition.

Ayoka looked around the milling crowd. She leaned in and whispered, "You need to wait behind the dressing room."

"No problem, I'll just—"

"No," Ayoka said. "I mean way on the far side. There's a tree around back."

There were trees all over the place.

"Uh, fine," Taylor said. "I'll just...wait behind the dressing room, then."

It didn't surprise Taylor that there were plenty of trees behind the dressing room. Even Topside, this part of the Ocmulgee Indian Mounds was near a wooded marsh.

What did surprise her was when she heard someone call her name. There wasn't another person in sight.

"Who's there?" she said.

"Taylor! Up!" the voice said again. This time she realized it wasn't a human voice. It was more like the squawk of a parrot or—

"A crow?" she said out loud as she scanned the nearest tree. A large black bird sat perched in a branch eight or nine feet up.

"Raven," the bird croaked. It fluttered to a lower branch so it could speak to Taylor face to face. "I'm only...borrowing." The bird, it seemed, could only speak in brief phrases of two or three words at a time. Taylor was astounded it could communicate at all. But what was it talking about?

"B-borrowing? What—?"

"Couldn't come...in person... My parents...still looking."

Parents?

"It's me, Taylor...Shanna." The raven snapped at a passing bug and swallowed it whole.

Taylor furrowed her brow. "This is some kind of..."

"Trick?" the raven said. "Of course! We say, 'faring forth.'"

"Faring forth," Taylor repeated.

"I'm still...in Tsuwatelda," the raven said. "But my consciousness...is here."

Taylor just stood there, nonplussed.

"You look good.... That color...suits you." There was something sad in the raven's croaky voice, and also something familiar.

"You're really Shanna?"

"It's me, *Neunhirri*."

Taylor looked at the raven wide-eyed. The first time she met Shanna, she had told her that her true name, the name that powered her magic, was Neunhirri. It was a secret only she and her birth mother shared.

"I wanted to come.... Chief Tewa said...too dangerous."

"So you...uh...fared forth?"

"Exactly."

Taylor stood there, mystified.

"How are your parents...dealing with...everything?"

She lowered her head. "Actually, I'm still not sure how to tell them."

"Taylor!" the raven scolded. "Over a month.... They deserve... to know!"

"Sure," she said. "It's just.... It's a lot to take in, you know?"

"Tell them," the raven squawked. "They can handle...better than...you think.... They love you."

There was a long silence as Taylor considered what her mom—or the raven, or whatever—had to say.

"Listen," the raven said, "I'm losing...my connection.... Have to go."

"C-can you come again later?"

"Might not find...an animal...that can talk," the raven said.

"Oh."

"Use your seeing stone!"

"I will."

"And learn...language of birds.... Very handy."

"How do I do that?" Taylor asked.

The raven gave a deep, throaty rattle. Shanna was gone. A second later, so was the raven.

When Ayoka re-emerged from the dressing room, she barely looked like herself. She wore a black, fringed skirt and a matching halter-top. Around her waist was a wide leather belt with elaborate loops along the edges, top and bottom. Fastened to the front was an animal pelt, turned so the skin part—dyed blood-red—faced outward.

On top of everything else, she was covered in war paint—her face, her stomach, her arms, and her legs all the way down to her bare feet were decked out in black and white stripes and whorls. Taylor realized Ayoka was wearing a feminine version of the same kind of outfits the stickball players had been wearing earlier. In fact, she clutched a pair of sticks in her hand that rested easily against her bare shoulder.

"Ayoka, Shan—"

"We'll talk later," Ayoka said with a wink, and then whispered "Too many ears around here."

Taylor smiled. She guessed Ayoka knew Shanna had hatched a plan to talk with her, but now she knew it for sure.

"Ready?" Ayoka said. Before Taylor could answer, the nunnehi girl strode forward. A line of competitors was forming several yards away. Most looked like teenagers. Older-looking players kept their distance but nodded encouragement to their younger teammates. Among these younger players, some like Ayoka had well-wishers tagging along, older men for the most part, but a few proud mothers were also in the group as well as several other kids Taylor's age there to support their friends.

Taylor followed as Ayoka took her place in line. When she reached the front, she held her sticks over a great stone bowl while an older fae poured water over them from a smaller ceramic cup.

As with the previous game, the Ichisi players wore red and the Tsuwatelda black. Both teams huddled around their coach, who gave them a pre-game pep talk that lasted for several minutes. Then everyone raised their sticks in the middle of the circle and joined in a thunderous war whoop.

At last, Ayoka motioned for Taylor to rejoin her.

Taylor followed the other supporters back to the playing field, but now she was given a seat much closer to the action, almost on the field itself. The other supporters of the younger Tsuwatelda players found their seats around her.

The musicians were still playing and singing, and by now the whole arena was filled with the haunting sounds of the music. A drumbeat rose to a crescendo as the players marched onto the field. It was another half-hour, however, before anybody even tried to settle down and start the game. The music continued to pulse through the arena like a living thing.

Taylor felt herself swaying to the music along with everyone around her. Jets of faery fire streamed across the noonday sky, a confusion of red and green and blue and gold. A thousand spectators seemed to become a single organism, wrapped up in the spectacle.

Only the guy in the "Wild Hunt" tee shirt seemed unfazed. He sat cross-legged on his blanket apparently unmoved. For a split second, he and Taylor made eye contact, but he immediately looked away.

There was something familiar about him; Taylor couldn't decide what.

Chapter 4

Magic and Monsters and Stuff

It was well past noon when the game finally began. The crowd cheered and whooped for their favorite players. Ayoka pumped her sticks in the air toward her own cheering parents, then toward Taylor.

Now Taylor could see the announcer she had only heard before. He was seated just a few yards away on a fringed white blanket. He stood and waved to get the crowd's attention.

As before, he said something in his native language before translating into English. "Welcome, honored guests. Before the chunkey tournament this evening, we are pleased to feature a junior stickball competition featuring players age twenty-five to fifty." The crowd cheered once more.

"Players to the field!" the announcer shouted. Both teams swarmed to mid-field.

A referee in white shorts and belted cotton trade shirt tossed a ball high in the air and then abruptly blinked away as both teams scrambled after it.

Ayoka's team ended up with the ball. A boy with pointed ears and blond hair in a long braid down his back trapped it in the cups of both of his sticks on a high flying leap. He hit the ground running at full bore toward the Tsuwatelda goal post, dodging the Ichisi defenders.

His teammates ran interference for him. Ayoka gestured toward a boy twice her size and shouted something in her own language. There was a flash of light, and the boy stopped cold as if he had run into a wall.

Meanwhile, another Ichisi player managed to ram the blond boy. The ball fell free, and another Ichisi player, a girl who looked college-age scooped it up without breaking her stride.

The Ichisi girl flung the ball across the field, using one of her sticks like a catapult. A teammate caught it and then blinked away just as two Tsuwatelda defenders surged toward him. They ended up smashing into each other, while he advanced toward the Ichisi goal.

He made a quick pass back to the first girl, who was now just inside the no-magic circle. She spun and launched the ball toward the goal. It struck the pole with a resounding thunk.

"Goal by Iti of Ichisi," the announcer said. "Two points!"

So it went for about thirty minutes of unrelenting, non-stop action. Taylor had to remind herself that this was only an exhibition game with under-age competitors. They were going at each other like wild animals—or nunnehi warriors in the heat of battle.

The crowd was into it, too. People shouted, clapped, and stomped their feet whenever their team made a good play. They chanted taunts against their opponents and generally got into it at least as much as the boys at Taylor's school got into a big football game.

Again, the "Wild Hunt" guy was the only person who seemed uninterested. He silently observed the game from the other side of the field. He barely moved. No matter how loud and raucous the fans around him were, he just sat there with his arms crossed and his mouth shut.

Taylor was sure she had seen him before, but that was impossible. Still, there was definitely something familiar. Taylor couldn't decide what. He seemed perfectly average: not too tall, not to short, not too thin, not too fat. He had fair skin, which set him apart from many in the crowd, but none of the distinctive body modifications that many of the Fair Folk seemed to embrace. His ears and eyes were shaped normally. He didn't have a tail or horns or anything like that. He might have been an ordinary Topsider if not for the fact that there he was in the middle of a hidden magical town, watching a magical stickball game.

Then she figured it out. She *had* seen this stranger before: a month ago. He was one of the changeling guards at Dunhough-key, the fae rath or castle hidden beneath Stone Mountain, Georgia. Taylor remembered two guards, but she only knew that one of them was named Bob.

Whoever he was, he pulled something from the pocket of his khaki shorts. It was a small brownish stone, about the size of a cell phone. He blew a gentle breath over it, then spoke to it.

It was a seeing stone, like the one Taylor carried in her beaded purse.

The man got up at once and climbed the slope toward the crest of the hill and the back of the arena.

If someone from Dunhoughkey was hanging around, it couldn't be good news. That was the territory of her grandmother.

To say Taylor and her grandmother didn't get along was an understatement. A month ago, Mrs. Redmane (and everybody called her "Mrs. Redmane") swore to make Taylor regret it if she ever set foot in any rath of the fae Chiefdom of Arradherry.

But what was one of her grandmother's goons doing here? Taylor had to know.

She slipped along the edge of the field, back toward the dressing rooms, and then out into the town. The streets were still quite busy, but there was no sign of her former prison guard. She stalked carefully forward, avoiding the crowds milling about by sticking close to the walls of buildings.

She paused to get her bearings. To her right was what she knew as the Great Temple Mound—now, however, with three large houses on top of it—and the Lesser Temple Mound beside and in front of it. Straight ahead was the Funeral Mound. Like the Lesser Temple Mound, the Funeral Mound was much bigger in the Wonder than it was Topside, and an earthen walkway wrapped around it.

Bob—or whatever his name was—stood at the base, talking to someone through his seeing stone. His back was turned; he didn't see Taylor approaching.

She paused to cloak herself in glamour. Taking a deep breath and letting it out slowly, she imagined a veil of magical mist swirling around her, blocking her from sight. It wasn't true invisibility, but it would work just the same as long as she didn't make a noise or trip over anything.

She inched forward. A break in the traffic gave her the opportunity to dart across the street and creep up on her grandmother's minion.

He put away his seeing stone.

Rats! Taylor thought. What was he up to?

His face betrayed no emotion whatsoever. He stood in front of the mound as if waiting for someone. After a few minutes, however, he started strolling north down Ichisi's main thoroughfare.

Taylor followed as quickly and quietly as possible—which wasn't easy in the heavy foot traffic.

The changeling stopped suddenly.

Taylor also stopped. She kicked a little bit of dirt as her foot landed on the path.

Bob (was it really Bob?—it could have been the other guy) turned around, slowly and deliberately.

Then he quirked an eyebrow in Taylor's direction. For a second, the two made eye contact. He gave her a polite nod.

Then he blinked out of sight.

Taylor's heart pounded like a drum. He saw her. She *knew* he saw her. But he didn't do anything, didn't say anything. He just nodded to her and vanished.

She didn't know what all this meant, but it couldn't be good news.

Anya Redmane is having me followed!

She didn't try to re-apply her magic mist. Best to be seen by everyone, just in case the Summer Court tried anything. The only thing she could think to do to get back to the arena as quickly as she could. She hurried back the way she came.

All the way back, she kept her eyes peeled for signs of Bob. He was nowhere in sight, however. By the time she made it back to her seat, her sense of dread had started to pass. There was no way Mrs. Redmane was going to try anything with a thousand people watching.

The match proceeded for another twenty or thirty minutes. It was every bit as fierce as it had been before, even though the players must have been at it for a couple of hours by now.

Ayoka had the ball. She held her sticks tightly together as she weaved in and out of Ichisi players, looking for a teammate to whom to pass. She dove to the ground to avoid an Ichisi lightning bolt that would have bored into her chest. She rolled, then sprang to her feet, leaped into the air, and stretched her arm high above her head, rocketing the ball toward a teammate.

At just that moment, the big Ichisi girl plowed into her. Ayoka landed flat on her back and didn't move.

The crowd gasped.

The referee called time-out just long enough for a couple of other fae to escort Ayoka safely from the field.

The game quickly resumed. The two fae sat Ayoka up on a blanket near Taylor, assessing her condition. She didn't seem to be in pain, just winded. Taylor wasn't surprised; it had to be nearly 100 degrees.

Someone handed Ayoka a jug of water. She poured half of it over her face before downing the rest in a single gulp.

"Are you okay?" Taylor said. The trainer (or whatever he was called) patted Ayoka on the shoulder. The nunnehi girl grimaced, but nodded to Taylor.

"That was amazing. You're really good."

"Thanks," Ayoka gasped. She lay down on the blanket and shielded her face from the sun with her arm.

"This heat is killing me! How do you even survive, living down here?"

"You get used to it," Taylor said. "In another couple hours, the sun will be setting, and—"

Taylor stopped herself. She had gotten so wrapped up in the game, and then with Bob, that she had totally forgotten the time. She pulled her cell phone from her purse. No signal! She studied the position of the sun in the sky. It had to be close to five o'clock.

"Oh, crud," she said. "I've got to go. My parents will be missing me."

"What? But the game isn't over! The next goal—"

"I'm sorry, Ayoka. I really am. I.... Good luck!"

She wove her way back out of the arena. Maybe she could make up a story for why she had to step out for a while. As she hustled through the streets, even though she knew it was hopeless, she tried her mom's phone number.

Taylor started to panic. By the time she got back to the Lesser Temple Mound, she was sweating at least as heavily as Ayoka. Her mouth was dry. Her breathing was rapid.

She trudged up the side of the mound, excusing herself when she nearly tripped over a little person on his way down.

She searched for the telltale shimmer where the portal to the Topside world was located. As she did before, she willed the portal into existence and jumped straight through.

She bounded off the mound, across the grass, back to the footpath, and down to the parking area. She fumbled with her bike chain, then jammed it into her purse and sped off as fast as she could pedal.

It only took her seven minutes to reach the entrance to the park, but traffic was backed up on the road outside—a stalled car had turned it into a giant parking lot. Ignoring the horns and shouts of motorists, she wove across the street and took off toward home.

She almost made it except for the tickle in her chest that warned her an asthma attack was coming on.

She cursed to herself. She hadn't had an attack in over a month, and now, of all times, was the worst time to get one. She pulled over to the side of the road and got out her inhaler.

Fortunately, she was able to head this one off. She took a couple of strong, slow breaths. She checked the time: 5:21. Her only hope was that her mom was stuck in traffic. Breathing a frantic prayer, she started off once more.

It didn't work.

She hadn't gone a hundred yards before her phone rang. She stopped again and tried to control her breathing.

"Hi, Mom."

"Taylor! Where are you?"

"I just...stepped out for...something."

"Stepped out! Young lady, when we say to stay home, we mean it. Where are you, anyway?"

Taylor looked around. She was in sight of the convenience store where her dad liked to get gas.

"Red-E-Mart. But I'm on my way home. Honest."

"You'd better be!"

"Yes, ma'am."

Taylor bit her lip and pedaled toward home.

Taylor sat on the sofa in the living room with her hands folded in her lap. Her mom sat beside her. Her dad stood and paced.

"Taylor," her dad said, "we asked you to stay home today for a reason. Something bad could have happened."

"I know."

"I almost had a heart attack when I got home and you weren't here," her mom added. "If anything ever happened to you.... If you absolutely had to go out, you could have at least called."

"I know."

"I'm sorry the Matthews weren't here today for you to hang out with. But your dad and I thought you were old enough to manage by yourself. It was just one day, Taylor."

"Taylor," her dad said, "we just want you to be honest with us. We don't like the idea of you sneaking around behind our backs. Do you understand?"

"I understand," Taylor grumbled. "You don't trust me. Why is this even such a big deal? I made it home safe, didn't I?"

"Honey, we do trust you. Really!" her mom said. "But there are people out there that.... We're just trying to protect you. You're very smart and you're very independent, but you're still only thirteen years old."

"I know!"

"Is that all you can say?" her dad said. "If you know all this, then why are we even having this conversation?"

"Fred," her mom said. Taylor understood the tone of her voice: Don't lose your cool.

"It's like something has happened to you, Taylor," her dad continued. "You mope around all day. You don't have any appetite. You snap at your mother and me for the slightest things..."

"Fred, come sit down."

"And now you're wandering the streets all day while we're at work. Look at your arms, Taylor. You didn't get that much sun just biking to the convenience store and back."

Taylor looked down at her arms, pink from her day in the sun.

Her dad took his seat in the easy chair beside her mom.

"Taylor," her mom said, "tell us what's wrong. Is something bothering you? Is something upsetting you?"

Taylor took a breath and concentrated on her hands. Was Shanna right? Could her folks really handle the truth better than she thought they could?

"Has that Shelby girl been picking on you again?"

"This has nothing to do with Shelby Crowthers!"

"Is it...," her dad began, his voice shaky. "Does this have anything to do with a boy?"

"Dad!"

"Please tell us what's the matter, sweetie," her mom said. "Help us to understand what's going on."

Taylor tried to imagine how she would feel if she were in her parents' shoes. She thought about all the other times they had been in her corner: the snooty librarian who thought she was too young for the stack of books she wanted to check out, the countless meetings with exasperated teachers, the unfortunate incident at church with the Communion wafers...

Maybe her parents really could handle it. One thing was sure, though. They had to find out some day.

Okay, here goes, she thought.

"All right," she began. Then she paused for a long time as she tried to figure out how to start. Her parents both leaned forward to listen.

"The thing is...I...sort of...met my birth mother."

"You WHAT?" both parents shouted at once.

"How is that even possible?" her dad said. Once again, he was on his feet, pacing. "We were told nobody knew who your birth mother was. Adoption records are supposed to be sealed. Julie, we need to talk to your boss, get some legal advice—"

"We can talk to Jim Caulfield later, Fred," her mom said. She turned back toward her daughter with an expression of concern. "G-go on, sweetheart. When did this happen?"

"About a month ago."

"And you met her *how*, exactly?" her dad said.

"It's kind of a long story. But the point is.... Okay, do you remember that TV movie we watched a long time ago, where the adopted kid got sick, and nobody could figure out what was wrong till they tracked down his biological family...and it turned out he had some kind of disease you only get if you're from certain ethnic groups?"

Her mom stretched out her hand. "Oh, dear Lord. You're sick, aren't you? That's why you haven't been eating—"

"No, mom, I'm fine. Really," Taylor said. "Maybe that wasn't the best example. Let me start over...."

"Y-yes?"

"Okay, let's try this.... You know those books I like to read, where a kid finds out he's...magical?"

"Like a wizard or a demigod or something like that?" her dad said, puzzled.

"Exactly," Taylor said. "Some kid has magical parents...but somehow he doesn't find out about it until later on. And then, all of a sudden, he's thrown into...I don't know...a whole different world that's almost like the normal world, except there's magic and monsters and stuff. And he doesn't know what to do, or how to fit in, or...or anything?"

Her mom shifted in he seat. She and Mr. Smart traded nervous glances. "So...," she finally said, "your birth mother.... We always assumed she had problems, leaving you at that hospital like she did. Are you saying she's—"

"A faery. Actually, a fae. It's... Never mind."

Her mom stopped mid-sentence and could do nothing but stare at Taylor for several uncomfortable seconds. "I was going to say, 'in trouble.' That is what you mean by 'monsters,' right? Something dangerous? Drugs? Gangs? That sort of thing?"

"Nope," Taylor sighed. "The monsters are pretty much real."

There was another long pause. Taylor's parents looked at each other in silence.

"I-I'm sorry," her mom said at last. "Just so we're clear.... When you said 'faery' just now, you were actually talking about...."

"Mischievous nature sprites, bogeymen, leprechauns. That sort of thing." She tried to put on a smile. "Weird, huh?"

Her mom leaned back on the sofa and stared at the ceiling, stifling a sob.

"Taylor," her dad said, "you know you can trust us, right? You know there's nothing you could tell us that would ever make us stop loving you?"

"Y-yeah."

"Then, why can't you tell us what's really going on? I promise we won't judge you. Just...just tell us, and we'll work it out together. All right? Sweetheart?"

"I'm telling the truth."

"Taylor, you can't honestly expect us to believe that your birth mother is...is..."

"Look, I know it sounds weird, but..."

"Weird?" Mr. Smart said. The color had drained from his face. "Honey, it's impossible. There's no such thing as—"

"But what if there were?" Taylor interrupted. "What if...what if magic is real? I admit don't understand it either, but you've got to believe me."

"Taylor," Mrs. Smart said, placing an arm on her shoulder, "Why can't you just tell us the truth. What were you doing today?"

"I was hanging out with a friend in faery-land."

"Don't take that tone with your mother."

Taylor sighed. "Whatever."

She got up and left without saying another word. Her dad started to go after her, but her mom gestured for him to let her go.

Chapter 5

Seeing Things

The six-inch tall woman was Jill's first clue that something was wrong.

She and William were tossing around a Frisbee at a nearby park with their cousins. Germaine, seventeen and a star on his high-school football team, kept throwing too far just to watch his cousins and his baby sister run after it. His last throw sent the neon-green disk into a clump of trees near the edge of the park.

Jill was closest, so after giving her cousin a disgusted scowl, she trudged off to find it.

The woman sat cross-legged on a tree branch roughly shoulder-high. She was cloaked in a gray haze, like fog on a lake. Even so, she radiated silvery light as if she were wired with a light bulb inside her.

Jill stopped short.

"Are you enjoying your vacation?" the woman said.

Despite the haze, Jill recognized her at once as the strange dark-haired woman from her dreams. She started to tremble. She opened her mouth to scream.

"Now, now," the woman said. "We'll have none of that." Something in her voice compelled Jill to obey. She stood silent and slack-jawed as the tiny woman continued to speak.

"We have business, you and I," she said.

Jill said nothing.

"You remember, don't you? Our conversation from the other night? You are a very gifted young lady, Jill Matthews. You have great potential."

Jill pondered what that could mean. Truth be told, part of her was curious what the woman was talking about. The other part, the larger part, refused to accept that what was happening was even real—even if it was happening in broad daylight.

"You can't deny who you are," the woman said. "Or *what* you are. Sooner or later, you will have to face reality."

"Look who's talking about reality," Jill said. "I may be going crazy, but I still know you don't even exist!"

"Point taken," the woman said. "But tell me, Jill. How do you *know* that I don't exist?"

"What? I mean—look at you! You're no bigger than one of my brother's old action figures. You're just...just..."

"Just what, precisely?"

Jill was about to say, 'a figment of my imagination,' but she stopped herself. Somehow, she knew that wasn't the right answer—as much as she hoped it was! Instead, she said something else, and her words surprised her even as they escaped her lips.

"You're just some kind of...projection."

The woman smiled.

"And you, Jill Matthews, are blessed with Second Sight."

There was nothing Jill could say to that because she didn't have a clue what it meant.

"Jill! What's keeping you?" It was William.

"Coming!" Jill called.

The tiny woman evaporated into the haze that had surrounded her. At the same time, she spoke over Jill's shoulder.

"You see things, my dear."

As soon as the woman spoke, Jill gasped and whipped around. There the woman stood at her full height. She gazed down into Jill's eyes with an intensity that burned a hole into her soul.

"Things that lie beyond what others of your kind perceive," she said. "It is a powerful gift...and a great burden."

"William! Germaine!"

"Wouldn't you like to see? Just a little bit?"

"Jill! Come on!" William said as he appeared from the other side of the tree. At the same time, the woman vanished in a flash of light.

Jill spun around.

"William...!"

"What's wrong?"

She turned back to the spot where the woman had been a second before. Now, there was only empty space. There was no wind, no sound of birds in the trees. The entire park seemed to hold its breath.

"Jill?"

William looked spooked. He was breathing hard, glancing this way and that. Germaine and Tonya were right behind him.

"D-did you see...?"

"I'm not sure what I saw," William confessed.

"What? I didn't see anything," Germaine said.

"Me neither," Tonya said.

Germaine noticed the Frisbee laying at the foot of the tree. "So are we gonna play or what?"

Jill just stood there, stunned.

"C-can we just go home now?"

"Aw, man! It's still light out! Another ten minutes?"

"No," Jill said. "I want to go home."

Germaine started to complain, but William cut him off. "You stay if you want," he said. Jill noticed he was trembling as much as she was. "We're going back to Maymay's."

"She did say we could have ice cream later," Tonya offered.

And that seemed to settle it. The four cousins walked the half-mile back to their grandmother's house. Germaine and Tonya led the way; Jill and William let them get out ahead of them.

The air was hot and muggy, even for seven o'clock. The sun hung low in the sky and bathed the trees in fiery hues. The colors seemed more vibrant than ever. With every rustling leaf, warm undertones infused the natural greens and browns with almost unearthly flashes of gold, silver, yellow, orange, and scarlet. The sky was as bright and blue as it had ever been, but beneath the blue was the encroaching purple and pink of sunset.

The breeze tickled the hairs on the back of Jill's neck. It wasn't an especially cool breeze, but it was welcome.

"You saw her, didn't you?" she finally whispered.

They walked silently past a couple more houses before William answered her.

"I don't know about a 'her'...but there was...something. Like a fog or a mist. But it only lasted a second."

Jill sighed. "It was real."

"What was real? What did you see?"

There was another long silence. They were only a few lots away from Maymay's house. Jill heard the concern in her brother's voice loud and clear. The measured breathing, the way he kept swallowing—his mouth was as dry as hers.

A cardinal flitted above the street, decked out in his lively red plumage. Jill spied his mate nesting in a nearby cypress tree, practically invisible with her more subdued coloration.

Jill struggled to put her fears into words. William had seen something, even if he wasn't sure what. Apparently, Germaine and Tonya hadn't seen a thing. She wondered why.

"I don't know what it was," she said.

By now, Germaine and Tonya were on Maymay's porch. There was a familiar creak, and the door opened to smiling faces and the smells of her grandmother's kitchen. Her cat, Merle, wove between Maymay's feet swishing his orangey tail.

Maymay beamed at her grandchildren. Her face almost literally glowed with love and pride. Jill became enthralled by her grandmother's kind yet wrinkled face. There was strength in those lines—the strength that comes from growing up black in the segregated South, the strength that refuses to pack up and move just because a hurricane washes away most of your city. Sure, Maymay was strong, but she never became hard or bitter. As much as Jill could read her strength, her love and patience and gentleness were just as apparent in the twinkle of her eyes and in her welcoming smile.

Halfway up the driveway, Jill realized something was different. It was like she was truly seeing her grandmother for the first time, ambling about with her walking stick with Merle at her feet. She didn't just see her face or her ample frame. Somehow, the deepest parts of her were as clear as day. And it wasn't just Maymay. She saw everything that way: the leaves, the birds, the sky. The air itself seemed to shimmer with life. The world around her was bursting with possibilities, with magic.

Her heart fluttered. They had finally reached the door. Maymay was waving them toward the kitchen.

"Don't say anything to Mom or Dad, okay?"

"Are you sure, sis? If something is wrong..."

"Nothing is wrong," Jill said. "At least, I don't think so."

The next morning, Jill woke up to a world exploding with color and sensation. The aroma of bacon and eggs stirred her to full consciousness. She was starving! She got out of bed and threw on her clothes while humming "Respect" by Aretha Franklin. It was as if someone had turned a giant, invisible dial and ramped everything good in her life up to eleven.

It was the Matthews' last full day in New Orleans. Germaine and Tonya and their parents would head home to Jackson, Mississippi after breakfast. Jill and William and their parents had planned to spend the day in the French Quarter.

Everyone milled around Maymay's tiny kitchen, filling their plates.

Merle hopped into Jill's lap and stared at her for the longest time. She shooed him away, but he just climbed back up and looked her in the eye.

"Maymay, the milk don't smell right." William held the open jug to his scrunched-up nose.

"I bought that jug two days ago!" Jill's uncle LeVon protested.

"I'm sorry, honey," Maymay told William. "Drink orange juice today, and your daddy can bring home some fresh milk this afternoon.

"Is your fridge staying cold enough, Momma?" Jill's mom said. "If we need to buy you a new one…"

"Now, Sophie. I've had that refrigerator for twenty years. If it needs replacing, I can take care of it." Maymay's voice was light and cheerful, but Jill couldn't help notice something odd about the way she glanced her way. "I won't have my children fussing over me when I can take care of myself. Ain't that right, Merle?"

Merle had taken up a position beneath Jill's seat. He turned his head at the sound of his name, then went back to staring at Jill.

After breakfast, William asked, "Are you sure you won't come with us to the French Quarter, Maymay?"

"You all go on," she answered with a grin. "I've got reading to catch up, isn't that right, Tonya?"

Tonya smiled, but Mrs. Matthews let out an exasperated sigh from the adjacent dining room where the other adults were eating.

"I can't believe my own sister would let her kids read that… stuff." There was a ferocity in her tone that took Jill by surprise.

"Sophie, we've had this conversation before," Aunt Odette said. "It's the first thing she's ever been excited about reading. What's the harm?"

"What's the harm?" Jill's mom said. "You grew up in New Orleans, too, Odette. You mean to tell me you're fine with all that voodoo nonsense?"

"It's just a story, Sophie. Nobody takes it seriously."

"That's what they *want* you to think," Mrs. Matthews said with a sidewise glance.

42

Jill's mom and aunt went back and forth, but Jill was distracted by something besides their words. She couldn't quite put her finger on it. It wasn't quite a shimmer, much less a glow, but something was different about their faces. It was like Jill didn't only hear the words, but sensed—even saw—the spirit behind them.

"The Bible is very clear..." her mom started. And there it was again, as if the subtle note of genuine love and concern in her voice was translated into an almost physical form.

"Sophie. It's just make-believe," Aunt Odette said. The same gleam or flicker or whatever it was surrounded her face. Goodness. Jill decided she was somehow seeing her aunt's goodness. It looked just like her mom's.

Jill glanced across the table at William, wondering if he was seeing it, too.

"Now, now," Maymay intervened. "I won't have my girls fighting under my own roof. Lord knows I had enough of that when you were children! Sophie, we all know you disapprove of that magic stuff in those books Tonya likes. That's one reason I started reading them myself, just to put my mind at ease. Now I'll admit, they're not my cup of tea, but they're not what you think. I can guarantee you my little grandbaby isn't going to start casting spells or whipping around on a broomstick just because she's filled her head with a little bit of imagination. You've got to let your sister raise her kids as she thinks best."

Aunt Odette started to say something, but Maymay rounded on her before she could even start.

"And Odette, there's no need for you to get your panties in a bunch because Sophie sees things differently." Jill stifled a giggle. Maymay shimmered, too, only stronger than either of her daughters. How in the world was she the only person seeing it?

"She and Charles have their own kids to raise," Maymay continued, "and they deserve the same right to set the ground rules in their house that you expect them to give to you and LeVon." She crossed her arms. "I thought I taught you both to live and let live."

She took a slow, deliberate sip from her coffee cup. Apparently, the matter was settled.

Mrs. Matthews excused herself and slinked away, but not before Jill heard her mutter something about poisoning children's minds.

Jill thanked her lucky stars she hadn't mentioned anything about meeting a faery last night in the park. That would definitely have not gone over well! She hoped William wouldn't say anything, either.

Jill's mom liked to take a stroll in the French Quarter whenever she came to visit her mom. It was her chance to browse the curiosities at the French Market and stock up on all her favorite sauces and mixes—not to mention buy some fresh, warm pecan pralines—at the New Orleans Cooking School.

A shopping trip might not have seemed like anything fun for Jill and William, but they knew Jackson Square could be counted on for at least a few minutes' entertainment. Today was no exception. On one side of the square, near the Café du Monde, a hobo clown twisted balloons into dogs and swords and airplanes in between goofy jokes. He had attracted half a dozen families with younger children to watch his show. A little further up the street was a juggler. In front of Saint Louis Cathedral, a band (guitar, harmonica, keyboard, and washboard) played "Sittin' on the Dock of the Bay," "Stand By Me" and other classics. Jill's parents held hands and leaned into each other, smiling. Passers-by dropped coins and bills into an open guitar case in front of their portable amplifier.

Another crowd had gathered around a magician doing simple illusions in front of The Cabildo, the old governor's mansion next door to the cathedral. While the elder Matthews enjoyed the music, Jill drifted toward this odd character in mismatched clothes with big, bushy eyebrows and a winsome smile.

He told stories and jokes as he pulled coins from the ears of children and puzzled their parents with card tricks. Everyone clapped when he made a dove appear from out of a wadded-up paper bag.

Jill studied him with wonder. It took her a minute or two to realize that she was seeing something in him, just as she had seen something in her mom at breakfast. She couldn't put her finger on what it was yet.

"William," she whispered as her brother came up beside her. "Is there something funny about that guy?"

"Yeah. Just look at him: red shirt, purple pants, and what's with the polka-dot tie?"

"That's not what I mean." Something about the street magician didn't add up. It was like he was wearing a mask or something. He pulled a young girl from the audience to be his assistant. Her dad smiled and encouraged her. As he bent down to ask her name, Jill figured it out. There was something wrong about the way he stooped over.

"How tall you figure he is?" she whispered.

"Five-seven," William answered. "Maybe five-eight."

Jill frowned. "I don't know. I think he's faking it."

"How can you fake how tall you are?"

"And now, ladies and gentlemen," the magician said, raising his voice, "Chelsea here is going to hold my magic box..." He gave Jill a sideways glance, like he had heard what she had said. "Now, I'm going to need another volunteer. You, young man." He knelt down beside a little boy about eight years old and showed him a handful of different brightly colored handkerchiefs.

Jill's vision blurred as she looked at him. If she squinted just right, she'd swear the man couldn't have been any taller than four feet, with big, pointy ears and long, nimble fingers. She gasped in spite of herself.

"Look again!" she whispered to William, more urgently this time.

William studied the magician as the boy picked one of the handkerchiefs. The magician threw it into the air, and it disappeared with a flash.

"Okay," William said. "So maybe he's only about five-five. So what?"

"Look at his ears!"

"Chelsea, do you still have the box?" the magician said. He gave Jill another impatient glance. Chelsea opened the box to reveal the same handkerchief that had just vanished into thin air. Everybody clapped. At the magician's urging, Chelsea took a bow.

"I'm going to take a break now, ladies and gentlemen. I hope you enjoyed the show!"

The audience dispersed. Several people dropped money in the man's upturned top hat. He began putting away his props in a weatherworn trunk.

Soon, only Jill and William were still standing around.

"Can I help you?" the magician said. The tone of his voice sounded anything but helpful.

"N-no, sir," Jill said.

"Then I'd thank you to keep your opinions to yourself." Gone was the jovial demeanor of the street magician. Now the man seemed visibly agitated. As he slammed his trunk shut, he flickered in Jill's vision. For a split second, she couldn't decide if his head was on top of his shoulders where it was supposed to be or somewhere in the middle of his chest.

"Some of us value our privacy."

"We're sorry," William chimed in. "My sister's just—"

The magician stalked away before William could finish apologizing.

"Sis, you want to tell me what that was about?"

"No idea," Jill said as she watched the strange little man disappear down Pirate Alley.

"And he honestly looked normal to you?"

"I guess. I mean, other than his outfit. Why?"

Jill shook her head. She turned around in a slow circle, taking in all the sights of Jackson Square: the sun-drenched trees, the stately white columns of The Cabildo, the crazy-quilt of colors and styles worn by tourists and locals alike. Some practically beamed with love and happiness, like the little girl walking hand in hand with her parents or a young couple having their portrait done by a street artist.

Others gave off a different vibe that made Jill nervous. A shady looking guy smoking a cigarette outside a café seemed distracted. He was up to something no good—he must have been. At least, something about him made Jill very uncomfortable. She instinctively took a step back and then scouted out her parents.

"No. It's nothing," she said, and walked back toward the musicians, now on the final notes of "Only You."

"Jill," William said. He gave her a look that said he knew full well she wasn't telling him the whole story.

Okay, it was something. She just didn't know what. And until she did, she figured she'd keep it to herself.

Some people value their privacy.

Chapter 6

Oak Hill

Saturday nights were the worst, especially in the summer. People would be surprised how many fool kids dared each other to walk through a graveyard in the middle of the night. Even a little country churchyard like his attracted them like a magnet. Silas's job was simple: make sure the little punks only try it once.

There hadn't been a new burial at Oak Hill Baptist Church in over forty years, but he figured that just added to the sense of mystery. Why prove your bravery in any old cemetery when you could go out to a really old, creepy one?

Silas had to admit the place did look pretty creepy after dark. The steeple stretched up toward heaven like a weathered, wooden spike. On a clear night when the moon was full, you could stand amid the rows of headstones and look back up the hill toward the church house and swear you were in another world.

He was in his usual spot in the bell tower. From that height, his keen eyesight gave him a clear view of the whole cemetery even on a cloudy night like this one. The air was silent and still. If not for a distant screech owl, Silas might have imagined he was the only living thing for a mile in any direction.

But something wasn't right.

It was just a tickle in the back of his mind at first: an odd, indistinct feeling that something was amiss. He didn't see anything or even hear anything. The dogs were somewhere fast asleep—as usual. Yet he couldn't help thinking someone was approaching. He'd have to go check it out.

Silas got up and stretched his muscles. He opened his trapdoor and slid quickly and quietly to the ground. He landed on the edge of the parking lot and skittered across the asphalt and into the graveyard. He shimmied up an old poplar tree and gazed at the horizon.

He sniffed the air. Nothing.

Then his bat-like ears perked up. There was definitely somebody out there. A minute later, he could make out the voices. They were talking about the usual foolishness: baseball, summer jobs, who's got the lamest parents, who thinks which girl is hot.

Silas grumbled to himself. *Dang kids better just keep walking*, he thought. If only he could be so lucky. He saw them now at the edge of the property. Three boys. Probably staying over at one of their houses nearby, looking for a little excitement. They all carried flashlights. One of them was shaking a bottle of spray paint.

Great.

He dropped silently from the tree back to the ground. The dogs were nowhere to be seen, the stupid beasts. Silas promised himself to have words later with the guy he got them from. Then again, if he couldn't handle three Jack kids up to no good without calling in the dogs, he might as well retire.

"This way's quicker," one of the boys said, stepping off the road and onto the cemetery grounds. The other two didn't look convinced.

"You're not chicken, are you?"

There was a brief argument involving the other boys' mothers and insinuations about what kind of skivvies they were wearing. Silas had heard it all before. It bored him, really, but what could he do? It wasn't his place to straighten out every budding juvenile delinquent in the county. He just had to make sure they kept off his yard.

He wrapped himself in glamour and stalked forward. The boys were now creeping among the gravestones.

Silas clambered up onto the tallest monument (Lt. Robert Bartimaeus Thorne, CSA, 1st Reg., 1837–1899). The boys were only a few yards away but, of course, they couldn't have seen Silas if they were looking straight at him. He grinned a sly grin and got to work.

He never wanted to show himself if he could avoid it. Too much of that and he'd have ghost hunters tramping around the place every night. His life had too many headaches without adding that. No, best to leave them guessing. Let their own imaginations do all the work.

Using glamour, he sent out the suggestion of the sound of a snapping twig.

One of the boys stopped cold. "W-what was that?" he said.

The others stopped to listen.

Once more, Silas created the sound of footsteps. This time, all three of them heard it. Flashlight beams swept out in every direction.

Now, we add a little bit of wind in the trees...

"M-m-mose?" a boy squeaked.

"It's just the wind, Jerome!" the first boy, obviously the ringleader, insisted. He called Jerome a couple of impolite names. The last boy, not wanting to look scared, joined in with Mose's ribbing.

Peer pressure! Silas thought. *When are these stooges going to wise up?*

The three inched forward. Mose wore a face of steely resolve. He shook his can of spray paint.

Silas cursed. He was going to have to escalate.

What'll it be this time? he pondered. *Ghoul? Ghost? Or maybe the classic black dog? That always gets their attention.*

He gestured, drawing more glamour under his control. He produced a low, baleful moaning, the kind that started at the edge of your consciousness and didn't really sink in at first. Maybe it was just a siren in the distance, or somebody's air conditioner running. Then it hits you that you're listening to the wail of something not quite human—at least not anymore.

The boys spun around. Once again, flashlight beams bounced off headstones. The third kid started to whimper.

Silas only grinned. If he played his cards right, he wouldn't have to become visible after all.

Suddenly, the night exploded with the sound of barking. The boys shrieked like little girls and scrambled back the way they came.

"What the—?" Silas boomed, but no one was there to hear him as he shouted and slipped off his gravestone perch.

"Dang it!"

He stomped off, wondering what the dogs had gotten into.

Finding them took a certain amount of skill because their bark got louder with distance. At a few hundred feet, the agitated baying seemed to come from everywhere at once. But Silas took a hunch and headed back to the church house. Sure enough, the sound diminished the closer he got. They had to be just around the corner.

Silas kept his mist of invisibility tight around him. He edged around the corner of the old, whitewashed building.

The dogs, a couple of redtick coonhounds, had cornered somebody near the edge of the parking lot. Whoever it was, he held the dogs at bay. Whenever one tried to get within biting range, it slammed against an invisible barrier and fell back, stunned. What was a Wonderling doing here?

Silas arched his eyebrows and sized up the intruder in about two seconds: pointed ears, glowing red eyes, built lean but strong, and with a face only a mother could love. He skittered forward. No matter how many times they failed to get through, the dogs continued to attack the invisible wall.

"Goodness! Mercy!" Silas called. "Down!" He let his glamour dissipate. The intruder noticed him for the first time.

One of the dogs backed off but growled a mean, rumbling growl and refused to take its eyes off its quarry. Silas snapped his fingers and the dog retreated to his side. The other dog, a female with a big patch of red covering most of her face and back, pressed the attack.

"Mercy! Heel!"

The female gave one last barely audible bark before backing off.

Silas rested his arm on Goodness's back and scratched the nape of his neck. He had more white in his coat than Mercy did, with red patches mainly on his face, shoulders, and haunches.

Silas looked up at the stranger. He was quite a bit taller than Silas. Most people were.

"You want to state your business, buddy?"

The stranger broke out in a stupid smile that did nothing for his overall appearance. "Silas Bludgitt!" he called.

Silas narrowed his eyes.

"Do I know you?"

"Dingle's the name."

The name didn't ring any bells.

"Yeah?"

"I'm here on official business for the Winter Court of Arradherry."

A cold shiver went down Silas's spine. The last thing he needed was a visitor from the Winter Court.

"I've got no business with them," he spat.

"You do now," Dingle said. "At least, you do if you know what's good for you."

"Are you trying to threaten me, bub?"

"I'm just passing on a message," he said. His demeanor was relaxed, almost cordial. It didn't fool Silas for a second. "You see, the Primus would appreciate if you'd do something for him."

"Yeah. Crom Cornstack is a really big fan of mine. What's he want? My autograph?"

Dingle shrugged.

"I'd think twice before I said anything else, Bludgitt," the intruder said. At the same time, he grew about six inches taller. "The Primus has resources. He can do things for people he likes."

"That's not the problem. It's what he can do *to* people he doesn't like that makes me nervous."

"Ancient history," Dingle said. "Things are different now. Things change in seventy years, you know? The Primus is ready to let bygones be bygones. I can't say he'll feel this way for long, but he does now. If I were you, I'd at least hear him out."

"Get off my yard," Silas said.

"If you insist. But first, two words."

Silas grumbled.

"Taylor Smart."

I should have known, Silas thought. If half the rumors he'd heard the past month were true....

"Who?"

"Never play poker, Bludgitt. You can't bluff worth beans."

"Okay, so her family are members at Oak Hill. What of it?"

"Let's just say she went and got herself on Crom Cornstack's naughty list. Ugly business. Headaches for everyone, let me tell you. Anyway, the Primus is looking for somebody to, erm, take care of her...so to speak."

"I'm a church grim," Silas said. "I don't 'take care' of little girls."

"Suit yourself," Dingle said. "There are plenty of people who'd jump at the chance to do Mr. Cornstack a favor. Especially people who have nothing to lose and everything to gain."

Dingle's tone turned sharp. Goodness and Mercy growled.

"I thought I told you to leave."

"If you insist," Dingle said. "But if you change your mind..."

"Out. Now."

Dingle bowed and blinked away.

Silas stood there for half a minute peering into the darkness, listening for any sign of movement. Finally, he convinced himself his visitor was really gone.

He exhaled.

"Come on, you two," he said. Goodness sniffed his face while Mercy licked his hand. The three of them trudged back to the church house together.

He sent the dogs out to the graveyard and clambered back up to the bell tower. As he replayed his conversation with Dingle in his mind, his hands began to shake and his heart began to pound. His mouth turned dry. He was suddenly, and quite explicably, wide-awake.

Getting strong-armed by one of the most powerful fae in North America had a way of doing that. It was a given that Crom Cornstack wouldn't like being refused. Least of all by Silas Bludgitt. The question was, what was he going to do about it—and how soon?

For several long minutes, Silas contemplated packing his bag and getting out of town at once. But he didn't like being pushed around and he was stubborn enough not to stand for it. No. By oak, ash, and thorn, he was staying right there. This was his home: it had been for the past seventy years. In all that time, he kept his head down and stayed out of other people's business.

He wasn't about to be intimidated.

And he sure as blazes wasn't going to do anything to an innocent kid just because some Gentryman snapped his fingers.

He sat and stewed and peered down upon the church grounds until gray morning light first crept over the horizon. He was surprised that nothing else happened during the night. There are lots of things a powerful fae could do to a church grim if he wanted to. Still, even the Winter Primus might think twice about trying something this time of year. The Summer Court could be pretty touchy about jurisdictions.

Whatever the reason, not being dead was something to be thankful for.

Silas stood and stretched. He wasn't sleepy, just stiff and mentally exhausted. He slipped through his trapdoor and crawled all the way down to his apartment in the basement. There, he splashed water on his gray, grizzled face and pulled a gap-toothed comb through what was left of his hair. He fixed himself a cup of coffee and a piece of dry toast for breakfast.

Cornstack or no Cornstack, he had to get going.

He put his coffee cup in the washbasin and padded out to the boiler room. From the tiny slit of window in the corner, he could see the sun peering over the horizon through the trees to the east. The Reverend always came early on Sunday to put the finishing touches on his sermon and pray by himself in the sanctuary. The dogs would have to be locked away by then.

He poured a handful of dry dog food into two tin plates. Like a lizard, he climbed up the wall to poke his head through the open window.

"Goodness! Mercy!" he growled. When nothing happened, he called again.

"Come on, you stupid beasts! It's time for breakfast!"

A minute later, he heard panting and the pat-patting of paws on the grass outside. *Good*, he thought. *The Winters do anything to my dogs, they'll be sorry!*

Goodness and Mercy appeared in a flash of light on the bare concrete floor. Goodness leaped up to rest his front paws on Silas's shoulders and tried to drown him with slobbery dog kisses. Mercy stood by wagging her tail.

"Get off me, you blamed flea-bitten mutt!" Silas pushed the dog aside with some effort just as the other one tried to get in on the action.

"Down, Mercy!" he barked. "It's time to lock you two out before the deathlings get here."

As if on cue, Silas heard the Reverend's car pulling into the parking lot.

"You two beat everything, you know that?" He grabbed up the plates of dog food and, holding them as high over his head as he could, led the dogs through the doorway.

In seventy years, no Topsider had ever found that door. Church custodians, furnace repairmen, and an unending stream of hide-and-seekers on youth group lock-ins had never seen anything but a rough plastered wall. Silas had hidden his front door behind the thickest mist of glamour he could manage, and reapplied it several times every week just to keep it fresh. He doubted even a Gentryman could see through the illusion he had created if he didn't know where to look.

"On second thought..." he mused. Then he stopped just long enough to add a little bit more.

On the other side of the door was Silas's true home. It was a lot like the portions of the church visible to Topsiders, only furnished in an older style—a country meeting-house from the 1800s restored to its original appearance and then converted into a private dwelling. It boasted hardwood floors, oil lamps, a Ben Franklin stove on the far wall, and simple handmade furniture.

Silas led the dogs through this modest apartment and out a door on the other side. There, it was down a flight of winding stairs and then out into a grassy field, sheltered from prying eyes, where Goodness and Mercy could enjoy themselves for a while beneath a bright, turquoise sky.

Silas set down the dog food on the porch and went back inside. He had plenty of time to make one last pass through the building and grounds before the earliest of the early birds would start trickling in.

He put on his Sunday suit—all but the jacket. Even in the Wonder, central Georgia was as hot as all get out in the summer. Since no one was going to see him, Silas didn't see the point of sweating like a pig all day. He left his thin burgundy tie on the peg behind his bedroom door where it had hung since before Vergosus Bright faded.

He halfway expected to find something deadly on the grounds. He wasn't disappointed when he didn't. He smirked with satisfaction.

Cars were already starting to trickle in. Sunday school teachers, deacons, a couple of eager beavers from the Golden Circle Sunday school class who were always early on general principle. Silas thought he had heard something about a missions committee meeting scheduled for that morning. All pretty ordinary.

He took his time walking back through the graveyard, studying every car as it pulled onto the property. He slipped around the back of the building, just as he did last night, to get a better look at the parking lot.

A green minivan pulled in. Silas recognized the man driving it, the woman in the passenger seat, and the slump-shouldered teenager in the back.

Mr. Smart hopped out and slammed his door shut probably a little harder than he meant to. He stalked around to the other side of the car, teeth gritted, while Mrs. Smart craned around to say something to their daughter. She jabbed a finger at the girl, who merely glowered back. A minute later, the two of them got out as well.

Silas crouched around the corner. There was no danger the two adults would see him, but the girl? The birds had been tweeting for a month about a daughter of Shanna Hellebore turning up. Taylor Smart was her name. Until last month, nobody even knew she existed. She was a pureblooded fae of the daoine sídhe, but raised as a Topsider. Silas scratched his head at the very thought. It sounded like something out of Edgar Rice Burroughs.

The Smarts trudged up the steps to the front door. None of them looked especially happy to be there. Nothing like a good old knock-down-drag-out in the car on the way to church to put you in the proper mood for worship.

Taylor lagged behind. Her mom held the door for her. She didn't say anything, but she didn't have to. The tension in the air nearly made Silas's ears pop. Taylor was practically shimmering with glamour, like a teakettle about to whistle.

Silas finished his rounds inside the church building. Beneath and between the walls and floors of the Topside structure was a maze of passages that could only be accessed through the Wonder. He slipped through a storage closet here, a radiator there, a crack in the wall in the library, and half a dozen other secret openings that no one else could see.

He kept telling himself it wasn't like Crom Cornstack to do anything in broad daylight—and less than two weeks before Midsummer at that. Still, you could never be too sure. He'd better keep an eye on that Smart girl, just to play it safe.

Midsummer or no Midsummer, trouble was coming. That was the one thing Silas was absolutely sure of.

Chapter 7

A Noble Calling

The shady guy with the cigarette was on the morning news the next day. Jill recognized him at once. The news reporter gave his name as his picture flashed on the TV screen and said he had been arrested the night before for some pretty serious crimes.

Jill didn't doubt it for a second. In fact, the whole thing sent a shiver through Jill's soul that didn't quite leave her during church with Maymay or even hours later when she and her family were on the plane, heading back home to Georgia. She knew there was something fishy about the guy when she saw him in front of that café. She couldn't put her finger on it, but she was certain then he was up to no good—just as much as she was certain of the goodness she had seen earlier in the faces of her mother, her aunt, and her grandmother.

Maneuvering through the crowds in the Atlanta airport, Jill struggled to focus on where she was going. She felt compelled to look into the faces of as many people as she could, searching for the truth about them their eyes would reveal. A young woman walked hand-in-hand with a man in army fatigues holding his baby daughter. Jill was sure she saw a golden aura surrounding the three of them. Another man, disheveled and twitchy, walked under a gray cloud of despair that sent shudders up Jill's spine. For every happy vision, there were two or three of the other kind. Eventually, she just looked at her feet.

On the ride back to Macon, she kept her eyes shut and pretended to sleep while William played *The Amazing*

Spider-Man on his Nintendo and her parents talked about grown-up things—bills and work and stuff.

As they turned off the interstate and toward home, nothing looked right.

Yes, all the familiar landmarks were there. It was just that they didn't look right.

The trees seemed to jut upward at weird angles, and the clouds looked odd, as if they had been artificially colorized or something. The late-afternoon shadows shifted against the modest brick homes like malevolent intruders looking for a way inside.

She hauled her suitcase to her room. Without stopping to turn on the lights, she heaved it onto the bed and then crawled up next to it. She lay there, relishing the stillness, until her dad called her to bring her dirty clothes to the laundry room.

"Coming!" she called. She forced herself to get up. She unzipped her suitcase and started emptying clothes into her laundry hamper.

Outside her window, a pair of glowing yellow eyes caught her attention. Her heart started to race, but she braced herself and went to investigate.

It was an owl, a big one. It perched on a branch not too far away where it could spy down upon Jill's bedroom. It looked at her, unruffled, as she stared up at it.

"This is ridiculous!" Jill told herself. "It's just a stupid owl." She turned away, but caught movement out of the corner of her eye. When she looked back, the owl was gone. In its place was a young man in blue jeans and a plain black tee shirt.

Jill began to shiver and quickly shut her blinds. "Not real," she told herself. "Not. Real."

She hauled her hamper down to the laundry room. She nibbled at her supper—Dad had stopped for fast food on the way home, but she didn't have much appetite. After rearranging the French fries on her plate for about twenty minutes, she announced she was tired and was going to turn in early.

That was a mistake.

She had barely fallen asleep when a familiar voice asked, "Did you have a nice flight?"

Jill was once again in Gethsemane Cemetery. Once again, the tall, dark-haired woman sat beneath the angel statue. She held a goblet in her hand, a huge black stone drinking cup like something that belonged in a medieval castle. The rim was adorned with angular writing and intricate carved Celtic knot work. A golden band circled the rim. The mysterious woman swirled its contents around and held it to her nose to admire the aroma.

"What do you want?" Jill challenged her.

The woman smiled. "I just wanted to see how you were doing. Is that a crime? We haven't had time to visit since the park."

"You did something to me, didn't you?"

"The Second Sight was already there, my dear," the woman said in a silky purr. "I simply helped it along a bit." She rose from her seat on the bench to approach Jill. "I trust the experience didn't disappoint. After all, it's not as if you can avoid your destiny."

"W-what are you talking about?"

"I expect you know. I'll bet you've always been an insightful young lady, haven't you? A good judge of character? Sensitive to people's emotions? That's part of your gift—but only a very small part." She cradled the chalice in her hands.

"Take this cup, for instance. It belongs to a satyr back in Louisiana by the name of du Marais. Anyone else looking into it right now would see nothing but water. But you, my dear, might see practically anything."

She's just trying to flatter you, Jill told herself. "Yeah? So what?"

"I'd offer you a peek, but unfortunately," she sighed, "it isn't real. This is just a dream, after all. And, regrettably, the cup isn't even in my possession." The woman gestured, and it simply vanished from her hands.

"What do you intend to do when your gift becomes even stronger, child? When your eyes are fully opened to the world all around you—or, I should say, the world you suspect is all around you, though as yet you don't even have the vocabulary to talk about it?

The colors, the details, the love she saw in her mother, and the darkness in the guy at the café—is that what she was talking about?

"There's no turning back, I'm afraid. It's who you are, Jillian Marie Matthews." As she spoke her full name, Jill felt a tingle pass through her body from her head to her feet.

"Y-you don't know that!"

The woman tsk-tsked. "And I suppose for your next trick you'll keep on being thirteen years old for the rest of your life? It doesn't work that way, my dear. The body matures. So does the mind...and so does Second Sight." She leaned forward. "However...."

"However?"

"However, it doesn't have to be frightening. Yes, I know you're frightened by some of what you've seen, just as the rest of it has thrilled you more than you can say. But if you knew how to control your gift, to open yourself to the Wonder only when you wanted, that would be better, am I right?"

Jill tried not to show emotion, but she wasn't sure she was successful.

"You need a guide, a mentor."

Jill stared into the woman's eyes. She tried to see, really *see*, what she was after. She didn't trust her, but she couldn't say the woman was telling her anything but the truth. Just the opposite: everything she said confirmed things Jill already suspected.

It was true that she got a spooky vibe off of cigarette guy, and felt it again when she saw his face on the morning news. It was also true that she got to see something in the members of her own family that was beautiful. Pure. The birds, the trees, everything in the world was full of...did she call it "wonder"? And Jill had been able to see it in living color. Getting to see all that almost made the other part worth it.

"I don't guess you're offering me this out of the goodness of your heart," Jill said.

"No," the woman said. "But if you're prepared to continue our conversation, it shouldn't be inside your head. Suppose I meet you in your bedroom?"

Jill looked up at the woman, looked at her timeless beauty, her cheery smile. She nodded.

She awoke with a start. She sat straight up, and there was the woman at the foot of her bed. Above her fluttered three tiny orbs of light, like fireflies buzzing around the woman's head, but bright enough Jill could easily make out the woman's features.

"Have a chocolate," she said, gliding around to Jill's side and extending her hand. It was a truffle, and not the cheap kind they sold at the grocery stores in February for people who forgot about Valentine's Day until it was too late to come up with a decent present. No, this was the real thing: Jill could smell the rich, dark chocolate even at a distance, and the fancy swirl on top traced the shape of a delicate flower.

"Don't be afraid," the woman said. "It's not poison." She popped her own truffle in her mouth and smiled. "I love these, don't you?"

Before she knew it, Jill had the treat in her hand. The rich chocolaty aroma was almost more than Jill could handle.

"When I was younger, they used to add spices to chocolate and serve it as a drink," the woman said. "It was...an acquired taste. Now this, on the other hand..."

Jill looked down at the truffle. Before she knew what she was doing, she had bitten it in two. It was raspberry crème, her favorite, and it was delicious. She finished it in two bites.

She looked up at the strange woman, who kept a respectful distance. She stood with her arms crossed, waiting for Jill to finish chewing.

"Who are you?" Jill said.

"I don't make a habit of giving out my name, child. Perhaps in due time. You can call me 'Godmother' for now."

The two regarded each other in silence.

"Okay then." Jill sat up straight and crossed her legs underneath her bed sheet. She peered into the woman's eyes, hoping for the kinds of subtle clues that had always helped her form an impression of people and whether she could trust them. Nothing. There was only one other person Jill ever had a hard time getting a read on, and that was her best friend, Taylor.

"You say you can help me with...with...."

"With seeing more than you're ready to bear? It would be my pleasure."

"And what do you get out of it?"

The woman raised one eyebrow. "Directness isn't always a virtue, my dear, especially not with one's elders." In a second, she composed herself. "But I can definitely understand your concern. When you are older and more adept in your craft, we will discuss how you can return my favor."

"I don't understand. What do you mean, 'my craft'?"

"I'd have thought a bright girl like you would have figured that out by now."

Jill simply looked up at the woman.

"Jill, you're a witch."

"I beg your pardon?"

The woman frowned wryly. "I've been wanting to say something like that for twenty years. To be honest, I expected a different reaction. You're a witch, Jill. Or perhaps I should say, you've got the makings of a witch, and I daresay a rather good one—once you've been trained up a bit, of course."

"Now, wait one minute," Jill said. "I am not a witch. I don't want to be a witch."

"It's a noble calling, my dear," the woman said. "A subtle science, an exact art that few can master. And, as I said, you've got the potential to be great. Let me teach you." She bent ever so slightly forward. There was excitement in her eyes. "I can help you unlock powers beyond your imagination. You have it within

66

you to command the elements, Jill, or foretell the future, or ride the wind."

"But I don't want any of that!"

"I see," the woman said. "Then perhaps you would prefer to be the girl who grew up seeing things that no one else could see, who worried her parents so with her rambling, who eventually got herself locked away for her own good. Hmm?"

Jill trembled.

"I'm a patient woman. I can wait for you to decide," the woman said. "Far be it from me to force greatness upon you when you're not prepared to receive it. And, as a show of good faith, let me do something about your Second Sight."

"Just take it away!" Jill said.

"Alas, that is the one thing that not even I can do, as I believe I have explained. But I can teach you control. Suppose I give you your first lesson free? Would that prove my good intentions?"

"W-what do I have to do?"

"Find yourself a cup or a bowl. A good-sized one is best, stone if possible, but wood or ceramic will do in a pinch."

"Y-you mean like the one you showed me before? In my dream?"

"Precisely, my dear!" The woman beamed with satisfaction. "But don't worry about finding anything so fancy as the one I showed you. The satyr's cup is a precious family heirloom—or was until fairly recently...but I digress. Gazing into a scrying bowl is a wonderful way to clear the mind and settle the emotions. I think if you give it a try, you'll find you're no longer troubled by things that go bump in the night."

The woman extended her hand. The three orbs of light collected in her palm and immediately extinguished.

"So long for now, child, and pleasant dreams." There was a brief flash of light, and the woman vanished.

Jill slipped to the window and peered outside. Nobody was sitting on the tree branch. No owls, either.

She got back in bed and pulled the covers tight.

She laid with her eyes wide open the rest of the night.

Chapter 8

Secrets

"How much longer you figure you'll be grounded?" Jill asked. She and Taylor were outside with the rest of the Oak Hill Baptist youth group, picking up litter on the church grounds. It was Wednesday night. As usual, the teenagers had been given something vaguely interesting to do while their parents were at the mid-week Bible study.

The sun hovered above the horizon, casting long shadows across the grassy patch back behind the sanctuary.

Taylor stalled. She didn't really want to talk about it. It might lead to awkward questions, questions she didn't feel like trying to answer in such a public place. She stooped over to collect an errant soda can.

"I'm guessing till the end of summer vacation," she finally said. "Church. Chores. Piano practice. That's about it: no cell phone, no computer, no TV. I'm just glad they agreed to let you come with us tonight."

"Hey, what are friends for? My folks figure the more church, the better. It was pretty easy to convince them to let me come with you. But are you ever going to tell me what you did to get in this much trouble?"

There it was. Part of Taylor was dying to tell Jill everything—you don't keep something this big, this blazingly important, from your best friend. Part of her, though, was still gun-shy after the way her parents shot her down when she tried to tell them the truth.

Jill gave her a good, long gaze. It was as if she needed glasses and kept squinting and relaxing her eyes to get them into focus.

Here was Taylor's chance. Surely Jill would listen to what she had to say, wouldn't she? She wanted to tell her. She needed to tell somebody who would believe her. But...what if Jill didn't?

"It's a long story."

"We got time for the short version?"

Taylor sighed. She wandered toward the church cemetery.

"We got in an argument," she said.

"Aha! Well, that clears everything up!"

"*Give me a break, will you?*" Taylor said. Without even thinking about it, she added the least bit of presence to her words—a glamour trick that let her project an aura of power and confidence. It had a way of shutting down conversations she didn't want to have.

"Oh no," Jill said slowly. "You're not trying that stuff on me. No ma'am."

"What?"

"That...that *thing* you do with your eyes, your voice. It might work on other people, but it's not going to work on me, thank you very much."

"Yeah," Taylor sighed. "It doesn't really work on my folks, either." Apparently it was harder to use presence on somebody you actually cared about.

The girls resumed their walk through the graveyard. Jill picked up a can of spray paint and tossed it into the garbage bag she was carrying. They had drifted a good distance from the rest of the group. Taylor realized this would be her last chance to talk to Jill in private for the foreseeable future.

"Jill?" Taylor said.

"Yes?"

"Do you ever think about...magic?"

"What do you mean?" Jill asked. She seemed suddenly tense.

"Look, I know your folks don't like you reading fantasy books and all that. I just wondered...do you ever...I mean...what do you think...?"

"Listen, Taylor," Jill said. "There's a reason my parents don't allow that stuff in our house."

"Hey, I'm not judging anybody. I just—"

"I know you're not," Jill said. "Can we just change the subject?"

Taylor stopped in her tracks. "Sure, Jill. Sure. Don't have a cow."

"What's that supposed to mean? Just because I don't read that stupid stuff—"

"Stupid? Come on, Jill, there's no reason to call it stupid."

"Yeah, well…" Jill trailed off, suddenly distracted by something behind Taylor. She looked over her shoulder but saw nothing but the rest of the youth group mucking around in the tall grass.

"What?" she said.

"N-nothing," Jill said. From the look on her face, however, it was anything but nothing. Taylor looked around again. Out of the corner of her eye, she sensed movement. A shadow flitted behind a headstone. It didn't look like it belonged there.

She scrunched her eyes, looking for anything hidden by glamour. If anything was there, Taylor couldn't see it.

"Look, Taylor," Jill said. "All I'm saying is, if magic *were* real…it would be really bad news, right? Regular people like us would just have to go along with it, you know what I mean? There's no way we could stop the wizards or vampires or whatever from taking over everything. What if some magical person were able to…I don't know, gain control over you somehow? Get in your dreams. Make you…see stuff." She shuddered.

"See stuff?" Something was going on with Jill; that had to be it. Danny Underhill had said that sometimes twins are born with Second Sight. They were able to see through glamour—or at least to sense when someone was using it.

"Just drop it. Okay, Taylor?"

"Sure. I'm sorry I brought it up," Taylor said. But she kept her eyes open. Something wasn't right, but she couldn't put her finger on it.

"Taylor, Jill! It's time to go in," Mr. Garvin, the youth director, called.

"Coming!" Taylor answered without looking at him. Instead, she scanned the churchyard.

That was when she saw him.

He wasn't glamoured at all. He looked like just an ordinary guy strolling down the street. Khaki shorts, tee shirt, ball cap.

Bob. Or the other guy. Whatever his name was.

Taylor gasped.

"What's wrong," Jill asked.

He kept on walking with practiced indifference. Taylor thought she saw him grin as he passed.

"It's time to go in," Taylor said. "Come on."

Taylor didn't like this at all. First he showed up at the nun-nehi town. Now he just happened to be taking his evening stroll past Taylor's church. There's no way in the world that was a coincidence!

The girls caught up with the rest of the group and went inside for lemonade. Taylor said hardly a word the rest of the night, and all the way home, she peered out the window of her parent's minivan to see if anyone—or any*thing*—was following them.

As soon as they got home, Jill strolled across the street to her own house. Taylor and her parents walked up to the front door in silence. She let her eyes dart from left to right, hopefully without her parents noticing it.

"Don't roll your eyes at us," her dad said.

"I wasn't," Taylor said. "I was just...never mind."

"No, Taylor. I want to know. What's going on? Are you ready to tell us the truth yet?"

"Fred," Mrs. Smart started.

"I've already told you the truth," Taylor said. "It's not my fault you don't want to listen."

"Now, everybody just cool it," Mrs. Smart said. Taylor sensed the pressure was building—again. Leave it to Mom to try to put a stop to it. Dad unlocked the door and the three of them stepped inside.

"Taylor, something about meeting your birth mother—"

"Shanna. Her name is Shanna."

"Alright," her mother continued, "something about meeting Shanna must have been very difficult for you. That's probably to be expected. We understand."

"You don't understand anything!" Taylor yelled. "If you did, you wouldn't be acting like this. Why can't you just believe me?"

"Taylor, just listen to yourself," her dad said. "Monsters? Bogeymen? Do you really expect us to believe that?"

"Yes, actually—because it's the truth." They just stood there in the living room, not knowing what to do or say next. Taylor paced back and forth. Presence pulsed out of her with every word, but it only seemed to throw up her parents' resistance. "I thought you trusted me."

"Please try to see this from our point of view," her mom said. "What you're telling us...it just can't be true."

"I think we need to have a talk with Pastor Mark," her dad said. "Maybe...maybe there's something he can do."

"Yeah," Taylor said. "Like tell you both to give me a break." She stalked off to her room and slammed the door.

Jill's dreams were filled with the odd little man she thought she had seen in the graveyard at Taylor's church. He was no more than three and a half feet tall, with big bat ears and a dull gray complexion. He had peered at Jill and Taylor from atop one of the gravestones, but then vanished as soon as Jill turned in his direction.

There was no convincing herself it was just her imagination. She just didn't know what it meant.

Then a familiar silky voice echoed around the edges of Jill's sleep. "Wake up, sleepyhead."

"Huh? What?"

The scene changed. Jill couldn't see anything but a swirling silver mist, and in the middle of it, the dark-haired woman who had apparently moved into her dreams on a permanent basis.

"Never say having me for a godmother doesn't have its benefits. I thought you'd like to know that your friend Taylor is in trouble."

Jill shook herself awake, or at least she thought she did. She was still floating in fog with only the woman for company.

"Taylor?"

"Yes, dear. Taylor. If you hurry, you may be able to help her."

Then the mist cleared, and Jill was in her bedroom, awake and alone.

Taylor's in trouble?

She looked at her alarm clock. It was after midnight. She pulled on the clothes she had taken off a few hours earlier: striped blue capris, cotton shirt, plain white sneakers. She threw on her red Bulloch Middle School jacket and looked around her room.

What kind of trouble?

She grabbed the flashlight she kept in her beside table in case of power outages and tiptoed down the hall, through the living room, and out the door as quietly as possible.

The street was as quiet as a tomb. She aimed her flashlight at the Smarts' house. There was no sign of smoke or fire. There were no strange cars in the driveway.

This is ridiculous.

She loped two houses down and across the street, then opened the fence to sneak into the Smarts' back yard. Taylor's room was in the back on the near corner. The apple tree outside her window swayed in the breeze.

She peered through the window into Taylor's room. She could just make out her friend's sleeping form.

A shadow skittered around the far corner of the house. Jill caught a glimpse of glowing eyes in the darkness. *That thing from the graveyard!*

"Taylor!" she whispered, tapping the glass with her flashlight. Taylor didn't move. Jill tapped again, louder—but hopefully not loud enough to wake up her parents.

This time, Taylor rolled over. A couple of seconds later, she sat up in the bed. Jill tapped once more, all the while keeping her head turned toward the fence and the danger lurking in the shadows.

Taylor saw her. She stumbled to the window, still half-asleep from the look on her face, and heaved it open.

"Jill? What's going on?"

"I'm not exactly sure," she confessed, never once meeting Taylor's eyes. "Is everything okay?"

"I guess," Taylor said. "What are you—?" She stopped. "What's that?"

Taylor pulled herself up on the window ledge and let herself drop to the ground outside. She peered into the darkness toward the back fence. Beyond was a little patch of woods. Plenty of places for someone to hide.

"Who's there?" she demanded. "Is that you, Bob?"

Who's Bob?

There was a flurry of movement. This time, Jill saw it, too. Then a huge, black dog burst out from around the corner of the house and bounded toward the fence. It stood in the middle of the yard, growling at something still unseen out in the woods.

A man emerged from the shadows. He waved his hand toward the dog, and it turned to something like smoke and drifted away. It was just a projection—like the tiny image of her "godmother" she saw back at Pontchartrain Park.

At the same time, the small gray creature at the corner of the house charged forward with a knife in his hand.

"Back off!" he yelled.

The other man backed away. He glared at Taylor and was suddenly gone in a flash of light.

In half a second, Taylor was on the gray creature. She marched out into the middle of her back yard, barefooted, dressed in her shorts and baggy tee shirt, her hair a mess from sleep, but she looked like she was about to rip him in half.

"Who are you?" she said. "Who are you working for?"

He spun around to face her, but he lost his footing and ended up on one knee. His knife fell to the grass. He gazed up at Taylor with something like terror in his eyes.

"Well?" she said. "Did the Hellebores send you?"

He shook his head.

"Then why are you here?"

He pointed to the apple tree. Jill scanned the branches.

High up, a huge owl took off, gliding down toward Taylor and the gray man. It bowled into him, and at the same time expanded until it was the size and shape of an ordinary man—the same man Jill had seen sitting in the tree outside her window.

Jill shrieked and clung to Taylor, almost bowling her over.

As the two figures wrestled in the grass, Jill and Taylor edged along the side of the house, trying to keep as far away from the fight as they could.

Jill jumped as the gray man shouted, "Ha!"

The man who used to be an owl growled and rolled away, grasping at his side.

The gray man pulled away his bloodied knife. Both men assumed defensive stances, breathing heavily, their eyes aflame with anger.

"T-Taylor?" Jill whispered.

The second man glared at him with glowing yellow eyes, then spread out his arms—which in an instant weren't arms at all but long, dark wings. At the same time, his body melted and compacted, and in an instant he flew off, once again in the form of an owl.

Somewhere beyond the back fence, a swirling column of gold and silver light sprung into existence. The owl flew into it and was gone.

"W-what...?" Jill stuttered.

"If you're looking for somebody working for the Hellebores, Miss," the gray man said, "I bet that's your man."

Taylor turned toward Jill, who could only look at her open-mouthed.

Jill came very close to crying. She couldn't decide if she needed to look at her friend or keep an eye on the third person in the yard. In the beam of her flashlight, she was finally able to get a good look at him. It was definitely the same thing she had seen earlier in the graveyard at Oak Hill. He was no taller than three and a half feet, with a dry, ashy complexion, thinning gray hair, and huge, pointed ears. His body was compact and stout, but his arms and legs were (relatively) long and slender. He reminded Jill of some kind of four-limbed spider, with long, spindly fingers ending in claw-like nails.

He was barefooted, but wore dark pants held up with suspenders and an over-large white rumpled shirt with the sleeves rolled up. He looked at Jill, and his eyes reflected the light of Jill's flashlight like the eyes of a cat.

"What's the matter, kid?" he said. "You never seen a church grim before?"

"I-I don't think we have those in the A.M.E. Church."

The creature scoffed.

"Jill," Taylor said. Jill started and turned her attention back to her friend.

"There's a secret I've had for a while," she said. She took another couple of deep breaths. "Something that I want to tell you."

She looked Jill in the eyes, those icy blue eyes that could bore into her soul if she'd let them. Then she looked to one side, where the gray man was sheathing his knife.

"Is that so?"

Chapter 9

Politics

Taylor scanned her back yard. The glare from Jill's flashlight kept her from seeing in the dark as clearly as she might have, but there was no mistaking the swirl of gleaming dust out past the fence.

"How long has that ring been there?" she said to no one in particular. She rounded on the little person. She hadn't exactly seen him before, but something about him was familiar. He had called himself a church grim, and that must have been the answer. She had sensed his presence at Oak Hill.

Jill started to say something, but Taylor held up a hand.

"*Who are you?*" she asked, and pushed a little bit of presence into the question. Between the little person and Bob and the shape-shifter—not to mention Jill!—she didn't know what to think. There was no need for him to know how bewildered she felt.

"Y-you can call me Silas, Miss."

"Thanks for the help, Silas. I owe you one."

"Taylor, what's going on?" Jill asked, increasingly frantic.

Taylor ignored her. "You're some kind of little person, right?"

"A goblin, if you please. And a church grim by vocation."

"Okay," Taylor said. "You can tell me what that means later. Right now, I want to know what's going on. And Jill! What the heck are you doing here?"

Jill looked at her in stunned silence. "I...had a feeling you were in trouble."

"I'll say!" Taylor said. "When Redmanes and the Hellebores both come calling..."

She turned back to the church grim. "We've got to talk. Someplace private, or my parents will flip. Will that ring back there take us to Oak Hill?"

Silas nodded. Taylor turned back to Jill.

"Jill, I can't explain now. Something tells me I need to get moving. But as soon as I can, we'll have a long talk about this, okay?"

"Forget it!" Jill said, finding her nerve. "We're talking now!"

"Meet me at Oak Hill," Taylor told Silas. "I'll be there in five minutes, tops."

"Wouldn't you like me to hang around, Miss? Just in case...?"

Taylor looked around again. She studied the treetops and the woods beyond the fence.

"Well...that's probably smart. Meet me by the ring, okay?"

"As you say, M—"

"*And stop calling me 'Miss'!*" She put a little too much presence into that sentence, and Silas whimpered a bit as he skittered across the lawn and hopped over the fence in a single bound.

"Taylor, I'm not leaving until you tell me what all this means," Jill said.

Taylor sighed.

"Then help me get back in my room."

Jill gave her a boost up to the window. Taylor crawled in and threw on her denim shorts, tennis shoes, and a teal polo shirt. She slung her beaded purse over her shoulder and slipped back outside. With another boost from Jill, she just reached the bottom of the open window and pulled it mostly closed.

"Follow me," she said. She and Jill retraced Silas's path across the back yard and over the fence—although the girls helped each other over rather than high-jumping it.

"Okay," Taylor said. "The thing is...I met my birth mother a couple of months ago."

"You what?"

"Yeah. And...well...she's not quite...human."

"What are you telling me? That you're some kind of space alien?"

"Not exactly."

They came across Silas standing beside a ring of mushrooms no more than five feet across. Taylor was certain it wasn't there in April when she had last been in the patch of woods behind her house.

"Are you ready?" she asked Silas.

"If you please," the church grim said, "This is a pretty small ring. I don't think it will hold up to three travelers at once. Suppose I go first?"

Taylor nodded.

"Taylor, what does he mean, 'travelers'?"

But as Jill asked her question, a sparkling mist rose up from the ring. Silas stepped into it and vanished. Jill's mouth fell open. She looked at Taylor and seemed even more confused that her friend didn't react to the sight.

Taylor regarded her friend. She realized she was shaking all over. Jill was in on her secret now. There was both relief and sheer terror in that realization.

"Do you believe in faeries?"

Jill stood there, dumbfounded.

"Your first time's probably going to be a little bumpy. I'm sorry." She offered Jill her arm. "Hold on tight."

Taylor drew up all her memories of Oak Hill Baptist Church: potluck suppers, Vacation Bible School, Christmas pageants. She let these memories congeal into a firm mental image of the place she wanted to go. Then, with Jill's arm wrapped around her own, and her free hand clinging to Jill's wrist, she stepped into the swirling mist.

The world suddenly seemed to stretch in impossible contortions as a flurry of images, dim and shadowy in the night, passed through Taylor's consciousness. It only took a couple of seconds till the two girls emerged at the other end.

They were standing in the Oak Hill cemetery.

Jill fell to the ground and threw up.

"Oh, crud, Jill. I'm really sorry."

Taylor bent down to put her hand on Jill's shoulder. Jill flinched, then rolled over and crab-walked away as fast as she could, eyes wide with fear.

"What...? What's going on?"

"Okay. You asked me before about the short version. Here it is. I'm a fae. What you would call a faery. I have magic powers—but not much. Just a couple of Jedi mind tricks, really.

"My parents were fae, too. My dad died before I was born, and my mom is in exile up in North Carolina. My grandparents are pretty important fae nobles. They're mad at both of us and, apparently, they've decided they want to kill me."

Jill summed up her reaction in a single word of which her mother would not approve.

"Silas, is there a place the three of us can go to talk?"

"Right this way, Miss—I mean, Taylor."

Silas led them to the church house. A couple of red-and-white hound dogs bounded toward them from around the corner. They circled the girls and growled. Silas snapped his fingers at them.

"Down!" he said. "They're with me, you mangy beasts! Leave them alone!" They followed the trio to the columned porch at the front of the building.

"Go on!" Silas commanded. "It's not light yet, get back to work!" He knocked on a wooden panel next to a drainpipe. A small doorway appeared.

"After you," he said. "Up the stairs to the right."

Taylor gave Jill a wary glance, then stooped down to pass through the goblin-sized opening. Jill followed close behind.

"Are y-you saying your parents were...like *him*?" Jill whispered.

"There's lots of different beings in the Wonder," Taylor said. "I haven't figured all that out yet. But my family all looks human, if that's what you mean."

They climbed the stairs with Silas close behind. It was a spiral staircase that took them all the way up to the bell tower. Taylor walked to the ledge and studied the view in the starlight. The thin crescent of the waning moon hung over the church like a curved silver dagger.

"The W-wonder? What's that?"

"It's what folk like us call home," Silas offered. "Faery-land, Arcadia, the Otherworld, whatever you want to call it."

"And that's where my attackers came from."

"Attacker."

"What do you mean? There were two of them. One was the shape-changer, probably sent by the Hellebores, and then there was Bob the changeling—or whatever his name is—that the Redmanes sent."

Silas shook his head. "He was a changeling, eh? I wasn't sure. But he wasn't sent to attack you."

"How do you know?"

"Because you saw him last night, right over there." He gestured toward the graveyard.

"Yeah, he's been following me for a couple of weeks, now."

"Then that settles it," Silas said. "Look, it's pretty simple. If you can see the guy who's tailing you, it only means he wants to be seen. If the Redmanes wanted him to kill you.... Well, pardon me for saying so, but you'd already be dead."

"They wanted me to know I was being watched," Taylor said. Silas nodded. "He was just meant to intimidate me."

"For now, at least."

"He was doing a darned good job of it."

"The Redmanes only hire the best."

"B-but the other one, the shape-shifter...."

"Now, he looked like trouble," Silas said. "I saw him hanging around earlier, in owl-form. When you went home, I saw him take off to follow you. I thought you might need a hand."

"Well, I'm glad you showed up," Taylor said. "But you...." She turned to Jill. "You 'just had a feeling' that I was in trouble?"

Jill gulped.

"Uh-huh," she said.

"You saw me last night, didn't you?" Silas asked. Jill nodded.

"Jill?" Taylor said.

"I'll bet she's got Second Sight," Silas said. "She's able to see through glamour."

"I've wondered about that," Taylor said. "You...but not William?"

"I think I'm a little bit more...advanced...than he is."

"Well, whatever. At least I can talk to you about what's going on now. I've wanted to do that for a long time. I just couldn't figure out how."

"That hell-thing," Jill said. "H-he really wanted to kill you?"

"Not a hell-thing," Taylor said. "My mom's mom is named Hellebore. Mara Hellebore." She gave Jill a quick run-down of her family history, the roles her grandparents played in the Seasonal Courts, how they feuded when their children fell in love, and how everything came to a head back in April.

"So yeah," she concluded. "I think he really wanted to kill me."

"I'd never have believed it," Silas said. "It's not like the Winter Court to try anything that obvious this time of year. Why, it's only two days past Midsummer! No way the Summer Court's going to take something like that lying down."

"I'm not sure the Summers would object too much if the Winters took care of me. I'm not exactly popular with them either, you know."

"It's the principal of the thing," Silas said. "The Summers hold power until the end of July. And besides, the Redmanes aren't the only faction in the Summer Court, you know."

"Dubessa?"

"Who's Dubessa?" Jill asked.

"Dubessa Fairchild," Taylor explained. "Her husband is the Summer Primus. Kind of like a king. I don't remember his name."

"Belas Wakefire," Silas supplied.

"Right. Dubessa and my grandmother have been rivals forever. That's why she stood up for me before. My grandmother wouldn't mind if the Winters killed me, but I bet it would seriously tick off Dubessa and her husband."

"They'd see it as a challenge to their jurisdiction," Silas said.

Taylor looked at Silas. "And they're only going to get stronger, aren't they?"

Silas nodded. "By definition. Midsummer is passed. We're heading toward autumn...and the Autumn Court is in Winter's pocket. Always has been."

"All right," Taylor said, shaking. "I am not liking this. I am not liking this at all."

Jill didn't know whether to focus on Taylor or the little gray man who had introduced himself as a church grim. She really wanted all of this to be a dream, but she couldn't make herself believe it. She had had plenty of bizarre dreams lately, but this was different. This was some kind of bizarre reality—which was at least ten times worse.

She watched Taylor pace back and forth saying, "I don't like this." She watched Silas, the church grim, sit on the ledge and nervously fiddle with his thin, gray fingers.

She's frightened, a voice said inside her head. It took her a second to realize it wasn't hers. Jill wasn't even dreaming, but her godmother was talking to her. She tried not to show her surprise.

You don't think I know that? she thought. *And what are you doing in here, anyway? This isn't a dream!*

"Why can't they just leave me alone?" Taylor said, pacing. "I do not like this!"

You could help her, the voice suggested.

What do you care? Jill thought. Then something Taylor had said tickled her memory. *You're that Fairchild woman, aren't you? The one that stuck up for Taylor?*

There were no words, but Jill could definitely feel a flush of satisfaction from her godmother.

"You're in a pickle, that's for sure," Silas said. "If the Hellebores are willing to try a stunt like that now, in the middle of summer...there's no telling what they'll do come autumn."

That's what this is all about, right? Those Winter people are getting into your business, threatening your rule. So you're taking Taylor's side again. Is that it?

Let's just say I have my reasons for wanting to keep your friend safe.

"Okay, let's back up," Taylor said. "Silas, are you absolutely sure that shape-shifter was sent by the Winter Court."

"Bound to be," Silas said. "A couple weeks ago I...uh...came to find out the Winters were looking for somebody to...take care of you."

"And by 'take care of,' you mean 'murder'?" Taylor said.

"That's about the size of it. Anyway, that's why I've been keeping my eyes on you, just in case something fishy happens."

"I'm pretty sure dive-bombing shape-shifters fall into the category of 'something fishy'! But what am I supposed to do now? I can't live in this bell tower the rest of my life."

"I suppose you could claim sanctuary in Ichisi," Silas said. "I doubt the Winters would want to raise a stink with the nunnehi."

"And then what? The Summer Court sent Bob to spy on me in Ichisi. What makes you think the Winters won't send somebody worse? I'd always be looking over my shoulder, just waiting for something bad to happen."

As I said, Jill, you could help her.

I'm listening.

She might pacify the Winter Court with a peace offering.

Are you kidding me? What's she going to do? Buy them all monogrammed sweaters?

Say it out loud, Jill.

It sounded crazy. Then again, the last few weeks had been a constant parade of crazy. Maybe it was time she just went with it.

"Maybe if she could give them some kind of peace offering..."

"What? What's that you say?" Silas said.

"I-I mean...if there was something they wanted...more than they wanted Taylor..."

"A bargain?" Silas said. "It's bad news to try to bargain with the sídhe. But..." He scratched his chin. "I've never yet known one of the Fair Folk to turn down a good bargain. It's dangerous—but it could work."

"But what could I offer?" Taylor said. "Crom Cornstack—my grandfather, for Pete's sake—told me to my face he thought I was a mistake. He came this close to blasting me to smithereens." She held up her hand, thumb and forefinger an inch apart. "I'm not exactly rich, you know. I'd have to become their slave for the next hundred years."

"At least," Silas added.

What do you suppose the Winter Court values most, Jill?

"Taylor, you know these people. What do they really want?"

Taylor shrugged her shoulders and stared at the ceiling.

"No idea at all?"

"Knowledge," Silas said.

"Knowledge?" Jill said.

"I was about to say murder," Taylor said.

"Murder's just a hobby," Silas explained. "The thing about the Winter Court is they think things through. That means they prize knowledge, clarity of thought. And they deal in secrets. They're probably the best spies in the entire Wonder, but they don't part with what they know until they find a way to use it for their own benefit. Till then, it's all stealth and misdirection."

"A lot like dwarves, then?" Taylor said.

"The Winters get along with dwarves about as well as any fae—which isn't saying much," Silas agreed.

"I don't see how that helps. I don't have any knowledge or secrets—at least, none the Winter Court would be interested in."

"What do you mean by 'clarity of thought'?" Jill asked.

Silas rounded on her, startled by the question.

"I think I understand," Taylor said. "It's like everything else: the Summer and Winter Courts see the world differently. The Summers are a bunch of hotheads. Shanna told me once that one of the things she liked about my dad was that he was so spontaneous. And Mrs. Redmane...well, let's just say she's not the most patient person in the world."

"You're on the right track, kid," Silas said. "Go on."

"I never had much dealings with the Winters—except for Shanna, of course. But even when she was a prisoner at Dunhoughkey, there was something calm and composed about her. Like she wasn't in any hurry. She was taking it all in, waiting to see what would happen next, ready to move when the situation changed."

"Yeah?"

"Yeah. And even before that, here's this girl who'd been locked up in a dungeon for over thirteen years, but it seemed like it hardly fazed her."

"That's what I mean by 'clarity of thought,'" Silas said.

Jill weighed all of this in her mind. Then it hit her. There was something her godmother said a few nights ago.

"So..." she began, tentatively. "Something like a scrying bowl...?"

"What's a scrying bowl?" Taylor said.

"How do you know about scrying bowls?" Silas said.

"I...must have heard of them somewhere."

"It's a kind of magical tool," Silas explained to Taylor. "You fill it with water and look into it."

"Why? What happens?" Taylor asked.

"It settles the mind, maybe shows you bits of reality you didn't know before. Really powerful fae can use them to see the future, even. But they're not exactly rare artifacts, kid. I bet the Winters have a dozen of them in every rath they rule."

Remember, the voice in Jill's head urged. And thankfully, she did.

"What…What if there was a special one? One they wanted because…maybe it was a family heirloom or something?"

Silas pulled himself up to his full height. His face narrowed into a scowl.

"What do you know?" he demanded.

Jill stared at him in shock. Taylor looked first at Taylor and then at Silas.

"I said, 'What do you know'?" In a second he was balanced on the ledge, stooped over Jill as she sat. He tilted his gray, misshapen head at an angle and peered into her eyes.

So long, Jill, the voice said.

"Silas, what are you talking about?" Taylor asked, springing to Jill's side.

"Look, I may not be the sharpest knife in the drawer, but if this little girl knows something she's not telling…"

"NO!" Jill shouted. "Back off! I want to tell you." She breathed deeply. Taylor put her hand on her shoulder.

She tried to say something two or three times, but couldn't find the words. Silas growled a low and rumbling growl. Taylor looked at her with concern.

"I've…been talking with somebody…. Somebody like you."

"Jill, what do you mean?"

"It's this Second Sight thing. It's been getting out of control lately. She said she could help."

"She?" Silas said.

"From the way you've been talking, I think it's that Du-something woman."

"Dubessa? Dubessa Fairchild?" Taylor said. "Long, dark hair? Fair skin?"

"Maybe. Whoever it is, she wants to help you, Taylor. At least, she wants me to help you. She's the one who told me about scrying bowls."

"Makes sense," Silas said. "If your Second Sight is in overdrive, spending some time with a scrying bowl might help."

"Th-that's what she said."

"But what do you mean talking about a family heirloom?" Silas's tone was once again sharp, accusatory.

"Something she showed me...in a dream."

Silas and Taylor now looked at each other with alarm.

"She came into your dreams?" Taylor whispered.

"Is she still in your head?" Silas said, nearly shouting. He pulled his knife from its sheath. "I've got some iron filings in the basement, missy, and don't think I won't use them!"

"No, no, she's not here," Jill said. And it was true: she searched her mind for any sense that her godmother was still inside but came up empty.

"Has she been riding you?" Silas said, angrier by the minute. "Has she?"

"Riding me? I don't understand."

"Taking over. Using you like a puppet."

"You all can do that?" Jill's eyes went wide.

"It's like faring forth, isn't it?" Taylor asked Silas. Then she turned to Jill and explained. "I saw Shanna do it to a raven."

"Animals are one thing," Silas said. His eyes never left Jill's. "It's against the Eldritch Law to ride any sentient being, even a Topsider. One's mind and body are one's own."

Jill's heart was now pounding so fiercely she was surprised nobody could hear it. "No," she said. "No, she's never done anything like that."

"But she told you something about a scrying bowl. A special one."

Jill nodded. "It's more of a cup than a bowl. In Louisiana. She said it belongs to a satyr named du Marais. Something about it being an heirloom. Wait! She said it used to be an heirloom."

"Like it's been stolen?" Silas said. "Like this satyr might not be the rightful owner?"

"I-I guess so. I just don't know!"

"It's okay, Jill," Taylor said. Then to Silas she said, "Do you think this cup could be something the Winters want back?" Jill might not have been able to read Taylor the way she could read most everybody else, but she had still known her long enough to know what to expect. Taylor was hatching a plan.

"I just don't like it," Silas grumbled. "Why don't the Winters go get this stupid cup for themselves?"

"Maybe they don't know where it is."

"Somebody's setting you girls up. You know that, right?"

Taylor nodded. And Jill was certain that Taylor was about to go off looking for the satyr and his cup.

"Politics!" he spat. "That's why I swore off politics seventy years ago. Somebody always gets hurt."

"Maybe so," Taylor said. "But it's the only lead we have."

Jill was about to volunteer to go with Taylor, but she didn't get the chance, because at that exact moment Silas's dogs started barking.

Chapter 10

Into the Night

In an instant, Silas had twisted around to scan the church grounds. There was movement in the graveyard. Goodness and Mercy were going nuts.

He turned back to the girls. They looked pretty scared, and none too keen for a fight.

"Stay down!" he barked. "And put out that flashlight!" He looked Jill in the eye. "You get in trouble, you ring the bell, got it?" He pointed toward the rope in the corner of the room. She glanced up and saw that it was attached to the bell itself.

She nodded, eyes wide.

"That okay with you?" he asked Taylor. She looked frightened, but she also nodded her consent.

With that, he flung himself over the ledge and scampered down the side of the bell tower. At the bottom, he bolted toward the graveyard. The barking grew fainter, more distant. He was headed in the right direction.

Silas let his instincts take over. After so many years, he was tuned in to his territory to a degree only a wood nymph or maybe a cymbee could match. And not just the physical aspects: he sensed the ebbs and flows of magical energy around Oak Hill Baptist like they were part of him. He approached Mercy, who stood silently barking behind the church, her tail wagging with anticipation. Something was coming through the overgrown lot behind the Oak Hill property.

Far to the right, Goodness followed movement beside the road. His barks reverberated across the graveyard as he bounded away from Silas's position.

"Be sharp, girl," Silas whispered, gazing into the tall grass, extending his magical senses toward whatever had Mercy so agitated.

Then he saw them: two sets of glowing red eyes in the distance. He unsheathed his knife.

"You can't have her! You hear?"

Two figures approached, with every step growing taller and taller until they reached the edge of the Oak Hill property. Silas barely came up to their knees, but he didn't have a choice. He took a breath and prepared to lunge at them.

Goodness let out a fitful yelp. Silas risked a look around. His other dog had been flung into the air by another attacker. This one hadn't yet grown to giant size, but he was just as fierce and obviously strong. The spriggan summoned a ball of fire into his hand and flung it after Goodness.

"No!" Silas shouted. He took a half step toward Goodness but could go no farther. A giant hand grabbed him around the waist. Mercy nipped at the giant's feet. Goodness howled in pain as the fireball exploded in front of him.

"Leave my dogs alone!"

"Or what?" the giant said.

Silas rubbed his jaw as he gazed into his attacker's face. It was Dingle: the spriggan from the other night.

Brother Mike, he swore to himself, *the Winters are moving already!*

Silas tried to summon some glamour. He wasn't sure what he could do to scare off all three of them, but if he could at least startle this one, he might break free and make a strategic retreat.

His eyes bored into Dingle's. He pushed out the illusion that spiders were crawling over the spriggan's arms and legs: hundreds of them, big, black hairy things with fangs dripping acid.

Dingle dropped him with a curse, but not before almost grabbing him again with his other hand. All he got this time was a handful of the church grim's long, sparse hair as Silas yanked himself away, hit the ground, and ducked behind the nearest gravestone. Goodness had pulled himself to his feet but whined in discomfort.

Silas skittered toward him, but ran into an invisible wall before he made it ten feet.

"Hand her over and you might live," the lone fae said, the one who fireballed Goodness.

He tested the barrier with his hands. It held firm and gave him a slight electrical shock as he pressed his weight against it.

"Three of you just to pick up one little girl?" Silas said. "Almost seems like Cornstack doesn't trust you, doesn't it?"

The spriggan gestured, and Silas felt the invisible wall shrink around him.

"The girl! Now!"

All three spriggans had now surrounded him, and all had shrunk back to their usual height. They formed a triangle around Silas. Goodness and Mercy were also trapped inside invisible barriers. Mercy stood up on her hind legs against hers; Goodness was still wobbly on his feet and tried to avoid brushing his blackened nose against the unseen wall.

Dingle drew back his cloak and summoned a ball of fire into his hand. He glared at Silas.

Just then, the church bell began to ring. The spriggans fell to the ground, clutching their ears. The barriers collapsed like soap bubbles. A second later, Mercy had barreled into nearest spriggan, knocking him to the ground.

Silas whipped around and gazed upward. A fourth fae clung feebly to the ledge of the bell tower. A fifth lay sprawled on the ground. Silas sprung to Goodness's side and gave him a gentle pat on the back, then wheeled around and scrambled for the bell tower.

The fae who had fallen off the tower heaved himself up and started crawling toward the parking lot. There, he took the form of an owl and disappeared into the night sky. The spriggans blinked away in fits and starts, four or five yards at a time.

Jill kept on ringing the bell.

Silas launched himself upward, grappling the tower five feet above the ground. He scrambled up the wall.

The one remaining fae wasn't looking too good. Silas heard a defeated moan: feminine, low, and raspy. He reversed his grip on his knife. Another second and he could pin her leg.

He slammed the knife into the wood, but his target howled and scrambled away at the last second.

"That'll teach you punks to give a church grim the home-field advantage," Silas said. But he doubted they'd stay away for long.

He called the dogs inside. As soon as he was sure the church-yard was clear, he threw himself over the ledge and into the bell tower.

Jill stood in the corner of the little room, grasping the rope. Taylor lay on the floor, twitching.

"We've got to get moving," Silas announced. "Can you move?"

Taylor groaned.

"I said, can you move?"

"Leave her alone!" Jill shouted. "Can't you see she's sick?"

"It'll pass," Silas said. "But that's the problem. It won't keep the others away, either, for long. So either help me get her downstairs or get out of the way!"

He draped Taylor's arm over his shoulders. Her knees drug the ground as Silas hauled her to his secret door.

"Wh-what's wrong with her? She was fine a minute ago."

"Church bells," Silas said. "Must have hit her like a ton of bricks."

"Church bells!" Jill gasped. "You mean I.... You mean you let me...?"

"Couldn't be helped," Silas said. "She knew what could happen." The three stumbled down the stairs toward the basement.

"I can't believe you let me do this to my best friend!"

"You probably saved her life," Silas said. "You want to tell me what happened up here?"

"I don't know!" Jill said. "We saw you and those...things. Then, the owl man from before landed on the ledge. You said to ring the bell if there was trouble, so I did. But you didn't tell me—"

"Like I said, it couldn't be helped. You did good." Silas shifted Taylor's weight on his shoulder.

"But...but...who...WHAT were those things?"

They emerged in the furnace room, where Goodness and Mercy were waiting. Silas opened the door to his apartment and the Topsider, the church grim, the sídhe girl, and the two dogs barged in.

"The ugly ones were spriggans," Silas said. "I don't know about the shape-shifter. Maybe a pooka with a bad attitude. Nothing I care to meet again." He heaved Taylor up onto the bed.

He tossed Jill a small metal jar. "Rub some of that on Goodness's nose. Hurry!"

She unscrewed the top. The salve inside smelled horrible, but she dipped her finger in it and gingerly applied some. The dog silently yelped at her touch.

"Why can't I hear it bark?"

"You're too close," Silas said. "The closer you are, the quieter they get."

"That's freaky."

"It's even worse if they're tracking you." His turned his attention back to Taylor, who still lay groaning on the bed. "How do you feel, kid? Has the nausea passed?"

She sat up slowly. She nodded and shivered.

"You're going to be a little antsy for a while. That's to be expected, but it'll pass." To Jill, he said, "Keep an eye on her. In extreme cases, church bells can cause hallucinations."

"You mean I'm *not* hallucinating?"

Silas just chuckled.

"I'm going to take you to Ichisi. They won't dare try anything there."

"No," Taylor said, her voice shaking.

"It's okay," Silas said. "You're coming out of it. You'll be able to travel pretty soon."

"No," Taylor said again. "Not Ichisi. I need to go find Jill's satyr. See if I can get his cup. Maybe he'll bargain for it. Maybe... maybe I could manage to steal it."

"Are you nuts?"

"Maybe, but they're just going to keep coming unless we do something. I'm not going to hide from them the rest of my life."

"I can't let you do that," Silas said.

"Me neither," Jill agreed. "There's got to be a better way."

"I wasn't asking for your permission," Taylor said. Her strength was returning, and her stubborn attitude with it.

"Taylor," Jill said, "this has got to be the stupidest plan you've ever had."

Taylor smiled. "You noticed. I'm touched." She stood up. Color was coming back into her face.

"Then I guess I'm going, too," Jill said. "I'm sure as heck not letting you do this by yourself."

"Jill, you don't know what you're asking," Taylor said. "You've never seen my grandparents up close and personal. They'll eat you for breakfast."

"Then I hope I give them indigestion."

"Sorry, Jill. No way."

"Then why don't you explain how you're going to find this satyr? Louisiana is a pretty big state, you know."

This at least made Taylor pause.

"I, on the other hand, have a pretty good idea where to start looking."

"Jill, listen to yourself. You don't even like sleepovers! Are you seriously going to go with me on a road trip to Louisiana?"

Jill sighed. "My godmother says I have a gift. If I can use it to help keep you alive..."

"But what about your parents?"

She felt her pockets. "Okay, so I forgot my phone. But we can stop along the way, right? Give them a call and let them know we're all right?"

Taylor bit her lip. "Are you sure about this?"

Jill nodded.

"Well, I'm not!" Silas said. "You girls are going to get yourselves killed!"

"Yeah, well..." Taylor muttered.

"Just one blasted minute," Silas said. He grabbed an old, weatherworn satchel from a hook on the wall and ran through the room collecting odds and ends and pitching them into it.

"This is ridiculous," he muttered. "It's suicide, is what it is! And with a Topsider tagging along, no less!"

He stormed over to the cupboard over his Ben Franklin stove, grabbed a small wooden bowl, and shoved it into his satchel. Turning to Jill, he said, "If you've really got the gift, then a bowl to scry with might come in handy."

"Thanks."

"If you're both so hell-bent on doing this, then I'm coming with you, and that's all there is to it! Now hurry up!"

He whistled for Goodness and Mercy. After a quick inspection of Goodness's injury—the healing salve had already started working—he turned them out the back door. He shouldered his pack and stormed back the way they all came with Jill and Taylor hurrying to keep up.

He stopped in the middle of the graveyard. The hair in his ears tingled. Magic was starting to twist around the grounds in malevolent patterns.

"I was afraid of that," he said. "They're back."

"Already?" Taylor gasped.

"Bells don't keep them down for long. You should know that."

Shadows flitted across his field of vision.

Silas raised his arm and opened a portal into the Wonder. The column of sparkling lights swirled and twisted like a small tornado.

"Where are we going?" Taylor asked.

"West," Silas said. "I'll lead. You just follow." He offered Jill his arm. She stooped over to grab him tight while linking arms with Taylor on the other side. She whispered a frantic prayer.

"Oh, dear Lord, just get me through this. Just get me through this. Just get me—"

She yelped as Silas pulled her into the portal.

They blazed through the night, whipping around the edges of the Wonder as Silas led Taylor and Jill over hills, through caves and woods, past ancient cemeteries and forgotten springs and rings of standing stones. Jill wailed like a banshee the whole way.

The noise didn't help Silas's disposition. Far sooner than he intended, he decided to exit the rings and give the poor girl a break. He pulled at her arm, but she yanked back defensively.

"Settle down!" he hollered. But it was hard to be heard over the sound of rushing wind. He pulled Jill toward him again, this time more firmly. She grunted and jerked away.

Silas lost his grip. The two girls spun out of sight.

He muttered a curse as he concentrated on the nearest portal.

Hopefully, Taylor would do the same.

He dropped into a ring of mushrooms somewhere deep in the woods. He stood braced for action, his ears perked up for any sign of the girls, his magical senses stretching into the pre-dawn darkness. *They could be anywhere*, he griped to himself. *Brilliant.*

He sniffed the air. The sweet, almost spicy aroma told him he had landed in the Wonder. That was just as well: it would be easier to do magic there than on human earth.

He didn't have any trouble seeing in the dark, but so far, he had neither seen nor heard the girls. Robins and swallows were his only company. He tuned into their cheerful morning song. Had they seen or heard anything?

It was no use. The only thing on their minds was finding a pretty she-bird to court. Silas really didn't care to listen in on a bunch of he-birds going on about what a catch they'd be.

Should he risk the direct approach? He didn't want to tweet his location. Those kinds of signals could get picked up pretty quickly in the Wonder. So far, it didn't seem like anyone had followed him, but his luck wouldn't last forever. In the end, he decided he didn't have much choice. He whistled a message in the language of birds: "*Anybody seen two girls?*"

"Tuck, tuck," a robin called, picking up the message. Another robin, farther away, echoed the first. A swallow chirped and gurgled the message deeper into the woods.

Silas stood as still as he could. There was a subtle pulse of magic in the air. Silas might have missed it, but there was no missing the shrieks of terror that followed or the sound of breaking branches or the loud thud as something—possibly two human-sized somethings—slammed into the soft, grassy ground.

A tree swallow chattered with agitation: "Cheep! Cheep!" "*This way! This way!*"

He bounded toward the sound.

"Cheerily, cheer up, cheer up," another robin tweeted. "*They're all right.*"

Good, Silas thought. *I can kill them myself!*

He came upon the girls face down in the grass and dirt at the bottom of a low hill. Just as the robin promised, they were pulling themselves up and brushing themselves off.

Silas produced a glowing orb of light and held it aloft. Taylor looked up at him, shocked and bewildered. Jill gazed out into the darkness. He planted his bare feet in front of her and waved his hand to get her attention. "I should have known better than to get messed up with some idiot Jack kid!" he yelled. "What were you even thinking? Ring-riding isn't the easiest thing in the world, you know! It takes concentration!"

Jill inched away. It was obvious she heard Silas, but her mind seemed elsewhere. "You could have ended up a hundred miles from here! You could have time-skipped and been bouncing around the Wonder for years! If I ever—"

"*Leave her alone!*" Taylor roared. Waves of presence hit Silas like a sledgehammer. He couldn't help but shut up. "She's not some idiot Jack kid. She's my friend!"

"S-sorry, Miss," Silas said, crumbling to his knees. But he still glowered on the inside. *Patience, Silas*, he told himself.

"She got scared, that's all."

Silas screwed up the courage to say, "Maybe."

"What do you mean by that?"

He took a couple of seconds to regain his feet and shake off the effects of Taylor's presence. "Begging your pardon, Miss, but we already know somebody's been hanging around inside your friend's head." His eyes narrowed to slits as he glanced in Jill's direction. "How do we know she's not still there?" Silas shifted the weight of his satchel on his shoulders. "It pays to be careful, is all I'm saying."

They all sat or stood in silence. The girls breathed heavily. Jill said, "What?"

"Hey!" Silas said. "Snap out of it! We've got to get moving. D'you hear?"

Jill shook herself out of her daze.

"First time in the Wonder," Silas commented to Taylor. "It takes a while for some Topsiders to get used to it."

"What... What's that smell?" Jill said.

"Grass," Silas said. "Dew, soil." He sniffed the air. "Maybe a little tree bark."

"It smells like the air after a thunderstorm," Jill whispered. "With maybe a little bit of cinnamon, or..."

"It smells like dirt," Silas scoffed. "Can we get moving, please?"

Taylor pulled Jill to her feet. She seemed fascinated by the sound her feet made as the scrunched on the grass.

"Where are we, anyway?" Taylor said.

Silas shrugged. "Somewhere in the Wonder. We were heading west. Alabama maybe?"

"The sun's about to rise," Taylor said, studying the eastern sky.

"Then my folks will be up soon," Jill said. She was finally starting to get used to her surroundings. "I'd better give them a call. Where's the nearest phone?"

"We'll have to go Topside for that," Silas said. "If you girls are ready to move."

Taylor helped Jill up. They took two steps and walked into a tree.

"Silas," Taylor said. "You need to get in front so you can shine some light on the path."

"You can't make your own?" he grumbled.

"Actually, no."

Silas let out an exasperated sigh. This girl can't even make faery fire and she thinks she can handle a satyr? "Hold out your hand," he said, irritated. When Taylor did so, he tilted his own hand and slid his fire orb into her palm. "It's kind of like a glob of concentrated glamour. Focus on it. Don't let it out of your mind for more than a second or two at a time."

"Thanks."

"Now, let's hurry up! We've got a head start, but that won't last long. We've got to get moving."

The three of them threaded their way through the brush, back toward the spot where Silas first landed. Taylor lost track of her faery fire twice. Each time, Silas kindled her a new orb and set it in her hand.

"It's almost light!" Jill fretted. "My folks will find out I'm gone any minute!"

"It's okay," Taylor said. "We've just got to get to find a phone somewhere." She brushed her fire orb away like it was a pestering insect, and it hovered beside her at head height as it slowly dimmed. She tried to rest her hand on Jill's shoulder, but Jill flinched away.

"We'll find you a phone," Silas agreed. "And a bus station."

"What do you mean?" Taylor said.

He glanced at Jill before addressing Taylor. "Like I said before, it pays to be careful. Are you sure it's smart to drag her along on this cockamamie expedition?"

The scowl rising on Taylor's face made him shudder, but he pressed on.

"All I'm saying is, if somebody wanted to sideline this quest of yours...well, you do the math."

"If you don't trust Jill, then come out and say it." Another wave of presence slid into Silas's consciousness. It wasn't as fierce this time, but it was just as compelling.

"You're just too young to remember Bailly Hen."

"What's that?" Jill said.

Silas shook his head.

"Ancient history," he said.

The church grim trudged on.

"You never answered Jill's question," Taylor said. "Bailly Hen?"

"It's a long story."

"Is everything a long story with you folks?" Jill said.

"Well?" Taylor said.

Silas figured it didn't look like they were going to leave the matter alone. "Well, I figure you've got as much a right to know as anybody," he said to Taylor. "It's your history, too."

"Go on."

Silas grunted. "The last time the Summers and the Winters went to war was seventy years ago. This was way worse than the little squabble they had when your parents eloped. Before it was over, just about every other fae chiefdom east of the Great River was pulled into it."

"So...like a civil war?"

"Exactly. The thing is, the ruling families of most of the major chiefdoms are related one way or another, so what affects Arradherry eventually spills over to the rest. That's how New Avalon got involved."

Taylor mouthed the name to herself.

"Anyway, Crom Cornstack made a deal for support from the Holly Court of New Avalon, and they started putting together an invasion force at Bailly Hen. They were set to ride south as soon as Midsummer passed."

A light went on in Taylor's eyes. "But there was a spy, wasn't there?"

Silas nodded. "The Summers got wind of the plan. Vergosus Bright himself fared forth. He rode one of the Holly warriors and learned the whole plan—numbers, time lines, travel routes, the whole thing."

"So the invasion failed."

"Failed!" Silas croaked. "It didn't even get started! The Summer Court launched a counterstrike on the eve of Midsummer. Topsiders say it was one of the worst tornado outbreaks in history, but that's not even half of it. By the time they were through, Bailly Hen was nothing but a blasted pile of rubble." Silas trembled as unsettling memories crept up and sent shivers through his body. "It was a massacre, I tell you. There's no other word for it."

They had reached the mushroom ring.

"So you'll forgive me if I take a very dim view of Fair Folk spies and traitors riding along while I'm trying to keep you safe!"

"I never asked you to come along!" Taylor blurted.

"Are you sending me home?" Silas barked.

Taylor stopped short. Even the birds kept their peace.

"You wouldn't last five minutes in the Wonder without somebody looking out for you," he continued. "This satyr you're looking for, du Marais? He's bound to be bad news. And forgive me for rubbing it in, but you don't even know how to make faery fire."

"You're right," Taylor admitted. "But I'm not sending Jill home, either. She says she knows how to find that scrying bowl, and it's the only lead I have."

There was a couple of heartbeats worth of silence, but it was enough for Silas to sense a frisson of magic that made his skin tingle.

"We better get moving," Silas said. "I've got a feeling we're not alone." He gave Jill another slit-eyed glance.

Chapter 11

Bisgarra Verry

Bisgarra Verry was a place of splendor, especially around Midsummer. The cheerful cottages around the rath itself were festooned with garlands of flowers and sparkling tinsel. The air was full of will-o'-the wisps of every size and every color of the rainbow. Bonfires blazed on the edges of town, where even in the pre-dawn hours daring young pisgies, pookas, and even the occasional satyr took turns leaping through the flames to the cheers of their fellows. Dryads danced in the moonlight while naiads splashed and played in a nearby stream.

Fair Folk and little folk alike greeted each other with smiles and bows. There was music and dancing everywhere day and night for days before and after the highest holiday of the Summer Court.

The great rath itself gleamed in the morning light, its white stone walls decked out in rich, golden hues. Inside, the doorways and bannisters were draped with green and gold bunting, and servants and courtiers on their errands greeted one another with shouts of "Happy Midsummer!" Claudia Fountain tried to find comfort in the beauty of it all as she made her way to the Chief Matron's chambers.

She bowed and smiled to passersby as she wove through the tapestried corridors of the Summer Court's capital. Claudia was taller than most of the denizens of Bisgarra Verry, and she cut an imposing figure in her royal blue business suit. She had inherited her father's height and his rich, chocolate skin. Like her mortal mother, however, her eyes were hazel. They reflected her mother's intelligence far more than her father's ferocity and raw power. At the moment, those eyes were also bright with determination. She could only imagine what the Chief Matron would have to say about the news she brought, but there was no way to avoid telling her.

Not for the first time, she realized the enormous risk she was taking. She was oath-bound to serve Mrs. Redmane, and had done so faithfully for decades. But her true loyalty lay elsewhere.

On days like this, it felt like she lived on a tightrope. Mrs. Redmane insisted on intimidating her granddaughter. Fair enough: what's the point of being a Chief Matron if you can't throw your weight around every now and then? Claudia understood that, and her fae half even respected it. But she wondered how Mrs. Redmane would react when she learned what Claudia had come to tell her.

Claudia had taken desperate action two months ago to prevent Mrs. Redmane's thirst for revenge from plunging the Courts into open conflict. Now conflict was brewing again, and it didn't seem there was anything she could do about it.

At last, she arrived at the great oaken double doors. The spriggan guard gave her a stiff salute and ushered her in.

"Chief Matron?" she said.

"Come in, Claudia," came the answer in an even tone. The Chief Matron was not in the antechamber but in a large and well-appointed private office to one side. The door was open, and Claudia stepped inside.

Anya Redmane sat behind a desk carved from a single gigantic tree trunk. She had the same sort of timeless beauty that all daoine sídhe possessed. In Topsider's terms, she might have been anywhere between thirty and fifty years old, but she carried herself with a grace and confidence that only comes with centuries of training. Her red hair hung loose around her shoulders. Her clear, green eyes sparkled with life and energy. She emanated a subtle pulse of presence—not enough to befuddle Claudia, but more than sufficient to assert her authority.

She held up a hand to signal Claudia wait a moment while she finished the letter she was writing. She gestured for her aide to have a seat.

"You have something to report?" As usual, Mrs. Redmane dispensed with the small talk.

"Miss Hellebore left her Topside house suddenly shortly after midnight."

Mrs. Redmane arched her eyebrows.

"Your tail reports they're headed west," Claudia continued.

"They?"

"A goblin was with her—the church grim from her place of worship. Also a friend of hers, a Topsider."

"Why would she take along a Topsider?"

"Bob wasn't entirely sure," Claudia said, "although he believes she has some degree of magical ability. Second Sight and perhaps some other talents. She spotted him the day before."

The Chief Matron sat back in her chair.

"They're headed west, you say?"

Claudia nodded.

"The grim confronted Bob and drove him away, but he picked up the trail quickly enough. Apparently there was some sort of disturbance. The grim had to tweet his location. Fortunately, Bob was listening. They're definitely headed west."

"You are quite sure?" Mrs. Redmane asked.

"Yes, Chief Matron. Bob reports something was said about trying to locate a satyr in that direction."

Mrs. Redmane's eyes widened. She leaned forward in her chair. Claudia steeled herself against a rumbling wave of presence.

"A satyr?" The Chief Matron had composed herself, but too late. It was obvious something was up.

"By the name of du Marais," Claudia said. The Chief Matron gasped. Claudia continued. "Something about a scrying bowl. They seem to think possessing it is important."

There were several uncomfortable moments of silence while the Chief Matron's eyes smoldered with growing emotion. Claudia wasn't entirely sure if it was anger or fear. It was certainly dismay.

"Is that so?" the Chief Matron said at last. Claudia noticed her fists clenched on the table. Anya Redmane might have been many things, but subtle wasn't one of them.

Her lips tightened into a thin, red line.

"Where is Lawdwick Vesper these days?" she said at last.

Claudia's heart skipped a beat, but she kept her composure. "The last I heard," she said, "he still lives in the forest somewhere south of Wanelawn."

"Excellent." The Chief Matron curled her lips into a grin. It didn't put Claudia any more at ease. If anything, it made her even more nervous.

"If the girl is headed toward New Cephalonia, Vesper will be able to intercept her."

Claudia nodded. It didn't escape her notice, however, that she had never mentioned Taylor Smart's destination.

"Scry him at once," the Chief Matron said. "Tell him... No, on second thought, I'll contact him myself."

"As you wish, Chief Matron."

"I never should have let the little monster escape me the first time." The Chief Matron sat up in her chair, took a breath, and smiled pleasantly. "Well, there's no use dredging up such upsetting memories. Thank you for your good work, Claudia. And Happy Midsummer."

"The same to you, Chief Matron."

Chapter 12

Runaways

Taylor and Silas held Jill tight between them as they stepped once more into the ring. Though Jill hollered and wailed, she managed to keep it together a lot better than she had before.

They spun out near a tranquil stream. The sky was still gray. They were traveling west, racing the sun.

Taylor kept her hand on Jill's arm. She was shaky, but at least she didn't throw up again. She tested her footing and wobbled into Taylor.

"Take your time," Taylor said.

"For that matter, have a seat," Silas said. He scanned their surroundings. "Over here."

Silas led the girls to a flat, open space and sat Jill on the ground.

"We're not going any farther till we know for sure she's safe," he told Taylor. Without another word, he pulled his satchel off his back and dug around in it until he brought out a leather sack from which he pulled a small plastic bottle, like the kind vitamins come in.

Taylor still didn't understand, but she let the church grim proceed. Jill still looked awfully shaky. From her expression, it was more about fear of what Silas was doing than the discomfort of ring-riding.

"Now, hold still," Silas said. "Keep your eyes shut tight. Don't open them for anything. Understand? And keep your jacket closed." He unscrewed the lid of the bottle and sprinkled a fine black powder over Jill's head.

"Hey!" she yelped, and scooted away. In the process, she managed to kick Silas in the shin. He jerked and dumped half the bottle down the front of Jill's jacket.

"I told you to hold still!" he said.

Jill tried to brush the powder off her shirt, off her face, and out of her hair. She made a face and spit it out when she accidentally tasted some.

"What is this stuff?" she asked, examining her blackened hands.

"Iron filings," Silas said. "How do you feel?"

"Filthy."

"How do you feel in here?" Silas pointed to his temple.

"I think I'm getting a headache."

"Good. That means it's just the three of us after all. The Fair Folk can't stand iron; it messes up their magic. If anybody was riding along in there, I guarantee they'd have said something. Now come on. Let's get you washed up."

Silas pulled a water bottle from his pack along with a small tube of liquid soap. He handed them both to Taylor. "Wash her off," he said. To Jill, he added, "Say something if it starts to burn or itch."

Silas shouldered his pack and headed off, leaving Taylor to help Jill clean up in privacy. Taylor squirted a drop of soap into Jill's hand and splashed her face with water. Then she poured half of the rest of the water over Jill's head to rinse her off. She took Jill's jacket and shook the filings off as best she could.

The two girls fell into step behind Silas, and he started moving forward again. The sun had now fully risen. Taylor could hear sounds of traffic in the distance. They were back Topside.

"Okay," Jill said. "I'm not being brainwashed or anything. Are you satisfied?"

"No. And you shouldn't be, either," Silas said. "You've still been awakened."

"What does that mean?" Taylor asked.

"Gifted," Silas explained. "Endowed. It means one of Your Kind has been rearranging the furniture inside your friend's head, probably hanging up a few pictures and bringing in a couple of lamps, too."

"I don't understand," Taylor said.

Silas gestured for Jill to lean over. When she did, he placed his hands on either side of her head and looked into her eyes.

"She's still shaking," he said. "That's not the ride, not after this long. You remember how she was acting while we were in the Wonder? Like her senses were all ramped up?"

Taylor nodded.

"Now that we're back on human earth, she's got the jitters."

They came to a footpath that sloped downward toward a paved road fifty yards ahead. Silas hurried his pace, but Taylor and Jill, with their longer legs, had no trouble keeping up with him.

"You're awakened, all right. Your godmother has created a bond between herself and you. She's used it to open up your Second Sight—and I doubt she did as careful a job as she should have."

"What do you mean?" Jill said, a note of panic in her voice. "What do I have to do to get rid of it?"

"You don't," Silas said. "Not until your godmother says so. You're in her debt, see? She's gifted you. That means she's eventually going to want you to repay her."

"Some gift!" Jill said. "I never asked for any of this!"

"Maybe you did," Silas said. "Or least, she thought it was something you'd like. The Fair Folk can be pretty tricky. Any offhand comment might have opened the door for her. Any gesture. Any token of her generosity you might have accepted without knowing what was at stake."

"No! I never did anything like that!" Jill stopped in her tracks. Silas and Taylor turned to face her.

"Think hard, Jill," Taylor said. "Silas is right. These people don't think about right and wrong the same way we do. Are you sure?"

Jill rubbed her hands on her capris. She shook her head. "I...I don't think so...." Then she looked up in fright.

"She gave me a chocolate."

Silas's expression, which was never pleasant, became even darker. Taylor cursed under her breath.

"What?" Jill said.

"Fae food," Taylor said.

"I was afraid of that," Silas said.

"She's bought in."

Silas nodded. "She's bought in."

Jill's eyes kept getting wider. "What?"

Taylor tried to keep the concern out of her voice as she spoke. "Eating any kind of food from the Wonder is...bad."

"Define 'bad.'"

"Not good."

"You are so helpful."

"It's hard to explain. Faery food unlocks your magical potential."

"If you have any," Silas added.

"Yeah," Taylor continued. "But there's more. Faery food changes you. Well, not people like me...but Danny says it can do stuff to people like you. Normal people. Topsiders."

"When you say change..."

"I'm not really sure." Both girls turned toward Silas.

"It's different every time," the church grim said. "The bottom line is that it creates a bond. You eat some, and it links you to the Wonder. You may have powers of magical perception now, but sooner or later, you're going to have to pay for it."

"I said I didn't want any of this!" Jill shouted.

"It doesn't matter," Silas said. "You ate. You've bought in. And if you took it directly from your godmother—she didn't just leave it somewhere for you to pick up on your own—that means you're bound to her as well. As far as the Eldritch Law is concerned, you owe her something."

Taylor and Jill both sucked in a breath.

Taylor reached into her bag and pulled out her seeing stone. "No offense, Silas, but this is a lot more complicated than I thought it was. A lot more dangerous. We need to call in reinforcements."

"Who do you think you're scrying?"

"A friend." She held the stone almost to her lips and whispered, "Dandan Underhill. Dandan Underhill. Dandan Underhill." Then she breathed on the stone and peered into the natural hole near one end of it.

A swirling yellow mist took shape before her eyes: a human form, crouched, with arms outstretched. In one of them, he held what looked like a sack.

"What are you doing?" Jill said.

"Go put your hand on her shoulder," Silas said. Jill complied. She gasped as soon as she did, for now she could see what Taylor was seeing.

The misty form of Danny Underhill appeared before them.

"Taylor?" he whispered. "Is that you?"

"Danny, I need your help! Somebody has done something to Jill. Where—?"

"Hold on!" the shade of Danny said. He ducked low to the ground and gazed overhead. His pointed ears perked up like a dog's."

"Danny, what's going on? Are those...feathers?"

From her expression of sheer bewilderment, Jill could see it, too. Danny was wearing a weatherworn denim jacket, but it looked like he had just come out of a no-holds-barred pillow fight. Feathers clung to his shoulders and poked out of his curly hair.

A second later, Danny raised himself up. He never got higher than a half-crouch, though, and his eyes kept darting from side to side.

"This is actually not a good time," Danny said. His eyes, Taylor could see, were glowing like they always did when he was agitated about something.

"Danny, Jill's in trouble! Do you think you could meet us in Louisiana? I really need your help."

Danny's shadowy projection hit the invisible deck. He let out a yelp.

"Louisiana. Got it. I'll do what I can, Taylor—Crud, what the heck was that?—but I ain't making no promises." The image vanished as quickly as if someone had turned out the lights.

Taylor muttered under her breath.

"I always said that boy was weird," Jill said.

"You don't know the half of it," Taylor said. "But he'll help us if he can."

Silas interrupted them. "We'd better get moving, you two. It looks like there's a town up ahead. Your friend needs to eat something. To be honest, a little breakfast would be good for all of us."

"Whatever you say," Taylor said.

They hiked along a county road for about a mile with woods to their left and a railroad track to their right. Other than two or three older cars and pickup trucks, the road was empty. Eventually they came to a sign from the Junior Chamber of Commerce that welcomed them to Mayfield, Alabama.

Jill looked at the sign, then down at Silas. She frowned.

"You're not gonna...I mean..."

"What," Silas snapped.

"Well...my folks say a black person needs to be careful about some of these small towns. But they never said anything about a gray person. Especially not a three-foot tall gray person with big pointy ears!"

"I'll have you know I'm three-foot-four," Silas said. "And if you were paying attention to the cars driving in and out of this place, you'd have noticed two things. First: the drivers are about half and half, racially speaking. We're not going to have to re-fight the Civil War to get a stinking cup of coffee in this town."

"And second?"

"None of them seemed to notice me at all. Now, why do you suppose that was, Miss Second Sight? Hmm?"

Taylor figured it out at once. She relaxed her eyes, opened them wide, and finally squinted, trying to find the right position to look beyond Silas's true form to the illusion he was projecting to Topsiders. A much larger man came into focus, nearly six feet tall, broad-shouldered, with a square jaw and a crew cut so spiky it almost hurt to look at it.

"Y-you're humongous!" Jill gasped. She saw it, too. Silas only chuckled.

"You're using glamour," Taylor said.

"Boy, nothing gets past you, does it?" Silas said.

"Glamour," Jill said. "Haven't I heard you all talk about that before?"

"It just means illusion," Taylor said. "Messing with people's minds."

"Waffle House!" Jill shouted. Sure enough, there was a Waffle House just down the street. The three picked up their pace. It wasn't long before they were sitting in a booth, studying the menu.

Once they ordered, Silas told Jill, "When I pay and get change, you can use it to call your folks. Hey, are you listening?"

"What?" Jill shook herself awake. "Sorry. I kind of zoned out there for a second." Taylor looked at her with concern.

"Your hands are still shaking," Taylor said. They stopped as soon as Jill became aware of it.

"Get some food in you," Silas said. "Then we'll see what happens."

When their food came, Taylor and Silas dug in right away. Jill took a few bites and then seemed to lose interest. She picked at her sausages and barely touched her eggs.

"What's wrong?" Taylor said. "It...it tastes all right, doesn't it?"

"I guess I wasn't as hungry as I thought."

Taylor and Silas traded glances.

"At least eat your toast," Silas said. "Jelly?"

Jill spread a little jelly on a slice of toast and nibbled at it halfheartedly.

Silas palmed the check and took it to the cashier. A minute later, he returned with a handful of bills and some change. He slid a stack of quarters toward Jill.

"Call your folks," he said. "They'll be worried."

Jill nodded. She scooted out of the booth and made her way to the pay phone in the back.

Taylor watched her go, watched her insert her money and punch the keypad. "Can we get Jill free?" she asked Silas. She looked past his glamour to see his true form. The church grim scowled, but he didn't seem angry. It was more like the expression someone had when they were talking about something unpleasant.

"I don't know," he said. "Maybe if... Nah, that won't work."

"What?"

"You'd have to convince her godmother to cancel her debt."

"Oh." Taylor knew enough about the Fair Folk and their ideas about reciprocity to know that was about as likely as wild boars taking wing.

"M-Mom, just calm down, okay?" Taylor and Silas both looked toward Jill. She rocked back and forth and kept her head down as she spoke.

"No, Mom. Nobody is hurting us," she said. "Taylor's with me. We're both fine. I promise."

Something else caught Taylor's attention. Their waitress was giving them a suspicious look.

Silas saw it, too. "We'd better leave," he said. He nodded subtly toward something over Taylor's shoulder. She craned her neck around to see a man in uniform—a county sheriff's deputy—nodding toward the waitress.

"Somewhere in Alabama.... I'm not sure exactly," Jill said. Her back was turned away from the dining area, but her voice carried just the same.

Silas slipped out of the booth and took a step toward Jill.

"Excuse me, sir," the deputy said. He was youngish, with a crew cut and ruddy cheeks. He was about as big as Silas's glamoured form, but lean and lanky.

"Is there a problem, deputy?"

Taylor immediately saw the problem. Three strangers in a small town, a dangerous-looking man and two teenage girls. One of the girls—who sounds a little bit frantic—is talking on the phone about whether anybody is hurting them. Is something fishy going on? Maybe, maybe not. But Taylor figured if she were a police officer, it was something she'd want to check out.

Taylor tried to slip out of the booth, but the deputy was in the way.

"Do you know this man?" the deputy asked Taylor.

"Of course. He's...he's somebody I know from church."

Jill turned around. Taylor tried to signal with her eyes that trouble was brewing.

"Gotta go, Mom," she said. "I'll call you soon. Bye. No, I promise. Bye." She hung up and hurried back to the booth.

Before she got there, the deputy spoke to her. "Miss, you want to tell me who this fella is?"

The question stunned Jill; Taylor could see it in her eyes. Jill was terrible at lying.

"Sure," she said. She had the same kind of expression Taylor was used to seeing on her when their math teacher announced a pop quiz. Far too late she added, "He's...m-my Uncle Silas."

"Your Uncle Silas, huh?" the deputy said with a frown. "Sir, please step over here with me. I need to see your identification if you don't mind."

"Of course, deputy," Silas said. The deputy pulled him away from the girls, but Silas didn't object. He reached into his pocket and pulled out his wallet. He thumbed through it, produced a small plastic card, and turned it over to the deputy. At the same time, Taylor noticed a fine wisp of fog rising from between Silas's shoulder blades and wafting toward the deputy.

He studied the card for several long seconds. Taylor glanced between him and Silas.

"Is everything in order?" Silas said.

The deputy lifted his eyes toward Silas. They looked dull and sleepy. He mumbled something.

"Perhaps you should sit down, deputy. You don't look well."

He nodded. By now, his expression was perfectly vacant. Silas turned toward the girls and motioned for them to leave. Taylor grabbed Jill by the arm and pulled her outside.

"Move," he whispered. "That little pishogue I put on the deputy won't last long."

"No kidding!" Jill said. She was glancing over her shoulder. Taylor turned to follow her gaze and saw the deputy lurching toward the door. They hadn't even gotten across the parking lot.

"Silas, you've got to do something," Taylor said.

"Just keep moving," he said. "The railroad tracks shouldn't be more than a couple of blocks that way."

"S-stop right there, sir!" the deputy stammered.

"Go!" Silas said. He whipped around to face the deputy. His body dropped into a crouch. Despite his command, Taylor and Jill stood there transfixed.

The deputy drew his pistol. "Put your hands above your head!" he ordered.

Taylor could only imagine what the deputy saw, but what she saw was Silas dropping his human appearance and extending a single, bony arm toward the deputy.

"Arghh!" he sputtered. He slapped at his arms and chest as if his body were suddenly covered with creepy crawlies. He fired his weapon toward the ground. Taylor shrieked and jumped. Jill grabbed Taylor's arm.

At the same time, Silas projected the image of a fierce, black dog. It reminded her a little of Danny Underhill's dog form, but a whole lot scarier. Silas's dog form was a huge, shaggy mastiff with glowing red eyes and fangs like white daggers. Also unlike Danny, Taylor could tell Silas's dog form was just another glamour. With a little concentration could still see both forms: Silas lunging for the deputy on two legs while the dog did the same on all fours.

Silas rammed into the deputy's belly headfirst, bowling him over. He grabbed the pistol, flung it across the parking lot, and then retreated.

"I said go!" he shouted. This time, the girls didn't hesitate. They crossed the street, nearly getting run over in the process, and kept on going. In no time, Silas caught up with them. Behind them, the deputy was calling for backup.

They followed the railroad tracks west. Silas insisted he heard a westbound train in the distance, but Taylor couldn't hear it.

Before long, Taylor started to get short of breath.

"Hold up," she gasped.

"Another fifty feet," Silas said. "We've got to get to the bridge up ahead."

Taylor shivered.

"I c-can't go on."

"What's wrong, Taylor?" Jill asked.

"The railroad," she said, huffing and puffing. "Iron."

"Iron only affects fae magic," Silas told her. "It doesn't do anything to your breathing. It's all in your head. Now come on!

"Her Kind don't do well with iron," he explained to Jill.

"You already said that," Jill said. "So why are we following the railroad tracks?"

"We can't travel through the Wonder. At least, not with you tagging along," he said. "We've got to stay Topside. With any luck, the railroad will give us a little bit of cover."

"Taylor, use your inhaler!"

Taylor waved her off. "I'm okay. Just let me catch my breath."

"I'm not loving this plan," Jill said.

"Then you're going to go ballistic when you hear the rest of it," Silas said. They came up to the bridge.

The church grim turned back to Taylor. "I don't suppose you know how to blink?"

She shook her head.

"Figures," he said. "All right, we're going to climb up the end post" He produced a two-foot length of nylon cord from his satchel. He pulled on both ends, and the cord lengthened. He pulled again. Soon, he had a good twenty or thirty feet of cord snaking around his feet.

He tied a loop at one end and gathered up the rest.

"Who's first?"

Taylor and Jill looked at each other with obvious concern. In the distance, Taylor heard a train whistle. Time was running out. She raised her hand.

"Okay," Silas said. "Slip the loop under your arms. I'll haul you up." With that, the church grim gave Taylor the looped end of the cord and scrambled up the diagonal steel beam with the other end. He tied it tight to a bracing at the top of the bridge and gave Taylor a thumbs-up.

She mounted the beam, which felt icy cold through the soles of her shoes. Silas was a lot stronger than he looked. He pulled her up with hardly any effort and guided her to sit straddling the nearest strut.

He freed her from the cord and threw it down to Jill. She pulled the loop over her head and arms. By now, all three of them could hear the chug-chugging of the train's engine.

Silas signaled to Jill and started to haul her up. She clung to the beam and inched up as carefully as she could.

"Hurry up!" he called. "Train's coming!"

"I know that!" Jill replied. But she didn't move any faster.

Taylor watched Silas haul the cord. He seemed to be operating more by feel than sight; his eyes were fixed on a spot in the distance where the tracks curved toward them from out of the trees.

"Come on!"

"What's the hurry?" Taylor said. "She's not on the tracks. She's not going to get run over."

"That's not the point," Silas said. "That train is our ride out of town."

"You can't be serious."

"If your friend doesn't get herself in gear, you'll see just how serious I am. I intend to catch that train, with or without her!"

He gave the cord a firm tug—hard enough to get Jill's attention but not so sudden it would make her loose her balance.

"B-but that train has got to be going...what? Fifty miles an hour?"

"Maybe more."

"Are you crazy?"

"Just desperate."

One more firm tug, and Jill joined them at the top of the bridge. Silas quickly untied the cord and collapsed it back to its two-foot length. He helped the two girls scoot out to the middle of the strut. He stood between them, apparently unfazed by the height or the narrowness of the beam.

"I say jump, you jump. Got it?" He didn't wait for either girl to say yes or no. He leaped over Jill's head and skittered back to the side of the bridge. He looked once more into the distance.

His face bore a look of deep concentration. He relaxed his body into a lazy crouch, his arms extended waist high, with palms turned up and outward in the direction the train would eventually come.

He took a couple of deep breaths and let them out slowly.

"What are you doing?" Jill asked.

"I'm trying to slow down the train, if you don't object!"

The train rounded the bend. Almost before it did, Taylor heard the squeal of brakes. Through the windshield, she caught sight of the conductor. His eyes were as big as saucers, and it looked like all the color had drained from his face.

Glamour? Taylor thought. She tuned her eyes to see what Silas had put in the conductor's mind.

She suddenly found herself sitting in mid-air over a smoking ruin where the bridge used to be.

Ah, she thought. *Bridge out.*

The brakes continued to squeal as the train barreled toward the bridge. Trains are a lot harder to stop than cars once they get going, but Taylor could see this one was at least slowing down.

Silas leaned out to get a good side view of the train just as the engine passed under his feet.

"Get ready!" he called.

The train coasted along, gradually slowing. It didn't come to a complete stop, however. In fact, it seemed to be holding at a pretty constant speed. Taylor feared the conductor realized he had only been seeing things.

The girls braced themselves. Taylor's heart was pounding like a drum. She concentrated on her breathing.

No asthma attacks! Not now!

Jill muttered to herself. There were tears in her eyes.

Silas sprinted along the beam back to his spot between Taylor and Jill and grabbed both of them by the hand.

"One...two...three!" He jumped, pulling the girls off the strut with him. Jill shrieked. They landed on top of a boxcar with a flop.

Jill yanked herself loose from Silas's grasp. She slid along the metal roof until she was teetering at the edge.

Silas cursed and bounded for her just as she rolled off.

"Oh, Brother Mike!" Silas cursed.

"Jill!" Taylor screamed. She crawled on all fours, finding whatever ice-cold handholds she could, to Silas. The church grim bent over, straining with a heavy weight, with his toes curled over the edge of the boxcar.

Jill's frantic shrieks almost overpowered the rumble of the train itself. Silas grabbed her by one arm. As she flailed helplessly, the church grim struggled to haul her along the side of the boxcar. She was bawling like a baby.

The door of the boxcar was partly open. There was plenty of room for a person to slip inside. Silas dragged Jill toward the opening and swung her in.

"You next," Silas called.

Taylor gulped. She took Silas's hand and allowed him to lower her over the side.

The church grim swung her into the boxcar, where she landed in a crumpled, trembling heap. Her left knee hurt like fire. She must have slammed it against the roof when she landed. She was out of breath, and her head was spinning. She resisted the urge to throw up. Jill looked to be in a similar state just a few feet away.

A second later, Silas joined them.

"Now, was that really so bad?"

Chapter 13

Sighted

"Bad?" Jill gasped. "BAD? That was the worst thing I've ever done in my life! You could have killed us!"

"Then maybe you should have stayed behind like I asked you." Silas had about reached his limit with Jill's constant complaining. Keeping Taylor out of trouble was one thing—she was dead if somebody didn't stick up for her, and it looked like fate had handed him the job—but bringing a deathling along was just asking for trouble.

"Listen here, you! Taylor is my best friend, and if she needs my help, I'm going to be there for her even if it scares me to death. What I *don't* need is any more of your lip!"

"It's okay, Jill," Taylor said.

"Like heck it is! This guy has done nothing but badmouth me ever since we met. Well, how would you like it if somebody turned your whole world upside down in about five seconds, huh? Oh, man, look at this! I tore my jacket!"

There was, indeed a long ragged tear down the right sleeve of Jill's windbreaker. Silas noticed blood underneath.

"Let me see," Silas said. "You need first aid." He reached toward Jill's arm, but she yanked it away from him.

"Don't you touch me!"

"Here, Jill. Let me see," Taylor said. She eased her friend out of her windbreaker and examined the wound on her arm. It didn't look deep, but it was long and angry-looking against her caramel skin.

"There must have been s-something sharp up on the roof. A n-nail or something."

"Are you still shivering?"

"It's just so c-cold in here," Taylor said.

"Being surrounded by thirty-plus tons of steel will do that to a fae," Silas said. He was rummaging around in his satchel. He brought out a roll of bandages, a small jar of healing salve, and the water bottle Taylor used earlier to wash the iron filings off of Jill.

"Take care of your friend," he said, and wandered to the far end of the boxcar.

It was old and creaky and thick with dust, but now that the sun had fully risen, a golden wedge of light shone through the open door. The constant rumble and the movement beneath Silas's feet soon ceased to be a distraction.

He watched from a distance as Taylor cleaned Jill's arm, applied salve, and then wrapped it in a clean, white bandage. She handed Jill her jacket back.

"You keep it," Jill said. "It looks like you need it more than I do."

Taylor shivered as she pulled it on.

"Here, kid," Silas said. He tossed Taylor a small package from his satchel. A hunk of fudge wrapped in plastic wrap.

"None for you!" Silas snapped at Jill. "You're in too deep as it is. But maybe this will build up Taylor's magic, keep her from feeling so cold. Go ahead, kid. Eat all you want."

He rummaged around in his satchel again. This time, he pulled out a small package of peanut butter crackers. He tossed this to Jill.

"Make it last," he said. "It's the only Topside food I've got."

Jill didn't open the snack. She just laid it beside her on the floor of the boxcar.

"So, how come iron doesn't hurt you?" Jill asked Silas.

"Different kind of magic," he said with a shrug. "Your friend... She's what we call a true fae. They're practically made of magic.

But that comes with its own weaknesses. We goblins are a little further down the food chain."

"Oh," she said. "I see." Her expression said she really didn't.

"Little folk magic is mostly pishoguery. Illusion. We can't really alter reality—not by much, anyway. But we're pretty good at messing with peoples' minds."

"You mean scaring the snot out of them."

"What can I say? You do what you're good at."

There was a moment of silence, then Jill spoke again. "And what about the bell? I mean, back in Macon?"

"Same thing," Silas said. "Magic is all about vibrations, frequencies. They hold the universe together."

"You're talking about m-music," Taylor said.

Silas nodded. "If you know how to adjust the frequency, you can do practically anything. That's why fae magic is based on music. It's hard-wired to the deepest part of you, Taylor. But something like a big church bell can cause a disruption. If it's on the right note, that is. Whoever cast the bell at Oak Hill knew what they were doing."

The train rumbled along. By now, they must have been a couple miles past Mayfield and heading west. Silas wished he knew how far it was to the Mississippi state line.

"Why don't you like me?"

Silas looked at Jill. Sitting down, she was only a little shorter than him.

"It's nothing personal."

"I don't care if it's personal, I just want to know. You act like I'm beneath you or something."

"You're not beneath me," Silas protested. "You're just in over your head. You don't even know what you've gotten yourself into. If your godmother is really Dubessa Fairchild, then frankly, I don't like your chances of coming out of this little road trip unharmed. If you don't get yourself killed, you're liable to end up enslaved so deep in the Wonder you'll forget what it's even like to be human."

Jill sucked in a breath.

"Do you always have to b-be so negative?" Taylor asked. She wasn't shivering as much now, but she still didn't look happy.

"Listen, Taylor, I didn't want to bring your little friend along in the first place. But it's hard to say no to a sídhe who's got her presence going full-bore, you know what I mean? I've got my own reasons for looking out for you, and I'm going to give it my best shot. But her?"

He started counting Jill's negatives on his spindly fingers. "She's a Topsider. She knows less about what to expect than even you do, and with all due respect, missy, you're not exactly up to speed even when it comes to your own magic, let alone what nasty things your enemies could do to you.

"And then, a powerful fae has fared forth into her. Maybe even ridden her. If that happened once, it could happen again. Her godmother could come back and none of us would even know it. If it weren't for the iron in this boxcar, she could be listening in even now. She thinks this lady's on your side, but do any of us really know that? What if she's luring us all into a trap? Did you ever think of that?"

It felt good to be free from the effects of Taylor's presence. Maybe it felt a little too good. Silas had been holding back for hours. He really wanted to let off some steam.

"Not only that, she's gone and bought in! Did you think of that? That means no matter how this turns out, even if by some miracle we find this du Marais and his stupid cup, and even if somehow we get it away from him, and *even* if that fixes things between you and the Hellebores, she's still bound to the Wonder, and especially to her godmother. I swear, it's almost like she blabbed her true name! What if her godmother makes her turn against us at the last minute? Do you think she'll be able to say no?" He scoffed.

"For that matter, I've already given her the only Topside food I had. We're going to have to stop somewhere and make a flipping grocery run or she's going to starve to death before we even get to New Cephalonia! Either that, or eat my rations and get pulled in deeper than she already is!

"And on top of everything else... Just look at her! She can't ring-travel without practically wetting herself. She shrieks like a maniac when she's afraid—and let me tell you, we're all going to be plenty afraid before this fiasco is over. If she can't pull herself together, then I still say we put her on a bus to Macon the first chance we get."

"Stop it!" Jill cried. "Just stop it!"

"That's right!" Taylor said. She pointed a finger at Silas. "I don't want to hear it. Understand?" Silas could tell she still didn't have any presence to project, but the fudge must have at least started making her feel more like herself.

"Fine," Silas said. "Have it your way." He gathered his salve and the rest of his bandages and stuffed them in his satchel. Then he brought out the wooden bowl he snagged from his cupboard.

"Then at least try to make yourself useful," he said. He set the bowl in front of Jill and filled it half-full with water from his water bottle. The girls' eyes widened as they realized it was once again completely full.

"What's this for?"

"It's for scrying. Why don't you see if you can find your satyr?"

Jill looked up at him, mouth half open, eyebrows furrowed.

"Look, just try to relax and concentrate on du Marais." He gestured toward the bowl. "See what happens. You might get lucky."

With that, Silas headed for the door.

"I'll be on the roof, trying to figure out where we are." He crawled up the inside of the open door and hoisted himself outward and upward.

The time alone did Silas good even though all that steel was enough to give even a goblin the shivers. He sat on top of the boxcar watching the world pass by, marking time by the sun as it slowly rose into the cloudy summer sky.

It wasn't all that different from a day seventy years ago when Silas's life changed forever. But he couldn't tell Taylor about that.

What would she do if she learned that he was the spy who brought about the massacre at Bailly Hen?

Politics!

He never liked politics, mostly because he never liked people. Leave him alone and let him do his job, and everything was fine. Why should it matter to him if the Arradherry Courts were having at it? Let the Gentry settle their own problems.

Then the Courts of New Avalon decided to start choosing sides. It seemed easiest just to go along and keep his head down. The Holly Court came out for Crom Cornstack—no surprise there. Silas figured the politicians would make speeches and the poets would sing their propaganda and that would be the end of it. It didn't have to affect him.

But then it did.

Silas wished he could chalk it up to the power of Vergosus Bright's glamour. After all, he wasn't the first goblin to crumble when the Summer Primus turned on the charm.

"You know you don't want to go to war," he said. His deep, green eyes reflected warmth and vitality as he strolled through Silas's former haunt back in New Avalon. "People are going to get hurt. Fae, little folk, dwarves: everyone. Let us settle our own disputes in Arradherry. Bringing another chiefdom into the conflict in would only make things worse."

It sounded so reasonable, so convincing.

"I know the Holly Court is itching to get involved. We both know that would be a disaster—no less for you than for us. But if we knew what they were planning, perhaps we could find a way to stop them before things get out of hand."

The Summer Primus made a strong case. It was hard to say no to such a powerful sídhe lord. In the end, he agreed to let Bright use him to spy out the situation at Bailly Hen.

Vergosus Bright heard the orders with Silas's ears, saw the massing troops with Silas's eyes. Silas felt him stir to anger inside his head as he took it all in. There was no pretending he didn't know how the Summer Primus would respond.

He wanted to be shocked when the Summers descended upon the place with unquenchable fury. He just couldn't convince himself it wasn't exactly what he had seen coming. Bright threw everything he had against the little rath. Silas barely got out alive. Most didn't get out at all. The Summers' vengeance was thorough. And then there came the repercussions: the accusations, the trials...and the teind.

Silas left New Avalon and never looked back.

Jill spent all morning trying to see anything but water in the scrying bowl, but without any success.

"It's not working!" she complained for about the hundredth time. "Why can't I see anything?"

"It's okay, Jill," Taylor said. "Maybe it just takes more practice."

"I'm starving. And I've stared at this stupid bowl so long my eyes are crossing."

Just then, Silas dropped in through the boxcar's door.

"Get ready to move," he said.

"Where are we?" Jill asked.

"Best I can tell, somewhere in Mississippi." He emptied Jill's bowl back into his water bottle, then stored both the bottle and the bowl in his satchel. "We're slowing down. This may be the last chance we get for a while to find you something to eat."

"I can't wait to get off this stupid train!" Taylor said.

"Don't get your hopes up. Trains are still the safest way to get you to Louisiana. We'll just find some food and come right back."

Taylor slouched, defeated.

The clouds had cleared out, but the bright, blue sky did little for Jill's spirits. They slipped off the train as soon as it stopped and skirted away under the cover of Silas's glamour.

The train station was drab and gray wherever it wasn't rusted and piled with junk, and the smell of oil, metal, and diesel fuel was overpowering. It almost made Jill's head spin, but at least they had something to look at beside the four walls of a dusty boxcar.

The church grim scanned the city beyond the station.

"Look over there. I bet you can find something at that gas station," Silas said. He handed Taylor a handful of bills. "I'll hang around and see where we need to go next," Silas said. "Don't be gone more than twenty minutes. And Taylor, use your seeing stone if you run into any trouble. Any trouble at all, you hear?"

Taylor nodded. "We'll be fine. I'm already feeling better."

"Then hurry up."

The girls sprinted across the tracks and sidled up to the wall of the transfer shed. They slipped through the fence, through an alley, and across the street to the gas station Silas had spotted.

As they reached the curb, Jill stopped to catch her breath. The sun beat down on both of them without mercy, but Taylor seemed to appreciate it. It just left Jill blinded and disoriented.

"Are you okay?"

"Just a little edgy," Jill said. "Why does the sun have to be so bright?"

"It's probably just your...uh...sight-thingy."

"I really wish it would do something useful for a change." She crossed her arms to keep them from shaking. "At least you're feeling better."

"I guess I am," Taylor said. "Are you ready?"

As Silas predicted, the gas station was home to a small convenience store. The girls picked up a box of crackers, a tin of Vienna sausages, a bag of cookies, a couple bags of potato chips, two bottles of lemon-lime soda, and three bananas. They got in line behind a woman about Jill's mom's age paying for her gas and a package of cigarettes.

Taylor cursed under her breath.

"What's the matter?"

"Look," Taylor whispered.

Jill followed her eyes to the TV behind the cashier. A news report was showing Jill and Taylor's seventh-grade school pictures!

The sound was turned down, but words near the bottom of the screen read "MISSING GA GIRLS SIGHTED IN AL." Jill felt a lead weight settling in the pit of her stomach.

The screen went to an artist's drawing of the glamoured appearance Silas had assumed at the Waffle House. Beside the image were bullet points:

Unknown suspect
• Possibly named "Silas"
• White, 5' 11"
• 40-45 years old
• Short light brown hair
• Large black attack dog

Beneath that was the phone number to a police tip line.

"Keep your head down!" Taylor hissed. Jill complied—though part of her wanted either the cashier or the woman in front of them to recognize them. She so wanted to go home!

But that wouldn't keep Taylor's messed-up family from trying to kill her. No, as much as Jill hated the idea, they had to keep going. They had to find a way to keep the Hellebores off Taylor's back. She sighed and lifted her head just enough to see what was happening.

It looked like the cashier was too busy finding the woman her cigarettes to be paying attention to the TV. As soon as she left, Taylor set their snacks on the counter and pulled out the cash Silas had given her.

The cashier took the money and bagged up their goodies. He looked sleepy and maybe even a little confused. Jill took a good look at Taylor and noticed tiny, almost imperceptible wisps of mist or fog rising off her. She was using some kind of glamour trick.

Taylor took the bag and scooted away while the cashier dully wished them a good day.

"What did you do to him?" Jill asked.

"I'm not sure. I just knew he needed to keep his eyes on me and not on the TV. I guess I threw a little glamour at him to hold his attention."

This whole best-friend-is-a-faery thing was going to take a lot of getting used to!

The girls slipped back through the fence without saying another word to each other. Jill was shaking. Seeing her picture on television was almost more than she could take.

"They think we've been kidnapped," she said at last as they waited for Silas in the shade of the transfer shed. "Mom and Dad must be worried sick. What are we going to do?"

"You don't have to stay," Taylor said while looking at her shoes. "Go back to the convenience store. Or go find a police officer. They'll get you home."

"But what about you?"

Taylor still didn't look up. "I'll manage."

"But what about your parents?"

A train whistle interrupted the conversation, but it didn't seem as if Taylor had much to say.

"We had a fight, remember? I'm not sure..."

"What?"

"I'm not sure they're up to being parents to a...to somebody like me. Probably better if I—"

"Now, just stop right there!" Jill said. "Don't be bad-mouthing your parents. As many times as they've stuck up for you? That fight you had. It was about...well, all this, right? You don't think they can handle it?"

"They've proven they can't handle it."

"No. Maybe they proved they don't know how to handle it—yet. But your folks are cool. You've got to give them time. They'll figure it out."

There was another long silence.

"Here comes Silas," Taylor said. Jill turned and saw the church grim trudging toward them. As usual, he didn't look happy. "You'd better go."

"Not till I can bring you home with me." She planted her hands on her hips and waited for Taylor to say something.

Silas walked up to them.

"We've got trouble," he announced.

Chapter 14

Horsing Around

Danny Underhill dared to rest a bit high in the branches of a great oak tree.

He had finally brushed the last of the feathers off himself and was pleased—though surprised—that he only had a few scratches to show for his troubles.

Those paissas mean business! he told himself, not for the first time.

From his vantage point, he had a decent view of his surroundings. Unfortunately, you couldn't see very far in a forest, even in the middle of the day. He thought about climbing higher, but first he had to catch his breath.

There hadn't been any sign of his pursuers for over an hour, but he didn't dare think he was home free. He took stock of his situation. He still had his seeing stone and his utility knife, but that was it. He got lunch from an apple tree a couple hours ago, but his stomach was rumbly. He could really use a little more sugar to build up his magical reserves, but that didn't seem possible.

Louisiana? he thought. *Why is Taylor Smart going to Louisiana? And why is she bringing her Topside friend with her?*

At the moment, he didn't see much chance he would be able to join her, no matter how much she said she needed him. Those paissas were pretty good trackers, even if he did have a head start.

And where is Louisiana, anyway? He was used to thinking in terms of the many competing chiefdoms of the Wonder. His grasp of Topside geography was a little sketchy, but he was pretty sure Louisiana was to the south and west, at the mouth of the Great River in what His Kind knew as the Chiefdom of New Cephalonia. It was maybe 700 miles away—assuming he could shake his pursuers.

He cursed when he heard voices in the distance. He let out a long, low breath and tried to calm his nerves and summon all the glamour he could to mask himself from view. Magical mist enveloped his body from head to toe, like a veil descending over him.

Thanks to his keen hearing, the paissas were still over a hundred yards away when they captured his attention. They were back along the same deer path he had been on since last night, speaking in their strange language, no doubt looking for signs Danny had passed that way.

Should he stay in the tree? It was tempting, but he wasn't sure his glamour could hold for long as tired as he was.

Then the wind shifted, and with it came a familiar smell: horses. In fact, if he listened closely, Danny could even make out the sounds of their hoofbeats and snorts. There were at least two or three of them, and hopefully a few more than that.

He might have a real chance of getting away, but he had to act fast. He reached into the pocket of his denim jacket. He had been saving one last apple for supper. With a sigh, he pulled himself upright and, steadying himself with his left hand, heaved the fruit as far as he could off to one side of the path. If they heard the sound of it hitting the ground, it might buy him a few more minutes.

As soon as Danny threw the apple, he blinked a couple yards further down the path into the branches of a poplar tree. Then he blinked again onto the low-hanging branch of a sycamore. He was exhausted, but he needed to get as far ahead of his pursuers as possible.

He dropped to the ground and landed on all fours. As soon as he did, he pushed all the magic he had left into a quick change. His limbs lengthened and darkened. His hands and feet hardened into tough, black hooves. His face and neck stretched out while his shoulders and haunches widened, filling with muscle. He felt his curly black hair grow into a shaggy mane.

As soon as he was completely transformed, he bolted down the deer path as quickly as he could. His horse shape gave him speed, but he wasn't quite as maneuverable in close quarters, and he feared tripping on his fragile legs. Still, he clopped along at as close to a full gallop as he dared. It wasn't long until he started wearing out, however. But up ahead, he could see an opening in the forest. He cleared a low wooden fence at the edge of the woods and found himself in a gently sloping pasture.

Just as he hoped, a herd of horses grazed at the bottom of the hill. Beyond them was a large, well-kept stable.

One of the horses, a big bay, started to whinny.

Slow down, Danny told himself. *Don't spook them.*

The other horses started at his sudden appearance. The big bay approached him along with a gray male whose eyes glowed with yellow fire, not unlike Danny's own. There were half a dozen more: two ghostly white, two black, one dun, and one dappled.

One of the black horses snorted fire and trotted behind the gray as he circled around Danny.

The gray whinnied. *Where do you think you're going?*

Uh..., Danny snorted.

Quick as a flash, the gray turned and gave him a fierce kick to the side. The black ploughed into him, trying to drive Danny off. He somehow managed to twist his body out of the way before the black's fore-hooves landed another blow.

I don't want no trouble, Danny whinnied. He knew how the game was played. This wasn't his first time being a horse, after all. He needed to become accepted by the herd. Then, he could lay low as long as he needed, build up his strength, and throw the paissas off his trail.

He trotted off in a wide circle until finally rounding back toward the horses. The bay followed at a distance, squealing and whinnying. By now, the rest of the herd had joined the ritual.

Danny didn't have much choice but to take whatever abuse they threw at him. He kept his distance as best he could, but gradually edged his way closer. The bay always whinnied and squealed when he did this, and one horse or another would charge at him to force him back.

The ordeal went on longer than Danny wished, but not longer than he expected. At the thirty-minute mark, he started getting hopeful he'd come out mostly unharmed. Other than a nasty bite to one ear and a couple more kicks to the ribs, he was hanging in there.

About forty-five minutes into the ritual, the paissas showed up at the edge of the woods. There were three of them: four to four and a half feet tall, black-haired, and dusky-skinned. Their ears peaked in subtle points like Danny's, and their eyes had a similar feral cast to them. They wore a mishmash of camouflage and buckskin and sported bows and quivers slung over their shoulders as well as bronze-headed tomahawks hanging from their belts.

The leader had barely made it over the fence when the bay sounded the alarm. *Two-legs!* he whinnied. The entire herd retreated to the far end of the clearing. It seemed the initiation ritual was postponed until they could take stock of the new threat posed by the strange intruders. All of them whinnied in alarm. Danny joined in. Nothing like a show of group solidarity to seal the deal, right?

"Fury! Lightfoot! What's going on?" Another fae came around the side of the stable. Danny froze, but the other horses seemed to take comfort from his presence.

He had fair skin and long, white hair. He was dressed in casual clothes: jeans and a green flannel shirt. His rounded ears branded him of distinguished birth, but he didn't carry himself with the kind of arrogance Danny was used to seeing in the Gentry. He ambled forward slowly and deliberately, as if he wasn't entirely sure of his footing. He wore his age a bit more heavily than most fae.

The gray trotted toward him, nickering. He pulled a treat from a pouch slung over his shoulder and offered it to him.

"Can I help you folks?" the old fae said.

The paissas approached. The horses moved to get out of their way. The black one that breathed fire blew orange sparks. One of the white ones jerked this way and that.

Tentatively, Danny fell in line behind the dun as he took up the rear. He kicked at him, but Danny stopped in time to dodge it.

"We're looking for a pooka," one of the paissas said. "Have you seen him?"

"A pooka?" the fae repeated. "Can't say as I have. Lightfoot, you haven't seen another two-legs, have you?"

The bay wagged his head left to right.

"Well, there you go, gentlemen. Lightfoot would know if anybody had passed this way. I've never known Lightfoot to miss something like that, and he's honest to a fault, that one is."

"They're shape-shifters, you know," a second paissa said. He eyed the horses, now huddled together at some distance from the conversation. "Are all these horses yours?"

"Of course not," the old fae said. "None of them are mine. They belong to Mr. Belas Wakefire. And I daresay he wouldn't take too kindly to trespassers on his land."

Belas Wakefire? Danny thought. *The Primus of the Summer Court?* His heart skipped a beat, and he let out a blow in spite of himself. Now he was the one getting jittery.

"Are you sure?" the first paissa said.

"Am I sure?" He scratched his head. "I'll have you know, young man, that I have been a stableman for the house of Wakefire for over seven hundred and fifty years. I think I know my horses," he sniffed. "Tell them, West Wind. Do I know my horses?"

The dun snorted, and Danny was certain he saw him roll his eyes.

"The gray one's the boss. His name is Fury. His sire was a wave-runner, but his dam was a fine saddle horse—a favorite of the Primus himself. And the two blacks and the dapple, those are Whitsuntides. The Primus brought them from overseas about twenty years ago..."

"There are three blacks," a paissa said.

"What's that?"

"There are three black horses in this pasture."

"That's what I said."

"You said there are two blacks and a dapple."

"You need to pay more attention, sonny. No, there's Snort and Midnight. They're the black ones. And...uh...Bloodhoof is the dapple..."

Danny looked around for the quickest way to escape. His heart started pounding, and his eyes began to glow.

The dun snorted. *Nice meeting you, kid.*

"No, no," the old fae said. "That last black one.... No, he's not a Whitsuntide."

The paissas reached for their tomahawks.

"He must be another saddle horse.... That's right, look at the fire in his eyes. Now I remember! The Primus said he was dickering with a Gentryman from back east about a horse. Yeah, that'll be him, all right."

"You're sure?"

"I know my horses, young man. Never let anybody say that Wictred Buckle doesn't know his horses."

The paissas didn't seem entirely convinced, but Danny knew their options were limited. You didn't just confiscate the property of the Summer Court of Arradherry, even if you did suspect it was really a pooka in disguise.

"Then we'll be on our way," the leader of the paissas said.

"I reckon you will."

The paissas blinked away with a flash.

"Aengus!" the stableman called. A young little person poked his head out the stable door, a ruddy-cheeked barn-brownie in a white cotton shirt and tan coveralls.

"Yes, Mr. Buckle?"

"Have you set up a place for the new horse?"

"New horse, Mr. Buckle?"

"Aye. The new hunter. Have you forgotten already?"

Aengus furrowed his brow.

"I don't rightly know about a new horse, sir. But I'll get right on it."

Chapter 15

Heading South

"Trouble?" Taylor said. "What do you mean?"

Silas gestured for the girls to follow him. He skittered around the corner, gesturing for them to follow. A small crack in the cinder-block wall of the transfer shed opened before him into a decent-sized opening. Jill remembered something similar back at the church.

Silas slipped through with Taylor close behind. Jill followed.

Inside was a tiny office with a desk, a couple of chairs, a coat rack, and a supply locker—all goblin-sized. Taylor and Jill had to stoop to keep from hitting their heads on the ceiling.

A second goblin rose from his seat behind the desk.

"This is Anthony," Silas said.

Anthony was shorter than Silas but clearly the same kind of creature: swarthy skin, bandy legs, and bat-like ears. His eyes were larger than Silas's, however. They were the biggest, bluest eyes Jill had ever seen. He gave the girls a pleasant smile.

He was dressed in an old-fashioned train engineer's coveralls and bill cap, but all in faded yellow, with a light blue, long-sleeved shirt underneath and a black kerchief tied around his neck. Pungent smoke wafted from his carved amber pipe and tickled Jill's nose.

Anthony extended his bony hand to both girls.

"These are the two I told you about," Silas said. "Taylor and Jill."

"Pleased to meet you," Anthony said. "Have a seat, have a seat." The two girls tried, not entirely successfully, to squeeze into the two goblin-sized chairs that faced the desk. Silas remained standing to one side.

"I ran into him while I was skulking around the main office, trying to get a look at today's schedule. Go ahead, Anthony. Tell them what you told me."

"Well," he said. He looked first at Taylor and then at Jill. He cleared his throat and began again. "I was telling Mr. Bludgitt here getting to New Cephalonia might be a problem."

"That's the part of the Wonder that connects to Louisiana and thereabouts," Silas explained.

"Right," Anthony continued. "But somebody knows you three are on your way, and they're not too happy about it."

"What do you mean?" Taylor asked.

"You hear things when you're in the transportation business. I've got connections a thousand miles in every direction. And everything I'm hearing from New Cephalonia tells me there's trouble brewing."

"W-what kind of trouble?" Jill asked.

"A nightwalker."

"I beg your pardon?"

"An elf," Silas explained.

"An elf," Jill dully repeated. "As in, one of Santa's helpers?"

"There's no way to know who he's working for," Anthony said. "But it doesn't really matter. You don't want to cross a nightwalker."

"There's different kinds of elves, just like there's different kinds of goblins," Silas said. "The ones that like to torment Top-siders—blast them with elf-shot, blight their crops, send them nightmares and such—we call those nightwalkers."

"And this one's right nasty, if you believe what folks have been saying," Anthony added. "Birds have been tweeting about him all day. He's down in the bayou, putting out the word about a sídhe girl traveling with a witch and a goblin."

"A witch?" Jill said. She would have jumped out of her chair in protest, but the armrests hugged her hips and kept her seated.

"Well, you're not fae or little folk," Silas said. "What else are we supposed to call you?"

"Witch just sounds so insulting." She crossed her arms.

"Semantics," Silas said. "Anyway, Anthony says this nightwalker has put the word out he'll reward anybody who tips him off to where he can find us."

"Who is he working for?" Taylor asked. "The Winter Court?"

"That, I haven't heard," Anthony said. "But I'd be careful if I were you. Dealing with any kind of elf can be dicey."

"Elves are cousins of the sídhe," Silas explained. "They're almost as powerful. 'Dicey' doesn't even scratch the surface."

"Wonderful," Taylor sighed. "Wait a minute, can you show me where this guy is supposed to be right now?"

"Of course," Anthony said. He pulled a rolled-up map off the top of the storage locker and unrolled it on the desk. Taylor scooted forward as best she could, trying not to bang her knees as she leaned over to study the map. It displayed a web of railroads from the east coast all the way to Texas.

"This is where we are," Anthony explained, pointing to a big red circle labeled Meridian. "From what I hear, the elf is somewhere down in these parts, along the Bogue Falaya River."

Taylor looked at Silas. "What are the chances this guy knows where du Marais lives?"

"Du Marais?" Anthony's eyes flashed blue fire.

"Could be," Silas said. "And if he does...."

"Then he's showing us which way to go," Taylor finished.

"Wait a minute," Anthony said. "Are you talking about Évastre du Marais? The satyr?"

"You've heard of him?" Silas asked.

"You're joking, right? I mean, you're not seriously looking for him, are you?"

"What if we are?" Taylor said.

Anthony shook his head. "You don't want to be messing with Évastre du Marais."

Jill leaned forward. Taylor and Silas traded worried glances.

"He's not your ordinary satyr. They say he's in tight with the ruling families of New Cephalonia."

Silas shook his head in disbelief. "How does a satyr have anything to do with the Gentry?"

"What's the matter?" Jill asked.

"Satyrs aren't exactly known for playing by the rules," Silas said. "Even by Fair Folk standards, they can be a little...unpredictable. Most of them are only interested in..." He frowned. "How old did you girls say you were?"

"Thirteen."

"Yeah, er, most satyrs are only interested in finding the next party. They're not what you'd call model citizens. If he's got ties to the Gentry, he really isn't your run-of-the-mill satyr. That could mean trouble."

"But...we knew we were heading for trouble when we left Macon," Taylor said. "We can't turn around now, can we?"

"No," Jill said. "We've got to find that cup, and that means finding the satyr." She felt her lip beginning to quiver. "It's the only way to get rid of my godmother."

"But it might not even work," Silas said. "Face it, Jill. She's got you right where she wants you."

"Maybe," Jill said. "But we've got to try. Show me again where this elf is?"

Anthony pointed a long, spindly finger at a spot on his map.

Jill studied the spot, then said. "That makes sense."

"What makes sense?" Taylor said.

"He's somewhere along this river, right? Well, it's not too far from there to New Orleans. See this big lake? That's Lake Pontchartrain. And just on the other side is New Orleans."

"So."

"So," Jill sighed. "Every time my godmother has talked to me about that cup, she's given me a dream. A vision. I don't know what to call it."

"Yes?" Silas said. He leaned against the map.

"She's shown me a place I know in New Orleans. It's the cemetery where my grandfather is buried."

"You think that means something?" Taylor asked.

"A cemetery can make a pretty good shortcut into the Wonder," Silas said. "Especially an old one."

"Do you think your godmother could have been giving you a hint?" Taylor said.

"Could be," Silas said. "Personally, I don't think we can trust anything Jill's godmother has told her—*except* that she wants us to find this satyr's cup."

"And when we find it, what?" Taylor asked.

"I don't know," Silas said. "But I doubt your godmother is going to let you keep it or bargain with it."

"Yeah, I've got that feeling, too," Taylor said, slumping her shoulders.

"So, what do we do?" Jill said. "Give up? Go back home?"

"And let the Winter Court pick me off whenever they want? And Mom and Dad, too?"

"We'll figure something out," Jill said.

"Like what?" Taylor snapped. "You don't have a clue what these people are like, Jill. They don't let anything—or any-one—stand in their way." She leaned back and closed her eyes. "Maybe we can get them off your back, Jill. But not me. I'll just have to keep running, I guess."

"Don't talk that way, Taylor. There's always a way. I know you. You've talked yourself out of tight spots before. We'll figure out what to do with the cup, then we can both go home and—"

"And what?" Taylor was shaking now. She looked like she was about to cry.

"I can't go home. Even without the Winter Court. My folks are never going to understand about...about..."

"Taylor Nicole Smart!" Jill said. "I think all this faery stuff has affected your brain."

"Fae!"

"Whatever! You know your parents love you, Taylor. They just need time to get used to it all, you know? Lord knows I do!"

"You don't understand!" Taylor said. "I told them everything and they didn't even believe me!"

"Taylor, listen to yourself. You told your parents you're a stinking *faery* and now you're upset because they didn't believe you?"

"Fae," Taylor said. "Please. 'Faery' is sort of rude."

Jill shook her head.

"They never asked for any of this," Taylor whispered, and now she really was crying. "How are they supposed to cope with a kid like me?"

Without a word, Jill placed her hand on Taylor's shoulder.

"I hate to interrupt this tearjerker moment," Silas grumbled, "but can we get going?"

Anthony took his cue. He grabbed a clipboard that hung from a nail on the wall. He flipped a page and ran a spidery finger halfway down the next.

"I can get you on the express to Shreveport..." he pulled a pocket watch from his overalls and checked the time "...if we hurry. Or, you can wait a couple hours and take a train straight to New Orleans. You should get there before sunset."

"Gethsemane Cemetery is the best lead we've got," Jill said. The others nodded their heads.

"New Orleans it is," Anthony said.

Taylor tried to reach Danny by seeing stone three times, but he didn't pick up. The last thing she needed to worry about was Danny being in trouble, but she couldn't help it. He was a nice enough guy, but he seemed to be really good at making enemies.

At a little after 2:30, Anthony led them across the rail yard under a deep cover of glamour. They skipped over railroad tracks and approached another train that was still being loaded.

Anthony double-checked his clipboard, then studied the long row of boxcars, counting from the front, and finally reading the letters and numbers painted on the side of one car in particular.

"This way," he said, and ducked underneath the boxcar itself.

Jill gave Taylor an apprehensive look.

"Hurry up," Silas said.

Jill took Taylor's hand, and the two girls followed after Anthony. At once, however, they had to let go of each other and get down on all fours to crawl across the gravel and railroad ties.

Up ahead, Anthony was applying a big, brass key to some kind of lock on the bottom of the boxcar. Jill heard a mechanical sound, metal striking metal, and the next thing she knew, Anthony had thrown open a trapdoor and had pulled himself up into the car.

She followed close behind and found herself in a little room. Anthony helped her and then Taylor up. Silas clambered into the room and smiled appreciatively.

It was no bigger than Jill's bedroom, with a low ceiling. That is to say, a Silas-sized ceiling. Jill and Taylor had to stoop to keep from hitting their heads. It had bare plaster walls painted dull light blue, a plain wooden table in one corner, a stack of old wooden folding chairs, and a cheap-looking sofa upholstered in tattered green vinyl with a hideous orange and black afghan thrown over the back. Whoever made it must have just been learning how to crochet, because there were a lot of obvious holes in it, and the whole thing was dotted with little knots of yarn where the maker seemed to have given up entirely. There were no windows. Apart from the entrance hatch, the only other door had one of those unisex bathroom signs on it. Jill was certain that, if worst came to worst, she could hold it in for a few hours. The only light was provided by a bare lightbulb dangling from the ceiling from a length of insulated wire.

"Perfect!" Silas said.

"Depends on your definition of 'perfect,'" Taylor said.

"The whole room is hidden from Topsiders," Anthony explained. "It exists in a pinched-off pocket of the Wonder. The trapdoor is the only way in or out."

"Sort of like my apartment," Silas said.

Jill's face scrunched up in deep thought. "But if we're in the Wonder, won't they be able to track us magically?" she said.

"No," Taylor said. "Too much iron." She shivered and closed her eyes. "I can feel it."

"Right," Anthony said. "At least, it's not very likely. You're still technically inside a steel boxcar. Any Fair Folk trying to find you would still have to get past that."

"Like I said, perfect!" Silas said.

"Yeah," Taylor said. She didn't look at all convinced.

Chapter 16

The Bayou

The train rumbled south for a couple of hours. Jill sat cross-legged on the floor, peering into Silas's scrying bowl and occasionally sighing, frustrated.

Silas rested, sitting in one wooden folding chair and using a second as a footstool. He bowed his head and kept his long, spidery arms folded across his chest.

Taylor curled up on the vinyl sofa with the knotty afghan wrapped around her shoulders. She was about at the end of her rope. The few hours of freedom in Meridian only made it harder when she once again had to crawl back into an ironclad cell.

It had been two months since she had last been wrapped in this much iron. The first time, she barely knew what magic was. Now, even though she was still a beginner, she had lived and breathed it long enough that she felt its absence. She didn't like the sensation. At all.

Jill was deep in concentration. But she was also nervous. She rocked back and forth so subtly that you didn't really notice at first. She tapped her knee with her fingers. Just a couple of nervous ticks, but Taylor knew it was unusual for Jill. Her friend was seriously freaked out by this whole magic thing.

At least, she hoped that was all it was.

What if it was something her godmother had done to her? What if she was craving another taste of faery food the way a drug addict craved the stuff that would kill him?

"What time is it?" Taylor asked.

"I'm doing the best I can!" Jill blurted.

"Jill, calm down. I just wanted to know what time it is."

Jill glared at her.

"Getting close to suppertime," Silas said. "Go ahead and eat a little if you want. It'll probably make you feel better."

"The only thing that going to make me feel better is to get this whole thing over with," Taylor said.

"Amen to that," Jill said. She turned to Silas. "You're sure you've never heard of this cup we're looking for?"

Silas shook his head. "To be honest, I still don't see how it's a big deal."

"Godmother said it was some kind of family heirloom. Something stolen from its rightful owners."

"If that's true, then the Hellebores would definitely want it back," Taylor said. "Reciprocity, right?" She turned to Silas. "Give and take. Settle your debts."

"Makes sense," Silas agreed.

"I'm sorry," Jill said, "but I just can't see what they think they're going to get by hurting Taylor!"

"Our Kind know how to hold on to a grudge," Taylor said. "And I'm right in the middle of a big one. I'm the Hellebore grandchild nobody wanted. Maybe they figured everybody else could get on with their lives if I were...out of the picture."

"That's just nuts! What sense does that make? How does killing an innocent person make anything better?"

"One's honor is one's life," Silas said. "That's the first precept of the Eldritch Law—and one the Fair Folk take very seriously."

"Maybe I'm dense, but I don't see anything honorable about painting a target on my best friend's back."

"Honor doesn't mean what you think it does," Silas said. "Honor means status, reputation. The better people think of you, the more honor you have. It's not something that exists apart from public opinion, so every fae wants to keep a close tab on what others are saying about them. If the opinion-makers turn against you, you're toast." He stretched and yawned. "I don't expect a couple of kids to understand."

"Please," Jill scoffed. "Did you miss the fact that we're in middle school? I could write you a book about kids trying to look fresh. You show up somewhere in the wrong clothes or get seen hanging out with the wrong people and the popular kids will tear you apart."

Silas considered this. "Yeah, that's more or less how it works. The better you live up to what's expected, the more honor you have. The more you fall short, the more you're disgraced. You lose honor."

"You're telling me the Fair Folk are basically just a bunch of immortal middle-schoolers with supernatural powers?" Taylor threw her head back and closed her eyes. "It's worse than I thought."

"I don't make the rules," Silas said. "But Your Kind *will* enforce them. They're like mirrors: they give you back what you give to them. You do them a favor, they'll repay you. But you insult them or try to trick them...."

"So back this spring, when my friends and I tricked the Hellebores..."

"You challenged their honor. They've got to respond."

"Can't I just say I'm sorry?"

"It's too late for that," Silas said. "The word has gotten out. It's not just about you anymore. It's about reasserting their status, defending the family name—and discouraging anybody else from challenging them in the future."

"But...." Jill struggled to put her thoughts into words. "We're still talking about killing somebody! Isn't that just a little extreme?"

"Not for Her Kind," Silas said. "The last time something like this bubbled up, it took a teind to settle it."

The church grim looked like he had swallowed a ball of cobwebs.

"It took a what?" Jill said.

"A teind," Silas said.

Both girls looked at him for the longest time. He didn't seem in a mood to explain himself.

"You might as well tell us," Taylor said. "It's not like we're going anywhere."

Silas bowed his head.

"'Teind' means tribute," he said. His voice was low, almost a whisper. He never raised his eyes. "It's the ultimate penalty for bringing dishonor on one's family."

There was another long silence. The train rattled along. Taylor sat up on the couch, still wrapped in the afghan.

"When a fae has done something terrible enough... unforgiveable enough...the offended party can demand a teind. It's very rare. It's only happened once in my lifetime."

Taylor thought about her mom's job as a secretary at a lawyer's office. "Like when you sue for damages in a lawsuit?"

"Worse." The church grim continued to gaze at the floor. Taylor shivered, but she wasn't sure it had anything to do with the temperature of the room.

"A teind...is a tribute of blood. It means sacrificing the children of the wrongdoers to pay for the sins of their parents."

Jill gasped. Taylor's mouth fell open.

"The...the children?" Taylor whispered.

Silas nodded. "To the fourth generation. One out of every ten. Chosen by lot."

"Th-they can't get to Shanna," Taylor said. "They can't get to my birth mother. She's too well protected."

"But they can get to you," Jill said. Tears trickled down her cheek. She scooted over to her friend and wrapped her arms around her.

"Is that what this is about?" Taylor asked. She shook like an old washing machine. "Is this Mara and Crom's way of getting back at their daughter? Through me?"

"Could be," Silas admitted. "But it isn't a teind. There's a formal process for that, and as far as I know, none has been started. No, this is just plain old-fashioned revenge."

"I can't help thinking about all those Bible stories," Jill said. "Pharaoh killing the Hebrew babies, or King Herod and the children of Bethlehem...." She trailed off, stifling a sob. Then she blurted out, "It just doesn't make any sense! How could they be so evil?"

"Not evil," Silas said. "Not exactly, anyway. The Fair Folk will do anything—*anything*—to preserve their honor. They don't follow what you'd call a black and white morality," Silas said.

"No," Taylor agreed. "More like purple and November."

"Still sounds like evil to me," Jill muttered.

Taylor noticed Silas's somber expression. It reminded her of something he had said that morning.

"You say there's only been one of these teinds in your lifetime. It was after that massacre you told us about, wasn't it? At that...chicken place?"

"Bailly Hen," Silas said. "And don't you *ever* speak disrespectfully about it again!"

"S-sorry!"

"But you're right. The Summer Court captured Bailly Hen through deception and reduced it to rubble. The Winters lost their allies, and it wasn't long until the Summers won the war. Arradherry's been pretty firmly in their control ever since. But that didn't keep New Avalon from demanding satisfaction."

"They called for a teind," Taylor said.

"And they got it. Every ruling family of the Summer Court was affected: the Redmanes, the Fairchilds, the Brights...all of them."

"The Redmanes? You mean Anya..."

"Yeah." Silas at last looked Taylor in the eye. "Your dad wasn't the first child Anya Redmane watched die."

It seemed all the air seeped out of the room. The lightbulb above them swung gently back and forth with the rumbling, rhythmic movement of the boxcar. Nobody seemed in a mood to say anything else.

Something hard and cold settled in Taylor's stomach.

"Aulberic had an older brother," Silas continued. "Lorcan. His name came up in the draw."

"And my grandmother just...handed him over?"

"Lots of folk wondered if she'd refuse. I mean, seriously. The son of the Primus and the Chief Matron? But if you knew what was good for you, you didn't say things like that out loud."

"Honor again," Taylor guessed.

Silas nodded. "You do what's expected. And like it or not, nobody is immune from a teind. Centuries ago, they'd let you designate a surrogate—a changeling maybe or some other underling. Then they decided that made it too easy. If you knew the stakes were high, you weren't as likely to demand a teind in the first place. You found other ways to satisfy your honor."

"Well, thank heaven for that," Jill whispered.

All at once, the three lurched forward. The train was slowing down fast—or at least, as fast as a freight train can slow down. The lightbulb swayed, casting agitated shadows on the walls and floor.

"What's going on?" Jill said.

"I don't know," Silas said.

A few minutes later, train squealed to a stop. As soon as it did, Silas moved to the trapdoor and unfastened the lock.

"You two stay here. I'll be right back."

He slipped open the door and dropped onto the gravel beneath the boxcar with barely a sound. Taylor shot Jill an apprehensive look. For the longest time, neither one of them dared make a sound.

When she couldn't take any more silence, Taylor said, "What do you think is the matter?"

Jill shrugged her shoulders. "This is my first quest, remember?"

Taylor tiptoed to the trapdoor. She opened it just enough to poke her head out and look around. It was still daylight. As best she could tell, they were somewhere in the woods. At least, she couldn't hear any traffic sounds or voices or anything else that would mean there were people nearby.

She shivered.

"Maybe we should go look for Silas." She eased the trapdoor all the way open. It creaked a little, but she kept it from making too much of a racket.

"He said to stay here," Jill said.

"You always do what adults tell you."

"Pretty much."

"That's an awful habit."

Taylor rubbed her shoulders. She had left the afghan back on the sofa. She was starting to get cold again. "We really ought to see what's going on out there."

"It's safer in here."

Taylor wondered if her friend was right. Any fae looking for them would have a hard time detecting them through the box-car's steel frame. She wasn't sure they were completely invisible, but Silas seemed to think they would be hard to spot.

At the same time, if they got caught inside the boxcar, Taylor would be worse than useless. Surrounded by that much steel, she would never be able to summon enough glamour to drive them away.

Her teeth chattered. Freezing to death didn't sound like much fun, either.

"I think we should risk it," Taylor said at last.

"You can't be serious!"

"We've got to, Jill. He's been gone forever. He could be in trouble." She grabbed her bag from where she had dropped it on the floor near the sofa.

"Listen, Jill. It's bad enough Silas went off without us. We need to stay together."

"Out there?"

"Once we get away from this hunk of metal, I can make us both invisible. Or mostly invisible. At least, I'm pretty sure I can. As long we don't make any loud noises or anything..."

"Well, if you're that confident, how can I say no?"

"Grab Silas's pack, just in case the train leaves without us."

Jill's eyes grew wide. "You're serious, aren't you?"

"Just come on, will you?"

The girls slipped down onto the tracks and crawled out from under the boxcar. Almost immediately, they felt the hot, muggy air. If the heat and humidity weren't enough, there was also a strong smell of rotting vegetation.

Once clear of the railroad, they found themselves walking on squishy, grassy ground. Mosquitoes and dragonflies were thick in the air.

"We've got to be somewhere on the bayou," Jill said.

"The bayou? Swamp is more like it."

"Bayou sounds better. My grandmother lived in country like this when she was little."

"I'm sure she misses it terribly." Taylor swatted a mosquito.

A thunderous noise shook the trees. It seemed to pound its way into Taylor's ribcage. It took her a second to realize it was the barking of a dog. She and Jill both spun around, looking this way and that, but there was no sign of movement.

"So, you said something about invisibility?"

"Right," Taylor said. "This way!"

She headed for the nearest tree with branches low enough to climb. Jill scrambled up first, then pulled Taylor after her.

The barking seemed to fade, replaced by the sounds of bodies swishing through the tall grass.

The girls both stood on the lowest branch huddled together, with Taylor hugging the trunk.

"Now just be quiet," she whispered. She closed her eyes and tried to concentrate. She imagined a misty veil forming all around her and Jill, covering them from top to bottom.

The barking got louder, then softer again. Eventually, it faded altogether.

They waited, Taylor's heart pounding.

"Is it safe?" Jill asked.

Taylor shushed her. "Dog!" she whispered.

"I don't hear it anymore," Jill whispered.

"I know." Taylor remembered Silas's dogs and how they sounded farther away the closer they came. If this was a faery dog, too, it was almost on top of them. Somewhere, someone grunted with exertion. Taylor was pretty sure it was Silas.

The barking started again. Taylor tried to pinpoint the direction it was coming from. To the left? Or was it straight ahead?

She looked up. The tree had one nice, low branch for the girls to climb on, but that was it. They were only four or five feet off the ground—whoever was running that dog could grab them in a heartbeat.

Across the way was another tree with good, evenly spaced branches. They could get twenty feet up if they tried.

"We're going to have to move."

"What?"

The barking was good and loud now, but Taylor still couldn't figure out where it was coming from. She got ready to jump. The barking got louder still.

"That tree over there," she whispered.

Jill saw it and nodded. She slipped her hand into Taylor's.

The barking started to turn soft again. The dog was rounding back toward them. It was now or never.

They jumped and bolted toward the other tree.

The barking dropped another notch in volume. *Not good!* Taylor thought. She ran just a few yards when the barking got loud behind her...or maybe in front of her.

The whole experience was disorienting, and she could tell Jill was feeling it, too. She yelped and ducked behind a nearby bush even though there was no sign of anyone else around.

Taylor stopped, stunned. It took her a second to remember that louder barking was a good thing. The way the noise seemed to come from every direction had her nerves on edge. She wondered if faery dogs didn't put out some kind of spooky canine glamour to keep their prey disoriented.

"Come on!" Jill said. She had retreated from her bush and was already halfway to their goal.

The girls were now so far apart, there was no way Taylor's glamour could keep Jill from being noticed. She hurried to catch up.

The barking had turned soft again, a nagging whisper behind her ears. At the same time, sounds of footsteps echoed in the trees. They, at least, sounded like they were coming closer.

She made it to the tree, and Jill hauled her up. They scrambled for hand- and footholds and inched their way upward.

Taylor concentrated on re-forming the misty veil around her and Jill.

Silas burst into view beneath them, his clothes splattered with mud. Close on his heels was a dog that looked like nothing Taylor had ever seen before.

First of all, it was green. At first, Taylor thought its rough coat was dark gray, but a second look confirmed it was a dark, forest green more or less the color of pine needles.

In addition to its unearthly color, it was huge—as large as a small horse, with paws the width of a man's hands. It whipped its long tail back and forth and glared at Silas with eyes that glowed like coals. It moved its mouth as if barking furiously, but Taylor could barely hear a sound.

The church grim turned to face the creature. He fell into a crouch and, as he had done outside the Waffle House that morning, projected the illusion of a fierce black dog. The hound fell back, but only for a second.

Another figure emerged from the trees. He was tall, fair-skinned, and dressed in muted greens and grays. The hunting knife strapped to his side was as big as a short sword. The bronze barrel of his shotgun glinted in the sunlight.

"Get him!" he shouted. He raised his shotgun to his shoulder.

The dog lunged forward, and Silas's illusion evaporated in a puff of black smoke.

It circled around Silas. It didn't tear into him, but Taylor guessed that was only because it was well trained. It didn't take much imagination to see the beast sizing up the church grim for his nutritional content.

Silas braced himself. The stranger had only to say the word, and he was dog food.

"Now," the newcomer said, shotgun still trained on Silas. "You ready to tell me where the girl is?"

Taylor couldn't bear to watch, but she couldn't turn away.

Silas stood there, arms outstretched defensively, tight-lipped and still as stone. The dog circled around him and growled an inaudible growl. The stranger kept his shotgun trained on him.

This can't be happening!

"Don't be a hero, goblin," he said. "Give up the girl, and I'll let you live."

Silas said nothing.

"Bitsy!" The dog padded over to the stranger. "Find the girl," he said as he pointed toward the tracks. From her vantage point in the tree, Taylor could just make out the roofs of the boxcars. What would happen if they found their empty compartment?

"We almost lost you when you switched trains."

"Is that so?"

"Oh, that's all right. I'd have done the same thing if I were you. It's nothing personal. And stopping a train isn't that hard. Now, are you going to cooperate, or does Bitsy get a new chew toy?"

Then there was an explosion of black smoke and a sudden, unearthly wail. Taylor gasped out loud. In the confusion, no one seemed to notice. She, however, noticed the sly grin on Silas's face. *More glamour!* She thought.

Bitsy barked in the distance.

Silas scrambled toward the nearest tree. The stranger fired his weapon. The muzzle flashed, and a sound like a thunderclap echoed through the woods.

The church grim fell to the ground.

"Silas!" Taylor shouted—then slapped a hand over her mouth.

It was too late: this time, the stranger heard her. He whipped around in the direction of her and Jill. The wood was suddenly clear and silent. The smoke and the noise of Silas's illusion were gone.

Bitsy was at the foot of the tree in no time. The stranger grinned as he opened the breech of his firearm and reloaded.

Taylor tried to settle down. She hoped she and Jill were still invisible. She summoned up as much glamour as she could, but if the stranger had already spotted them...

"Which one of you girls is Selena Hellebore?"

So they weren't invisible. That was bound to complicate things.

"Or maybe you go by your deathling name? Taylor Smart?"

Taylor looked around for something to throw. Anything to defend herself. If she gave herself up, would the stranger let Jill go free? Even if he did, he didn't seem the type to take her to the nearest town and give her change to call home.

Taylor dropped to the ground. She imagined herself as powerful, imposing—not a scared teenager but an immortal princess of the daoine sídhe.

"*You need to go. Now*," she said, and she threw all the presence she could into the words.

For a second, it even worked. The stranger lowered his weapon, as if he just realized he was taking aim at his boss or something.

But then the dog started yelping—at least it looked like it was yelping; Taylor couldn't hear a thing—and jumping around again. The stranger's expression hardened. He wasn't buying her act any more.

"Are we through now?" he said. And then, with no warning at all, he fired point-blank into Taylor's chest.

She crumpled to the ground. The last thing she heard was the sound of Jill screaming.

Chapter 17

Licorice

Danny dined on hay.

He would have preferred roast beef and potatoes, but that was out of the question. First, Aengus the stable boy always seemed to be hovering around grooming the horses, filling their feed trough, and inspecting their legs and hooves. On top of that, he was clearly confused by Danny's mere presence in the pasture.

"I just don't remember nothing about a new horse," he said to himself. "Now, if Mr. Wakefire wants him a new saddle horse, then that ain't none of my business. I'm just a hired hand. It just strikes a fella a bit odd, is all."

He rubbed Danny's back as he offered him a piece of apple. "Mr. Buckle says I must have forgot about you, but I ain't sure that's so. Mr. Buckle, he's the stableman, and he knows his business...but he ain't as sharp as he used to be." He leaned in conspiratorially. "I think he's getting ready to fade, if you asked me. They get like that sometimes, right at the end. They lose track of things, get all turned in on themselves, and then all of a sudden...poof!"

Even when Aengus wasn't taking care of them, he liked to sit on the fence rail and play soothing music on his panpipes. There was no way Danny could sneak off without being noticed. And with those paissas around, he didn't dare.

But even if he could have found himself a nice slice of roast (with mashed potatoes and gravy...), Danny couldn't have eaten it. For the time being, he had a horse's stomach, after all. He'd have never been able to digest anything but the grasses and grains Aengus put out for him.

As the hours passed, Danny came to terms with the hay. He knew as well that the longer he stayed a horse, the more the taste would grow on him. His appetites and even his instincts would become more horse-like. Already he noticed himself getting jittery at any sudden noise. He found himself scanning the horizon on the lookout for wolves. Every now and then, he turned his eyes upward, looking for griffins.

All the while, the other members of the herd kept reminding him that he was the newcomer. Fury, the gray one, was the leader. The only horses that even came close to challenging him were Lightfoot, the big bay, and Snort, the fire-breathing black. The others fell in line behind those three: Midnight, Bloodhoof, and the dun, West Wind. Finally, the two silvery white horses, Froth and Glitter, were lowest in the pecking order. But even those sneered at Danny with impunity.

Danny knew that if he just put up with it, the horses would finally realize he wasn't a threat to anybody's position. The truth was all he wanted to do was get out of there. That just wasn't possible until things cooled off with the paissas. Maybe after dark, he could blink away and hopefully figure out where he even was.

Only West Wind seemed uninterested in asserting his dominance. He only reared at him once or twice early on, and Danny got a sense that was just to keep up appearances. He was, in fact, the first in the herd to act like Danny belonged. He seemed to keep aloof from the other horses, content to wait his turn at the feed trough and roll in the grass by himself while the others grazed.

Danny ambled over to him after lunch, cautious not to get too close too soon.

I won't bite, West Wind nickered.

Thanks.

Why were those two-legs chasing you?

No sense of humor, Danny snorted.

West Wind snorted in reply and rolled his eyes in a way that said he understood.

That afternoon, a stranger appeared. Danny started. The other horses cast him a wary eye before returning to whatever they had been doing. He was a handsome young sídhe in green riding clothes of the sort that were in fashion a hundred years or so ago in the Topside world, with a sword and a flintlock pistol strapped to his belt and a gold circlet in his wispy, auburn hair. Aengus followed close behind.

"Will you be wanting Fury, Sir?" he said.

"I haven't decided," the sídhe said. He leaned against the fence and studied the herd.

"I don't expect trouble, but one never knows. If Cornstack tries anything, I'll need a good, fast horse with a good disposition. Say, where did that new one come from? The black one?"

"Him?" Aengus said. "He just got here today. I'm not sure where from exactly, Mr. Wakefire, but Mr. Buckle had some dealings this morning with some Indian fae I ain't never seen before."

Wakefire! Danny's eyes glowed yellow. *That's the Summer Primus or I'm a unicorn. And what does he mean 'Cornstack'?* Crom *Cornstack?*

"So Buckle acquired him, did he? He'll be a fine horse then. What do you know about him? Already broken, I suppose?"

No, no, no! Danny thought. *This is not happening!*

"Seems pretty even-tempered to me, Sir. And he's got a good, smooth gait. I don't know how he'd do in a fight, but I reckon he'd make a fine riding or hunting horse."

"Then bring me tack, Aengus. Let me see what he can do."

The next thing Danny knew, he had a bit in his mouth and a bridle fastened around his head. He flinched; it had been over a hundred years since he had last worn horse tack. The bit felt odd in his mouth, but familiar enough that he didn't complain too loudly.

He considered his options. He could buck and fight, and the Primus might pick another horse to ride. That would be great.

But what kind of trouble would he make for himself by acting up now? He still needed to lay low until sunset. And what kind of trouble would Buckle get in for supposedly buying a belligerent horse?

Belas Wakefire smiled. He extended his hand toward Aengus and snapped his fingers. The stable boy handed him a blanket, which he quickly draped over Danny's back. Then he slung a saddle onto Danny's back and deftly tightened the girth.

Danny did not want to go riding!

Then he thought about Taylor. She was in trouble, and so was her friend Jill. Danny bet anything Crom Cornstack figured into that trouble somehow or another, and if Belas Wakefire was going to visit the Winter Primus, then maybe Danny needed to be there, too. He chomped the bit in agitation.

This is going to ruin my whole weekend.

"Very good," the Primus said. "He's been well trained, that's plain to see. And he looks like he's got some spirit."

Danny became self-conscious of his eyes' yellow glow. He tried to settle down.

"Aye, sir, that's always a good sign. He'll make a fine saddle horse, for sure, once he gets to know you."

"Oh, he seems perfectly content right now," the Primus said. Without another word, he slipped his foot into the stirrup and hoisted himself up onto Danny's back.

Danny pinned his ears and shifted his feet but managed to suppress his instinct to buck.

I can't believe I'm doing this, he thought.

"I believe I'll take him for a ride, Aengus. If he meets my expectations, you can groom him and have him ready to travel in the morning."

He kicked at Danny's sides and yanked on the reins. If possible, Danny felt even worse about this turn of events than he did before.

Amateur! he thought. But he ambled forward anyway. The Primus turned him toward the gate with the reins, and soon they were on their way down a woodland trail with the stable fading into the distance.

"Good boy," the Primus said. "What shall I call you? Blackie? Blackjack?"

Danny whinnied. *How about Lightning? That's a good name for a horse.*

"How about Licorice? Do you like Licorice?"

Not as much as I like Lightning!

"All right, Licorice, let's see what you can do." The Primus kept kicking him until Danny sped up to a canter. They rode past tidy stone farmhouses as well as barns and various other outbuildings, some sized for fae and others for little folk like Aengus.

After a few more minutes, the Primus spurred Danny to a gallop. *Take it easy!* Danny whinnied. *We'll get there, I promise!*

The trail had curved back toward the pasture by this time, but the gate was shut. The Primus pushed on.

"Can you jump, boy?"

You can't be serious!

Danny started to slow down. His head told him he could probably clear the gate with no problem. His horsey instincts made him second-guess himself. He just didn't like the idea, not with his ribs still sore from the initiation the other horses had given him earlier.

But the Primus wouldn't let up.

"Come on, Licorice. Show me what you've got!"

Danny had no choice but to barrel on. With every step, the gate seemed to grow higher and higher. He really didn't want to even try to jump the gate, but he didn't like the one alternative he saw around it.

At the last minute, he simply did what came naturally. He blinked, vanishing in a flash of light and reappearing a heartbeat later on the other side of the gate.

"Well, I'll be dogged!" Aengus called. Danny could hear him whooping and laughing. The Primus turned him toward the stable boy, and Danny could see him slapping his knees and grinning from ear to ear.

"You should have told me he's a blinker!" the Primus said.

"I didn't know myself!" Aengus wiped the sweat off his forehead.

"Buckle's done it again, by Danu! Isn't that right, boy?" He patted Danny's neck. By now, they had ridden to where Aengus was standing. "I should have known he was a blinker from the fire in his eyes. Let me cool him down with a lap or two around the pasture, and then I'll leave him for you to groom."

"As you wish, sir."

"I'll be back tomorrow. Have him ready to go by sunrise, do you hear?"

Aengus nodded. "I'll have him ready, sir. You don't need to worry about that."

"Licorice, you and I are going riding tomorrow. And I'm going to show that blowhard Crom Cornstack he's not the only fae with an eye for horseflesh."

Chapter 18

Captured

Jill screamed all the way down the tree and halfway to the stranger before she realized that charging a man with a shotgun and an attack dog the size of a Volkswagen was a monumentally stupid thing to do.

"Hold it right there, kid," he said as he took aim.

Jill stopped in her tracks. Her pulse pounded in her temples so hard it was giving her a headache. Her breath was forced. Her limbs were shaking. It was a miracle she hadn't already fallen over.

She might have looked the stranger in the eye, but two bronze shotgun barrels demanded her full attention.

He was nearly six feet tall, with a lean but broad-shouldered frame. He quirked a cocky smile. Behind his dark sunglasses, a white-blond eyebrow arched.

His clothes were the color of smoke, from his wide-brimmed hat to his knee-high boots. They even seemed to change shades of gray as he moved, as if real smoke were swirling through them. His long, cloak whipped about easily in the gentle breeze. The whole ensemble was made of the same material, which—Jill gasped when she realized—was partly transparent. But instead of revealing the contours of the man's lean muscles, revealed instead fleeting glimpses of the trees and undergrowth behind him.

He wore a utility knife strapped to one leg and a canteen and a small leather satchel slung over his shoulder.

"Bring me the goblin," he said.

Behind him, Silas let out a feeble moan. He was still alive.

Jill dropped to her knees beside Taylor. She rolled her over on her back, both relieved and confused that there was no blood on her shirt. There weren't even holes where the shotgun's pellets must have torn into it.

The universe started to spin at unpleasant angles.

"They're not...?"

"Dead?" The stranger chuckled. "The boss lady wants the girl alive."

"B-but...you shot her. In the chest." Jill would be the first to admit she led a fairly sheltered life, but she had somehow gathered that shooting a person at point blank range usually resulted in a severe case of death.

"You think I don't know how to mix elf-shot?"

Jill didn't even know what elf-shot was.

"They're just paralyzed, missy. If I'd wanted them dead...." He left it to Jill to finish the sentence.

"Bring me the goblin," the man said again. He bent down and hauled Taylor up onto his shoulder, all the while keeping his firearm pointed at Jill. "I'll take care of this one."

First, he snatched Taylor's purse. Then he slung Taylor across Bitsy's back and fastened her hands and feet together around its belly with a leather strap.

"And be quick about it!" he said.

"He's a church grim."

"Don't matter to me."

Jill tentatively approached Silas. He looked up at her with half-open eyes and tried to say something, but his mouth wasn't working. He looked like he had been drugged.

She tried to heave him up onto her back. Not a great idea. Silas was about as big as a five-year-old and weighed a lot more than Jill expected him to.

The stranger sighed his impatience.

Jill finally grabbed hold by both arms, dragged Silas across the ground, and laid him at the stranger's feet.

As he did with Taylor, the stranger hoisted Silas up onto Bitsy's back and bound him in place. The dog panted loudly. With its shaggy coat, it must have been twice as uncomfortable as Jill was—and she was practically drenched with sweat from all the running and screaming she had done.

He came toward Jill while pulling a third strap of leather from his coat pocket. He spun her around, pulled Silas's satchel off her back, pulled her wrists together, and bound them in about half a second. It was like the straps knew what to do and tied themselves in a knot. No, she thought. It wasn't *like* that; that was exactly what happened.

"This way," the stranger said, gesturing with his shotgun. He slung Taylor's purse and Silas's pack over his shoulder.

The stranger and his dog walked behind. He directed Jill to turn now right, now left, as they weaved their way through the bayou. Always, he kept his shotgun with its paralyzing elf-shot trained on her.

In the distance, Jill heard the sound of the train lurching back into motion.

Fantastic. As if it wasn't bad enough to be captured at gunpoint and marched through the bayou, now she was missing her ride.

Silas groaned again. Taylor did, too. Apparently, she was also shaking off the effects of the elf-shot.

"Stop," the man said. Jill stopped beside a massive, moss-draped cypress tree. Above her, four mesh bags dangled from high branches. They must have made it to the stranger's base camp.

She slowly turned toward him. He pulled first Silas and then Taylor from their mount. Each flopped to the ground. The stranger tied their wrists behind their backs and propped them up against the tree.

"Have a seat," he said.

Jill backed up and used the tree for support as she lowered herself to the ground.

The stranger dropped their confiscated purse and satchel to the ground. He pulled something from his pocket. It was a pale, gray stone with a hole through the middle. He held it to his mouth and whispered a name. "Claudia Fountain. Claudia Fountain. Claudia Fountain."

It was what Taylor had done to communicate with Danny Underhill, their classmate from last year who, it turned out, was also some kind of supernatural creature.

"Vesper here," the man said. "Your boss said to call you with any news. Well, you can tell her I got the girl." He peered into the stone. He must have heard someone speaking on the other end, but Jill could only hear the buzz of dragonflies and the croaking of frogs.

"No, no problems at all. The only thing is, there were two others with her. What do you want me to do with them?"

The sun was low in the sky. Jill imagined wandering through the woods in the dark, trying to find the nearest road.

"A church grim," the man—Vesper—said. "And another girl... How should I know? She might not even be Our Kind. She doesn't act like it, anyway."

He listened some more.

"All right, if you say so. But we haven't eaten all day... I know, but it's been a long day. Your boss made me get up early. And it's still a pretty good hike to the nearest ring.... Give me a while to pack up. I'll bring her in."

"Her," Jill noted. Not "them." That didn't sound at all comforting.

Vesper pulled his own satchel off his shoulder and set it on the muddy ground. He gave Jill another suspicious glance and then vanished in a flash of light. Jill yelped.

He reappeared above her, straddling the branch where he had stored his supplies. He unfastened one of the bags and dropped back to the ground. He moved with an eerie grace and made hardly any noise at all as his boots touched down the grass.

He rummaged around in the bag and brought out a package wrapped in white paper. He undid the wrappings to reveal an entire ham shank—and apparently one taken from a pig as oversized as Vesper's dog.

He whistled. His dog loped toward him, its tongue lolling. He dropped the ham shank at her feet and rubbed her shoulders as she tore into it.

"Who's a good dog?" he said. Bitsy wagged her tail.

Vesper found a wooden pail in his bag.

"Don't go anywhere!" he growled. He vanished again, but returned only half a minute later in another flash of light. Now, the pail was sloshing with water.

He set the pail down some distance from the tree, and Bitsy found it soon enough. Then from his own backpack he retrieved a tin of food. It reminded Jill of some kind of army rations.

He sat cross-legged on the ground, his shotgun beside him. He rummaged in his pack for a plastic knife and a sleeve of crackers.

Silas groaned.

"Wh...? Wh...?"

"Wake up, Silas," Jill whispered.

The church grim struggled to open his eyes. His left eye stayed partially closed, and the left side of his mouth drooped. But at least he was awake, or close to it.

"Huh? Whuh?" Taylor mumbled.

"You see, missy? Your friends will be just fine."

"No thanks to you!" Jill said. Vesper only laughed.

All she could do was glare at him.

Beside her, Silas pulled himself up to a seated position. He was awake but groggy. He struggled against the cords on his wrists. With some effort, he eased up into a crouch. It looked like his left leg was still asleep. At any rate, he didn't get far before Vesper simply touched his shotgun and shook his head.

The church grim lowered himself back to the ground.

"What are you going to do with us?" Jill asked. She tried to sound brave. She would have settled for not sounding frantic.

"My contract is just for your friend there," Vesper said. He spread a dab of potted meat on a cracker.

By this time, Bitsy had finished her supper and was resting in the shade of a massive willow.

"You didn't...answer her question," Silas said, his voice slow and deliberate like somebody just waking up, or maybe a little bit drunk. "What...are you going...to do with us?"

Vesper shrugged his shoulders. "Nothing. As long as you all don't take a notion to follow me, we're good."

Jill's heart sank. He was leaving them to fend for themselves in the middle of the Louisiana bayou. If they didn't get eaten by an alligator or swallowed up in a sinkhole, the mosquitos would eat them alive. And given the events of the past day or so, she realized she couldn't disregard other threats her Maymay used to tell stories about: zombies and tainted keitres and rougarous.

She glanced at Silas. His face still looked droopy, his expression listless. The chances of him swooping to the rescue were pretty slim.

Vesper vanished again and suddenly appeared on his branch, where he untied the remaining bags one by one and dropped them to the ground. He was packing up. In a few minutes, he and Taylor would be gone, and she and Silas would be alone in the wilderness.

A desperate thought crept into her mind.

No. There had to be another way.

But once Vesper left with Taylor, it was over. She might never see her friend again. She might never see anything again.

She shut her eyes and shook her head.

She sighed and then tried to focus her thoughts into a mental message addressed to parts unknown.

Godmother?

"Come on, Bitsy," Vesper called. "Up and at 'em." The dog came padding to Vesper's side. He gave her an affectionate neck rub.

Godmother...is there any chance you could give us a little help here?

Jill felt the hairs on her neck get twitchy, like something was sneaking up behind her. She looked left and right, but there was nothing to see. Vesper was fastening his bags together into an overlarge backpack.

Don't trust him. The thought came to Jill from out of the blue.

Duh! she told herself. Then she realized she wasn't alone inside her head. Her godmother had returned.

There is a faery ring about a mile to the west, she said. *Cross the stream behind the big oak tree. Watch out for alligators.*

Vesper turned in Taylor's direction.

Sure thing, Jill thought. *I'll just rip these cords apart with my bare hands, disarm a dangerous magical bounty hunter, and fight off his dog. Shouldn't take more than twenty seconds.*

Vesper heaved Taylor onto his shoulder.

You really don't understand the benefits of having someone like me in your life, do you?

Not from where I'm sitting, no.

Then pay attention, the voice said. *You're going to put the elf and his dog to sleep. Do you know any lullabies?*

Say what?

We're going to perform some magic, child. You and I. I'll provide the power, but you will have to direct it. Do you understand?

She didn't really, but her whole body suddenly started to tingle. She glanced past Silas to Taylor, now being strapped once more to Bitsy's back. Her friend seemed agitated but too weak to put up a fight. Jill tried to call out to her, but the words wouldn't come.

Her heart fluttered. A fine haze seemed to rise up from the ground, but only she could see it. At least, Vesper didn't act like he noticed.

That should do, the voice in Jill's head said. *Now very softly, child, you need to sing a lullaby.*

Jill's eyes widened. *You're serious, aren't you?*

Silence. The haze swirled and eddied around her. Vesper still didn't see it.

Slowly, tentatively, Jill began to sing. "Hush, little baby—"

"Huh?" Vesper whipped around.

"Nothing!" Jill squeaked.

Not so loud, Jill's godmother said. There was the slightest hint of impatience in her disembodied voice.

Are you sure you can't just do this part?

Are you formally granting me permission to take over?

Jill gulped.

On second thought, let me try again.

She took a breath and started again, more softly but a bit more steadily.

"Hush, little baby, don't say a word.
Mama's gonna buy you a mockingbird."

This time, Vesper didn't turn around. He was busy heaving his supplies onto his own back. Bitsy nuzzled his elbow.

"And if that mockingbird don't sing,
"Mama's gonna buy you a diamond ring."

The swirling haze had congealed into a tiny, twisty tornado of sparkly light, barely visible—yet Jill could see it clearly. It reached out blurry tendrils toward Vesper, Bitsy, Taylor, and Silas.

Vesper had leaned against the cypress tree, wiping sweat from his brow. The dog started to whine.

"And if that diamond ring turns to brass,
Mama's gonna buy you a looking glass."

Jill was piecing out what was happening. The haze must have been the magic her godmother talked about drawing up from the Wonder. Her singing gave it shape, turned into some kind of sleeping spell. She felt her voice grow stronger, more confident.

Vesper's eyes grew heavy.

"Taylor?" she called.

Don't worry about Taylor, child! Concentrate!

"But..."

The dog chuffed and lifted her head, eyelids barely open.

"If that looking glass gets broke,
Mama's gonna buy you a billy goat."

There was no denying the magic was working now. Vesper had slumped to his knees, sound asleep. The dog snored and panted.

Jill felt wide awake.

Now focus, child, her godmother admonished. *Don't cry out if you want this to work!*

Something moved behind Jill. If not for her godmother's warning, she would definitely have shouted as something small and hairy brushed past her hands.

She felt something wet and rough against her wrists. She craned her neck to see what was happening, but to no avail. She had a pretty good guess, though. By the time she finished the next verse, her suspicions were confirmed.

Her hands fell free of the leather strap that had bound them. Jill twisted around in time to see a single mouse scampering away. She rubbed her wrists.

Bitsy snored, but never awoke.

Taylor groaned in her sleep.

"Taylor!" Jill whispered.

The next thing is to wake your friends, Jill's godmother said. *Some water from the elf's canteen should do the trick.*

Vesper was only a few feet away. Jill scrambled across the ground to him, pulled his canteen off his belt, and rushed to Taylor. She undid the straps that tied her to the back of the dog and rolled her over onto her back.

Once you reach the ring, head south. You'll know the way from there, I think.

"Taylor!" she whispered again. She grabbed her friend by the shoulders and pulled her up to a sitting position. She splashed water in her face.

Taylor groaned. Jill called her name once more, and Taylor slowly opened her eyes.

The dog was fast asleep, as was Vesper.

Jill scrambled to Silas and gave him the same treatment. As soon as he started to stir, she ran back to Taylor.

"Get up, girl," Jill said. "We've got to get moving. Now!" Taylor opened her eyes.

Behind them, Silas grunted.

"You coming?" Jill asked him.

The church grim stumbled to his feet. He found his pack and started rummaging through it.

"Give me a minute," he said. He rubbed his eyes and yawned. "I can work a spell to find the nearest entrance into the Wonder."

"There's a faery ring about a mile from here," Jill said. "To the west."

"Is that so?" Silas said, arching his eyebrow.

Jill ignored him. "Are you ready to move, Taylor?" She glanced around the clearing. Vesper and his dog were still asleep, but the elf mumbled and rolled over onto his side.

"We don't have much time."

Chapter 19

A Race to the Ring

Hiking through the bayou was a sweaty, dirty ordeal, but Taylor didn't dare slow down. There was no telling how long it would be before Vesper was awake and on their trail.

Silas took the lead, as usual. Taylor envied his quick, agile steps as he navigated a living maze of tree roots, vines, quicksand, and spider webs. Jill followed close behind the church grim with Taylor taking up the rear.

Jill had said it was only a mile to the faery ring, but it took forever to get there. The sun was going down fast. Long, dark shadows obscured the way.

Silas produced a fiery orb to light the way. Taylor tried to do the same, but she still didn't have the knack of it. The obstacle course she was running made it too hard to concentrate.

"Got to be around here somewhere," Silas grumbled.

"Have we gone a mile?" Jill asked, huffing and puffing. "Feels more like two."

"Close to a mile," Silas said. The sun had dipped beneath the trees. The church grim's faery fire stood out against the encroaching darkness.

"How about that spell you mentioned?" Taylor said.

"Might as well," Silas said. He pulled off his satchel and reached in it for a small plastic bottle.

"Give me some room."

Suddenly, the bayou erupted with the thunderous sound of a baying hound.

"Hurry!" Taylor said.

"Really? Why?" Silas smirked. He released his fire orb. It floated lazily above him.

"Stay put!" he barked. Jill and Taylor froze in their steps. "And I could use a little more light, if you think you can manage."

Taylor gulped but nodded. The barking of Vesper's dog echoed through the trees, making it hard to tell what direction they were coming from.

Taylor tried to settle her thoughts. She imagined a veil of magic mist encircling her, wrapping her up like a blanket. So far, so good. She had at least gotten enough practice to recognize the feel of her magic when she called it up. She focused on her true name and extended her right hand as if ready to receive a gift.

Just like glamour, right? she told herself. *That's what Silas said.* But instead of letting the magic settle all around her, hiding her from sight, she willed it to gather in the palm of her hand. All the while, she imagined a fully formed fire orb bursting to life at her command.

Neunhiri, she thought with each exhaled breath. *I am Neunhiri, Laughter in Winter.*

This time, it actually worked! A ball of faery fire sprung into being, bright and cold in her outstretched hand.

Silas nodded with approval. He took two or three slow, deep breaths, his head tossed back and his eyes closed. He chanted an incantation, then unscrewed the lid of his bottle and emptied about a tablespoon of fine powder into his hand. It glowed faintly in the shadows.

The sound of Vesper's dog was getting steadily quieter. They were on the trail. Taylor hoped Silas's spell worked—and fast!

Silas tossed the powder into the air. Instead of falling to the ground, however, it hung there for several impossibly long seconds, glistening like frozen miniature fireworks. As he completed his incantation, the cloud spun into a tiny dust devil and whipped away through the trees.

"That way," Silas said. He didn't say anything else or even wait to see if the girls would follow. He just hoisted his satchel and started hiking away.

Taylor and Jill followed. Bitsy was getting closer. Taylor could barely hear the dog at all over their own footsteps.

"Gonna be a race," Silas commented.

"We can make it," Taylor said. She wasn't sure she believed it, but it felt good to say it out loud.

"Even if we enter the ring, he'll try to come after us."

"Are everybody's shoes tied?" The last time somebody chased her through a ring, she lost a shoe. Since her pursuer was grasping on to it at the time and losing it meant losing him, it was a pretty good trade.

The three stumbled into another clearing. A tiny ring of mushrooms, no more than five feet across stood out on the grass.

"Crud," Silas said.

"What?" Taylor said.

"A ring that size is going to be too weak. I don't know if it'll bear all three of us at once."

"It bore Vesper and Bitsy," Taylor protested. "Plus all Vesper's gear. That's got to be at least four hundred pounds."

"It's not about physical weight; it's about magic. Too much magical energy at one time, and the ring will collapse on itself."

"But how is that a problem for us? You said yourself church grims don't have all that much magic to begin with. And all I can do is a couple of glamour tricks."

"You're a sídhe, even if you are young and ignorant. You've got more magic than you know, little girl. But I wasn't talking about you. There's another variable I still don't think we've accounted for." He gave Jill a suspicious gaze.

"The three of us can probably make it. But we sure to blazes don't need any hitchhikers. If there's anybody else in there—" he pointed toward Jill's forehead "—we're all going to have a very bad day. Are we clear?"

Jill gulped.

185

Bitsy's barks were so quiet Taylor could hear the dog and the elf disturbing the undergrowth with their passing.

"It's just me," Jill said. "No hitchhikers. I swear. Now, can we please get out of here?"

Silas warily extended his hand toward her. "No screaming this time."

"I'm not making any promises."

A column of swirling, sparkly light spun up from the ring. Jill took the church grim's hand and offered her other one to Taylor.

"Where are we going?" Taylor asked.

"South," Jill said. "Toward New Orleans."

"Stay right there!" an angry voice yelled. Vesper stepped into the clearing, his shotgun at his shoulder.

"Now!" Silas growled as he dragged Jill and Taylor into the ring.

The trio was suddenly plunged into wild darkness. As they spun through the Wonder, images of murky woods and moonlit lakes assaulted them, disorienting Taylor and frightening Jill. At her side, Taylor could hear her friend whimpering, but she didn't cry out.

They whipped around like rag dolls in the teeth of an enormous, playful puppy.

Then everything went wrong.

They bobbed to and fro, buffeted by fierce turbulence. Jill didn't scream, but she let out a frightened squeal, and Silas grabbed her wrist with his free hand.

Something wasn't right. The ride was too bumpy. As if that weren't bad enough, Taylor started to feel a weight dragging behind her. For a second, she panicked, fearing Vesper had managed to grab hold of her. But there was no one there. Still, she felt like she weighed three hundred pounds.

"Something's wrong!" she shouted.

She felt the tug of Jill's hand. Her friend was gritting her teeth, struggling to hang on to her. For some reason, Taylor was slowing them down.

"Hold on!" Silas yelled. Taylor could barely hear him over the roar of the wind.

"Taylor!" Jill shouted.

Taylor's hand was sweaty. It was getting hard to keep a firm grip.

"Don't let go!" Jill shouted.

"Exit up ahead!" Silas shouted. "Just another—"

Taylor couldn't hold on for another second. Her hand slipped out of Jill's, and she spun away into the Wonder.

"Crap," she muttered. But she knew what she had to do. She settled her thoughts and held on to the only thing she could: her true name. She let the syllables bathe her in their cool, peaceful, resonance.

Silas said there was an exit ahead. She imagined her glamour reaching out, probing the darkness for it. Her mind fastened on a fleeting image: a broad river snaking through the bayou, reflecting the glimmer of a thousand stars.

She settled her mind into that image. She tried to perceive every detail and, as she did, it became clearer in her imagination.

She fell out of the Wonder and splashed into murky water.

Chapter 20

Carrot and Stick

The stable door creaked open at an atrocious hour.

"Up and at 'em, Licorice!" Aengus called. His voice was way too cheerful for Danny, who shook his head and pinned his ears as the stable-brownie approached him, bridle in hand.

Danny took stock of his situation. Was it really only Friday? It felt like he had been a horse for a week and not merely about twelve hours.

Some way to start the weekend, he thought.

Before he knew what was happening, Danny had the bridle over his head and he tasted the cold metal bit in his mouth. Aengus led him to the pasture. He nibbled on grass as Aengus fit him with a green saddle blanket (Danny assumed it was green; with his horsey eyes, he didn't see colors exactly the way he was used to seeing them) and an ornate etched-leather saddle with golden fittings. The stable-brownie decked him out with a leather band from which hung a dozen tiny jingle bells.

"Mr. Wakefire'll be here any minute," Aengus said. "So try to do what he tells you."

Easier said than done, Danny thought, when Mr. Wakefire didn't seem to know the first thing about handling a horse. A sweet smell tickled his nostrils. Aengus offered him a piece of apple, which the pooka gratefully accepted.

As promised, the Primus of the Summer Court of Arradherry appeared not much later. He was dressed pretty much as Danny expected: an effete flurry of green and gold and robin's-egg blue. Most ridiculous was the green silk duster, flitting in the gentle breeze like a cloak, with buttons in the shape of golden oak-leaf clusters all the way down the front. It was kind of outfit no real equestrian would wear, but that a rich wannabe might think made him look the part.

Behind him trudged Wictred Buckle lugging a set of saddlebags and struggling to keep up.

The Primus was deep in conversation with his seeing stone. "New Cephalonia, you say?"

That got Danny's attention. Taylor had been heading to New Cephalonia.

"No, of course, Dubessa. Best to keep an eye on the situation."

Dubessa? So the Primus was talking to his wife, Dubessa Fairchild. Danny paced nervously. The last time around, Dubessa was in Taylor's corner—but only because she knew it would get under Anya Redmane's skin. Danny knew it might not be convenient for Dubessa to support Taylor this time, and he didn't trust her or her family any further than he could kick them.

"Vesper? *Lawdwick* Vesper?" The Primus whistled. "You're right, darling. They're definitely up to something if they've got the likes of *him* working for them."

Danny wracked his brain, trying to remember the name Lawdwick Vesper. He rocked from side to side in frustration when nothing came to mind.

"Easy there, boy!" Aengus rubbed his shoulder.

"Send Andred Thornberry," the Primus said. "She's very good at this sort of thing. And have her take that jinn she's been seeing. What's his name? Bacary?"

By now, Belas Wakefire had come alongside Danny and his handler. Buckle flung the saddlebags over Danny's back and began fastening them to his saddle.

"I doubt the Hellebores are involved, darling. The world would come to an end before they'd partner with the Redmanes on anything. But if I learn any different from Cornstack, I'll let you know."

And Danny suddenly remembered with a shiver of dread who he was on his way to see.

The Primus listened for a while, impatience spreading across his face.

"Oh, you don't have to worry about that," he said at last. "Cornstack can see the writing on the wall. He knows he'll have to deal with us sooner or later."

Another pause.

"Yes, I'll tell you everything as soon as I return. Goodbye, darling." The Primus slipped his seeing stone into a pocket of his trousers. He patted Danny on the shoulder.

"Well, Licorice, are you ready for a little ride?"

Danny pinned his ears. *Let's just get this over with*, he thought.

Wakefire climbed into the saddle.

"Well, Buckle, it looks like your Licorice here is about to have his first test."

"Aye, sir," the old fae said. "He'll do you proud, I'm sure. I knew he was a prize when I first laid eyes on him."

The Primus kicked Danny in the sides, and he trotted toward the gate. Danny was fairly sure he heard the old fae asking Aengus, "What did he mean, *my* Licorice?"

They trotted out the gate and down the country road the same as they had the night before. The first orange fingers of sunlight reached over the tops of the trees. In a dozen humble barns and cottages, farm folk were busy with their morning chores.

Wakefire steered Danny down an unfamiliar lane that gradually widened until it opened up on a ring of standing stones, each as tall as a house. They stopped long enough for the Summer Primus to open a portal to somewhere else in the Wonder.

"Be sharp, boy," he said. "I don't think Cornstack will try anything—but you can never tell with the Winters."

Danny instinctively shied away from the pillar of swirling, sparkling dust, but stopped himself before he bolted. It wasn't the portal he was afraid of, he realized. It was the prospect of getting anywhere near blasting range of the Primus of the Winter Court.

And then Danny realized his rider must have been having similar thoughts.

"We'll just play this cool," he said, more to himself than to his steed. "Cornstack is the one with the most to lose here. Don't let him forget it."

Danny's eyes began to glow, not with aggression but with panic.

"That's the spirit, boy!" Wakefire said, patting Danny's shoulders. "Let's go get him!"

Danny trotted into the portal and immediately lurched forward as the maelstrom of fleeting sights and sounds enveloped him. Riding a faery horse through the Wonder isn't at all like ring-travel with a human companion. In that case, like when Danny accompanied Taylor on her first adventure, only the fae traveler knows what to do. Danny had to focus on their destination and provide the magical energy to get them there.

Horseback riding is different. For one thing, the horse usually isn't informed where they're going. Now, some faery horses are very smart. Most can understand at least a little bit of human or fae language—and some can even speak it. But riders being what they are, it isn't likely the horse is brought into the planning phase of a journey. In the magical scheme of things, the horse is more than a mere tool, but not quite an equal partner.

What the horse does provide is raw power. That's important when there is likely to be trouble on the other end. If the horse does all the hard work in getting there, the rider doesn't have to expend his own magical reserves. He can show up fresh and rested and ready to blast away if necessary.

Wakefire was the one guiding this trip; Danny just had to supply the magical energy to get them there—wherever there was. He was relieved that the Summer Primus at least knew enough horsemanship to guide him through the Wonder without incident. They blazed across farmland and forests, hills and streams, graveyards and standing stones, at a steady pace—breakneck and dizzying to any Topside observer but fairly unhurried as far as ring-travel goes.

Wakefire said nothing. The only sounds were the torrent of wind that whipped Danny's shaggy mane into a tangle and the jingling bells on his harness.

Finally, Danny leaped out of the whirlwind and onto a grassy hillside. Behind him stood another ring of standing stones that shimmered and hummed as the portal closed. Above them, the turquoise sky was partly cloudy. It seemed dimmer than when they entered the ring-system. They must have headed west, and the sun hadn't yet caught up with them. It was easily light enough to travel safely, but Wakefire spun out three golden orbs of faery fire to accompany them.

He clicked his tongue and kicked Danny to get him moving. They trotted up the hill and into a patch of trees at its top. Then they headed down a well-worn trail on the other side.

Wakefire stopped underneath an ancient oak tree and dismounted long enough to work a bit of magic on that portion of the trail. Some kind of ward, Danny guessed, though he didn't recognize the incantation. It made sense: things could go wrong in a hurry when somebody like Crom Cornstack was involved. If they had to make a run for it, a booby trap to slow him down could make a world of difference.

Once the spell was ready, Wakefire climbed back on Danny's back and spurred him forward.

The trail led down to a stream and followed its winding course for couple miles or so. At last, Wakefire brought Danny to a halt near the head of the stream: a natural spring gushing up out of the earth and filling a cold, clear pond.

He let Danny approach the pond and drink.

It wasn't long before they both heard the sound of jingle bells, soft but constant. Wakefire pulled up on the reins. Danny snorted in spite of himself.

The other rider appeared from the opposite direction to the one Danny had taken. He was a huge, broad-shouldered man, long-legged and square-faced. His hair, so blond it was almost white, hung down his back in a long braid. His beard hid most of his face and forked into two similar braided cords gracing his barrel chest. What Danny could see of the rider's face was adorned with tattoos, a spidery mosaic that made him look something less than natural.

He was dressed in black and white and burgundy: practical riding clothes, but of the finest make. His only ornaments were a silver bracelet on his left wrist and a silver device on the band of his open-crease hat displaying intricate Celtic knot work and flanked by sprigs of holly.

Around his head floated four tiny pinpricks of silvery light, will-o'-the-wisps smaller but brighter than those Wakefire had conjured.

From where Danny was standing, the man's horse was at least as impressive. He was a pure white charger, easily big enough and strong enough to carry his massive rider. He was decked out in white and burgundy tack with silver bells on a band across his breast.

Now that *is a horse*, Danny thought. Self-consciously, he stood a little bit straighter and lifted his head.

The horse and rider faced Wakefire from across the pond.

"Belas," the other fae said, his voice even and restrained.

"Crom," the Summer Primus said. He slowly led Danny back downstream. The Winter Primus mirrored him on his own horse.

"You said you had something to discuss."

"A matter of mutual concern," Wakefire said. "Ride with me. Cross the stream, and we can talk."

Tricky, Danny thought. Running water tends to ground out magic. A lot of fae didn't like crossing streams or rivers for that reason. Wakefire was issuing a challenge: put down your weapons.

There was a quiet splash in the water. A water nymph had come up to see who was disturbing her pool and quickly decided she wanted no part of what seemed to be unfolding.

Crom Cornstack sat motionless on the opposite bank for several heartbeats. At last he said, "I find your lack of trust discomfiting, brother Primus."

"If I didn't trust you, *brother Primus*, I would not have suggested a meeting on neutral ground."

Once more, the Winter Primus sat and pondered. But this time, it was only for a moment.

"One might be tempted to say you chose neutral ground so you would be absolved of your obligations under the Law of Hospitality."

Danny felt Wakefire's body tensing.

"If you're afraid, Crom, say the word, and I'll pledge your safety for the duration of our meeting."

Another trap, Danny thought. If Cornstack demanded safe passage now, he lost face. If he didn't, he left himself open to possible attack.

The Winter Primus spoke again.

"I can afford to overlook your petty posturing," he said. "And in any case, it is fitting that I defer to the Summer Primus at the peak of his season." With that, the Winter Primus nudged his horse into the stream. One by one, his fire orbs extinguished as the horse splashed through the water. Only one was left, stranded on the far side of the stream. It lazily floated away into the trees.

As soon as the Winter Primus's horse climbed up the near bank, Wakefire pulled Danny around and set him trotting downstream, following the same path they had taken to reach the spring.

Atop his charger, Crom Cornstack quickly caught up. The two Primuses rode side by side through the woods.

"So, Belas, what is this matter of concern you wished to discuss?"

"The future," Wakefire said.

"The future?"

"And our places in it." Wakefire nodded. "The seasons change, Crom, as both of us know full well. Things have a way of circling back to how they used to be."

"I've no patience for riddles, Belas."

Wakefire scoffed. "A startling admission from the Primus of Winter, Crom, and one I hardly believe."

They passed underneath a stately Virginia pine. Wakefire's fire orbs threaded through the branches, testing their freedom while circling their creator every now and then.

"Then consider this," Wakefire continued. "Anya Redmane will not be the Chief Matron of Summer forever."

Cornstack's lips pulled taut beneath his whitish mustache. "Do I smell a plot afoot, Belas?"

"A plot? Of course not. I am oath-bound to support my Chief Matron—and she me." He chuckled ever so slightly. "Perhaps what you smell is reality."

"You think the old crone is weak," Cornstack said.

"And you don't? My wife tells me you were there at Judaculla Rock. Or are there gaps in your memory?"

"I remember full well the unfortunate incident involving my former daughter." For the first time, Danny sensed a hint of frustration in the Winter Primus's voice. He pricked his ears, imagining the Cornstacks' reaction when they realized their daughter had slipped through their fingers, free at last after fourteen years as their prisoner.

"I trust the girl is well?" Wakefire said—innocently, Danny was certain. No one knew that Shanna Hellebore had escaped her parent's dungeon except those like Danny who had helped to pull it off.

"It will be gratifying to see her again soon." There were several ways to take that statement. The one that came immediately to Danny's mind made him bare his teeth and shudder.

"Even so, Crom, you saw then that Anya is not entirely stable. Eventually, she will fall—with Fairchild's help or without it. And rest assured the House of Fairchild already has plans in place for just such an eventuality."

"If Summer is in turmoil," Crom said, his voice measured, "then surely it is Winter's duty to help restore order?"

"I am telling you, Crom, there will be no turmoil. The transfer of power will be quick, orderly, and thorough."

"And you expect me to believe this...why?"

"Because I am giving you my word."

"An empty promise, from all I can see. If you Summers could plan ahead, you'd never have assaulted Bailly Hen."

Once more, Wakefield's body tensed. "We do not speak of Bailly Hen."

Careful, Danny thought. *Not a good topic with the Summer Court.* Some wounds don't heal, even after seventy years.

"You lost a daughter to the teind, didn't you," Crom said. "Wasn't her name Illuna? And the Redmanes a son who might have married her some day and brought your two houses together. Lorcan, if I remember correctly."

The fire orbs blazed like tiny suns as they swirled around Wakefire's shoulders.

"If you value your life, Crom, you'll hold your peace."

A wave of presence rippled from Wakefire to Cornstack. Cornstack barely flinched, but both Danny and the Winter Primus's horse shuddered. The other horse backed up and gave a deep, thunderous blow.

"Easy, Blixem." Cornstack rubbed his mount's massive shoulders.

Blixem, huh? Danny thought. *At least one of us gets to have a cool name.*

Wakefire spoke slowly and deliberately. "The faults of the current Chief Matron reflect poorly on the rest of the Summer Court," he said. "But don't assume the house of Fairchild is similarly handicapped. By Danu, Crom, you'll regret it if you do."

Crom Cornstack sat up in his saddle. Danny peered up at him, trying to read his expression. He saw the Winter Primus bite his lower lip. He averted his icy stare, if only for a heartbeat. Was Wakefire actually getting to him?

"The Summer Court isn't going to follow an oath-breaker, Belas," he said at last.

"I have no intention of breaking my oath," Wakefire said, raising his hands in protest. "You would convene the Deep Council before the sun had even set."

"Of course," Cornstack said. "And I would lead the Wild Hunt myself if you were the quarry."

"I'm glad we understand each other."

"So why are you telling me these things? You want my assistance, I take it? A fellow conspirator who isn't oath-bound to Summer?"

Wakefire chuckled under his breath.

"I don't need Winter's help, Crom. I never have. As I said, I have merely called you here to discuss the future. What will be the relation between our two Courts once the house of Redmane falls?"

"Ah," Cornstack said. "Now I see. You've brought me here to bribe me. Dangle a carrot in front of me to pacify me while you do whatever it is you have planned, eh?"

"Actually, Crom, I'm fresh out of carrots. I'm afraid what I have in mind is actually more like stick." He stroked the topmost golden button on his duster, and the slightest whiff of magic rippled outward. Danny realized they were under the tree where Wakefire had worked his spell.

At the same time, Wakefire kicked Danny forward with such force he blinked five yards. As soon as they reappeared, he tugged hard on Danny's reins and spun him around to face Cornstack.

Danny snorted with awe.

In the split second it had taken to blink away, Cornstack and his horse had been entwined in snaky strands of lush, green ivy. All four of Blixem's hooves were wrapped tight with the stuff, and Cornstack's arms were bound to his side, his hands still on the reins but buried in a knot of living cord. It didn't just come up out of the ground. It also fell from the trees. The result reminded Danny of a wriggling green spider web.

Oak, ash, and thorn! Danny cursed. *What's Wakefire trying to do, get us both killed?*

Cornstack steadied his horse. He didn't shout, but his icy glare might have frozen a river.

"Treachery, Belas? You disappoint me."

"I'm afraid I don't quite have your glacial patience, Crom," Wakefire said. "I don't have time to dicker—and it isn't as if you have any real choice in the matter. Things are changing. The Summer Court is shaking itself from its long slumber." He nudged Danny closer as he jabbed a single finger at Cornstack. "I can make the transition easy for Winter...or not."

Cornstack pressed his lips together. "If you know what's good for you, Belas, you'll release me at once. I *may* even let you live."

The air seemed to get colder—but only for a second. Wakefire gestured, and the ivy that bound the Winter Primus began to glow with golden light. This time, Danny could see Cornstack swallow.

"You still don't understand, Crom. I don't fear you, and I certainly don't need your help. The house of Fairchild will be ascendant, and things will then be quite different from the stalemate we've had for the past seventy years." Wakefire paced Danny back and forth. "The purpose of this meeting is simply to negotiate the terms of your acquiescence."

Blixem whinnied and tried to back away, but to no avail. On his back, Cornstack struggled futilely to pull himself free. The ivy glowed brighter with every flexed muscle.

"Do you honestly think you can rule Arradherry without Winter, Belas?"

"Oh, I have no intention of destroying you, Crom. Merely containing you."

"Containing us?"

"It's nothing personal. It's just that the Winter Court has always struck me as better suited to support than to command. Every strong leader needs a few musclebound thugs to threaten his enemies with." Wakefire smiled. "You should be a natural."

"Winter will fight you, Belas. Whatever you do to me. My forces in Tobarty alone will give you more than you can handle."

"Yes, your rath at Tobarty has been a fine weapon to point against the Nunnehi Lands for all these years." Wakefire brushed a stray hair from his forehead. "I'm inclined to let you keep it."

"*Let us* keep it? You go too far, Belas." Cornstack's presence radiated outward so strongly that Danny reared. Of course, it had no effect on Wakefire's enchanted ivy. Presence was a glamour trick to confuse the mind; it had no effect on matter—even magically animated matter. Wakefire himself seemed unaffected, though. Danny snorted and struggled to stay calm.

"The Winter Court has held Tobarty for five hundred years. It is second only to Cair Cullen among the Winter raths. And you dare speak of *letting us* keep it?"

"Crom, Crom, Crom," Wakefire chuckled. "You're losing your cool. You. Losing your cool. That's funny. But I'm willing to work with you. Honestly, I am. It goes without saying you have long been an asset to the Chiefdom of Arradherry. I hope you will continue to be so for centuries to come."

The Winter Primus grumbled. With his deep basso voice, it sounded like a distant avalanche. He took a couple of deep breaths and regained his calm.

"We can share power, the same as always," Wakefire said. And you can still count Kern Barrows as your lieutenant."

"I'm sure the Autumn Primus will be thrilled with your magnanimity."

"Scoff if you like, Crom, but I have no intention of upsetting the applecart. Change for change's sake only brings chaos. That wouldn't be good for the Chiefdom. It wouldn't be good for me."

Cornstack glared at his counterpart. "But?"

"But Redmane will fall. When they do, things will be quite different in the Summer Court. Fairchild will assert Summer's ancient primacy. You don't have to like it, Crom. But you do have to accept it."

There was a long silence.

Crom Cornstack blinked.

Then he sighed.

"What do you want?" he spat.

"Pledge me you will keep your distance. Let events unfold in the Summer Court as they will without any interference from Winter."

Wakefire gestured again with his finger, and a single slender vine snaked around Cornstack's neck. It rested there writhing gently.

"I will not interfere in Fairchild's plans for dominance of the Summer Court," Cornstack said.

"Good. Oh, and there is one more thing."

Cornstack raised a single eyebrow.

"A token of fealty," Wakefire said. Danny could feel him shivering with excitement on his back. "Something to let others know you accept your rightful place in the order of things. It could go a long way in pacifying all four Courts in what could be a very delicate time."

"Yes?"

"I propose...a readjustment of forces," Wakefire said. "To be announced at the very hour in which Anya Redmane is deposed."

Wakefire leaned forward in his saddle and almost whispered.

"Give me Tobarty."

Cornstack rumbled again, a growling earthquake of barely contained fury.

"Never!"

Wakefire gestured. The glowing tendril around his neck tightened at once, and the entire spiderweb of ivy burst into open flame. Cornstack cursed. His horse whinnied in panic and reared as much as his entangled limbs would let him. With another gesture, the flames extinguished and even the golden glow subsided.

"It seems a single rath is a small price to pay for peace. Or are you really that curious to see what Summer can do?"

"And *you* would defend our borders from the nunnehi?"

"You say that as if you doubt Summer's determination to achieve our goals. I would think the last five minutes would have taught you better than that."

"Tobarty has always belonged to Winter!"

"Things change."

"Not Tobarty," Cornstack growled. There was yet another long, uncomfortable silence. The Winter Primus pressed his lips together.

"I would be willing to give you Ledoga."

"I might have accepted Ledoga if not for your own obstinacy, Crom. No. Summer shall have the honor of defending the eastern border," Wakefire said. "Tobarty. Or we are done here—and Danu help you when Fairchild comes to power."

"This is extortion."

"Swear it, Crom. By your own true name."

Cornstack bit his lip.

"At such time as Anya Redmane is deposed," he began. The words sounded heavy and leaden in his mouth. "Winter shall make the rath of Tobarty a present to the house of Fairchild. I so swear by my own true name."

Wakefire sung an incantation. Above, clouds started to gather. Thunder rumbled.

"I'm glad we understand each other," Wakefire said. A single drop of rain fell on Danny's nose. "The rain will break the spell that binds you. You should be free in ten or fifteen minutes, I expect."

He kicked Danny's side and turned him back toward the standing stones. A gentle drizzle began to fall.

"Well, Licorice," Wakefire sighed. "That actually went rather well."

Danny silently agreed, but it didn't help his frazzled nerves.

He was actually thinking the whole thing went a lot easier than it should have.

Chapter 21

Dreams and Visions

Silas and Jill spun out and slammed into another huge cypress tree. Silas saw it coming about a second too late, but he twisted his body around to shield the Topside girl from most of the impact. His left shoulder exploded with pain and he let out a fierce, barking curse. Then Jill head-butted him in the gut and took his breath away.

They slumped to the squishy ground, bruised and breathing hard.

"Worst. Road-trip. Ever," Jill muttered. She gasped. "Taylor?"

"Got to be around here somewhere," Silas said. He conjured a fire orb so he could see Jill's panicked face.

"It's just me, I swear!" Jill cried. "Godmother isn't here! Stop looking at me like that!"

Silas wasn't aware he was looking at Jill any way in particular, but there was no denying what he thought. He looked her up and down and offered a noncommittal "Uh huh."

Jill got up and offered Silas her hand. He chose to pull himself to his feet. His shoulder was tender beneath his torn and bloody shirt. He must have found a nasty branch when he crashed.

"What are we going to do? What are we going to do?" The girl was starting to sound frantic again. Just what Silas needed.

"Will you hush for a minute?" he barked.

He pulled his satchel off his back and tried to hang it from his right shoulder, keeping weight off the left one. It was a tricky maneuver when his left arm wasn't entirely ready to cooperate and his right hand was busy being a light fixture.

"I'll carry that," Jill offered.

Silas frowned.

"Just hold it for me," he said. He rummaged through it until he found his plastic bottle of faery dust. He tossed the fire orb into the air. It hovered over them, dim but serviceable.

"Is that the stuff you used to find the ring?" Jill asked.

Silas nodded. "It's sensitive to magical energies. Maybe it'll pick up where Taylor landed. If we're really lucky, it'll pick up Taylor."

"What's in it?"

"The usual: hollyhock, whiskers of a black cat, sunbeams, oregano. That sort of thing. Now stand back." He glared at her. "We don't need any interference."

He worked the incantation while driving away the thought that he was quickly running out of faery dust. He had hoped to use it to find the satyr's domain. As carefully as he could, he tapped about half of the remaining dust into his hand and tossed it into the air. As before, the dust hung in the air, making a tiny golden light show before twisting into a swirl and sailing off through the murky bayou.

"Taylor's that way?" Jill asked.

"It's the closest thing we've got to a lead," Silas said. "Let's go."

They searched for Taylor most of the night by the light of Silas's faery fire. His shoulder still hurt, and it soon got stiff. He had some healing ointment in his satchel, but he didn't want to use any until he saw whether Taylor needed it worse than he did. He tore the sleeves from his shirt and, with Jill's help, rigged up a passable sling to keep his injured arm still against his body.

After three or four hours, the two rested beneath a tree. Silas could hear things splashing in water somewhere nearby. He had no way of knowing if it was catfish or water moccasins or alligators—or worse, something spooky from *his* side of the pond.

Scratch that. As near as he could tell in the dark, they *were* on Silas's side, somewhere in the Wonder. The air had a familiar perfume to it that was absent Topside. And on top of that, Jill had seemed to calm down after the initial panic of losing her friend passed. She breathed deeply of that perfumed air, and it brought a subtle smile to her face that even she probably wasn't aware of.

She wasn't the agitated, erratic girl she had been before.

She had gotten another fix.

"You need to rest," Silas said. "The sun won't be up for another few hours. We're not getting anything done in the dark."

"B-but Taylor—"

"I'll keep an eye out," Silas assured her. "Try to sleep."

Jill dreamed she was in Gethsemane Cemetery at the grave of her Pawpaw. The sky was steely gray and the air was pleasantly warm, though a stiff breeze was blowing in from the north over Lake Pontchartrain.

She stood in front of her grandfather's crypt of weathered white stone. The hairs on the nape of her neck started to tingle. She knew what was happening before she ever turned around. There on the bench beneath the statue of an angel sat her godmother.

Jill stared at her. She wanted to burn holes in her with her eyes. Then she remembered how the faery woman had helped them escape from Vesper and she didn't know what to think.

"Thank you," Godmother said.

Jill's mouth fell open. What?

"I saved your life," Godmother continued. "I thought you might have told me 'Thank you.'"

Oh.

She gave it a moment's thought but just couldn't bring herself to thank her godmother. After all, she was the one who got her into this mess in the first place. Instead, she said, "We can't find Taylor."

"Now, that is a problem, isn't it?"

"I don't suppose you could give us any hints?"

"Jill, sweetie, I could give you so much more than mere hints."

"Don't call me sweetie!"

Godmother crossed her legs and folded her arms in her lap.

"You have a gift, child," Godmother said at last.

"You've told me that already."

"But perhaps now you are ready to listen. Tell me, child. Who is Taylor Smart?"

"W-what do you mean? She's my friend. We've been best friends since fourth grade."

"Why?"

"I don't understand."

"Why is Taylor Smart your best friend?"

Jill started to sweat. She wasn't sure why.

"We've always been friends."

"Have you really?"

"Well...like I said, we met in fourth grade. Is that what you mean?"

Godmother smiled. The scene faded.

Jill was nine years old and hanging around the school playground with Taylor. It was recess. Other kids were playing tag. Jill and Taylor were sitting on the swings talking about the latest shows on the Disney channel.

Jill and her family had only moved to Macon from Atlanta that summer. They had been busy unpacking the moving truck for several hours when a smiling white lady and a girl about Jill's age showed up with lemonade to welcome them to the neighborhood.

She immediately sized up Mrs. Smart as a kind and patient soul. Her daughter Taylor? Well, that was a different story.

Jill didn't have words to describe it, but even at nine years old, her first impressions of people were usually right on target.

And more often than not, she had a pretty good sense of how people were feeling.

Taylor wasn't giving off any vibe at all, at least that Jill could pick up on. Was she eager to make new friends? Nervous about meeting strangers? Perturbed to be dragged away from whatever she'd been doing a second before her mom called her to help with the lemonade? Jill didn't have the slightest idea.

And that made her very curious.

A few weeks later, the two girls started the fourth grade. Starting at a new school was as rough as Jill expected it would be, but she eventually settled in. Riding to and from school with Taylor every day at least gave her someone to commiserate with.

Then came that day on the playground. It was recess. Jaquarrius Evans started teasing her because she had spilled ketchup on her shirt at lunch. That was the first time Jill had ever seen Taylor put the whammy on anybody.

"Hey, new girl!" he said. "Why you so clumsy?"

Taylor sighed and exasperated sigh. "Leave her alone, Jaquarrius." She didn't raise her voice. She sounded more bored than angry.

"Why you sticking up for her, huh? What she ever did for you?"

Taylor turned red in the face.

"Did you not hear me?" she said. She jabbed at Jaquarrius with her finger. "I said, *Leave her alone.*"

Something in the tone of her voice, something in her icy blue eyes, made Jaquarrius take two steps back.

Taylor put her hand on Jill's back and walked her away.

"Jerk," she muttered.

Soon, it was November. Just before Thanksgiving was Jill and William's birthday. Of course, Taylor was invited to the party. Her mom even came to help out with the games and refreshments.

Jill wasn't supposed to hear the moms talking in the kitchen, but she wanted to show everybody the silver cross her Maymay had sent her from New Orleans, and that put her in the hallway at just the right time.

"It looks like you all have settled in all right," Mrs. Smart said.

Jill's mom nodded and smiled. "It was hard to leave Atlanta, but it was the right move. Charles loves his new job. We've found a great church. And Taylor and Jill get along so well. It's a real blessing."

"More than you know," Mrs. Smart said. "Taylor has always struggled getting along with girls her age. Fred says it's because she's an only child and used to being around mostly adults. Plus, she's really bright—I don't mean to brag, but—"

"You're not bragging, Julie. I can see what a bright girl Taylor is. Everybody can."

"Well, it makes it even harder for Taylor to fit in with other nine-year-olds. And the questions she asks!" Mrs. Smart shook her head. "But I think there's more to it than that."

"Oh?"

"Sophie, I think Jill is the first real friend Taylor has ever had. I don't know what your daughter is doing, but Fred and I are amazed at how she's brought Taylor out of her shell. She's been a godsend to all of us. And I mean that literally."

"Well, let's hope and pray those two get to stay friends for a long, long time."

"Amen!"

The scene faded to black, and in the darkness, a woman's voice softly echoed from every direction.

"Why is Taylor Smart your best friend?"

Jill lurched awake. It was morning. Friday morning, she realized. Birds were singing. The warm air hadn't quite become a muggy, soupy sauna yet.

Silas stood ten yards away on an uprooted tree trunk. He glanced in Jill's direction when he heard her stirring. He hopped down and walked toward her.

"How's the shoulder?" Jill asked.

"It's still attached," Silas said.

"Well, that's a good sign." Jill took a long, deep breath. "Taylor?"

"Still out there somewhere. She might have landed Topside, though. Probably better for her if she did, but it'll make her harder for us to find."

"I've got an idea about that." Jill chose her words carefully. She didn't want to mention her godmother at all, given Silas's attitude on the subject, but she had a growing feeling that crazy fae woman really did give her a nudge in the right direction.

Silas grunted. Jill took it as an invitation to keep talking.

"I...I think I should try scrying for her."

"Because you've done such a fantastic job of that so far, no doubt."

"Just let me talk, okay?" Jill sat up straight, which made her almost as tall as Silas standing. "I've been thinking," she continued. "Maybe I haven't been able to find the satyr because I don't know anything about him. But Taylor and I...we're practically sisters. I bet I could find her if I tried."

"The rule of contagion," Silas said.

"Huh?"

"The part is the whole. If you've got a piece of Taylor, it can help you find the rest of her."

"Maymay says folks she grew up with were touchy about getting their hair cut or their fingernails clipped. They thought witches could use those things to curse them."

"She's right," Silas said.

Jill gulped. That wasn't the response she was expecting.

"But I don't have anything like that of Taylor's."

"Sounds like you've got something better." He tapped his chest. "In here."

Jill nodded. "Will that work?"

"Magic works because you believe it works." Silas turned to rummage through his satchel for the scrying bowl. Jill just looked at him.

209

"Run that by me again?"

Silas sat down on the grass and put the bowl between himself and Jill. He gestured, and she sat cross-legged facing him.

"Okay," he said. "Magic."

"Go on."

"Do you have electricity at your house?"

"What kind of question is that? Of course we do!"

"No offense. I don't get out much. Electricity used to be a pretty big deal. Not everybody's house was rigged for it. But you've got this energy source, right? It'll do anything you want it to: toast bread, light up a room, play music. You name it. You just have to build the right kind of gadget and plug it in. That's kind of how magic works."

"So, I'm supposed to be some kind of toaster?"

"The spell is the toaster. You're the plug. Except you're not making toast. You're making a connection between you and Taylor. Something that will help you zero in on where she is."

"I guess that makes sense," Jill said, frowning. "And if I believe it'll work...?"

"Chances are, it probably will."

Jill bit her lip. There was still a piece of the puzzle she wasn't quite grasping.

"Then shouldn't...shouldn't everybody be able to do magic?"

"Not everybody's wired for it," Silas shrugged. "Wired. Get it? You can have the best toaster in the world, but it won't help you unless you've got someplace to plug it in. You've got to be born with the gift, or else awakened by a powerful fae—something like that."

"Godmother said I had a gift before she...did what she did." Jill shuddered. "But Mom and Dad aren't magical. They're as ordinary as they come."

"Sometimes the magic just appears out of nowhere," Silas said. "Twins are good for that. And sometimes it skips a generation. The point is, you've got to be able to tap into the Wonder.

That's where the power of magic—the electricity, you might say—comes from."

"I've heard you and Taylor talking about the Wonder, but I still don't understand what you mean."

Silas scratched his chin and looked across to Jill. "The Wonder is more than just a place. It's a frame of mind." He gazed at the sky as if he might chance upon the right words written on the clouds.

Tentatively, he began again. "Have you ever seen the Grand Canyon? Or been caught outside in a lightning storm? Or watched a mother give birth? Have you ever been in church when the choir brought the house down and the whole place felt like it was alive with energy?"

Jill nodded apprehensively. "Not all of that...but yeah. I think I know what you're talking about. Are you saying that's the Wonder?"

Silas shook his head. "It's only a byproduct. The Wonder reaches into your world, maybe just a little bit, whenever Topsiders recognize they're in the presence of something beyond themselves, something bigger than they are."

"Like...God?" Jill said.

"You can believe whatever you want about that," Silas said. "But whatever you believe, you know what it's like to come face to face with beauty, genuine heart-stopping beauty. Or mystery. Or power. Or terror. Feelings like that bring the Wonder into focus. Some say it even gives it substance. And places that inspire those kinds of feelings usually make pretty good gateways into the Wonder itself."

Something clicked in Jill's consciousness. "Is that why you hang out in a cemetery?"

Silas nodded.

"And scare the crap out of people?"

"Have you been paying attention at all?" Silas snapped. "The boundary between the Wonder and Topside can be awfully thin in a graveyard, and Topsiders aren't the only folks lurking around. People—I mean your kind of people—have no idea how bad it could really get." He jabbed a thumb at his chest. "That's where I come in."

"You..." Jill began, stumbling over her words. "You scare people off...to keep them safe?"

"Like I said, there's a fine line between the two worlds in a graveyard. You don't want to accidentally run into anybody from the other side. But none of this is getting us any closer to Taylor, is it?"

"I guess not." Jill turned her attention to the scrying bowl. She took a couple of deep breaths and tried to process everything Silas had told her.

"Try to get a clear mental image of Taylor," Silas said. "Then reach into the Wonder. Not with your head, with your heart. With your gut. Focus on something that fills you with awe. Something bigger than you. Then use that feeling to pull just a little bit of magic into your image."

Jill nodded.

She sat still for the longest time, conjuring up a picture of Taylor in her mind. She imagined every detail: her pale blue eyes, her smirking grin. Once or twice, Silas reminded her to relax.

Then she tried to reach into the Wonder. She wasn't sure exactly what she was supposed to do, but she tried to imagine the feeling she had when her godmother had provided the magic for her sleeping spell. She tried to sense the ebb and flow of magical energy brushing against her skin.

She wiped a trickle of sweat from her forehead.

"Nothing's happening," she complained.

"Focus," Silas said. He didn't sound angry for once. He wanted to find Taylor, too.

"I've got an idea," she whispered. She found herself trembling, both at the audacity of what she had thought to do and the look on her mother's face if she ever found out.

She pulled her necklace from around her neck. It was a small silver cross, the birthday present her Maymay gave her when she was nine.

She clutched it tight in her hand, breathed a wordless prayer, and peered into the bowl.

Nothing continued to happen.

Jill took another deep breath. She locked her mind on the image of Taylor she had summoned up. In her imagination, she fixed the image at the bottom of the scrying bowl. She imagined fingers of magical energy snaking out from her mind and heart and boring deep into the water.

Then, something started to happen. There was a ripple in the water—at least, she thought that was what she saw.

"Hold on," she whispered. Silas moved closer.

"Do you see anything?" he asked.

Jill furrowed her brow and peered into the water. She saw something, but not anything like what she expected.

Seated on a porch was a young man, bare-chested with elfin features and a cup of wine in his hand. (Jill didn't know how she knew it was wine, but she was certain that's what it was.) He had scruffy good looks. Actually, he was gorgeous. Jill had to work to pull her attention off him and notice the woods all around. Another man approached, one she may have seen before—maybe in a nightmare.

"They're coming," this second man said. His voice was garbled, like he was far away and underwater. "They may look weak and unassuming."

"But appearances can be deceiving, is that what you're getting at?" The young man spoke in the kind of musical Creole drawl Jill loved to hear in Louisiana.

"I'm simply offering you the courtesy of a warning," the other man said. "Taylor Smart is not to be trifled with."

The young man raised the cup to his lips—a black stone cup, Jill realized with a start, adorned with ornate carvings and rimmed with gold.

"Neither am I," he said.

Then a foamy wave washed that scene away and replaced it with another.

It was Taylor's face. Even though she was blurry and out of focus, Jill could tell she looked scared. Person-sized shapes moved in the background, even less distinct than Taylor's own form. Jill watched as Taylor backed away from them.

But there was something else. Jill felt a weight on her chest, on her arms and legs. Her ears started to pop. The sounds of the bayou became muted, distant. She suddenly realized what the blurry haze meant.

"She's...in the water," she said.

"You see her? Good job!"

"No, not in the bowl. I mean...she's *literally* in water. It's like a lake or a river or something. I—I can't really explain it. I just know she's underwater." She didn't dare look away. The vision might fade. The indistinct figures continued to hover around Taylor.

And then, a foamy wave washed away the image and replaced it with another.

With effort, Jill pulled her eyes away. "She's in trouble!" She shuddered. "Somebody's trying to hurt her."

"There's a river nearby," Silas said. "I found it last night while you were sleeping."

"Do you think that's where she is?"

"All we can do is go look."

"Then we'd better hurry!"

Chapter 22

The Abita Brothers Band

Taylor woke up to the sound of music. Fiddle, accordion, and some kind of percussion.

What had happened since she hit the water was mostly a blur. She remembered the sting of the water against her skin. She remembered thrashing about wildly, trying to find the surface, while her lungs nearly exploded for lack of oxygen.

Then there was a sudden downward jerk. A cold, rough hand had grabbed her by the ankle. She kicked hard but couldn't break free. A second later, a slimy, tingly...something...wrapped around her like a blanket.

Part of her was sure she was dead. She knew she couldn't hold her breath as long as she had been doing.

Then everything went dark. She must have passed out or simply fallen asleep. She woke up disoriented, exhausted, and cold, with her ears throbbing from the music. It was a happy, fast-paced tune somewhere between the blues and bluegrass.

It went on for who knows how long while Taylor struggled to open her eyes. When she finally managed to stir, she hoped she was still dreaming.

She was lying on a couch in an old-fashioned sitting room decked out with rustic furniture covered with embroidered throw pillows, doilies, and colorful quilts and afghans. There was a musty smell in the air, as if the place hadn't been swept in a while. It tickled her nose, but only for a minute.

She was dry, however, and that surprised her after her plunge into the river. Someone had covered her with a warm

215

purple and green quilt. She decided to lie still until she could figure out what to do.

The musicians continued to play. Taylor took one look at them and let out a stifled squeal.

They were white. Not Caucasian—from their features, Taylor thought they might be multi-racial. But their skin was white: pale and scaly like a trout's.

One wore a calico dress and tied her long, black hair in a braided ponytail. She played a fiddle and kept time by tapping her bare, webbed toes on the hardwood floor. The other two were male. The accordion-player was the largest of the three, and the ugliest. His wide mouth and bald head made him look even more fish-like than the others, and his lips curled into a grin that was well on the way to becoming a leer. He wore denim overalls and a flannel shirt that might have been red in an earlier century.

Last, there was a smaller male wearing some kind of washboard tied around his neck with rough twine. His muslin shirt was overlarge for his body, and his rough, gray work pants had patches on the knees. His body swayed this way and that as he scraped his washboard with a spoon in each hand. His enormous eyes were orangey-brown and didn't seem to blink.

Taylor tried to control her breathing. Her captors must not have noticed she was awake because they kept on playing.

The tune was vaguely familiar, but it just wasn't coming to her. Maybe it was the unusual pace and the rhythm. Maybe Taylor was still too groggy to really pay attention.

They went through the whole song again before she finally figured it out.

They were playing "It's a Small World"—or at least a jazzed-up, syncopated version of the song from her Grandma Miller's favorite ride at Disney World. Visions of cherubic animated dolls in costumes from around the world began to creep into Taylor's consciousness.

She realized she was getting a headache.

"Tubby!" The music stopped abruptly as the woman (or whatever she was) spoke. The bald guy with the fish lips grunted, and his accordion wheezed to a stop.

"She's awake," the fiddle-player said in a lazy drawl.

There was no use pretending. Taylor pushed herself into a sitting position.

The smaller guy pulled off his washboard and stood up.

"You hungry?" Baldy asked.

Taylor just stared at him, frightened.

"We ain't gonna hurt you, chère," he said. "How 'bout some bacon and eggs? Teema, we got any of that bacon left?"

"A little bit," the woman said.

"No!" Taylor found her voice. "I mean...I'm not hungry. Thanks."

"You got to eat something," the woman—Teema—said. "How you gonna learn your part on an empty stomach?"

Taylor rubbed her ear. Did she hear right?

"Learn my part?"

"We been lookin' for a fourth member for our band," the other man, the accordion-player, said. "The Abita Brothers are the hottest zydeco band on the bayou, leastwise until we lost our guitar player."

"Et by a nekkid bear," The washboard-player explained. "They's a big 'un out there on the bayou."

"We call him Bubba," Teema added.

"You don't play, do you? It don't have to be guitar. Maybe the drums? Or the piano?" Taylor noticed there was an old and scuffed upright piano on the far wall.

"It don't matter," Baldy said. He rose to his feet, and his accordion sighed a plaintive note as he set it on his chair. "Ol' Catfish there can teach you to play just about anything. Ain't that right, Catfish?"

"Sure enough, Tubby," the washboard-player said with a grin. He had moved to the back of the room and was rummaging through a big steamer chest. To Taylor he said, "You got a preference?"

"Look," Taylor said, "there's been some kind of mistake. I'm not here to join your band. I've got somewhere I need to be."

Catfish and Tubby had started to chuckle. "It don't work that way, chère," Tubby said. "We done caught you swimmin' in our river. That makes you fair game."

"I-I don't understand."

"We done claimed you," Tubby said. "Fair and square."

"Come three days, you'll be an okwa naholo, just like us," Catfish added.

"More like two and a half," Teema said. She had arrived with a plate of bacon, which she set on the end table beside Taylor's sofa. "Now, eat up, chère." She winked at Tubby. "You'll feel better once you do."

"A little food'll make all the difference," Tubby said with a grin. Behind them, Catfish also chuckled at the joke.

Then Taylor figured it out.

"You want me to buy in, don't you?"

Tubby's mouth dropped open. Catfish swore.

"You're a smart girl," Teema said. Her wide lips curled into a wry grin. Her eyes flashed with something like appreciation. "It figures, the way you didn't get all panicky when you woke up. Most folks just thrash around, hollerin' like they seen a ghost. Not many of you deathlings know the old stories any more."

"Just eat up," Catfish said. "We're wasting time jawin' when we could be playin'!" He returned to his seat with an old, battered guitar. "I'll teach you a couple of chords and then we'll take it from there, all right?"

Taylor swallowed. Her eyes darted around the room, but there didn't seem to be any way out except the front door, which she had finally located on the far side of Tubby.

Think! she told herself. Three *things* had captured her and wanted to turn her into one of them. That meant she had to be somewhere in the Wonder. The fact they had offered her some of their food pretty much proved it: they knew if she bought in, it would be that much harder for her to return Topside.

She took a short breath when she realized something. It wasn't much, but it might give her the element of surprise.

"You think I'm a deathling," she said.

"You mean you ain't?" Catfish said, suddenly suspicious.

She might not have another chance.

Taylor had no clue what an okwa naholo was, but they couldn't have been as powerful as the daoine sídhe. As long as she could fake her way around how little she really knew about magic, she might have a chance.

She took half a second to gather up all the glamour she could. *Be confident*, she told herself. She let her true name stir in the pit of her stomach. Then, with all the presence she could muster, she said, "*No.*"

Catfish scooted back in his chair. Tubby gasped while Teema slapped her slim, white hand across her mouth.

Taylor took a chance and rose from the sofa. She was the shortest person in the room, but standing up helped her feel more in control of the situation than she really was.

"*Now, are you going to let me go...or what?*"

Nobody moved. Tubby, Teema, and Catfish froze like statues. There was no sound but Taylor's breathing.

Tubby shifted his impressive weight from one webbed foot to the other. The floorboards creaked.

"N-now, don't do nothin' hasty, chère," Catfish said, once more rising slowly to his feet. "Tubby...?"

"I hear you, Catfish. I'm thinkin' the same thing myself." Tubby wiped his hands on his trousers. "Teema, you seen my holey stone anywhere?"

"It's on the piano," she said. She was already backing toward it, extending a hand behind her to feel for it, never letting her eyes move from Taylor's cold-blooded expression.

Tubby gazed at Taylor. "I don't know what some Gentry kid's doing in these parts..."

Teema reached out and slipped a small, round stone in Tubby's hand. The effect of Taylor's presence was wearing off.

"*That's because it's none of your business,*" Taylor said. She hoped she was coming across as angry rather than terrified. Tubby shuddered, but shook off whatever magical effect Taylor's words had on him. Something else had captured his imagination. Something that was worth standing up to Taylor's presence.

"*Au contraire,*" Tubby said. "It's definitely our business. You see, there's a nightwalker that's lookin' for you. Word's out all over the bayou that whoever finds you is in for a mighty big reward."

Great.

"So you just sit back down, chère, and let me fetch him to come get you."

Taylor's options were disappearing quickly. As much as she didn't want to spend the rest of her life playing back-up with a band of fish-monsters, being turned over to Vesper sounded even worse.

There was nothing left to do but make a run for it.

She screamed at the top of her lungs. It was the loudest, most blood-curdling scream she had ever let loose. And just as she let it fly, she rammed straight into Tubby with all her might.

The accordion player ducked out of the way instead of standing his ground. That was fine with Taylor, because there was no way she'd have been able to bowl over anybody that huge.

She was at the door in a second. She flung it open—and almost took a step.

Just outside the door was a wall of water. A giant rat swam past at about eye-level. An alligator appeared from nowhere and gobbled it up in a single bite, and just as quickly disappeared leaving nothing but a murky cloud of silt.

The entire house was underwater.

Taylor spun back around.

"Have a seat, chère," Tubby said, gesturing toward the sofa. His grin turned into a smile revealing a mouth full of tiny jagged teeth. "You might as well make yourself comfortable."

As soon as Tubby made contact with Vesper, the three okwa naholo went back to rehearsing. They played "It's a Small World" all morning long and into the afternoon. It nearly drove Taylor to tears. She hoped they would move on to something else soon, but as time passed she began to fear it was the only song they knew.

When they insisted she pick up a guitar and join them, she tried to beg off. Eventually, however, she agreed to play the piano. If she was going to get shanghaied into an underwater zydeco band, she was at least going to put all those years of lessons to work.

Humoring her captors by joining their jam session might have kept Taylor alive. It wasn't doing much for her sanity. By the time Tubby announced it was time to go meet "the elf," she almost giggled with relief. Then she remembered "the elf" and his dog had already tried once to cart her off to Mrs. Redmane.

With hardly a word, they dragged her from the piano bench, hauled her to the door, and shoved her outside into the murky water. She struggled in the slow-moving current and lost whatever air was in her lungs in a flurry of bubbles.

"Just breathe normal," Tubby said. He kept his cold, white hand on her collar.

Taylor held out as long as she could, but her lungs soon ached for another breath. Her head started to swim. When she couldn't hold out any more, her mouth flew open of its own accord and she took a fitful gasp that filled her lungs with water.

For some reason, she didn't drown. She twisted toward Tubby, who just smiled back at her with those needle-like fangs.

"I done claimed you, remember?"

"Woulda been nice to keep you," Catfish said. He and Teema were swimming along close behind. "We coulda used a piano player."

Breathing underwater had never been one of Taylor's top choices for a super power. She wasn't that great a swimmer, and even in the Louisiana bayou, the water felt cold.

Now that she was actually doing it, however, she marveled at the underwater world through which she swam. With her eyes adjusting to the haze, it was almost as if she were wearing goggles. Frogs and turtles scuttled along the river bottom. Above her, the golden sun glistened on the surface waves, creating patterns of light against a blue-green backdrop. An alligator kept its distance, wary of the unusual intruders into his domain—if this indeed was his domain! Taylor got the impression the Abita Brothers Band were the real threat in these waters.

They reached the surface. Taylor began coughing water out of her lungs as soon as her head broke the water. Tubby dragged her to shore until her feet found solid ground beneath her. She and her three captors trudged through the muddy shallows.

She was sopping wet and shivering when they at last emerged from the river. The noonday sun felt warm on her face, though. Soon she wasn't cold at all, though her waterlogged clothes were itchy and uncomfortable.

Tubby and the others didn't seem to mind.

They stayed close to the river. One of the three always kept an eye on Taylor while the other two watched the perimeter of their little clearing for signs of an approaching elf, but apart from a couple of dragonflies and a huge green snake languishing high above on a tree branch, there were no signs of animal life.

Somewhere in the distance, the gekkering of a fox startled them all. It only lasted a second, then everything returned to lazy silence.

"Tubby, are you sure this is the place?" Catfish asked.

Tubby grunted.

"He shoulda been here by now," Teema added.

"He's a little tied up now," a female voice said. Suddenly all three okwa naholo were on their guard. Teema, the closest to Taylor, clapped a long-fingered hand around her upper arm.

"So why don't you just hand the girl over to me." A woman stepped out of the trees. She couldn't have been more than five feet tall, with short blonde hair, a perky button nose, and slightly pointed ears. She was more cute than beautiful, but she was really cute. One part Barbie, one part Tinker Bell. Three months ago, Taylor would have thought all faeries looked like that.

She was dressed in denim cutoffs and a green sleeveless blouse with a leafy print pattern, cinched at the waist with a golden-buckled belt.

Catfish sneered. "Move along, girlie," he said.

Tubby flexed his fingers. A hazy distortion started to form in his palm, as if he were holding a baseball that wasn't quite invisible.

The newcomer had noticed, too. "Don't even think about it," she said. As if to underline her point, she gestured toward the ground. At once, the ground began to rumble and pull itself apart as a snaky mass of tree roots found its way to the surface.

Tubby, Teema, and Catfish spun and dodged. Tubby extended his hand, but the woman sidestepped his blast with effortless grace. Catfish swore as he toppled to the ground, his ankles wrapped in slithering roots.

The woman's green eyes flashed with fury, and she hurled a blast toward Tubby. This one found its mark, and the giant okwa naholo fell backward with a yelp.

Teema pulled Taylor away from the fracas. She had only taken a couple of steps toward the water, however, when she yanked Taylor to a halt. A gigantic snake—probably the same one they had noticed earlier—had positioned itself between Teema and the river.

It flashed a pair of fangs as it coiled up into a slithery knot. Teema extended a hand, five fingers wide, and a shimmer of light told Taylor she had put up some kind of magical shield.

Teema looked over her shoulder at her fellow band members. Taylor followed her gaze and saw Tubby and Catfish rolling on the ground, wrapped up tight in a tangle of creeping roots and vines.

Teema yanked Taylor's arm and scurried off down the nearest pathway, cursing all the way.

"Let me go!" Taylor shouted, but Teema seemed not to hear her.

They wound through the woods. The path, it turned out, wasn't actually much of a path. It was more a wide place between two trees that soon became overgrown with brush.

Teema let out an exasperated yell.

There was a flurry of activity in front of them: a flutter of huge, black wings as an enormous vulture landed in front of them. As soon as it hit the ground, it started to shimmer. Then it began to grow, and as it grew it replaced its expansive wings with well-muscled arms. Its legs grew, too, and in just a few seconds it was no longer a bird at all but a man: a short, bald, dark-skinned man with a pointed beard and fiery yellow eyes, dressed all in white and sneering savagely.

"Not so fast," he said.

Teema snarled.

The vulture-man made a pushing motion with his hands, and suddenly the entire wood was filled with blinding light and the sound of thunder. Taylor and Teema both fell to the ground.

"Bacary!" the woman in green shouted from a distance.

"It's all right, Andred," the vulture-man answered in a slow, satisfied drawl. His accent was exotic, musical. Taylor was barely aware of movement over her: a body being dragged away.

"I'll take care of these three," the man said. "You find the nightwalker and keep him busy until I catch you up."

"How long?"

"Not too long," he said. Taylor dared open her eyes in time to see him standing over her. Small as he was, he had hoisted Teema up onto his shoulder and was carrying her like a sack of flour.

He looked down at her with a white, toothy grin. "Her friends are close."

Chapter 23

A Narrow Escape

Jill couldn't decide whether or not the big bird fluttering overhead was the owl she had seen back in Macon that had morphed into a man. It flew overhead a couple of times, but she only ever noticed it after it was high in the trees. Was it purposely trying to avoid being seen? Was it spying on them? Jill only knew it gave her the creeps.

She and Silas had wandered through the bayou all day. She was hot, dirty, sweaty, and ready to be anywhere else. But there was nowhere else to go. Taylor was out there somewhere, and she was in trouble. Jill knew her friend was somewhere in the river—either caught in the current or holding on for dear life to a floating log or unconscious on some muddy bank.

As soon as they had reached the riverbank late that morning, Jill knew they were heading in the right direction. She couldn't explain it, but she was sure Taylor was close by.

The hours dragged on with no sign of her. They called her name, but no one answered. They waded through the shallow fingers of streams that fed into the larger river. Nothing. The only signs of life were a family of pelicans that took flight as Jill and Silas drew near.

"Are you sure you saw water?" Silas said.

"I'm sure!" Jill answered, testy and impatient. She was tired of Silas's constant distrust. She wanted to find Taylor, but she also wanted to prove she could do something useful.

She took a deep breath and continued. "She's got to be around here somewhere." Jill gazed across the river to the other side. One of the pelicans plunged into the water and came up with a fish in its mouth. A bit more hesitantly, Jill added, "She's not that great a swimmer."

Silas grunted. "You want to give the bowl another try?"

"I guess," Jill said. She started as the huge bird disappeared into the trees above her. It wasn't an owl but a vulture. She caught herself shaking.

"Just give it to m—"

There was a sudden flash of light and a sharp crack, an explosion that rumbled through the air and nearly knocked her off her feet. "What was that?" she shouted.

Silas reached up and slapped a bony gray hand across her mouth. "Stay here!" he whispered. He knitted his brow, suddenly serious, and dropped into a fighter's crouch. He sloughed off his satchel one-handed—the only way he could with his injured arm—and left it at Jill's feet.

Before Jill could protest, the church grim had drawn his dagger and disappeared into the woods.

No sooner had he left her alone than the sound of thunderous barking assaulted Jill's ears. Vesper was back!

That's the last thing I need! she thought. She looked for a good place to hide. Bitsy's deep, mournful bellows got louder and then softer. It was impossible to tell what direction they were coming from, much less how close they might be.

Silas sprung into view with Taylor on his heels. She was rubbing her eyes, but seemed otherwise unharmed.

Jill started to call Taylor's name but stopped herself. She gave her friend a brief hug. She might have taken longer but for two things. First, Taylor smelled like a swamp. Second, Silas wasn't slowing down. He ran past Jill and gestured for both girls to follow. The look on his face said hurrying would be advisable.

The three charged onward. They sent a small flock of ducks into the air while they threaded their way through narrow, muddy deer paths.

A fox crossed their path, noticed them barreling toward it, and darted back into the undergrowth.

They scrambled through the woods away from the river. The barking was getting steadily louder. Jill thought dogs that got louder the farther away they were had to be stupidest thing she had ever heard of.

Silas came to a halt.

Taylor was breathing hard and leaning on her knees. For the first time, Jill noticed how terrible her friend looked: her hair was a mess, her face was streaked with mud, and her clothes were wet and dingy.

She realized she and Silas didn't look that much better.

"Which way?" Taylor gasped. She stood up straight and raked a tangle of hair out of her face.

Silas shushed her and raised a hand for quiet. His bat-like ears stood straight up.

Taylor's eye opened wide. Finally, Jill heard it, too. It was a low rumble from somewhere in the woods, a rattling drone pitched so low Jill could feel it in her gut. Something was close. And it was big, too. Bigger than Vesper's dog, Jill was certain.

"What is it?" she whispered.

"Shh!" Silas scowled at her.

Then came a terrible, raspy huffing and puffing, a barking noise that no one would ever confuse with the bark of a dog. Ponderous footsteps followed like the thud-thud-thud of a creeping headache. At the same time came sounds of wood splintering—full-grown trees being snapped in two.

"Bubba," Taylor said.

"Run!" Silas called and darted down the deer path.

The thing, whatever it was, roared so loud Jill felt it in her jaw. The next thing she knew, Taylor had grabbed her wrist and yanked her away.

The three ran as fast as they could with the new horror smashing through the woods behind them. They followed the path until it opened on a clearing where the grass was as tall as Silas.

The church grim scanned the edge of the clearing then took off in a different direction. Jill and Taylor sprinted behind him.

"Ah!" Silas called. Jill realized they weren't in a clearing at all, as she had thought. They had wandered onto a finger of land that jutted out into the river.

They were trapped with water on three sides and, on the fourth...

It crashed into view, pulling down a young cypress tree in the process.

Jill whimpered.

It was nine feet tall, massively built, with naked grayish-brown skin like an elephant's. That was where the similarity ended, though. The creature—whatever it was—was like a huge bear with about three times the recommended allotment of fangs. A pair of tusks as big as traffic cones jutted upward from its maw. It stalked forward slowly, its enormous body swaying this way and that.

It rumbled an irritated growl.

"You have got to be kidding me!" Jill complained. Her knees went weak and wobbly.

"Please tell me we're not going to swim for it," Taylor said.

Silas shook his head. "Naked bears can swim faster than we can," he whispered. "Our best bet is to scare him off." The church grim pushed his way to the front.

Jill almost laughed out loud.

"Taylor, get ready to disappear," Silas said.

Taylor gulped. "Okay, but—"

"No buts! If I... If we get separated, find the nearest ring. There's got to be one around here somewhere. Get to du Marais." He checked to see if his makeshift sling was secure. "Jill can help you find him."

"Silas, I—"

"Good luck, kid. I wish I could have done more."

The creature was only a few dozen feet away.

Silas roared and started forward, throwing glamour as he went. He took on the appearance of a huge, black dog. This time, however, he projected the illusion of a beast nearly as big as the creature that was bearing down on them.

At the same time, Jill sensed a mist settling around her. It was Taylor's glamour. It dimmed her vision with a light gauzy haze, which was just fine because she couldn't bear to see what was going to happen next, anyway. She turned her head and buried it in Taylor's shoulder.

Another growl rung in Jill's ears, higher and louder than the bear-thing's. Silas was doing his best to scare the thing away. The ground shook beneath the creature's feet. It roared again. It was a terrible sound. Then there was a massive thud, louder than anything Jill had heard so far. She dared to steal a look.

The creature had circled around so that its back was to the girls. Jill couldn't see Silas's black dog illusion, much less Silas himself. But she still heard barking, so she knew Silas was still out there somewhere.

"W-will your Jedi mind tricks work on...*that*?"

"To be honest..."

The beast swung back around. There was an eerie stillness in the air, interrupted only by the creature's rumbling growl.

"...I'm not exactly sure," Taylor said. Animals could usually figure out that something was up. At least, that's what Danny Underhill had told her once.

The beast lumbered toward the girls. Where was Silas?

Taylor wondered if using presence would give them a better shot of escaping, but she didn't dare drop the magical mist that—hopefully—would at least confuse the beast. It had to be Bubba, the naked bear the Abita brothers had mentioned.

Hell hounds. Naked bears. Just once, couldn't it be kittens?

She stood as still as she could. The chorus of "It's a Small World" nudged itself into her consciousness.

She hardly dared to breathe as the beast lumbered closer. It didn't stop until it was three feet in front of them. It sniffed the air but looked blankly ahead. At least for now, Taylor's glamour was holding up.

Jill held onto her arm so tight it hurt, but she didn't make a sound.

There was a rustling in the trees—soft at first, but growing louder and more constant.

Taylor tried not to become distracted. Everything depended on staying invisible.

Birds took flight. Someone—or some*thing*—was causing a commotion in the underbrush. Taylor kept still as a stone, but her eyes darted back and forth. What was going on over there?

A sharp whistle captured Bubba's attention. It swayed to one side—it was way too big to actually spin around, but it tried its best.

Taylor found the source. The Barbie doll fae woman who had helped her escape from the okwa naholo leaned out from behind a tree with her hands on her hips and a playful smile on her face. Taylor was pretty sure it didn't mean friendship, no matter what the song said. The beast took a ponderous step toward her.

With its second step, it let loose a roar like a peal of thunder.

It broke into a trot in Barbie's direction. Just then, there was a flash of light and a deafening sound, a hundred pops and cracks and fizzles as if somebody lit a whole box of firecrackers and threw them at the monster's feet. A ball of fire exploded against its shoulder. It roared again and stopped in its tracks.

It took a second for the smoke to clear. When it did, the naked bear charged forward, now in the opposite direction.

Barbie whistled again and summoned a bright, blazing light into her hands. Bubba paused and grumbled and changed course once more, now turning back toward the woman. It roared, angry and confused.

Another fireball exploded, this time on the monster's haunch. It yelped and practically leaped into the air, landing with a thud that shook the ground and almost bowled Taylor and Jill over.

The beast charged into the trees, disappearing from sight.

Only then did Taylor remember Silas.

She sprinted forward. "Silas?" she called as loudly as she dared.

"Hrnsh," Silas groaned.

There was movement in the tall grass. Taylor and Jill both moved toward it.

"Silas!" Jill cried.

The church grim looked shaky as he slowly pulled himself to his knees.

Jill offered him a hand up.

"You're all right," Jill said. "I was afraid you were…"

"I'm fine," he said. "The brute just knocked the wind out of me." He stretched his neck this way and that and adjusted his sling.

A bruise was forming over one eye, however, and he didn't look awfully sturdy.

Then his eyes grew wide, as if he had just woken up. He looked at Taylor.

"You drove him off?"

"I wish!" Taylor said. She scanned the trees. "We had help. Two fae, one was a woman. I didn't see her partner, but it had to be the same man who helped me escape earlier."

"Helped you escape?" Silas said. "What are you talking about?"

Taylor filled Silas and Jill in on her recent adventure and especially about the blonde woman and the shape-shifter who had sprung her from the okwa naholo.

"And as soon as he set me free," Taylor concluded, "as soon as he saw that I was okay…he just blinked away. I think they took care of Vesper, too."

The three looked at each other in stunned silence.

Silas frowned. Eventually, he told Jill, "Looks like your godmother really wants Taylor to make it to du Marais."

She gasped. "I-I hadn't thought of that."

"I wouldn't think of anything else if I were you," Silas said. "Your godmother's using us, plain and simple. If she's not poking around in that skull of yours, she's got her goons tailing us."

"I'm not so sure that's a bad thing right now," Jill said.

"Right now? I'll take it," Silas said. He headed back the way they had come. "It's later that I'm worried about."

"Later?" Taylor said as she forced her legs to start moving again.

"Say we find this du Marais. Maybe we somehow even manage to get his cup. What then? What's in it for her?"

"How should I know?"

"Exactly. You don't. Neither do I. Neither does Taylor. But I guarantee she's not helping us out of the goodness of her heart. She wants something. Once she gets it, who's to say we're not disposable?"

Taylor sighed. The images in her head of dancing animatronic dolls didn't make her feel better. They were getting on her nerves.

They got back to the trees. Silas gestured for Jill to give him back his satchel. When he struggled to handle it with his injured shoulder, Jill offered to help him find the last of his faery dust. After his simple incantation, the dust flew back into the woods the way they had come. Since they could no longer hear Bubba— or any other threat—they decided to risk backtracking to the river.

After a few hundred yards, Silas climbed a tree to get his bearings—not a simple feat one-handed! Once he was back on the ground, he shepherded the two girls through a thick patch of weeds and onto a different deer path.

"You found something?" Jill said.

Silas grunted and pressed on, picking up speed.

Before long, they found themselves in an open, overgrown field. In the distance were the ruins of an old plantation house. Silas headed toward it.

"Bound to be close," he said.

"What?" Jill said.

"The graveyard." He stopped long enough to scan ahead of him from left to right.

"Graveyard?" Taylor said. "Do Our Kind even have graveyards?"

"Not generally," Silas said. "But Topsiders do. It didn't make much sense to carry the dead into town to be buried at the church. There'll be a patch of ground around here somewhere..."

"Wait," Taylor said, looking up at the turquoise sky. "We're still in the Wonder, right?"

"We're somewhere in the Shallows," Silas said. "The line between the Wonder and the human earth is pretty thin around here. Topsiders built this place, but it brushes up to the Wonder. You might say it overlaps. There!"

Silas pointed to a bare patch of ground in the distance and picked up his pace. The three crossed the bare foundation stones of buildings that time had long since swallowed up. A couple of tiny gravestones, so weathered that Taylor couldn't begin to read them, were the only proof that they were standing on hallowed ground.

"Probably a graveyard for the slaves they kept here," he said.

"And we're here because...?" Jill asked.

"Because it's the quickest way out of the bayou," Taylor said. "A graveyard works like a ring, doesn't it? It's a portal through the Wonder."

Silas nodded. "Not always, but yeah. I think there's enough magic swirling around this one for it to work. We just need to decide where we're going."

"New Orleans," Jill said. Silas and Taylor looked at her.

"The cemetery, right?" Taylor said.

Jill nodded. "It's still the only lead we've got," she said. "And Silas is right. Godmother wants us to succeed. She's been helping us all along. She hasn't been making me dream about Gethsemane Cemetery for nothing. It was a message. A clue. If we can make it there, we'll find du Marais. But..."

"But what?" Silas said.

"I...I haven't had a chance to tell you," Jill began. "When I had my vision of Taylor, I think I saw du Marais, too."

"You what?" Silas thundered.

"It was just for a second. I saw the cup. And there's something else you need to know." Jill took a deep breath. "I think he knows we're coming."

Taylor cursed.

"How?" Silas said.

"I saw somebody with him. I didn't get a clear look, but somebody was telling him that Taylor was on her way. That he should be careful."

"Well, isn't that just...peachy!" Silas grumbled.

"Okay," Taylor said. She started pacing back and forth. "Okay, so that's going to make it a little bit harder."

Silas scoffed.

"But we can still do this," Taylor offered, as much to convince herself as the others. "We'll just have to...maybe take our time. Survey the situation. Figure out the best plan of attack. Knowledge is power, right?"

"You're serious," Jill whispered.

"I don't see that we have a choice at this point," Taylor said. "Vesper is still out there somewhere, plus who knows how many other nasties."

"I hate to say it," Silas said, "but you've got a point."

"Then let's go!" Taylor said. "Er...Silas, you can get us there, right?"

Silas scratched his balding head. "It's tricky if I've never been there, but there are ways." He motioned for Jill to sit down. He sat down facing her.

"You've got to help me picture it in my mind," he said. "Maybe not all of it, but at least part of it. Tell me about where your grandpa is buried."

Jill took a deep breath.

"There's a big oak tree," she began. "And there's a bench... under a statue of an angel. It's the angel Gabriel. He's got his trumpet to his lips like he's about ready to start playing."

"That's good," Silas said. "What about the grave itself? A lot of graves around New Orleans are above ground."

"That's right," Jill said. "It looks like a big, white marble box. And there's an empty spot next to it...for Maymay some day."

"What's the inscription say?"

She sniffled and took another breath. "Gilbert Joseph Blay. May 14, 1939 to March 5, 2009."

"Anything else?"

She nodded. "In sure and certain hope of the resurrection."

"Okay, kid," Silas said. "You did good. Now hold onto those memories. Picture the place in your mind as clearly as you possibly can."

Only then did Taylor realize a haze had settled over the graveyard. A swirl of gold and silver dust had begun to rise at her back.

Jill and Silas got up. Silas was deep in concentration, opening a portal.

"Now," Silas said, "before we go in, we're going to need a plan. We'll try to spy out the situation like Taylor said, but if he's ready for us, that plan'll go to pot in a hurry. If it does, we won't have many options. None of us can blink. I can manage one, maybe two good blasts. That's not a lot of firepower. If du Marais isn't in a mood to talk, we could be in trouble."

"Presence?" Taylor said.

Silas waited a second before answering. "Maybe. If he thinks you're somebody he needs to respect..."

"I don't know," Taylor admitted. She slumped her shoulders. "Never mind. What if I can't pull it off?"

"Seriously?" Jill said. "You've been pulling that trick on people as far back as I can remember."

"It's not the same," Taylor said. "Topsiders are one thing, but it won't be as easy with a fae. He might be able to push it back on me, convince *me* to do what *he* wants."

"I hadn't thought of that."

"You've never met my grandmothers."

"Well, like you said," Jill said, "Godmother seems to want us to succeed. Maybe she'll come through for us one last time."

"Yeah," Silas said. "But I'll be honest. I don't like the idea of having to rely on somebody we don't even know, whose motives we don't understand."

"If her godmother really is Dubessa," Taylor said, "she stood up for me before. She may not like me. Strike that. She definitely doesn't like me. But I think keeping me alive gives her some kind of pleasure. I'm something she can throw in Anya Redmane's face."

"A win here gives her bragging rights," Silas said. "That's for sure."

Taylor nodded. "And I've got to believe getting all three of us out in one piece makes her look even better."

She looked around the dilapidated, overgrown graveyard. The swirl of lights had grown both larger and brighter.

She looked at Jill. "Ready?"

Jill bit her lip and nodded.

"Alright," Silas said. "Let's do this."

He looked at the swirling lights and then at Jill. "We have got to do this right this time," he said. "No hollering. No fighting. I absolutely have to concentrate or it's not going to work. Got it?"

"Got it," Jill said.

"Taylor, you were listening, too. You've got to hold the same picture in your mind. Understand? Let Jill get in the middle with you on one side and me on the other."

"Right." Taylor gulped, and the three got into position.

She focused on the scene Jill had described. The image of the angel stuck in her mind, so she concentrated on that. With every breath, she repeated to herself her true name. Soon she felt a warm tingle in her chest that spread out to the rest of her body.

The sparkling swirl of light had formed the familiar pillar of an opening into the Wonder.

Jill held her hand so tight it hurt.

"Ready?" Silas said.

"Ready," the girls answered.

"Then let's go."

They stepped into the whirlwind. Taylor concentrated hard on the statue Jill had described and on her true name. They bounced around the Wonder for just a few seconds, spinning over lush swamps and hidden springs, until finally stepping out onto solid ground.

"W-what the...?" Jill gasped.

Taylor looked around. They had stepped out beside an ancient burial mound in the middle of a grassy field. A church steeple towered in the distance. There wasn't a gravestone in sight.

"Look alive!" Silas whispered. He drew his dagger.

There was a flash of light, and two figures suddenly appeared in front of them—a man and a woman. Silas dropped to a crouch.

He wore faded jeans and Converse high-top tennis shoes. Instead of a shirt of any kind, he had a leopard pelt wrapped around his neck like a cape. His arms were covered with tattoos.

He was fairly tall, just barely an adult, with curly reddish hair, twinkling green eyes, a dimpled smile, and the hint of a scruffy beard. His body had a lean, almost catlike grace.

The woman rested her head on his shoulder. She was as good-looking as her boyfriend, with wavy brown hair, subtly tapered ears, cut-off denim shorts, and a powder blue tank top under a black leather vest.

Her cow-like tail swished behind her.

"There's no need for violence," the man said. His accent was both refined and easygoing. His eyes flashed, and he waved his hand. Silas's knife flew off into the grass. The woman smiled.

"Maybe you'd like to tell me what all this is about."

Taylor tried to muster her presence. She stepped forward and said, "*This doesn't concern you.*"

He smiled again. "Now, I'm not so sure about that. I hear tell you all have been looking for me. I reckon I've got a right to know how come."

He gave a slight bow.

"The name's du Marais. Shall we step inside?"

Chapter 24

The Circle of Power

Danny spun through the kaleidoscopic maelstrom at a brisk pace. He figured Belas needed to blow off a little steam. That was fine, because he was shaking in his hooves. A good gallop through the Wonder's ring system might calm his nerves.

At last, they came to a stop amid grassy rolling hills. Belas pushed Danny forward at a trot.

"That went well," he commented to no one in particular.

Danny wasn't convinced, but he was in no position to argue.

Soon they rounded a bend in the road and entered a stretch of farmland. The spring wheat looked healthy and full. In another couple of months, Danny judged, farmers could look forward to a bumper crop.

He took in the sights and smells of the fields, listened with pleasure to the work songs of the Fair Folk going about their farm chores—green-haired poleviks with skin the color of topsoil; grotesque, hairy gruagachs; not to mention hobs and brownies of every description.

The Primus of Summer nodded to them as he passed the barn where they were working. When a gruagach milkmaid began to sing a song in his honor, he stopped to listen. Danny felt Belas's legs tense, however. He was in too big a hurry for such delays, but honor demanded he give attention to his people.

As soon as the songstress finished, the Primus joined the others in their applause, asked the girl her name, and exchanged pleasantries with her and her fellows. The morning shaded into noon as he inquired about crops and seeds and orchards and sunshine and rain.

Can we get on with it? Danny thought.

Not nearly soon enough, Belas bid his farewells and picked up the pace.

They passed through more farmland on their way to a large, stone rath on the top of a distant hill. The place looked familiar. It didn't take long for Danny to realize where he was. He had passed this way more than once in the past forty years.

They were headed to Bisgarra Verry, the seat of the Summer Court.

And Belas was in a hurry. He kicked Danny into a canter, and it wasn't long until they were passing through the fields that surrounded the rath itself. Workers were cleaning up after the recent Midsummer celebrations, taking down the colorful pavilions and collecting stray pieces of litter.

Belas finally let Danny slow down as they approached the outer gatehouse. The guards—two menacing slant-eyed giants—saluted their Primus as he passed.

Once through the gate, Danny was trotting to the stables. Belas slipped from the saddle as soon as Danny came to a halt. A wrinkled, red-faced stable hand loped out to meet them. Below his pant legs, Danny spied horse hooves. His ears were also long and pointed like a horse's and they swiveled forward as he addressed his Primus.

"Afternoon, Mr. Wakefire," the stable hand said in a thick Russian accent.

"Thank you, Chort."

"Mrs. Fairchild said you was coming. She wants you to go see her as soon as—ah, here she comes, now."

Dubessa Fairchild was indeed striding across the outer courtyard toward her husband. She had a gleam in her eyes and a stern look on her face.

"Dubessa," Belas said, "The meeting was a success. My plan worked like—"

"Later, darling," Dubessa interrupted. "I have news as well. Something is afoot."

Belas gestured toward the stableman without looking at him. "Take care of Licorice, Chort."

Belas offered Chort the reins. "Don't you worry about that, Mr. Wakefire," the stableman said.

Danny sidestepped to position himself to hear the rest of Belas and Dubessa's conversation.

"This has to do with Vesper, doesn't it?" Belas asked.

Dubessa nodded. "And more. But we should discuss this further in the keep..."

No! Discuss it right here! Danny pleaded. But to anyone listening, it only sounded like a frustrated blow.

"Now, you come with me," Chort said. "Licorice, huh? You must be new. But don't you worry none. Chort'll take good care of you." He gave Danny's reins a gentle tug, just enough to get his attention.

"Come on, Licorice, let's get you cooled down and fed."

Chort led him into the stable and untacked him with practiced ease.

Danny had to admit he appreciated being relieved of his saddle and walked around the outer courtyard. Chort seemed like he knew a thing or two about horses, and when he finally led the pooka to the stables themselves, a couple of other hands had already prepared him a trough of fresh hay.

Free from his bridle at last, he nibbled a bit and swished his tail.

Alfalfa, he noted. *Bisgarra Verry always did have the best chow.*

But he still needed to get out of there. He hadn't had a chance to contact Taylor in forever. If she was still heading for New Cephalonia, she would need his help. Plus, there was no mistaking Dubessa's unrest about whatever it was she needed to tell Belas.

And he wasn't in a position to help anybody cooped up in the stables. He had to get free somehow and then figure out a plan.

"Chort, you want me to give Mr. Wakefire's saddle a good cleaning?" a stable hand said. He was a tow-headed stable brownie, probably kin to Aengus back at the horse farm, but a little bit taller and a little bit younger.

"*Da*," Chort said. "And then take break. Something is up, Murghad. We may be needed later. We should rest while we can."

Murghad arched an eyebrow. "You don't think this has anything to do with Mrs. Redmane, do you?"

Chort shrugged. "Nobody tells me nothing. Just make sure horses are taken care of and tack is ready to go. Tell Steve, Gilno, everybody. Understand?"

"Whatever you say, Chort." The little man sucked in a breath and hefted the saddle onto his shoulder.

Danny took his time finishing his lunch. After the morning he had, he didn't have much of an appetite even for alfalfa hay. One of the other hands led him to a stall while Murghad polished Belas's saddle like it was a national treasure.

Hurry up! He shifted from side to side, craning his neck to see over the stall door and keep an eye on what was happening.

At last, Murghad finished, and all the hands stepped out to the courtyard to smoke. Danny only had the other horses to worry about. He hoped none of them could talk. But he couldn't wait any longer.

He backed into the corner of his stall, as far from the door as possible. With a bit of effort, he resumed his two-leg form. Keeping the same shape for so long made his muscles ache, but he would get over it soon enough.

Blinking away from the stables without being seen was fairly easy, and Danny didn't have any trouble weaving through the tangle of shops and humble homes that ringed the inner wall. He used to be oath-bound to Anya Redmane, after all. For the past forty years, Bisgarra Verry was the closest thing he had to a home.

But that could be a problem, however. If the house of Fairchild was really plotting something big, something that would take down the house of Redmane and change the balance of power in the Summer Court once and for all, then Danny could be walking into trouble.

He didn't dare try to glamour himself to change his appearance. There were too many Fair Folk about who would see through any kind of magical disguise. The last thing he wanted to do was raise anybody's suspicions. All he could do was keep his head down, walk toward the keep, and try to look like he belonged there.

The guards at the inner gate stopped him long enough to ask his name and his business.

"Uh, Danny Underhill," he said. "M-Mrs. Redmane said she'd give me a good reference if I ever needed one, so..."

"The Chief Matron is away," the guard said, his arquebus resting on his shoulder. He looked Danny over. Actually, he more or less glared at the pooka. Danny did his best to look hapless and unassuming.

"You can leave a message with her staff if you like."

"Thank you, sir."

Danny passed into the inner court with a bow. The guards weren't usually that surly. Maybe they knew something was up, too.

He repeated the routine at the entrance to the keep itself, where the Primus had his main residence and the business of the Summer Court was usually conducted. The Chief Matron's office would be ahead on the right. Once he was sure no one was looking, he turned left toward the Primus's private apartments.

More guards walked the halls on their rounds. What was up with all these guards? It was starting to look to Danny as if somebody—maybe more than one somebody—was expecting trouble at the heart of the Summer Court.

He walked more slowly and softly now, all the while working out what he would tell anybody who stopped him.

A tug on his collar jerked him into a side passage. Before he could say anything, a hand clapped over his mouth and a voice whispered, "Quiet!"

Danny heard the creak of a door opening in the main corridor. He was pulled further down the hall and behind a great marble bust of Finnuala Fairchild (of the Tír na nÓg Fairchilds).

Footsteps echoed in the corridor. Danny heard a woman's voice say, "I'll send word as soon as I learn anything."

"Are you sure you don't need me with you?" Belas Wakefire asked.

"Best you stay here, darling. Until we know her plan, we need a strong presence here at the rath."

Dubessa Fairchild stopped in front of the side hall long enough to kiss her husband lightly on the lips.

"Then I'll hope to see you soon," the Primus said.

Dubessa spun away as her husband paused, then strode boldly in the other direction.

It was a full ten seconds before the hand slipped from Danny's mouth. He already knew who it was, however.

"Claudia!"

"Danny, what are you doing here?" Claudia grabbed Danny's arm and pulled him out of the Primus's apartments.

"It's kind of complicated," he said. "But I think Taylor Smart's in trouble."

"She's not the only one."

Claudia led him without another word back through the keep in the direction of the Chief Matron's apartments. She pulled a large, brass key from her pocket, slipped it into the lock on a great, oaken door, and pushed Danny inside.

Her office was bare and efficient, with a small writing desk and bookshelf to one side and a door leading to her private quarters to the other. The back of the room was taken up with a circle of unbroken silver inlaid in the hardwood floor. It was inscribed with a simple, looping three-cornered design of Celtic knot work.

Claudia tossed a cushion into the circle, the twin of one already positioned in the center, and grabbed a huge roll of parchment from her desk. She gestured for Danny to enter the circle and then knelt to touch the silver ring and breathe a quick incantation.

"Now we can talk freely," she said.

Danny nodded his approval as he lowered himself to a cushion. A circle of power would keep anybody from snooping on them—at least using magic.

"The keep is usually pretty empty this time of day," Claudia said. "We shouldn't have to worry about eavesdroppers—but keep your voice down, just in case."

"Claudia, what in the world is going on?"

Claudia sat on the cushion in front of him. "All I know is that your friend Taylor is in the middle of it. The Chief Matron put a tail on her. A nightwalker by the name of Vesper."

"So I heard," Danny said. He gave her the short version of all he had learned during his recent excursion with Belas Wakefire. Claudia sat stunned for about a minute, staring into his golden eyes.

"Then the Fairchilds are making some kind of move against the Chief Matron," she said at last.

"Sounds like it," Danny agreed. "They done got Winter to sit this one out, so they must feel pretty good about their chances—whatever they got planned."

"Vesper is the key," Claudia said. "And, therefore, Taylor. She's stumbled upon something that must be very dangerous for the Chief Matron. You should have seen how she reacted when she learned Taylor and her friends were headed to New Cephalonia. She didn't waste any time sending Vesper to intercept her."

"And when Mr. Wakefire found out, he sent in his own goons—Andred and Bacary."

"I know them," Claudia said. "They can be very...effective."

Danny nodded. "I reckon if I was with the Fairchilds, it would make sense to put a tail on Vesper, get in his way if I could. Whatever Mrs. Redmane wanted, I'd sure as blazes want the opposite."

"Exactly," Claudia said. "She's nervous. She's likely to be reckless. People are going to get hurt. And Danny..." She sucked in a long, steady breath. "I'm not sure we can count on Winter staying out of this, no matter what Cornstack promised."

"I was thinking that way, too," Danny said. "Something about the way that whole thing went down still don't sit right with me."

He clenched his fists. "By oak, ash, and thorn, Claudia, I've got to find Taylor. I don't know what all's going on between the Fairchilds and the Redmanes, and I don't especially care, but I've got to try to keep Taylor safe. She don't deserve to be in the middle of this."

"I figured you'd say something like that," Claudia said. Something rumbled in her voice, unseen power and determination. It made Danny shudder.

She rolled out the parchment between them on the floor. It was a map.

"The Chief Matron had me track Vesper's progress—that is, until she left to oversee the matter personally. He lost them here, on the Abita River, just north of Lake Pontchartrain."

Danny studied the map.

"Do you figure they're still in that neck of the woods?"

"Could be," Claudia said. "But if I were you, I'd look a little further to the south."

Danny looked into Claudia's eyes. There was something there he couldn't quite read—but he knew he could trust.

"Then I better get going," he said.

Chapter 25

Évastre du Marais

"You're the satyr?" Jill blurted.

"Pleased to meet you," the young man said. He extended his hand to Jill, who jerked hers away.

"But...but...what about the horns? The goat legs?"

Du Marais smiled an easygoing smile. His girlfriend suppressed a giggle.

Jill's heart fluttered, and she felt her cheeks warming. There was no doubt about it: Évastre du Marais was good-looking! A sideways glance at Taylor told her she was thinking the same thing.

"You're thinking of a faun," he said. "Easy enough mistake for a Topsider—and yes, *Monsieur*, I know who you all are." He had seen Silas's hand shoot up and answered the church grim's question before he could ask it.

"This is Lily."

She nodded and swished her tail.

"This way, if you please." The satyr turned toward Silas, "If you'll keep your knife sheathed, I won't object to you carrying it."

Évastre du Marais strolled away from the burial mound toward the woods. Jill kept her eyes on the church steeple to her left until they passed into the trees. Silas retrieved his knife, and he and Taylor followed close behind.

As soon as Taylor caught up, Jill whispered, "How come we're not in New Orleans?"

"I do hope you'll forgive me for that," du Marais said. "I'm not used to so much attention. It seemed you were in such an all-fired hurry to find me, I might as well bring you the rest of the way."

"You brought us here?" Taylor asked. "You pulled us off course? How is that even possible?"

"Right," Silas said. "You'd have to have a relic from one of us—blood or hair or fingernail clippings. And you'd have to know at least one of our names. It's the only way."

"As you say, Mr. Bludgitt." Du Marais shrugged. "But we'll have plenty of time to chat once you've...ah...put yourselves together."

Jill was suddenly aware of how awful the three of them looked. She ran a hand across her face and straightened her shirt.

She started to feel woozy, and it wasn't just because of the satyr's good looks. Something in her gut told her they were heading deeper into the Wonder. Magical power seemed to course up and down her arms, tickling her skin. She suppressed a giggle. Du Marais turned in her direction, and she quickly dropped her eyes to the ground ahead of her.

Ahead was a huge live oak. Its branches were full of birds of every sort, singing their evening songs. A rabbit bounded away them deeper into the woods.

Du Marais slipped around the tree's massive trunk. Jill and the others followed close behind. On the far side, there was a knot in the wood about three feet off the ground. Du Marais passed his hand in front of it, and the entire tree began to shimmer.

"You all look like you've had a rough time of it," du Marais said. "Why don't you come in and clean yourselves up?"

"In there?" Jill said. Nobody seemed to hear her.

Silas said, "Are you offering hospitality?" He folded his arms in front of him. "In accordance with the Eldritch Law?"

"Of course," du Marais said with a smile. His teeth, Jill realized, were as white as pearls.

"And you swear to honor your obligations as our host?"

"You're quite the stickler, aren't you? Very well." He cleared his throat and raised his right hand. "I welcome you three into my domain under the Law of Hospitality," he recited. "For whatever time you abide with me, I pledge to hold your life and well-being as sacred as my own. I will not injure or defraud you, nor in any way bring shame upon myself by failing to honor this sacred obligation."

Jill glanced at Taylor, who seemed just as confused as she was.

"I believe, sir, that it's your turn."

Silas grunted. He raised his hand and said, "We receive your welcome under the Law of Hospitality, and we pledge to honor the sacred obligation of beholden guests in your domain." He glanced at Taylor. "So we're going to be good guests and not wear out our welcome. Right?"

Taylor nodded.

"Well, now that that's settled, let me see about drawing some baths and finding you some fresh clothes. After me, if you please."

Du Marais poked his head into the shimmering knot in the wood—and vanished. His body shrank and twisted and disappeared into the knot as if he had been sucked down a drain.

"That was just weird," Jill said.

"Yeah," Silas agreed. "Well, in you go."

"What?"

"The tree is a portal to someplace even deeper in the Wonder. We'd better follow before we lose him."

"I get it," Taylor said. "Come on." And she bent down like du Marais had done and just as quickly vanished into the tree.

"I'll be right behind you," Silas said. He glanced around. "I don't like what some of those birds are tweeting. We'd better hurry."

"The birds are...? Wait, you speak *bird*?"

Silas nodded, distracted.

"Something's coming. They're not sure what, but birds in the Wonder usually have a good sense about such things. The satyr has offered us protection. I don't like it, but it's better than nothing. Now, in you go."

Jill stood in shock for only a second. With Silas's nudging, she bent down as she had seen Taylor do.

Crossing the portal felt exactly like it looked. It wasn't painful, just disorienting. Jill felt as if her entire body was being sucked through a straw the size of a pool noodle. The only thing she could see clearly was a bright spot straight ahead. The tree, the woods, Silas—the entire outside world—dissolved into a kaleidoscope of lights and colors and soon vanished behind her.

She stood on a manicured lawn dotted with shrubs and flowerbeds. Taylor and du Marais stood beside her, and straight ahead was the biggest mansion she had ever seen. It was pure white, with a colonnaded porch that ran the entire length of the front. She had barely begun to take it all in when Silas appeared behind her.

Her senses were overloading with the wonder of this place. The scent of perfume was on the wind. The colors of the leaves and flowers were more vibrant than anything she had ever seen. The marble columns of the mansion practically blazed with pure, white light.

"It's bigger on the inside than on the outside," du Marais explained as he skipped up the steps and onto the porch.

"Apparently," Taylor said.

He opened the front door and ushered his guests into a vast foyer festooned with paintings, bronze statues, a crystal chandelier, and a Persian rug that was an intricate maze of greens, blues, and browns.

Zydeco music was playing somewhere. For some reason, Taylor growled in disapproval.

"Richard!" du Marais called, clapping his hands. Someone who must have been the butler soon appeared. Richard was a ruddy, blue-eyed blond only a couple inches taller than Silas.

"Lily, please draw a bath for Miss Smart and Miss Matthews and do something about their traveling clothes. Some of my mother's things are still in her old room. If you can find anything that will fit them, I'd be much obliged."

"And Richard, please see that Mr. Bludgitt is properly cared for." He glanced at Jill. "And alert Carlos the four of us will eat Topside food tonight. I think the Creole Café still does carry-out."

He extended his arms toward the three of them. "Welcome to my domain," he said. "Dinner is at seven. I look forward to seeing you then."

He bowed deeply and excused himself through a side door.

The guest room was bigger than any hotel room Jill had ever seen, complete with a walk-in closet, a balcony, two four-poster beds, and a bathroom she could have gotten lost in.

While Taylor took her bath in the claw-foot tub, Jill paced back and forth in the bedroom in her borrowed robe, examining the clothes Lily had brought for the girls.

Lily stood at the edge of the bed and held up one dress after another for Jill's consideration. She settled on a light green sleeveless dress that reached almost to her knees, with matching sandals and a beautiful golden brooch in the shape of an oak-leaf cluster.

Taylor had been harder to fit. She was a lot slimmer than du Marais's mom, apparently. But she found a cobalt blue short-sleeved shift with a modest neckline that didn't look too bad even though it was kind of baggy on her. At Lily's insistence, she accessorized with a necklace and laurel wreath, both fashioned of pure silver.

Lily carried off their dirty clothes in a laundry basket, promising they would be cleaned and ready for them after dinner.

Everything was too beautiful for words: the clothes, the room, the grounds—and especially their host! It all left Jill with a dizzy, disoriented feeling. She was giddy with excitement and a little nervous. Her heart raced. Try as she might, she couldn't block out the flurry of sights, sounds, and smells that assaulted her. Not for the first time, she wished she was back home in Georgia—or at least at Maymay's house where things were normal. After all, New Orleans couldn't be that far away.

A few minutes before seven, Lily returned dressed in a short white dress and her hair done up in an elaborate braid. She escorted the girls downstairs to the formal dining room, where Silas waited in a perfectly tailored goblin-sized suit. He tugged at his bow tie, and Jill noticed that he no longer wore his arm in a sling.

Évastre du Marais entered the room dressed almost the same as when they had first met him. He had traded in his leopard pelt for a solid white tuxedo jacket, but he wasn't wearing a shirt underneath it, and he still had on his jeans and tennis shoes.

He slid easily into his seat at the head of the table and beckoned his guests to join him. Lily sat immediately to his right and ran her fingers up and down his arm.

Carlos, a brown-skinned fae with pointy ears and amber eyes, brought bowls of soup to the table. To Jill, it smelled like heaven. Taylor scrunched her nose.

"Just try it," Jill whispered as she gave it a taste. "It's crawfish bisque. It's good."

"It looks spicy."

"It's not spicy. Why do you have to be so fussy?" Jill shook her head. Taylor tried the soup but wouldn't admit she liked it.

Du Marais took a sip of his wine. "Now, down to business," he said. "You've come a mighty long way. I reckon it's about time you all told me why."

Taylor, Jill, and Silas traded looks.

"To be honest," Taylor began. "We're not a hundred percent sure."

The satyr leaned back in his chair. A quizzical expression passed over his face. Quizzical but not exactly patient.

Jill focused on Taylor. She knew more than any of them what was really going on. She needed to speak up.

"Just tell him—"

"I'm getting to it, okay?" Taylor blurted.

"All right," Jill said.

Taylor composed herself and turned toward du Marais. "All we know is..." she started again. "...Well, the truth is, I'm not too popular with the Winter Court of Arradherry."

"From what I hear," the satyr said, "that is a bit of an understatement."

"Yeah, maybe." Taylor bit her lip. Jill knew that expression. Taylor had figured out a plan of attack. "I sort of got in the middle of a feud between my two sets of grandparents."

"Your grandparents?" du Marais said. "I heard you're Shanna Hellebore's daughter. Is that what all that was about?"

"Y-you know about my mom?"

"No more than what everybody knows. She ran off with Aulberic Redmane, didn't she? The whole thing nearly brought the Courts to open warfare. Both families have been at each other's throats ever since."

"That's about the size of it, yeah. And now, it looks like the Hellebores are out to get me." She gazed up at the satyr and took a deep breath.

"Unless..." She was about to say something about the cup, Jill knew it. Bless her heart, for all her smarts, Taylor could learn a thing or two about diplomacy.

"M-Mr. du Marais?" Jill interrupted. "You've got so many pretty things in your house. W-where did they come from?"

"Hey, I'm talking here!"

"Well, now it's time to let Jill talk," Silas grumbled. She gave Taylor a raised eyebrow. *Slow down, Taylor*, Jill thought, hoping her friend could read her mind. Something told her they'd have to go slowly. She didn't understand about the Law of Hospitality or whatever Silas called it, but she was pretty sure trying to steal the cup they were looking for would be bad for all three of them. Apparently, that's how Silas saw it, too.

But why was everybody suddenly so on edge? Jill felt her heart beating faster than it should have. Every little sound made her jumpy. At first, she thought it was a side effect of being deep in the Wonder again. But looking around the table, she wasn't the only one feeling it.

"Most of this is my mother's," du Marais said.

Carlos entered to take up the soup bowls.

"She lives across the Great River these days. I go see her every Hallowmas. But this is her old stomping ground. My daddy built her this place when they first got married."

"She gave it to you?" Silas said.

Du Marais gritted his teeth. "Daddy was a Gentryman named Leatherleaf."

"I don't know that family," Silas said.

"Well, at any rate, he left us when I was little. Momma said the place had too many memories for her to carry."

"How sad!" Jill blurted.

"You're very kind," du Marais said. Jill blushed and averted her eyes. "But that was over sixty years ago. I barely remember what Daddy looks like, to be honest. Momma says I favor him, though. But we lived here a good, long time. When I grew up, she figured I should take care of the place. Keep it in the family." He gestured vaguely at the room. "Momma wasn't much for all this finery. Wood nymphs never are.

"Carlos!" he suddenly shouted. "What's keeping the salad? Hurry up, you oaf!"

"I-it's okay," Jill said, startled by du Marais's outburst. "I'm not in any hurry. Are you in any hurry, Taylor?"

"You better believe I'm in a hurry," Taylor snapped. "Are we going to have to wait till dessert before we can bring up—"

"Girls! Settle down!" Silas pounded the table. "You're acting like a couple of..."

"What?" Jill snapped.

Silas rose from his seat. His eyes were focused on the French doors and the lawn outside.

Du Marais followed the church grim's gaze. "Danu," he breathed.

A fine mist had settled over the lawn. It moved in so fast Jill could watch the trees and flowers fade into a dim, silvery haze before her eyes.

"Is there something you'd like to tell me, Mr. Bludgitt?"

"We got company," Silas said.

"Obviously," du Marais said, rising. "Friends of yours?"

The mist had quickly become a thick fog. Jill could barely see the flowerbeds outside, much less the trees at the edge of the lawn. A flurry of indistinct, barely perceptible sounds filled her head and made it hard to concentrate—footsteps, whistling winds, the howls and shrieks of animals.

"That's not fog," she said. "It's some kind of magic."

"Nothing gets past you, does it?" Taylor scoffed.

"And I still want to know what you had to do with this!" du Marais shouted.

"You mess with Évastre, you mess with me, dearies!" Lily blurted as she jumped up from her seat.

"Now listen here," Silas blurted. "You can't honestly think—"

"I welcomed you into my home under the Law of Hospitality. Is this how you treat your host?"

"It's not us!" Silas said.

"Oh, and that fog is just a coincidence. Is that it?"

"*Stop it!*" Taylor shouted. With the words came a ripple of presence that pushed du Marais back into his seat.

"Everybody, settle down!" Jill said. "The fog—the magic—it's making us, I don't know, jumpy or something."

Precisely, a voice inside Jill's head said.

"You again?" Jill said out loud.

"What?" du Marais said.

"Shut up," Taylor said with an angry glare. She turned to Jill and said, "It's her again, isn't it?"

Jill nodded.

Your enemies have started their assault, Godmother said. *They've laid a curse on the entire area. If you don't shake it off, you'll soon be at each other's throats.*

"You couldn't have given me a little more warning?"

"Who is she talking to?" Lily said, her eyes wide. "Is somebody riding her?"

Du Marais took a step toward Jill, but Taylor was between them. She threw up a hand to block the satyr's advance. As she did, she seemed to scoop up a handful of energy, and when she shouted at him, it erupted against his chest.

Du Marais fell backward.

Silas sprang onto the table, his knife drawn. He glared at du Marais.

"Wait!" Jill said. She stretched out her hands, one toward Silas and the other down toward du Marais as he struggled to sit upright on the floor.

We'll do this just like before, Godmother coaxed inside Jill's head. *But you've got to hurry. I have other matters to attend to. I can't stay long.*

Jill kept her hands spread out and tried to settle herself. She whispered a single word: "Peace." She closed her eyes and said it again, drawing out the syllable as long as she could. The magical energy welled up in her chest. It was far more powerful than the sleep spell back in the bayou. It radiated to the tips of her fingers and then out into the dining room just barely in her control. Her arms began to tremble.

The third time, she sang the word. A long, low note that seemed to wrap everyone in its warm embrace: "Peace."

Silas shook off his anger and sheathed his knife.

Taylor helped du Marais to his feet.

"Did I...? Is that what it's like to..."

"Uh huh," Silas said. "You blasted him."

"I am so, so sorry!"

The satyr rubbed his temples. "I need a drink."

"We don't have time for that," Silas said. "Whoever's out there is playing for keeps."

"No doubt about it," du Marais said. "Looks like we're going to have us some company."

Taylor gazed out the French doors at the blanket of fog that now enveloped the entire lawn.

"Mr. du Marais," Silas said, "we're oath-bound to help you defend your home. Just say the word."

"I'm much obliged, sir. I've got some pretty strong wards… but I'm not sure they'll be enough."

"In that case," Taylor said, "maybe we ought to skip straight to dessert."

Chapter 26

The Fog of War

"How can you think of dessert at a time like this?" Jill said.

"She'll need it if she wants to use magic," Silas said. "She's already wasted a blast. It'll be a while before she can manage another one. Sweet treats will help her recharge."

"Another one?" Taylor said. "I don't know how I did the first one!" She was still trying to shake off the edginess from whatever magic their enemies had thrown at them. She had blasted du Marais on pure instinct. There was no way she could do it again, no matter how long she had to recharge!

And Taylor really needed to recharge. Blasting the satyr left her sluggish and dazed. Her arms felt like they were made of lead. It took all her effort to stay focused on the conversation.

She barely realized it when somebody—maybe Lily—set a dish of bread pudding in front of her.

"I'm going to assume I'm the only one here with any combat experience," Silas continued. He had taken off his jacket and loosened his tie. His satchel was by his feet. Taylor wondered how long she had been fazed out.

"The first order of business is to secure the house," Silas said.

"The house and grounds are warded," du Marais said. He was also finishing off his dessert while he talked. He had changed out of his tux and back into his leopard-pelt cape. Lily was at his side, her body tensed. She looked as frightened as Taylor felt.

"Blinking won't be an option—for them or us," the satyr said. "To be honest, I'm surprised their curse got through."

"That worries me, too," Silas said. "They may have an in we don't know about. We'll have to be sharp. That fog out there is a perfect cover. We need some way to see past it, find out what's going on out there."

"I've got an idea about that," du Marais said, slipping into the kitchen.

At some point, Carlos and Richard had joined the others in the dining room.

"If you two can lock down the back of the house," Silas told them, "Taylor, Jill, and I can take the front."

"Sounds like a plan," du Marais said. He was returning from the kitchen carrying a great stone cup. It was dark gray, almost black, and trimmed with gold. There were bold, angular letters etched around the rim.

Jill gasped.

"I...I've seen that before," she said. "Godmother showed me."

"This was my Daddy's," du Marais explained. "I don't know about no godmothers, but maybe we can use this to see what's going on out there. I'm no great shakes at scrying, mind you; I usually just use it as a drinking cup. But we don't have much choice. Unless one of you thinks you can do it."

Taylor and Silas both glanced toward Jill.

"Jill," Silas said, "why don't you stay here. See if you can help du Marais."

She nodded, but she didn't look convinced.

"Lily," the church grim continued, "can you keep an eye on the back lawn? Let somebody know if you see anything?"

Lily nodded.

"This way," Silas said. He took Taylor by the arm. She set her dessert dish on the table as he led her toward the front door. Silas pulled back the blinds and peered into the fog.

"Sunset's not for another half hour," Silas grumbled. "I can't see a blasted thing out there!"

"I hear drums," Taylor said.

"Don't trust 'em," Silas said. "It might be the enemy. It might be just a pishogue."

"A glamour trick?"

"Why not? You think magical combat is just lobbing fireballs at each other? That's how amateurs do it." He absentmindedly tapped the flat of his knife against his thigh. "I used to think that way, too."

Taylor wiped her sweaty hands against her dress.

"So, what do we do?"

"Nothing yet. Somebody makes a move on the house, we stop them. Hard. Any way we can."

"Okay. You know this is my first siege, right?"

"In theory, we're safe as long as we stay inside."

"In theory?"

Silas looked worried. "A home—even a deathling's home—can usually keep most magic out."

"So how could they throw that curse on us at dinner?"

"Three ways," Silas said. "One, you heard how du Marais talks about this place. It was his father's, but his father left him. His mom never felt at home here. I bet he never has, either. Once a house stops being a home, it loses its protection.

"Two, he might have accidentally given somebody permission to come in. Maybe he let somebody in who's working for the enemy. Maybe he brought something in that they can claim as their property."

"Like a family heirloom scrying cup?"

"Yeah, exactly like that. Or somebody pulled a glamour trick on him and he just didn't know what he was doing. A threshold can be pretty strong magic, but there are ways around it."

"You said there were three ways," Taylor said.

"Maybe whoever these people are, they're just that powerful."

"Oh."

"It still won't be easy, though. That trick at the dinner table worked because it was subtle. It must have been working on us for at least half an hour before we started turning on each other.

That's how you get through a threshold: low and slow. Try to barge in fast and hard and you'll limit what you can do. But du Marais invited us in. That's our advantage. We'll have all our magic. They'll have to leave most of theirs at the door."

"I'm still not sure how I blasted Mr. du Marais," Taylor said. "I wouldn't count on me doing it again."

"I already told you," Silas said. "Blasting and fireballs and such is just a part of it. Pretty small part if you ask me. The key is to play to your strengths. You've got a pretty strong presence. Maybe you've got a couple other glamour tricks under your belt. Use that."

"And if that doesn't work?"

Silas shrugged. "Improvise." He pulled his satchel off his shoulder and passed it to Taylor. "I've got a few iron filings left in there. A magic rope. A water bottle. Be creative."

Taylor was not encouraged.

"Thanks. I think I'd rather—"

Silas held up a hand. Something was happening outside. There was a shout and a flash of light Taylor could clearly see despite the fog. Dark shapes scrambled across the lawn.

"What's going on?" Taylor whispered.

As if in answer, there was a flash of light, made even brighter as it diffused through the fog. Someone let out a strangled cry. A gray person-sized lump lay still on the grass. A second shape spread its wings, flew straight up, and disappeared into the fog.

"People are fighting out there!" Taylor said with a gasp. "I mean, fighting each other!"

"Give me a break," Silas groaned. "Are Summer and Winter *both* here?"

"Uh, you're the expert and everything," Taylor said, "but sounds pretty bad to me."

"Yeah, it's bad all right."

"Okay. Just so we're clear."

"Both sides are probably gunning for you, Taylor. So, new plan: I'll hold the front door. You find a place to hide and cover yourself in the thickest glamour you can. And take Jill with you. Got it?"

"No!" Taylor said. "We have obligations as Mr. du Marais's guests, don't we? I know I can't do much, but I'm sure as heck not going to run and hide when—"

There was another shriek outside, then a thud. Somebody hit the outside wall with a groan.

Ponderous footsteps shook the house. Silas peered out the window.

"It's Dingle!"

"From the Winter Court?"

"You know him?" Silas asked.

Taylor nodded. Now she looked out the window. The ten-foot-tall spriggan was tossing Summer Court fighters left and right. A shot rang out, and Dingle spun around and dropped to the ground.

"Taylor, you just aren't safe here."

"I'm not running away!"

Jill screamed. Taylor sprinted to the dining room.

"Incoming!" Jill called. She was staring into du Marais's cup, a look of terror in her eyes. Taylor wondered what her friend could see as she peered into the water. It mustn't have been pleasant.

There was a crash above them. Someone—or something—had landed on the roof.

"Carlos!" du Marais called.

"I'm on it, boss!" the fae shouted from the kitchen. Footsteps hurried up the back stairs.

"What was that?" Taylor asked.

"I don't know," Jill said. "Some kind of flying snake, I think." She gazed into the cup like it was a radar screen. "But here comes something else. Small, but dangerous. I can't describe it, but it feels very dangerous, whatever it is." She looked toward the French doors. "That way!"

All eyes followed Jill's. A gray shadow slipped across the bottom of the window glass. Du Marais pulled back the curtains.

A fox stared up at him, then glanced around the dining room. It scampered away just as the satyr threw the curtains shut.

"We better move," he said. "Miss Matthews is right, that beast could be dangerous. Our Kind can hop a ride in an animal, use them to spy things out from a safe distance."

Jill muttered something that might have been "Not just animals."

Something rapped the window—hard.

"Get down!" du Marais shouted. He and the two girls hit the floor as an explosion shook the house. Outside, the sky itself seemed to catch fire. Inside, the thunderous boom left everyone stunned.

Silas barged in. "What was that?"

"Hand grenade?" Lily suggested.

"Hand grenade?" Jill said. "Faeries are attacking the house with *hand grenades*?" She pulled herself up by the edge of the table.

"The house is practically magic-proof," Silas said. "Sometimes you've got to do things the hard way. If they can weaken the physical structure—"

As if on cue, a rock as big as a baseball sailed through the window. Shards of broken glass scattered everywhere.

"Everybody out!" Silas called. "They've broken through!"

But he had barely finished giving the order when a willowy, fair-haired figure dressed in smoky gray crashed into the middle of the room. In a single, graceful motion, he took du Marais down with a roundhouse kick.

It was Vesper, the same creepy fae they'd barely escaped in the bayou. He had ditched the sunglasses, but he still had his shotgun. He slammed the butt of it into Silas as the church grim lunged toward him. He slammed against the china cabinet and crumpled to the floor, nursing his still-tender left arm.

Jill clutched the cup in front of her. Water splashed everywhere.

Vesper was on her in half a second, but Silas had regained his feet and was already lunging with his knife. The nightwalker punched him in the jaw with his right hand while yanking the cup from Jill with his left. With a triumphant cackle, he dove through the shattered remains of the French doors.

Du Marais grabbed Vesper in a flying tackle, and the two crashed out onto the back porch. They rolled around, each struggling to best the other. In the commotion, Vesper lost track of the cup, and it rolled across the floor, down the steps, and onto the grass.

Jill was bent over Silas, trying to shake him awake.

Taylor eyed the cup. That was what this was all about, even though she still didn't know why. But if she could get away with it, she might be able to bargain with the Winters.

She bounded onto the lawn and scooped it up. Now, all she had to do was find the way back to the live oak, back to the burial mound and the Topside world.

No sooner had she set a sandaled foot on the grass than she was nearly bowled over by a flying body flung by an angry spriggan. Shotgun fire pierced the air. Somewhere, someone gasped in pain. Faerie hounds were barking, whispers in the fog. Taylor ducked and scrambled for the front yard, clutching the cup like a football.

She had to circle the mansion in the fog while staying as far away from the fighting as possible. It sounded like a much better plan in her head than it did in real life, but crouching there on the lawn, she didn't see any alternatives. She took a breath and charged to the left, keeping as close to the wall as she could.

Something grabbed hold of Silas's satchel, forcing Taylor to stop with a jerk. The momentum spun her around and left the satchel five feet away on the ground.

Vesper trained his shotgun on her. His silver-gray eyes bore into her.

"Just give me the cup, dearie, and nobody else gets hurt."

Taylor took a breath. She looked around for a way out, but she could barely see anything in the fog. She cradled the cup tighter.

There are some things a thirteen-year-old girl should not say, but Taylor said one of them, anyway.

Vesper lurched suddenly forward, his eyes rolling back in his head.

Behind him stood a Native American fae in jeans and a black tee shirt. The wispy residue of a blasting spell curled up from his outstretched hand. He gave her a wink and a sly half-smile. A head start?

A second later, he had transformed into an owl and taken flight.

Taylor didn't understand what the owl-man was up to, but she didn't have the time to analyze it. She dove for Silas's satchel, then spun around and started to run again.

Another two seconds, and she was rounding the corner and sprinting onto the front lawn. Any second, she knew her asthma was going to start acting up. And, of course, she had left her inhaler upstairs when she changed clothes.

Don't think about that, she told herself. *Just get out of here!*

Jill was springing down the front steps.

"Taylor!" she cried.

"Where are the others?"

"They went to get the servants, to get them out safely."

"Safely? What do you mean?"

As soon as Taylor asked, she saw the answer for herself. Thick, black smoke was spewing from an upstairs window. The mansion was on fire.

"We've got to get out of here," Taylor said. "Do you remember the way back to the live oak?"

Jill nodded and pointed over her left shoulder. "I'm pretty sure," she added.

Taylor sighed. Pretty sure would have to do. "Let's go!" she called. The two girls sprinted forward. Jill took the lead, but kept turning back to make sure Taylor wasn't falling too far behind.

"Go on! I'll catch up!"

But Jill only made it a few steps before a billowing mass of greenish smoke stopped her cold. She doubled over and acted like she was going to retch. A second later, Taylor smelled it, too.

"Augh! That's vile!" she said.

"Who farted?" Jill asked. And that was exactly what it smelled like. It was the most heart-stoppingly awful odor of flatulence Taylor had ever been forced to endure. She fell to her knees and clapped a hand over her nose. Tears welled up in her eyes.

"A dying elephant maybe?"

"I can't see!" Jill cried.

"Hold on," Taylor said. She tried to pull herself together. Her eyes burned, but they had to get moving. She got up and stumbled forward. The noxious vapor was starting to dissipate.

"Can you move?" she asked.

"Yeah," Jill said. "Give me a hand."

Before she could help Jill up, though, someone slammed into Taylor, and she went sprawling to the ground. The cup tumbled out of her grasp and across the lawn. She groaned in defeat as a dark, elfin shadow leaped over her and scampered after it.

"Ha!" the shadow exulted. Taylor looked up to see the African fae who had driven off the naked bear. His partner had called him Bacary. He wore a wide, white grin, and his eyes flashed eerie yellow in the semi-darkness.

"I thought you were on our side!" Taylor screamed.

Bacary only grinned and winked. He grabbed the cup and ran back the way Taylor had come. Jill was already running after him, wobbly but determined. Taylor sprung to her feet and tried to follow.

There were more blasts and the report of elf-shot. Taylor even saw a few fireballs getting lobbed this way and that. About a dozen fae skirmished on the lawn. The whole top of the mansion was engulfed in flames.

Something fell to the ground thirty feet in front of Taylor. At first, she thought it was some kind of ball. As she got closer, she realized it was moving.

"Mew."

It was a cat. Or rather, it was some sort of ghostly representation of a Siamese kitten. It was about the right size, but it shimmered when it moved like it was at least partly transparent. It stretched and yawned...and started to vibrate.

Another one, a Calico, fell ten or fifteen feet to the right. Taylor jumped over the first one as she caught up with Jill.

And then the first cat exploded. It wasn't a large explosion, but clear fluid flew everywhere, and it was loud and bright: a fiery, furry cataclysm that shook the ground and sent Jill, Taylor, and Bacary ducking for cover.

A similar ghostly beagle puppy fell near Jill, wagging its tail. Then another cat. Both cats and the dog began to vibrate. Bacary dodged and weaved as another couple of dogs fell in front of him.

The second cat exploded. The fae who had been darting across the lawn fell back to the trees. Taylor looked for cover as another handful of cats and dogs landed, rolled to a stop, and started to vibrate.

"Give me a freaking break!" Taylor said.

Bacary dodged a glowing Pomeranian puppy that struck the ground ten feet to one side. It was the cutest little dog Taylor had ever seen—and then it blew itself to bits and threw Bacary ten feet backward. When he got back up, it was in the form of a huge, black vulture. Grasping the cup in his talons, he took to the air.

Jill stopped to track the fae's movement. He weaved in the air, deftly avoiding further volleys of cats and dogs. On the ground, Taylor and Jill dodged a rain of fiery cuteness.

"There!" Taylor said, pointing over the back lawn. She panted hard, but so far, no asthma. "We better follow him!"

Jill nodded and took off. Whoever was responsible for the fuzzy, adorable inferno was backing off. Apparently, there were only so many exploding house pets available.

Taylor stood for a second with her hands on her knees, then bolted after Jill.

The back lawn was a scorched and pockmarked disaster area. The fog was starting to dissipate, but it had done its work.

Silas, Lily, and du Marais were nowhere in sight. A dog yipped in the distance. The vulture spun in slow circles over the lawn.

A crack of gunfire rang out, and the vulture dropped out of the sky and resumed human form as it hit the ground.

The shooter sprung out from the woods. It was a sandy-haired figure in camouflage pants and a tee shirt that said "The Wild Hunt – 1997."

It was Bob the changeling.

He smirked at Taylor as he jogged past her toward where Bacary had crash-landed.

"Oh, no you don't!" Taylor shouted and ran after him.

Jill overtook Taylor, but Bob still managed to get there first. He kicked Bacary in the face, then took three steps to where the cup had rolled away.

He turned his shotgun butt-down and raised it over his head, ready to smash the prize they had all been chasing.

Dingle slammed into him from behind. The two rolled on the grass, but Dingle grew to giant size and flung Bob away like a rag doll.

"Ha!" Dingle shouted. He lumbered toward the bowl.

Before he could get there, however, Jill dove for it. She snatched it away and started back around to the front of the mansion. Taylor stood facing Dingle, who was now shrinking to his usual five-five or so height. She took a deep breath and tried to imagine a veil of magical mist swirling around her, wrapping her like a blanket.

"*Stop!*" she called, and she threw as much presence into the word as she could manage.

Dingle did, in fact, stop. All the fight seemed to drain out of him with a single breath. But Taylor didn't wait to see how long the effect would last. She spun around and sprinted after Jill, around the corner, back onto the front lawn.

She rounded the mansion just as Jill went flailing to the ground. The shaft of a spear passed through her body—and then vanished into thin air.

She hit the ground with a thud and didn't move. She didn't move at all.

Taylor was at her side in a heartbeat, calling her name.

The fog was mostly gone.

The sun had set.

A light appeared, a glowing golden orb of faery fire in the hand of the cute blonde fae Taylor remembered from the bayou. Barbie's mean big sister, now decked out in blue whorls of war paint, a feathered headband, and leather arm braces.

Taylor started to rise to her feet.

"If you've hurt her, you sorry—"

She shushed Taylor. Only then did Taylor realize Barbie had recovered the cup.

"Finders keepers," she said as she skipped away.

Jill grunted and started to move. Taylor tried to coax her to sit up.

The blonde fae approached a dark-haired figure, tall and statuesque, who appeared out from of nowhere.

This woman smiled a broad, triumphant smile and accepted the cup from the hand of her underling. Her dark green gown whipped about in the breeze.

"Well done, Andred," she said.

Taylor helped Jill to her feet and glared at Dubessa Fairchild.

"What did you do to Jill?" she demanded.

"Simple elf-shot, child," Dubessa said. "She's only stunned."

Jill was, in fact, standing up by now. She looked groggy, and she continued to lean on Taylor for support, but she was shaking it off.

"Is that how you treat your goddaughter?"

Dubessa raised an eyebrow. "Goddaughter? Whatever do you mean, child?"

Taylor took a step back, pulling Jill with her.

"You...you're Jill's godmother, right? You've been helping her...helping us get here so you could get to that cup..."

"Taylor," Jill whispered, shaking her head. "That's not her."

The world started spinning. Taylor felt sweat trickle down her neck. Apart from the blazing mansion behind them, the lawn was silent. It was just Taylor and Jill and Dubessa and her minion, Barbie (though apparently her real name was Andred).

"I'm afraid you've confused me with someone else," Dubessa said.

"Someone like me, perhaps?" another woman said.

She had appeared from out of nowhere, just as silently as Dubessa. It wasn't blinking: more like she had been there all along under a heavy glamour. She was cold and beautiful, with jet-black hair and a thin, pale face. Her business suit was opalescent gray.

"Mara?" Taylor gasped. She had only met her once before, and only for a few minutes, but there was no mistaking her cold beauty, her piercing dark eyes.

Dubessa handed the cup back to Andred and raised her hands in a defensive posture. Swirls of energy coalesced around her palms. She was getting ready to blast.

"G-godmother?" Jill said.

"Wait," Taylor said. "*She's* your godmother?"

Mara Hellebore smiled and crossed her arms.

Chapter 27

The Satyr's Cup

A second hand grenade exploded above the mansion.

As soon as Silas heard Carlos shout "fire!" he turned to du Marais. "Get the others out," he said. "I'll see about Carlos."

He bolted toward the back stairs before du Marais could argue. As he bounded upstairs, he gathered up his rage, his sense of injustice, and began to focus it into a magical attack. The smell of smoke filled the second floor, and a thin, gray haze made Silas's eyes water.

They were outnumbered, outgunned, and their defenses were down. It was Bailly Hen all over, just on a smaller scale.

Not this time, Silas thought. He pushed forward despite the smoke.

At the end of the hallway, Carlos struggled against a door. Someone was trying to break through. Silas sprang to help him—but too late: the door exploded open.

A fae leaped into the hallway. He was tall and wiry, with reddish blond hair and a devilish grin. He pushed Carlos down and made a lunge toward Silas. The church grim repulsed him with a blast that sent him diving to the floor. The pulse of magic jetted over the intruder's head, though. It landed against the far wall, where it cracked the plaster.

Silas cursed. It would take time to build up his magical reserves for another blast—time he didn't have.

The fae once again lunged for him. This time, Silas shouldered into him and flung him to the floor. He used his skill and his lower center of gravity to his advantage. The two struggled, but Silas wasn't going to back down, especially against an opponent who had crossed a threshold unbidden and sacrificed most of his magic to do so.

The smoke in the hallway was getting thicker. The church grim backed the intruder into a guest bedroom. With another deft maneuver, he slammed the fae into—and through—the window.

But the intruder didn't fall to the ground. Rather, he transformed in a flash of light into a fiery, flaming serpent and soared into the sky.

A firedrake! Silas thought. *Just what we need.*

Silas looked around the room. Taylor's bag lay at the foot of the bed. He got an idea. He grubbled through the bag as quickly as he could and brought out Taylor's seeing stone. He hefted it in his hand. It was black and smooth and the perfect weight.

Now he dove out the window, grabbing the top windowsill and swinging himself up onto the outside wall of the house. He scrambled to the roof and spied the firedrake's location.

He was soaring downward toward the mansion, a living dive-bomber gathering magic for a single, fiery assault.

Silas grinned and sent the black stone hurtling. It struck square in the fae's flaming forehead. Rather than blazing into the mansion, he dropped unconscious onto the back lawn.

The smoke, however, was even thicker now, and Silas hadn't heard a peep out of Carlos since the firedrake took him out. Silas called his name. No answer.

He slipped through the window and barged into the hallway. Carlos was coughing and leaning on an antique hall table.

"Let's go!" Silas called. He came up underneath the satyr's chef and offered his shoulder for support. Carlos braced both hands against Silas's shoulders, with Silas reaching up to steady his arms.

The heat was nearly as oppressive as the smoke. They had to get out now if they were going to get out at all. And it was only a matter of time before the firedrake came to and attacked again.

They half-stumbled down the stairs, through the kitchen, and out the side door onto the lawn.

Du Marais, Lily, and Richard were dodging an oncoming attacker in a Wild Hunt tee shirt. Du Marais held both hands toward him, palms outstretched, and blasted the attacker in the chest, who then fell face-first to the ground. The satyr's blast bought Lily and Richard time to reach a gazebo at the edge of the lawn. Du Marais took charge of Carlos, and the remainder of the group reached the platform.

Silas began to summon glamour. If he could keep the gazebo hidden, they might have a chance. But there was a problem.

"Where's Jill?" he asked.

"She thought she saw Taylor on the lawn," du Marais said. "She just took off."

"You've got to stay low," Silas told the satyr. As he spoke, he began to weave his magic around the area. "You're the target, you understand? We've got to get you clear of the area."

"I will defend my home!"

"First we need to sort out who's here—and what they want." Silas paced across the open platform, gazing upon the fog-covered lawn.

"Somebody's after your scrying cup," he said. "Whoever it is cast that suggestion at dinner to confuse us."

"And sent in that confounded elf," du Marais added. Silas nodded.

"But we've also got some help out there, somewhere. This fog is keeping everybody buttoned up wherever they're hiding. I hear a lot of movement, but I think that's just pishoguery. There's a spriggan on the grounds. Then the elf, the firedrake that broke in upstairs, and the one you just took out. There aren't too many more than that, I'd bet."

The satyr peered into the fog. "I can't see a blasted thing!"

"Call it a blessing," Silas said. "If you can't see anything, neither can they."

"So, what happens when the fog breaks?"

"We'll cross that bridge when we—"

An explosion shook the gazebo. Everyone braced themselves against support posts or fell back onto the wooden benches that lined the structure.

There was a second explosion, followed by a young girl's angered shout.

"Taylor!" Silas said. He traded glances with du Marais.

"Find her," he said. "I'll take care of my people."

Silas sprinted onto the lawn and into the path of a cocker spaniel puppy that rolled and frolicked on the grass. It didn't look entirely natural. It was a magical construct of some kind, and as soon as Silas spied it, it started to vibrate.

This can't be good, he thought. Instinctively, he leaped over the dog and kept running. A second later, a third explosion knocked him off his feet.

He started to call Taylor's name, but dodged instead as a vibrating English tabby dropped out of the sky and practically into his arms.

He spun around and dove back toward the gazebo. The fog was starting to clear, which only gave him a clearer view of the cuddly conflagration dropping from the sky.

Another cat fell onto the roof of the gazebo. It stalked around the edge of the roof.

"Get out!" Silas called.

Du Marais helped Carlos out of the gazebo and toward the woods as Lily and Richard dove for cover. The structure exploded in a rain of splinters and cat hair.

A chunk of wood slammed into the back of Lily's head. Du Marais called her name as he spun around.

"Get to the woods!" Silas called. There was no time to see to Lily's injury. He hoped du Marais could take care of her.

They weaved through a barrage of exploding house pets on a desperate race for the woods.

A Welsh corgi trotted into Silas's path. He kicked it out of his way, and it blew up in mid-air. The church grim tumbled forward.

"Hurry!" he yelled.

He put his head down and barged ahead at full speed. He only made it a few yards, however, before running into something solid. He staggered backward.

The spriggan was braced against his charge, shoulder down, eyes straight ahead.

Du Marais was suddenly at Silas's side.

"Dingle!" he shouted. "What's ?"

Silas was nonplussed. "You know him?" He debated rushing the spriggan, but thought better of it. He glanced in du Marais's direction. The satyr stood there, dumbfounded. He glanced at Lily. Richard was with her, wrapping her head in a strip of cloth torn from Carlos's chef's apron.

"Who do you think alerted him to your quest?" the spriggan asked with a shrug. "Or provided the wherewithal for him to bring you here?"

Silas squeezed the grip of his knife. He didn't know what else to do.

"You gave him my name?" Silas said.

"And Miss Smart's. Oh, and a bit of your hair. A little trophy from our meeting in the graveyard two nights ago."

Silas instinctively drew a hand across the back of his head. He backed away from the satyr and trained his blade first on him, then on Dingle. Richard had managed to get Lily and Carlos upright. The three of them were wobbling toward the tree line, but more spriggans were converging on them.

"I don't appreciate being lied to," du Marais said.

"When did I lie?" Dingle said with a grin. "When I met with you this morning, I told you a sídhe girl and her two friends were heading your way, and that they were sure to bring you a good deal of grief. I told you they were being followed by others who meant you harm, and offered the service of the Winter Court of Arradherry to, ah, deal with the situation."

Du Marais gestured toward the burning mansion and the pockmarked lawn. "Do you call this 'dealing with the situation?' My girlfriend's badly injured. Not to mention my servant."

"Without our fog cover, the enemy would have eaten you alive. As it is, everyone gets out alive—and with only a bit of property damage."

"And the fuzzy little cataclysm?" Silas asked.

"Our allies tend to have a flare for the dramatic, I'm afraid."

"Allies?"

"Yes. Speaking of which, it's time we met them, don't you think?"

Dingle signaled to the spriggans guarding Lily, Richard, and Carlos. They escorted the three away—one of them had to carry Lily—while Dingle and one of his lieutenants manhandled Silas and du Marais around to the front of the smoking hull of the mansion.

The scene caused Silas's heart to sink.

Jill was slumped over Taylor's shoulder. The two girls stood between two dark-haired women. One of them had two attendants at her side: a dark-skinned man with a pointed beard and a blonde woman in war paint, holding a spear. Silas recognized the other woman as Mara Hellebore. If the Chief Matron of the Winter Court deigned to make a personal appearance, the worst was yet to come.

"Y-you're Jill's godmother?" Taylor said. Mara took a subtle bow.

"Brother Mike!" Silas cursed.

"Godmother?" the other woman asked. "What is she talking about, Mara?"

"Nothing for you to worry about, Dubessa, dear," Mara said.

Dubessa? Silas thought. Now he knew who the other woman was: Dubessa Fairchild from the Summer Court.

Waves of presence nearly bowled Silas over. The two sídhe women were bearing down on each other like they meant business.

"Perhaps you'd like to explain it to me?" Dubessa said. Her stance was tense, guarded. Mara had her off balance.

Mara and Dubessa, flanked by her attendants, circled slowly around Taylor and Jill. Taylor was nervously humming a song Silas didn't recognize.

Dingle and his lieutenant took up positions behind their Chief Matron. Both women, Silas noticed, were gathering magical energy, getting ready to blast.

He struggled against Dingle's grip.

From somewhere in the woods came the high-pitched gekkering of a fox.

"You don't trust me, Dubessa? And after I did all this work to bring you a gift?"

Dubessa stood still. Suddenly aware of the cup in her underling's hands, she stretched out her hand. She raised the cup while conjuring an orb of golden faery fire by which to see it clearly.

At the same time, Mara nodded to Dingle. The spriggan grabbed du Marais by the collar and threw him to the ground at Dubessa's feet, nearly bowling Taylor over in the process.

Dubessa stood there, open-mouthed, as her fingers traced the bold, angular lines of the letters that rimmed the cup. Wordlessly, eyes wide, she rotated the cup to show Mara the writing.

Mara simply smiled.

Dubessa's attention was now captured by the satyr kneeling before her. She looked as if she had seen a ghost.

"L-Lorcan?" she muttered in disbelief. "Impossible...I..."

Silas squinted at the cup. It was dark, but his eyes were used to seeing things at night.

"By oak, ash, and thorn...," Silas whispered. He gazed at du Marais, then back at Dubessa.

"What?" Taylor said. "What's going on?"

"*Mongruad*," Silas said, reading the word on the cup. Why hadn't he paid attention to the writing before? "It's Gaelic. It means..." Silas fell silent, dumbfounded.

"What?" Taylor insisted. "What does it mean?"

"It means..."

"It means 'Redmane,'" Dubessa said. Her voice was weak, distracted. She sounded completely overcome with shock.

"Redmane!" Taylor said. "As in Anya Redmane?"

Dubessa nodded. Her eyes fell once again on du Marais.

"How do you come by this cup?" she asked. Her voice betrayed deep emotion, but it was once again finding its strength. "Speak truly, satyr. I will tolerate no deception, do you understand?"

Silas remembered what the satyr had told them earlier: the cup used to belong to his father. His mind darted ahead. He didn't like where it took him.

"My daddy passed on that cup when he left us," he said.

Silas's heart pounded wildly. He struggled once more against Dingle's iron grasp, but the spriggan was far too strong.

"Your father was Lorcan Redmane," Dubessa said. The faery fire that circled above her head grew brighter and redder.

"My father's name was Leatherleaf. Rossa Leatherleaf."

"Don't lie to me, boy," Dubessa said. Her voice simmered with barely controlled rage. "Your father was Lorcan Redmane. You have his eyes. His jaw. You may have known him by a different name, but there is no hiding whose son you are." She hefted the cup. "And here is the proof."

"Who's...?" Taylor started. Before she could finish her question, her mouth formed a silent "Oh" as she remembered the conversation on the train. She shifted uneasily, trying to shield Jill from Dubessa and from Mara in turns.

"A boy who should have died," Dubessa said. "Seventy years ago."

"He was your uncle, dear," Mara said. Her silky voice was unfazed if not positively amused. She was reveling in every detail of the conversation. "The son of Anya Redmane, consigned to the teind to pay for the sins of his house."

"And yet..." Dubessa turned toward du Marais. The magic she had gathered up sent a shiver through Silas's body. The hairs on his neck stood up straight. "He apparently survived."

She furrowed her brow as she gazed at Mara. "You knew."

"Not at first," Mara confessed. "But soon enough. Waiting for the right time to tell the world has been excruciating, I must say."

"But...how?"

"I must plead ignorance of many of the details," Mara said.

"I will know the truth!" Dubessa said, her voice now smoldering with rage. She lifted her head to the sky and shouted, "Present yourself!"

"It's over!" Mara shouted into the woods. "I suggest you do as Dubessa asks!"

There was silence broken only by crickets.

Mara turned toward the woods. Everyone else followed her gaze.

A red fox ambled into view.

"It's time we all heard this sordid tale," Mara said. "It is well overdue, I must confess. But there is no time like the present."

"Indeed," Dubessa said.

The fox warily approached the circle.

"A fox?" Taylor said. "I don't understand. What...?"

"Why don't you ask her?" Dubessa said.

Taylor glanced at Silas with questioning eyes. The church grim merely wagged his head. Taylor turned again toward Dubessa.

"Don't be shy," Dubessa addressed the fox. "We all want to hear this."

"I must agree with Dubessa," Mara said, her eyes flashing, her voice exploding with giddy delight. "I'm itching to know."

Silas braced himself.

"What does the fox say?"

The fox growled. It stood up on its hind legs as it began to grow. It's limbs stretched and bent into human proportions while its narrow muzzle melted into its face.

In a second, the fox was gone, replaced by a tall, red-headed woman with regal bearing and eyes ablaze with fury and fear.

Anya Redmane joined the circle.

Chapter 28

Paying the Piper

Taylor's eyes opened wide as the woman unfolded from her animal shape and stood before them. The fox she kept running into since they arrived in Louisiana was Anya Redmane! The Chief Matron of the Summer Court of Arradherry stood tall and defiant, but looked exhausted even so.

She and Jill were trapped in a triangle of some the most powerful fae in North America. She wasn't the least bit encouraged by the fact that two of them were her grandmothers.

To one side stood Anya Redmane, bold yet weary. To the other, Mara Hellebore, arms crossed. Taylor could practically feel the confidence she exuded—and which had very little to do with the glamour she projected.

At the third point of the triangle was Dubessa Fairchild, who seemed to be the only one of the three who didn't know what was going on. From the look on her face, Taylor judged she didn't like the possibilities in the least.

Vesper slipped out of the shadows. The nightwalker's expression reminded Taylor of a wild animal in a trap. He was angry...and afraid. He circled at some distance from the three sídhe Matrons, unsure where to stand. He kept in a low crouch and swayed while giving Anya suspicious sideways glances.

"Y-you...?" Taylor struggled to put her thoughts into words.

"Is there anything you'd like to say, Anya?" Mara asked. "Anything at all?" A smile brightened her moonlit face. It wasn't the kind of friendly smile children around the world were likely to sing about.

Taylor kept turning, dragging Jill along with her, trying not to present her back to anyone for more than a few seconds. Something told her magic was about to start flying. She wasn't in love with the idea of getting caught in the crossfire.

Jungle princess Barbie kept her eyes glued to Dubessa. She held the shaft of her spear so tightly her knuckles had gone white. The eyes of the African fae beside her began to glow.

"Yes, Anya," Dubessa said. Magic crackled around her, making her whole body shimmer. She stared daggers into Anya. "I for one want to hear it."

"This is about the massacre, isn't it?" Taylor whispered. "Bailly Hen, right?"

"Indeed," Dubessa hissed.

"Lorcan... Lorcan was sentenced to death...to pay for the crimes of the Summer Court. Silas called it a teind."

"They carried him away," Dubessa said, shuddering. "They carried him away, along with my Illuna. I *saw* him carried away!"

Taylor gasped and almost let Jill topple over. The pieces of the puzzle were coming together.

"She gave them a fetch instead," she said. Taylor didn't know much about fetches, but Danny had once told her the basics. A well-made fetch could be indistinguishable from a real person— at least for a while. "Lorcan got away..." She looked at du Marais, now slack-jawed and obviously frightened. "Had a kid..."

"Your cousin," Mara offered. "Isn't it a small world?"

Don't say that! Taylor thought.

"He was only eight years old," Anya whispered, head bowed.

"You know the Eldritch Law!" Dubessa shouted. As she spoke, she raised her right hand, then, jerked it down while making a fist as if grabbing something out of the air. She thrust her hand toward Anya, and a shimmering distortion arced toward her.

The Chief Matron of Summer staggered backward two steps. She fell to one knee with a gasp of pain.

Vesper sucked in a breath. He shook his head and muttered a single word: "Oath-breaker." He looked toward Dubessa.

Dubessa took two steps toward Anya. "You know the sanctity of the teind is inviolable!"

Only Mara's restraining hand kept Dubessa from blasting the Chief Matron again. Instead, she turned toward Vesper.

"You served Mrs. Redmane in good faith, nightwalker," she said through gritted teeth. "You have no part in her guilt."

The elf bowed and turned his back on the circle. As he walked away, he veiled himself in shadows and vanished without a sound.

"You sent him away, didn't you?" Taylor said.

"I had no choice," Anya said.

"She sent him to New Cephalonia," Mara explained. "Changed his name. Shielded his identity in a web of pishoguery."

"Except for this," Dubessa said, staring at the cup.

"For a while," Anya said. Her words came in halting fits between sniffles. "We would use it to talk."

"Then he learned what you did. Didn't he, Anya?" Dubessa seethed. "He learned that his own mother had become an oath-breaker!"

Anya only nodded.

"You saved his life," Taylor said, bewildered. "Yeah, sure, you broke the law. But the law is full of crap! Nobody should have to sacrifice their children just to satisfy some twisted idea of honor!"

"Silence, child!"

Dubessa turned on her with venom in her voice.

"Have some respect for our ways—even if you have been raised by deathlings!"

Mara threw back her head laughed out loud. "You Summers are always prattling on about law and tradition, aren't you, Dubessa? But now the truth is evident for all to see." She gestured toward Anya. "Look at the high esteem in which you hold our most sacred rites."

"She doesn't speak for the Summer Court," Dubessa said. She glared at Anya with murder in her eyes. "Not anymore."

She clenched her fists. Taylor stepped back. Jill gasped. She saw it too, then: the swirl of magical energy gathering around Dubessa.

Before she could let loose her blast, Anya raised her arms in a defensive gesture. A heartbeat later, a wave of magic surged from Dubessa and glanced off Anya's invisible shield.

Anya then let fly a flurry of sparks and loud, shrieking, fiery streamers. In the confusion, she ran for the woods, covering herself with a veil of invisibility.

"Get her!" Dubessa shouted.

Bacary leaped and became a vulture in midair. His girlfriend sprang in the direction Anya had run.

All this time, Taylor realized, Mara had been content simply to observe.

"You did this," Taylor said.

"Of course."

"You arranged for us to come looking for Mr. du Marais's cup. You didn't want us to steal it. You just wanted Dubessa to find it. You wanted her to discover the truth about Lorcan Redmane."

"Didn't I just say as much?" Mara gave her a subtle smirk. "I don't believe you're as bright as people say you are."

"But Dingle..." Silas said. "Dingle said Cornstack had his sights on Taylor. He tried to recruit me to kill her!"

"He recruited you to *take care* of her," Mara said. Dingle chuckled. "And I must say, you've done an admirable job."

Silas struggled against Dingle's iron grip, but it was hopeless. He spat a curse at Mara. She tittered politely.

At last, she addressed du Marais.

"I have no quarrel with you, satyr," she said. "But I cannot speak for the Summer Court...or for those who lost loved ones at Bailly Hen. You're free to go. Or stay. It really doesn't matter to me."

Du Marais still looked like he'd gotten the wind knocked out of him. In the past few minutes, he had learned that everything he thought he knew about where he came from and who his parents were was a lie, an illusion. Taylor could relate.

"Where are my servants? Where is Lily?"

"Safe," Mara said. "Mr. Maywhistle can take you to them if you like."

He glanced at Taylor—at his cousin. He looked unsure what to do.

"It's okay," Taylor said. "Take care of your people." Get out while you can, she meant.

Du Marais nodded. Mara nodded to the spriggan who guarded him. The two removed themselves from the circle.

"You are free to go as well, my dear," Mara told Taylor. "You and your hobgoblin have proven...quite useful."

"I am nobody's hob!" Silas sputtered.

"Only me and Silas?" Taylor said. "What about Jill?"

"Ah." Mara grinned. "My goddaughter and I have some unfinished business."

Jill shivered despite the sweltering heat.

"The two of you are excused. Jill will be coming with me."

Jill's head was finally clear. She eased herself off of Taylor's shoulder, finally confident she could stand up on her own, but Taylor wouldn't let go of her arm.

"What do you mean, she's coming with you?" Taylor said.

"We've made a bargain. I've kept my part of it. It is time for Jill to honor hers."

"Now, wait a minute!" Jill said. "I'm not going anywhere!" She pulled her arm free from Taylor's grasp and squared her shoulders.

"*Do not challenge me,*" Mara said. The words hit Jill like waves in the ocean. She averted her eyes. She wondered if she should bow or even fall on her knees.

"I'm sorry," she squeaked.

Taylor, however, was not bowed. "Cut that out!" she demanded. "You've got no right to take her anywhere!"

"Right? Oh, child, I have every right." Mara seemed to grow larger. At the least, she was more imposing. Jill didn't know if it was faery magic or just her godmother's natural charisma. Either way, her voice was electric.

"I awakened her Second Sight. I protected her on her quest—and through her, you and your hobgoblin as well."

"You did that for your own sake, not hers!"

"She received food from my own hand, Taylor. She has bought in to our world—and of her own free will."

She's right, Jill thought. *It's my own fault.* Then she wondered where that thought came from. Certainly not from her! Mara's magic was twisting her mind, making her compliant.

Are you inside my head, Godmother?

There was no answer, which Jill took as a good sign, all things considered.

"And now, you're just going to carry her off?" Taylor said. "Make her your slave?"

"Not slave, child. I'm not a barbarian."

"But you want to take me away," Jill managed to say.

"Our Kind occasionally stumble upon Topsiders that promise to prove useful to us. If you had read your Spenser, you would know the relationship often proves beneficial to both parties." She spread her arms wide.

"It is a great honor to become a knight of the house of Hellebore. Do you think I've given you power, Jill? You don't know the half of it. I can make your wildest dreams come true."

Mara gestured. Jill's green dress, now dirty and torn, morphed into a beautiful ball gown. At the same time, glittering silver sparkles fashioned themselves into earrings, a necklace, and silver-studded sandals. Her hair became perfectly coifed and set with priceless emeralds.

"There are advantages to having a godmother, you know," Mara said. "Don't let prejudice blind you to that. Winter isn't only barren cruelty. It is also hot chocolate or a warm fire in the fireplace. Sledding and building snowmen in the park. College football. Presents under the Christmas tree."

"I don't believe in Santa Claus."

Mara chuckled. "But you take my meaning. As my chosen knight, you will have unimaginable power."

She gestured again. Jill's ball gown transformed into a black and silver surcoat over a coat of silver mail. A sheathed sword appeared out of nowhere, strapped to a belt around her waist. A shield rose out of the ground and sprung to her left arm.

"I thought knights had to be men," Jill said.

"Deathling language can be quite limited," Mara shrugged. "Technically, you will be my *padam*, my right hand. But don't worry, you'll have plenty of time to grow into the role. Centuries, in fact."

Once again she gestured. Jill's armor and weapons vanished, replaced by khaki pants, a red polo shirt, and a name badge: "Jill. Trainee."

"You stand on the verge of greatness, Jill. That is what I promised. I can be very patient. But it *is* time to go."

Jill struggled not to kneel at her godmother's feet. Her mind was fuzzy. Probably the lingering effects of being elf-shot. She wasn't sure about any of this, but if Mara said it was okay....

"*No!*" Taylor yelled. "*Jill, don't move!*"

Jill snapped to attention.

"Wait. What?"

"She's not going with you!"

"Don't defy me, Taylor," Mara said. "You cannot win."

"Taylor," Jill said. Putting the words together in her mind was a challenge. She only half believed it—but that was enough. "I...I want to go home."

Mara huffed a disgusted sigh. "Then go, if that is your preference."

Jill started. Was it really that easy?

"But first I'll take back what I've given you." She took a deep breath. As she did, she raised her hand, palm forward.

Jill sensed her body growing lighter. A weight was being removed. It was exhilarating—for a second. Then she felt tightness in her chest. Her skin seemed to dry out and shrink against her bones and muscles. It was like life itself was being sucked out of her.

She stumbled onto Taylor's shoulder.

"Jill, what's happening?"

She shuddered. A dark cloud loomed over her consciousness. All the color seemed to drain from the world. All the sensations. All the joy.

Her throat was parched. She was tired. Nothing mattered. Not anymore. Everything was dull, dead.

"You've grown accustomed to magic flowing through you," Mara said in a low growl. "This is what it's like when it gets taken away."

Jill started to shake with fear, and more than fear. A sense of desperation assaulted her. She was falling into a bottomless pit of gloom.

And it was all her fault.

"N-no."

"This is what your pathetic life will be like till the end of your days, child."

"Jill! Stand up, girl. Don't pass out on me!"

"Your contract has come due, Jill. Will you honor it...or not?"

Jill collapsed in a sobbing heap on the ground. She gasped for breath. She struggled to find in her heart a reason to keep on living. Taylor bent over her, urging her to hold on. She could barely make out the words.

"This is your last chance," Mara said. "I will be paid what I am due."

She screamed. The despair, the emptiness, was unbearable.

"No!" Taylor shouted. Jill pounded the ground. How could this keep getting worse? She wanted to die.

"No!" Taylor shouted again. "You don't have to do this!"

"Don't I?"

Jill wiped at her tears, but they kept coming. Taylor stood up. All Jill could see was her sandaled feet.

For several long seconds, the only sounds were Jill's gasping breaths and the crickets in the woods.

"No, you don't," Taylor said. She expelled another breath. "I'll pay."

A Deal with the Devil

The reactions were sudden and stark.

Silas shouted "No!" as he strained against Dingle's grasp.

Dingle, stunned, whispered "Danu" and almost lost his hold on Silas.

Jill shook her head and croaked Taylor's name.

Mara took a step backward. Her eyes wide, and a wide grin spread across her face. She was the only one who seemed happy with Taylor's proposal.

"Don't do it, Taylor!" Silas shouted. Bargaining with the sídhe was a crapshoot at best. At worst...he didn't want to think about it.

It was obvious, however, that Mara *was* thinking about it. She lowered her hand. Jill breathed easily. She didn't move, however. Buying in was easy. Silas had never known of anybody buying out, and now he knew why.

"You are prepared to pay your friend's debt?" Mara asked in her silkiest voice.

"Sports teams buy out players' contracts all the time."

"Jill is a witch, not an athlete."

"Doesn't matter. I'd rather she be on my team than yours."

Taylor, just shut up! Silas thought.

"You agree to feed her with your own magical energies? To kindle her gifts? To see to her training as I would have done?"

Taylor started to speak.

She took a deep breath.

She nodded. "As soon as I learn how."

"And in return?"

Another long pause.

"Once Jill is trained and fed and whatever...you can come for me."

"I cannot take you on as my knight," Mara explained. "Knighthood is only bestowed upon deathlings. You're... overqualified."

Silas sighed with relief.

Taylor slumped her shoulders.

She lifted her head toward Mara. Silas could read the growing fury in her eyes. She threw back her right foot and slowly pivoted so she faced Jill head-on and turned her left shoulder to the Chief Matron. Her right hand slipped quietly into Silas's bag. What was she up to?

"I'm not going to let you take my friend," she said.

"So you say," Mara said. "I must admit, though, that your offer intrigues me."

Jill pulled herself up to her knees. "Taylor, you don't have to do this."

"Well?" Taylor said.

Mara swayed slightly, comfortably.

"I'm prepared to let you have her in exchange for proper consideration."

"Taylor!" Silas growled through gritted teeth.

"Captain Dingle, kindly do something with the hobgoblin."

Dingle pulled Silas off the ground and slapped a hand over his mouth.

"I'm listening," Taylor said. "What do you want?"

Mara smiled broadly. "A favor."

"A favor."

"To be performed at a time of my choosing. Something it will be fully within your power to do."

Taylor gulped. "I see."

"And you will have no right to refuse me. Absolutely none. Are we clear?"

Silas squirmed and tried to bite Dingle's hand.

"Are we clear?" Mara's tone was hard and cold as ice.

"Taylor, don't," Jill said.

Taylor nodded.

"Say it."

She took another glance at Jill, straining to stand up. Silas could see that both girls were shivering. Taylor took a deep breath.

"In exchange for Jill's contract, I promise to do you a favor. You decide what it is and when you want me to do it." She bit her lip. "I'll do whatever you ask."

Mara arched an eyebrow. "And...?"

"I so swear...by my own true name."

Mara bowed deeply and flashed another brilliant smile. "Well, it has certainly been a pleasure doing business with you."

"Drop dead."

"And now, it seems my work here is done. I will be seeing you in due time, Taylor. Of that you may be certain." She bowed again and turned to Dingle. "Captain, the other two are no longer useful to me. Please be sure and kill them before you leave."

Silas growled and kicked. Dingle jerked to attention.

"What?" Taylor gasped.

"Chief Matron...," Dingle said. "Are you sure...?"

"Quite sure. Now, hurry up. My husband will be expecting us."

"You promised Jill her freedom!" Taylor shouted.

"I merely transferred my obligations toward her onto you, dear. If you want her and your other little friend to go free, that's now your responsibility. It certainly isn't mine. Dingle, if you please?"

Dingle sighed. "Yes, Chief Matron."

"No!" Taylor yelled. She lunged forward, putting her whole body behind it. In her right hand was a small leather satchel. Silas recognized it at once, recognized the open plastic bottle inside, and kicked even harder against Dingle's knees.

From the bottle spewed a fine black powder. It jetted across the distance between Taylor and Mara.

Mara screamed and clutched at her eyes as soon as the iron filings struck her face. She tried to blast Taylor, but sent the spell bending wildly into the night.

Silas felt Dingle's grasp loosen and took his chance. He wrenched his body free from the spriggan's hold, tumbled to the ground, and came up sprinting toward Taylor and Jill.

"This way!" he yelled. He didn't have to say it twice: Jill and Taylor were already on their way toward the edge of the lawn.

Silas looked ahead. Only then did he realize he didn't know where the portal was that would take them back to the burial mound and, hopefully, to safety.

Mara was still spewing profanities. Dingle had grown to giant size and was quickly gaining on them with earth-shaking footsteps.

"That way," Jill said, pointing.

"You sure?" Silas said.

Jill nodded. "There's a kind of shimmer. That's got to be it."

"Then get out of here. Now! I've got a spriggan to take care of."

He pushed the girls forward while he drew his knife and turned to face Dingle.

"Come on, you poxy oaf! Are you ready for a rematch?"

He scrambled beneath the spriggan, slashing at his legs. Dingle roared and spun around.

"Let's go!" Taylor called. She dared one last glance over her shoulder. Mara was stalking toward them. Her face was red and splotchy and streaked with what looked like black soot, but which Taylor knew was a fae's worst nightmare: iron.

As the girls sped toward the portal, she imagined the full-face brain freeze Mara was getting. She hoped it would slow her down enough for them to get away.

So far, her plan was working. But they had to make it out of the Wonder—and soon.

"This is it," Jill said.

"Where?"

"All over. It's like this whole field is thick with magic."

Taylor couldn't see anything, but she had to trust what Jill was telling her. She settled herself down enough to evoke her true name. She raised a single hand, like a conductor at the head of an orchestra, and a sparkling swirl of dust rose around her.

"Ready?" she asked.

"Let's get out of this place."

They stepped through the ring and arrived in the empty field with the burial mound. Taylor spun slowly around.

"Where's the church?"

"What?"

"There was a church around here. Remember? I can't see it in the dark."

"That way!" Jill called. Taylor started running. "At least, I think it was that way!"

Girl can see magic but she's got no *sense of direction.*

Then Taylor caught sight of the steeple, just where she remembered it.

"Hurry up!" she yelled. For once, Taylor was outpacing Jill. She hung back, though. If she couldn't protect her friend, this whole adventure was a waste of time.

As she turned back to offer Jill her hand, she saw Mara emerge from the portal.

The two girls ran as fast as they could. They threaded their way through a thin strip of trees that separated the field from the churchyard.

If they were lucky, Mara wouldn't be able to blink with a face full of iron filings.

They emerged on the grounds of an old country church. Taylor gazed upwards—and groaned.

"Where's the bell tower?"

The church had a tall, narrow steeple. Too narrow for a church bell.

Mara bellowed with rage as she charged toward them, rubbing her tear-streaked eyes on her sleeve.

Taylor grabbed Jill by the shoulders. "Where's the stinking bell tower?"

"Look behind you!"

She spun around. Beside the church was a small open structure, just big enough to shade a big brass church bell from the elements.

"Don't move!" Mara thundered.

Taylor backed away.

"I said, 'Don't move!'" A crackle of lightning sizzled through the air, barely missing Taylor as it harmlessly struck the side of the church house. Jill shrieked and hit the deck.

The building was undamaged. Mara wasn't firing on all her magical cylinders. She probably had enough cylinders to burn an average thirteen-year-old girl into a crispy critter, though.

The Chief Matron of Winter stalked toward Taylor.

"You try my patience, child." The wind picked up. It whipped Mara's hair.

"You got what you want!" Taylor said. "Leave Jill alone!"

"That is not your decision to make." She produced a dagger from inside her jacket.

Taylor only had a couple of seconds. She bounded toward the church bell. It had a long handle on one side topped by a big brass ball. Taylor gritted her teeth and threw her weight onto the handle.

The bell creaked and swayed.

"Get away from there!" Mara called. She gestured as if to unleash a blast of magic, but it fizzled in her palm.

"No chance, Grandma," Taylor said. She heaved the handle upward and dragged it down again with all her strength.

The bell tolled a rich, resonant note. Taylor felt suddenly nauseated. Mara groaned.

She gritted her teeth and rang the bell again. She could feel the undertones coursing through her body. She started to swoon.

Mara had dropped to her knees.

She grabbed the brass ball. One more ring.

She felt sick to her stomach.

Taylor wanted to ring the bell once more, but all she could do was hang on to keep her footing.

With some effort, she focused her eyes on Jill who was now standing over an unconscious Mara. She tried to tell Jill to get out of there, but she couldn't find the strength to speak.

She stumbled to her knees.

Everything went black.

"Please God please God…"

"Back up. Give her some air."

"Can I do anything? Would clapping my hands help?"

"What?"

"I don't know! I'm new at all this, okay?"

Taylor felt something cold and wet on her lips. Someone was offering her a drink of water. She was lying on grass. She could smell the pungent aroma of flowers.

"Is she going to be okay?"

"I ain't sure yet, but I think so. You better sit down. If your buddy says you got elf-shot, you're gonna need to rest for a while."

"Buddy's name is Silas."

"Pleased to meet you, Silas. I'm Danny."

Danny? Here?

"Taylor? Are you all right?"

She opened her eyes. An orb of faery fire made her blink, but even in the semi-darkness she made out the curly hair and pointed ears.

"Danny."

"How do you feel? Can you move?"

She tried to sit up, but her stomach rebelled at the idea.

Her head hurt. She wasn't sure where she was. The last thing she remembered was…

Taylor gasped. "Mara!"

"Gone," Jill said. Despite what Danny said, she was nudging in to see Taylor. "We got away."

"The spriggan chased me as far as the burial mound," Silas added from somewhere beyond Taylor's field of vision. "When I heard the bell ring, I knew you two were in trouble."

"The bell got Dingle, too?"

"I wish!"

"He must have been too far away," Jill said. "And by the time Silas and I got to you, Mara was waking up, too. She didn't look too good, but she was mad as a hornet."

"And you fought them both off?"

"Didn't have to," Silas said. "Thanks to Danny here."

The pooka grinned from ear to ear.

Jill wore an expression of pure awe.

"It was...I don't even know how to describe it." She shook her head as if she couldn't believe what had happened. "There was this loud noise. Some kind of...polka band, I guess. Then all of a sudden, there were flashes of light—every color of the rainbow... I think I saw exploding pumpkins... And then came the stampede..."

"Chickens everywhere," Silas said. "I thought we were goners. Then *this* guy appears out of nowhere starts calling for Taylor."

Taylor's mouth dropped open. She tried once more to sit up.

"You set loose a stampede...of *chickens*...on Mara Hellebore?"

"I noticed a chicken farm on my way in," he said with a devilish smile. "It's pretty easy to rile up a chicken. And all I really needed to do was keep Mrs. Hellebore and her henchman busy while I got you three to safety."

"From now on, you're in charge of distractions," Taylor said. She looked around. She was surrounded by a sea of huge marble boxes. Over Danny's shoulder she caught a glimpse of an angel statue.

"We're in New Orleans," Jill said. "The cemetery I told you all about. Silas figured it would be a good place to stop and hunker down for a while."

"A short while," Silas said. "Your godmother knows about this place, after all. Once she's back on her feet, we'd best be long gone."

"You were all three pretty banged up," Danny commented.

"What time is it?"

"Past midnight," Danny said. "Are you hungry? I can go get you something."

She shook her head. "Maybe later. I could use an aspirin, though."

"No problem, Taylor. I'll be back as soon as I can."

"Wait," Taylor said. It was all coming back to her now. She wiped away a tear as she looked first at Jill, then at Silas. "What about Mara? She's won, hasn't she?"

"Big time," Silas said. "Mrs. Redmane has been disgraced. The best she can hope for is banishment from Arradherry. And since she's been the Chief Matron for about 150 years, that's bound to throw the whole Summer Court into chaos."

"Perfect time for Winter to make a move," Danny said. "Is that what you're thinking?"

Silas grunted.

"Mara orchestrated the whole thing. She waited decades for just the right time to expose Évastre du Marais to the world. It wouldn't surprise me if she's had a hand in advancing the house of Fairchild, either. A strong rival to the Redmanes inside the Summer Court means less risk for them."

"So Dubessa is the new Chief Matron?"

"As soon as they can call a meeting and work through all the formalities," Silas said. "I'd bet my life on it."

"And while Dubessa's busy getting Summer shaped up the way she wants it, Mara and Crom get a free hand to do whatever they've got planned," Danny added.

"Well, that royally sucks."

"You might say that," Silas said.

"And I'm in her debt," Taylor said.

"That," Silas said, "was about the stupidest move I've ever seen."

"Yeah, well..." Taylor shrugged. How could Silas possibly know what Jill meant to her? You risk anything for your best friend. For your only friend.

"Seriously," Silas continued. "You don't make bargains with the sídhe. You just don't. Nobody ever wins that game. Ever. Do you understand?"

"I get it, okay?" Taylor snapped. "But what was I supposed to do? Let Mara take Jill away? She needs to go home. She's got parents who love her more than anything. She's got a brother who's...not that terrible. If somebody's going to get sucked into the Wonder, it makes sense it should be me instead."

"Your parents love you, too," Jill said. "And nobody's getting sucked anywhere. Not today, anyway."

"I guess."

"Let's just go home. Both of us."

Taylor nodded.

"Besides," Danny spoke up, "we may be forgetting something here."

Taylor looked up. Danny had a twinkle in his eyes.

"Sure, Taylor made a deal with a duine sídhe. All things being equal, that's pretty bad. I mean, the things they can do to a person.... It gives me the heebie-jeebies just thinking about—"

"How exactly is this helping?" Taylor said.

"You gotta remember: Mara made the same mistake. She made a deal with a duine sídhe, too, didn't she?"

"I didn't think of that," Taylor said.

"Huh. Me neither," Silas said.

"So you think Taylor can get out of this?" Jill asked.

"Aw, heck no," Danny said. "By oak, ash, and thorn, nobody gets out of a deal with the daoine sídhe. But what she *can* do is twist it to her advantage. Make Mara wish she'd never agreed to Taylor's bargain. We just got to figure out how."

"Okay," Jill said. "That sounds...hard."

"But not impossible," Taylor said. She felt her confidence returning.

"And don't forget: Mara didn't get everything she wanted," Danny said. "I mean, you three got away."

"Barely!"

"Good enough," Silas said. "And Danny's got a point. Remember what I told you about the Fair Folk and honor? Mara had the three of us right where she wanted us. One of the most powerful fae there is, and here we are, safe and sound. We stood up to her. *You* stood up to her, Taylor."

"And you didn't cast a single spell," Jill said. "All you did was stuff anybody could do—even me."

"Exactly," Silas said. "The Gentry are at the top of the food chain. A powerful sídhe like Mara has more magic in her little finger than I've got in my whole body. But at the end of the day, who leaves her scarred and dazed and knee-deep in chicken poop? A pooka, a church grim, and a couple of teenagers."

Silas's eyes twinkled. "That's going to leave a mark."

Taylor wasn't so sure. She didn't feel like a conquering hero. She felt like a kid who'd been beaten up by the biggest bully in the schoolyard. "So what happens now?" she asked.

"Move to a different part of the cemetery, just in case Mara comes calling," Danny said. "Then try to get some sleep. All three of you. I'll go find Taylor some aspirin and scrounge up something for everybody to eat. I'll be back by sunrise. We can figure it all out then."

Easy for him to say, Taylor thought. Her own grandmother had used her—and even tried to kill her best friend.

Sure, sure. They'd all sit down and try to figure it out over breakfast. Eggs. Toast. Maybe a side of bacon, fresh orange juice. More like a stale burrito from the nearest gas station, the way this weekend was going.

But Taylor knew what she wanted to do.

If it was the last thing she did, she was going to make sure Mara never hurt anybody ever again.

Chapter 30

This Isn't Over!

Danny returned with a sack full of plums shortly before dawn, plucked, he said, from a Topsider's tree. Jill didn't want to eat anything stolen, but the pooka assured her he "paid" for them by making sure the owner would have a bumper crop of pears in another month or so. She didn't understand what that meant, but Taylor assured her Danny knew a thing or two about agriculture.

Maymay only lived two or three miles away—an easy enough walk for Jill and Taylor as long as they started early, before the heat and the sun could get the best of them. That, then, became the plan. Hidden under a thick mist of glamour, Danny and Silas walked with them for most of the way. Once they entered the Pontchartrain Park neighborhood, the pooka and the church grim bid their farewells. Jill figured it would be startling enough for her and Taylor to show up unannounced on her grandmother's doorstep. One look at either of their two companions would probably send her over the edge.

And so two girls walked the last few blocks alone. That was fine, because they definitely had things to talk about.

"So...," Jill began. "Does this mean you're my godmother now?"

"Good grief, I hope not!" Taylor said. After a long pause, she added, "I should have told you what was going on with me sooner. It might have kept you from...from..."

"From taking candy from a stranger?" Jill scoffed. "That wasn't your fault, Taylor. That was me being stupid."

"No, if you knew…if I had told you…maybe I could have warned you. Messing with my relatives is trouble."

"So I've heard."

"How do you feel?"

"A little jumpy, maybe. Kind of…distracted. Not as bad as it was before, though. How about you?"

"I'm just mad," Taylor said. Her voice was cold and sharp. "I don't like being lied to. I don't like being used. And I sure don't like anybody messing with my friends!"

Taylor was talking with her hands. Jill sidestepped to get out of their way.

"At least it's over."

"Over?" Taylor shook her head. "Don't you understand? This isn't over! One of my grandmothers just made sure the other one is a wanted criminal. And while the Summer Court figures out what to do next, Mara has pretty much given herself all the time she needs to take over everything. Plus, I've got a cousin out there on the run somewhere, and maybe an uncle I've never met. Is she going after them next?"

"I don't know," Jill said. "Sorry. I wasn't thinking."

Taylor sighed and bowed her head.

"What are you going to do?"

"I'll tell you what I'm *not* going to do," Taylor said. Despite the warm, morning sun, the temperature seemed to drop five degrees as she spoke. "I'm through getting pushed around by my own family. Any of them. Do you understand? That is *so* not going to happen again. Ever."

Jill nodded.

"I've got to learn magic. Big time. And as fast as I can. If they try anything else, then by oak, ash, and thorn, I'll be ready."

"By oak, ash…Taylor, you've got to settle down."

"Teach them to mind their own business. Stay away from my friends…. If they even look at you the wrong way, I swear…."

"Taylor!"

"What?"

"Maybe before you go all nuclear on everybody, we could just go home? These sandals are killing me!"

Taylor stopped cold. She looked down at herself and must have only then realized she and Jill were still wearing their party dresses from the night before, now stained and frayed and sweat through.

She looked back up at Jill with an embarrassed half-smile.

"Yeah," she said. "Home sounds good."

Jill ushered her forward. Maymay's house wasn't too much farther.

"And I haven't forgotten about you, Jill. Mara said something about feeding you with my own magic. As soon as we get home, I'm going to talk to Silas and Danny. Figure out how to do that. I bet it'll help with the jumpy feeling."

"Yeah. I guess."

"Are you okay?"

Jill looked straight ahead and walked almost half a block before answering.

"I just..." She took a deep breath. "How in the world am I going to explain all this to my parents?"

"Once you figure it out, promise you'll let me know!"

Taylor hung her head as they walked. Jill saw her wipe a tear from her eye.

"It'll be okay, Taylor."

They walked a few more paces.

"And you know this how?" Taylor said.

"Do you remember in sixth grade when you got detention?"

"Which time?"

"When you convinced Jacquarrius Evans that Tenika Watson liked him?"

"I do not recall such an incident," Taylor stated flatly.

"You might not," Jill said with a grin, "but I'll bet Jacquarrius and Tenika do. And so does everybody who saw the fight you and Tenika got in afterwards."

"It wasn't a fight," Taylor said. Jill could tell she was struggling not to laugh. "Just a difference of opinion."

"A loud difference of opinion. Expressed in very colorful language, if I remember right."

"Your memory may be playing tricks on you," Taylor said. Her face was turning pink. She couldn't hold out much longer.

"So tell me this," Jill said. "What did your mom and dad do when they found out?"

The building explosion of laughter faded like air escaping a balloon.

"They hit the roof," Taylor said. "They said mouthing off to teachers was bad enough, but embarrassing my classmates in front of everybody and nearly getting into a fist fight was too much. They said I'd gone too far—even for me."

"And?" Jill motioned for Taylor to turn at the corner. Maymay was only a block away.

"And they grounded me for three weeks."

"And?"

Taylor sighed. "And eventually everything got back to normal."

"You see, Taylor, that's what I love about your folks. As big a pain in the neck as you can be—"

"Hey!"

"...they have always loved you."

A couple paces later, Taylor said, "This is just going to be so hard."

"Hard," Jill agreed. "Not impossible. Give them time."

"How'd you get so smart?" Taylor said.

"I'm a witch," Jill said. "We know things."

They continued up the street until they reached a familiar yard and the cozy house that always held such warm memories for Jill. Bathed in the morning light, the colors seemed vibrant and alive, full of warmth and love and peace. She grinned, then quickly closed her eyes when she started to feel woozy. When she opened them again, everything was mostly back to normal, although the buzzing of a passing bee seemed louder than it should have been, and the sweet smell of blooming flowers nearly took her breath away.

They reached the door.

Jill rang the doorbell. Almost immediately, Maymay swung open the door and wrapped Jill in a fierce hug. She started to cry in spite of herself.

"Oh, my baby!" Maymay sobbed. "We have been so worried!"

"I'm sorry, Maymay! I didn't mean to make you worry. I tried—"

Jill's grandmother shushed her and patted her on the back. It seemed she only then noticed Taylor standing on the porch.

"And who is this?"

"Maymay, this is my friend Taylor," Jill said. Her voice quavered a little. "Can we use your phone?"

Maymay took off her glasses, rubbed her eyes, and put her glasses back on, never averting her gaze from Taylor.

"Jill's friends are always welcome in this house," she said. Without another word or gesture, she pivoted on her walking stick and strolled toward the kitchen. The good thing about grandparents, Jill decided, was that some things didn't need to be explained.

Taylor stepped inside behind them.

"You can call home in a minute," Maymay said. "But you need to calm down first or you'll give your mother fits. Have you eaten? I have some leftover biscuits."

"That would be nice," Jill said.

Maymay gestured, and Jill led Taylor into her grandmother's kitchen. A plate of biscuits, butter, and two different kinds of jam were already on the table along with three simple place settings. Maymay never ceased to amaze Jill. It was almost as if she knew visitors were coming. Merle the cat tickled Jill's bare legs as he weaved around beneath her.

The three sat down. Merle jumped into Jill's lap. He meowed, looked across the way at Maymay, and leaped to the floor.

Danny's fresh fruit was okay, but Maymay's homemade biscuits were beyond description. Taylor and Jill both dug in, and soon the plate was empty.

"Now, talk to me, sweet girl," Maymay said.

"Yes, ma'am?"

"I'll call your momma for you if you like—and yours, too, Taylor—but I need to know something before I do."

Taylor muttered a word of thanks, her mouth still stuffed with biscuit.

"Thanks, Maymay. I'd appreciate that," Jill said. But she was afraid of what her grandmother wanted to know first. Was she going to get hollered at? Get a lecture about running away from home and worrying her family sick? She prepared to flinch.

"Wh-what is it you want to know?"

"Now, settle down, Jill. I'm not going to hit you." Maymay chuckled. It put Jill at ease—slightly.

"All I want to know is...How are we going to tell your mother about you using magic?"

Taylor's eyes instantly fixed on Maymay. Jill's butter knife clanged against the tile floor.

"Uh..."

Jill's pulse started racing as her throat became dry.

"You don't need to pretend, Jill. I saw the signs when you visited last. Milk turning sour. The way Merle kept checking you out—and still is!"

"You...you knew?"

"I had my suspicions. I could tell something was up from the way you were acting. Like all your senses were in overdrive." She chuckled at some unspoken thought. "I might have known you'd be the one. The way your mother is so dead set against it."

"What do you mean, you might have known?"

Maymay smiled a broad, proud smile. "Magic," she said. "Sometimes it skips a generation."

Jill looked at her grandmother with eyes wide. Taylor nearly fell out of her seat.

"You?" Jill said.

Maymay nodded. "Oh, I put it down years ago." She shook her head. "Cleaning up after one bunch of rampaging pixies is enough for a lifetime, let me tell you." She shook her head and stifled a smile.

"So, you...what? Retired?"

"Mostly."

Even after the faeries, goblins, hell hounds, naked bears, and exploding house pets, this was too much. Jill held onto the edge of the table because it felt like the room was starting to spin.

Then it hit her.

Jill looked her grandmother in the eye and spoke in an accusing tone. "You told Momma those books about the kid wizard that Tonya likes aren't your cup of tea."

"Honey, magic just does not work that way," Maymay said. "Swishing wands around, hollering at each other? In Latin? Please! But if Tonya likes it, who am I to discourage her?"

"Does...does Momma know?"

"Your momma was just a little girl when I got out of the business." Maymay got up, pulled the cordless phone off its base, and ambled back to her seat. "This is going to be rough on her. We'll have to give her time to get used to the idea.

"Now suppose you girls tell me what you've been up to. Hmm?"

Jill's grandmother listened patiently for over an hour. When the girls finished their story, she sat silently, stroking Merle's furry head as he rested on her lap. Finally, she picked up the phone.

She talked to Jill's mom for a long time and then passed the phone to Jill. Jill and her mom talked some more. Meanwhile, Jill's grandmother took Taylor into the living room and sat her on the sofa. She dug a cell phone out of her purse and had Taylor dial her home number.

Someone picked up on the first ring. "Is this Mr. Smart?" Maymay said. "Mr. Smart, my name is Rosaline Blay. I'm Jill Matthews's grandmother in New Orleans."

Taylor watched. Jill's grandmother gave her a wink.

"Yes, Jill's parents have called me every day... I'm sure you are... Mr. Smart, the reason I'm calling is that Jill and Taylor are here with m—. Yes, they're fine. Yes, she wants to talk to you, too."

Taylor's throat felt dry. She swallowed.

"She's right here, but before I give her the phone, Mr. Smart, there's something I need to tell you... No, sir, your daughter is just fine... It's just, well, she wants you to know she's sorry about the way she's been acting the past few weeks... No sir, it's nothing like that..."

Taylor reached for the phone. Jill's grandmother held up a hand.

"Mr. Smart, the thing is... How can I put this? Taylor is a unique young lady... I know you've got no reason to believe me, but I really think you should hear her out... All right. Here she is."

Taylor snatched up the phone.

"Taylor? Are you all right? You're not hurt?"

"Daddy, I want to come home!"

"Of course, sweetheart. Your mom is checking air fares right now..."

"Daddy, I'm sorry I blew up at you like I did."

"It's all right, Taylor. We can figure this out, whatever it is."

"I...I hope so. But we really, really need to talk."

"Oh, Taylor. You can always talk to me."

She swallowed.

"I know," she said. "I love you, Daddy."

"I love you, Taylor." On the other end of the line, her dad sniffled. "We're going to get you home."

"Daddy?"

"Yes, Taylor?"

"There's something I need to tell you, and I need you to just listen. Okay?"

"Okay, Taylor. Whatever you want to say."

She took a breath.

"Okay, then. Here goes..."